TERMINAL SECRET

MARK GILLEO

20/20 PRESS

ALSO BY MARK GILLEO

Favors and Lies
Love Thy Neighbor
Sweat

2020 Press, LLC.

Copyright © 2017 by Mark Gilleo

Visit the author's website at www.markgilleo.com

ISBN: 978-0-999-0472-0-0

ISBN: 978-0-999-0472-1-7 (ebook)

First trade edition: September 2017

10 9 8 7 6 5 4 3 2

ACKNOWLEDGEMENTS

I would like to thank the following people for their input and/or editing assistance: Dave Allen, Chris (Coach) Barker, Tim Davis, Diana Ellis, Claire Everett, Sue Fine, Scott Forrest, Joel Frost, Michele Gates, Jeffrey B. Krieg, Dan Lord, Carroll Reed, and Nancy Williams. Without your help, I would still be muddling through drafts of this manuscript. I would also like to extend my gratitude to Dennis Dobrzynski for his medical input and suggestions. Any errors or omissions are mine and not his. Additionally, I would like to extend gratitude to my editor, Nora Tamada, for her skill and professionalism.

Last but not least, I would like to thank my wife, Ivette, for all of her support.

DEDICATION

This book is dedicated to my father, who has valiantly battled cancer for ten years, smiling through radiation, chemotherapy, countless medications, and endless needles and body scans. He is a testament to the power of the human spirit.

CHAPTER 1

IT'S ALWAYS EASIER to break the law wearing a tuxedo.

Dan Lord teetered on the top of the security fence, both hands resting on the flat crossbeam of the large metal structure. In between his hands, and for as far as he could see in either direction, sharp metal spikes shot upward like menacing teeth. Music from the small live orchestra on the other side of the property floated across two acres of manicured lawn and gardens.

Dan lifted his right leg and slipped his polished black shoe between an adjacent void in the spikes. He took one look behind him, paused for a final view from the top of the fence, and threw himself over. The ground shook as his weight transferred to the soil, his legs absorbing the downward energy as he bent at the knees and landed in a crouched position.

He stood, brushed off the bottom of his pants, and straightened his black bow tie. He looked up at the fence, all ten feet, and hoped that he would be using the front door of the lavish residence for his exit. If not, he would be forced to have another dance with the fence spikes on his way out, most likely with security personnel in pursuit.

Dan checked his watch and then patted the front of his tuxedo jacket. He acknowledged the small square outline of his digital camera and confirmed his lock pick set had survived the journey through the woods—an area of no man's land near the terminus of Klingle Road in Washington, DC.

A few paces from the fence, Dan's foot found the crushed gravel path that ran through the property behind the residence of the Deputy Chief of Mission for the Indian Embassy. Dan weaved to the right, past a large gazebo. He noticed the outline of a well-dressed couple with roaming hands seated on a small bench in the dimly lit corner. At the next bend in the gravel path, he intercepted a glass of champagne from the tray of a passing waiter.

As the path widened and the lights from the residence stretched forward, Dan stepped onto firmer ground. Pausing, he digested his surroundings. A large square fountain filled the center of the entertainment area. To the left, the live eleven-piece woodwind and string ensemble continued to play. Dan performed a quick headcount and estimated attendance at just over two hundred. A respectable size for any garden party. He had no idea if it was an equally respectable number for the festival of Dussehra, the Hindi celebration of good over evil.

"Spectacular home, isn't it?" a woman's voice interrupted.

"Incredible," Dan agreed, turning in the woman's direction.

"I don't believe we've met," she added.

Dan smiled. The woman was attractive. Mid-thirties. Dirty blond hair. She wore a proper black dress that subtly pushed her chest front and center. The intentional uplift was neither overtly promiscuous, nor possible to ignore.

Dan extended his hand. "Dan Lord. Attorney at Law."

"An attorney? There's no shortage of those here. What kind of law do you practice?"

Dan considered his current assignment. "International labor," he replied. "And you? To whom do I have the pleasure?"

"Abigail Downs. Foreign Service."

"Oh, really? I was actually a diplomat brat growing up."

"Anyplace interesting?"

"All of them were interesting. Some more than others. How about you?"

"Did two years in the UAE. Another three in the Philippines. Been back in DC for the last two years. I'm heading to Moscow in the spring. I'm in intensive language training now."

The woman's voice seemed to fade as Dan glanced over her head and made eye contact with a waiter on the far side of the fountain. Dan gave an almost imperceptible nod and politely ended his conversation with the woman in the black dress.

"If you'll excuse me, I have to go," he said, gently touching the woman on the arm. He took two steps, turned back around, and added, in Russian, "Good luck in Moscow. And try not to look too surprised the first time someone attempts to bribe you for a visa at the embassy."

The woman was still working through the translation in her head as Dan turned and weaved his way through the crowd of party guests.

Dan approached the waiter as an inebriated man grabbed a handful of grape-leaf wraps off the server's tray. A second later, Dan was alone with the waiter, pressed against the edge of a large boxwood. Dan grabbed an hors d'oeuvre off the tray and waited for the waiter to provide the information he had paid for.

"I think the two women you're looking for are located in the bedrooms downstairs. There are locks on the doors. On the *outside* of the doors. If they're in those rooms, then someone has to unlock the doors from the hallway in order for them to get out. There are small windows at ankle level on the other side of the house. The windows are blacked out."

"How many people are in the house?"

"A couple dozen. Plus the waitstaff and caterers. It's a big place. Ten bedrooms and at least that many bathrooms. Most of the guests are outside. It's beautiful weather for a garden party."

"General security?"

"A half-dozen security guards are on the premises. A couple of dignitaries arrived with their own security, on top of what was here for the event. Everyone had their IDs checked at the door and their names matched to an invitation. From what I've seen, no one is watching the basement. Access to the downstairs is through a door at the end of the hall, on the right side of the kitchen, as you enter from the front of the house."

"The right side of the kitchen, as you enter from the front," Dan confirmed. "I assume the hall will be obvious once I get inside."

"It should be. The kitchen opens to the living room and the main foyer. There are two halls off the kitchen. The hall on the left leads to one of the bathrooms. The hall on the right leads to the basement door."

"Sounds easy enough."

"No one knows what's *really* down there, behind the doors," the waiter added.

"I have a good idea."

"So you say."

"I don't intend on leaving without proof," Dan said.

"What's the plan?"

"I'm going to access their location, make a couple of quick videos, and then disappear."

"And if you have problems?"

"I'll handle them. The element of surprise is on my side. I'm just a drunk guest in a tuxedo who got lost in a big house while looking for the john."

"And if there's a guard downstairs?"

Dan winked. "He'll never know what hit him."

The waiter nodded nervously and looked around. "Are we done? I need to keep moving."

"Yeah, we're done. Thanks. I'll take it from here."

"I hope it works out."

"Why wouldn't it? We have karma on our side. We're celebrating the festival of Dussehra, the triumph of good over evil."

"Sorry if I don't share your enthusiasm. Seems like evil does its fair share of winning these days."

"Not tonight," Dan replied, turning towards the house.

*

Twenty minutes later, the sound of breaking glass on the far side of the house was inaudible over the live music permeating the property. Dan cursed as he brushed aside glass shards from the windowsill and eyed his tiny exit. The small basement window was near the ceiling of the bedroom wall and Dan pushed a wooden writing desk beneath the window to expedite his departure. Behind him, on the other side of the room, the closed door to the bedroom thumped heavily, an unseen shoulder slamming into it from the hall. For now, the weight of the bed and dresser resting in front of the door was keeping security at bay on the other side of the threshold. It wouldn't last forever.

Dan ambled to the top of the desk and shoved one arm through the broken window frame. He looked back at the two women in the room who jumped onto the bed to add weight to the barrier.

"How long do you think it will take?" one of the Indian women asked, looking up at Dan wide-eyed.

Dan paused and glanced at the camera in his hand. "I'll send this video to the press later this evening. After that, your employer will have some explaining to do. As a diplomat, he has immunity from criminal prosecution. But illegal enslavement isn't going to be completely ignored. Pack your bags. Be ready to go," Dan said.

The sound of the doorframe cracking, combined with growing grunts of desperation from the hall, propelled Dan through the narrow window opening. He stifled his own grunt as a shard of glass still attached to the window frame ripped through his tuxedo jacket and dug into his flesh. He could feel skin tearing and the warmth of blood on his shoulder. He gritted his teeth through a series of curses and pushed through the pain at the expense of a larger wound. Seconds later he pulled himself through the window, stood on the grass, and plotted his exit. He followed the brick walkway from the side of the house to the front yard, where a large man stood stoically at attention. Dan made eye contact and smiled. No one checks the ID of people on their way out of a party.

"I don't want to ruin anybody's good time but a couple of drunk guests started getting a little frisky on the other side of the garage, if you catch my drift."

"Do they still have their clothes on?"

"Not for long. It may not be good PR for the party if someone sees them. Just thought I would mention it."

The man looked at Dan and nodded. "I'll check it out."

"Have a good night."

"You do the same."

By the time the lone guard assigned to the women in the basement broke through the bedroom door, Dan was a half-mile away, wearing jeans and a T-shirt with a black backpack slung over his still-bleeding shoulder.

CHAPTER 2

DETECTIVE EARL WALLACE of the Washington Metropolitan Police rolled out of bed and climbed onto the elliptical machine. Five feet away, his wife was still asleep. After a quarter century of middle-of-the-night beepers, phone calls, and progressively intense snoring, only the sun and her alarm clock would wake her. She no longer heard him come and go—the holster, the gun, the handcuffs—all rattling and clanking in the darkness. She was the wife of a detective and, like most others in her predicament, she molded her life around her husband's. The first five years of their marriage had been peppered with a thousand sleepless nights. A thousand strikes of the sleepless chisel that transformed her into a work of art, capable of seven hours of shuteye, regardless of what her husband did.

Wallace hit the red button on the elliptical and increased the resistance. He could still feel the pain in his calves from yesterday's workout. *Weakness leaving the body,* he reminded himself. Now, if the new limp would just leave with the weakness.

He was the first to admit he had allowed middle age to sneak up on him. Fifty had been a particularly difficult milestone and the years since had reminded him that his body wasn't what it should be. He'd blamed the first additional twenty pounds around his midsection on natural weight gain. Weight he thought he could afford to have on his bones. His knees disagreed. Then came another twenty pounds. Followed by ten more.

When high blood pressure reared its ugly head, a pill a day put the concern to rest. Surging triglycerides—something he had never heard of—arrived next on the scene and served as the impetus to cut alcohol and donuts from his diet. With the exception of the occasional digression, Wallace took his sacrifices in stride. It wasn't until a skyrocketing cholesterol reading stole the bacon off his plate that he decided to fight back. Steal all of a man's little devils and there may be no angel left in him either.

When the bacon thief came knocking, the clothes hanging on the handles of the elliptical machine sitting in the corner of the bedroom found their way into the closet. On a rainy Sunday afternoon, with the thoughts of losing forty pounds in mind, Detective Wallace had found himself in running shoes, nose-to-nose with an instruction book written in twelve different languages.

The first fifteen pounds had dropped as if a fat-busting fairy had waved a magic wand over his slightly graying head. Another twenty-five pounds and he would be out of the big men's section of the department store. And as much as he wanted to attribute the weight loss to the elliptical, the real secret was in his diet. And he had tried them all. Meat only. Only carbs. No carbs. Veggies and fruit. Anything liquefied. Ultimately, too many options resulted in no results.

So Wallace took all of the variables out of the equation. He would eat whatever he wanted one day, and eat nothing the next. It worked for him. In the moments when hunger struck, the thought of yesterday's indulgence lingered fresh enough to be rewarding. He could shut his eyes and still taste the previous night's dinner. When that failed, the promise of tomorrow's feast was enough to keep him motivated. The one-day off, one-day on diet.

Detective Wallace spent thirty minutes on the elliptical in a pair of boxers and a white T-shirt. He spent an equal amount of time shaving his gray whiskers, showering, and getting dressed.

The first call of the day arrived while Wallace was in the kitchen making coffee and eyeing the food he would eat tomorrow. The day's *Washington Post* rested on the kitchen table next to his empty coffee cup. Wallace answered on the third ring.

"Yo."

"Hey, Sarge. We have a murder in Spring Valley."

"Nice neighborhood. Robbery gone bad?"

"Doesn't appear so."

"Domestic?"

"Negative. A professional woman was shot on her doorstep as she left the house."

"In Spring Valley?" Wallace confirmed incredulously.

"It gets better. You might need to see this in person. The news trucks just arrived. It should be on the TV momentarily."

*

Wallace parked his unmarked police car along the curb and took a sip of his coffee. He got out of the car and squinted at flashing lights from various emergency vehicles filling the neighborhood street. Yellow crime scene tape stretched across the front yard. A forensic photographer snapped pictures on the front porch.

Detective Matthews, a mulatto with Puerto Rican and South Pacific islander thrown in for spice, spotted Detective Wallace as he stepped away from his car. Matthews weaved through the activity in the front yard to meet Wallace before he reached the driveway.

The two detectives exchanged handshakes.

"So this is how you want to be remembered?" Wallace asked. "Forty-eight hours left on your temporary transfer and you call me with the first murder in this district in two months."

"Go ahead. Bust my balls. But by the end of the week I will be back in Anacostia, where the murder rate is ten times what you see in the rest of the city."

"And I'll be left cleaning up this mess by myself."

"I'll give you all the help you need. As long as you solve it in the next two days."

"You got a suspect in your pocket?"

"Nope."

"What exactly do we have? Talk to me," Wallace said, removing his notebook from his breast pocket.

"Twenty-eight-year-old black female. Shot on her doorstep as she stepped outside. Briefcase in hand. Looks like she was on her way to work."

"Weapon?"

"Forensics says we're looking at a rifle, based on the wound and spray pattern. We won't know for sure until ballistics are complete and the ME gets a look at the body."

"How many shots?"

"One. Right through the chest."

Wallace looked around. The park across the street was fifty yards away. A mix of trees surrounded the large playground in the center. The street beyond the park was another hundred yards in the distance.

"Are we talking about a rifle shot from long range?"

"That's our guess."

"Jesus. Let's keep that quiet as long as we can. We don't need panic over a possible sniper."

"No, we don't."

"What do we have on the victim? Is there a husband or boyfriend in the picture?"

"No husband. No family."

"A single, black female in a wealthy, predominately white neighborhood?"

"Does that mean something to you?"

"Just talking out loud," Wallace responded, never taking his eyes off his surroundings. "Who reported the body?"

"A neighbor out walking the dog happened to look over and see a pair of Jimmy Choos sticking up on the porch. Ran over, called 911. She's sitting on the garden bench in the corner of the yard if you want to talk to her."

"In a minute. What else?"

"No one heard anything. Forensics said the victim has been dead for a couple of hours."

"Which means she was shot early."

"The stiffness meter and body temperature indicate somewhere around six o'clock."

"The sun wasn't up yet but there's plenty of light in the neighborhood. Good streetlights. Lights in the park. Even if no one saw anything, I can't believe no one heard anything."

"So far, no one has come forward."

"Occupation?"

"Attorney."

"Well, then we have motive. Everyone I know hates at least one lawyer."

"She's a tree hugger. Was a tree hugger. Worked for the EPA. Sued big corporations."

"More motive. You been inside yet?"

"I took a quick look."

"Anything related to the crime?"

"Not on the surface. You want to take the full tour?"

"Just give me the highlights," Wallace replied. "Then I want to talk to the woman who found the body."

CHAPTER 3

DETECTIVE MATTHEWS STOOD next to Detective Wallace's desk at District Two Headquarters and extended his hand. Wallace grabbed the hand and pulled the man in for a chest bump.

"I'm going to miss you," Wallace admitted.

"I'm only going twenty blocks."

"Once you cross the Anacostia River, it's a different world."

"I'll see you around. And you can always come visit."

"I did my time in the war zone. I like what I have now. BMW break-ins and iPhone hold-ups."

"And the occasional sniper."

"Yeah, I do have one of those."

"Yeah, you do. By the way, word is that your new partner is meeting with the Captain as we speak."

"Please tell me it's not a young white male. I've had a bad run working with young white guys. The last time I ended up interrogated, in the news, and on involuntary leave without pay."

"It's not a young white guy. Two out of three, though."

"A young brother?"

"Try again."

"No way…"

"Oh, yeah. Name is Emily something or other."

"Shit. Emily?"

"Some new blood transfer detective from the fast track program. I hear she's from Northern Virginia. She should be right at home with you and all those BMW break-ins and iPhone hold-ups."

"I think it's time for you to leave."

"Later, Sarge. Keep me on speed dial."

As detective Matthews turned away, Wallace heard his Captain's voice rise above the din of the Robbery and Homicide division, calling his name.

*

Emily Fields stood from the wooden chair in the Captain's office as Wallace entered the room. The Captain, late fifties with white hair, gave the introductions.

"Wallace, this is your new partner, Detective Emily Fields."

Wallace looked his new partner in the eyes as they shook hands.

"She comes to us from Fairfax County. She's been a detective for two years across the river. Came to DC for the long hours, infrequent pay raises, and higher crime rate. Show her the ropes. Keep her out of trouble."

"Yes, Captain."

"I'm looking forward to working with you," Detective Fields said with a smile, flashing a set of dimples.

Wallace eyed his new partner, his mind devouring the details. Five seven or eight. Athletic build. Brown eyes. Brown hair pulled back in a braid. Attractive. Certainly better looking than his last partner, or any partner he'd ever had for that matter. He could already hear the catcalls.

Finished with his exterior assessment, Wallace turned towards the Captain. "May I have a word with you in private?"

The Captain nodded at Detective Fields, who stepped through the door and waited outside the glass wall of the Captain's office.

"I know we discussed it, but I don't know if I'm ready for a new partner just yet."

"You worked with Matthews for the last few months."

"That was different. He's been around. He knows the city. This girl is from Fairfax. She doesn't know anything about DC. And this fast track detective transfer program is bullshit. We have plenty of cops here in the city who want a crack at detective."

"And they will all get their shot. This program does not take existing job slots. The transfer program positions are all new, funded for transfer detectives. Agreed to by the police union."

"I still don't like it."

"You know what I like? I like the fact that Detective Emily Fields has a master's degree in criminal justice and an undergrad double major in criminal justice and information systems. She speaks Spanish, which will help with the MS-13 problem. She tested off the charts in every category of the transfer training program."

"The program is bullshit designed by a bunch of bureaucrats."

"Then I guess you're unaware I helped design the curriculum? Everyone accepted into the program has to go through the District's police academy. You can imagine there aren't many mid-career officers willing to put up with a second tour through any academy. And Detective Fields is my first and only choice from the program since it started."

"Sorry for the insult, Captain."

"How long have we known each other?"

"Longer than I've known my wife," Wallace replied.

"A long time. What's the problem with her? She has police experience and detective experience. Just not much DC experience."

"I don't know if I have the training side in me anymore. May not be good for her. May not be good for me."

"I know you're still dealing with Detective Nguyen's death. We all are. He was your partner, but he was everyone's friend. And we all have to move on."

"I just don't know if I can train another young detective."

"Don't train her. Mentor her. Let her watch. Let her learn. You're the best detective I've got. This police force needs new blood with advanced IT and cross-cultural communication skills. We're being gutted by other jurisdictions that pay more. The bottom line is that we can't produce decent veteran detectives without training a few young ones first, and we can't attract and keep the good young ones without someone experienced to guide them."

"Yes, Captain."

"Get acquainted with her. Share your cases. Get to work."

*

Detective Wallace stepped from the Captain's office, forced a smile, and then flicked his head in the direction of the staircase.

Five minutes later they were in traffic on the Q Street Bridge with the treetops of Rock Creek Park a hundred feet below them. Detective Wallace sipped coffee from a Styrofoam cup as he drove with two fingers of his free hand.

"I thought we were going over some of your cases?" Detective Fields asked from the passenger seat of the unmarked dark car.

"I am. We are. Consider this your first lesson in DC detective work. I'm not sure how it works in Virginia, but the only thing at the station here is paperwork and bad coffee. The less time you spend there, the better. Use it as a resource. Forensics. Evidence. Databases. Those are all part of the job. But don't confuse them with *being* the job. The job is out here. Gathering evidence. Talking to people."

"Roger that. Can I ask a few questions?"

"Shoot."

"Where are you from?"

"For all practical purposes, I've been in DC forever."

"I heard you have thirty years on the force."

"Easy, Detective Fields. I'm approaching twenty-five years."

"I'm only repeating what I heard. You look good for someone closing in on sixty."

Wallace spilled some coffee on his hand and drifted into the other lane. "Sixty? Jesus."

"Just kidding. I put your age closer to fifty."

"You know what they say…"

"Good genes."

"No. 'Black don't crack,'" Wallace said.

"I've heard the expression."

"Don't hold back on my account. I have thick skin. Thick black skin. And if you and I are going to work together, we are going to have to get past a few things. I'm black. You're white."

"Oh, here we go. I heard race might be a problem in the District."

"Now, wait. Hear me out. I'm not sure how it works in the suburbs, but this is how it works here. I know we probably come from different backgrounds and have different taste in music, food, and whatever else floats your boat. But as your partner, you can tell me anything and I will keep it to myself. I will have your back at all times. I expect you to have mine. And I will most certainly not be offended when you say 'black.' Out here, we have white perps, black perps, Asian perps, Middle Eastern perps, Hispanic perps. Those are the basic groups. And if they don't fall into any of those groups and you're still unsure how to describe someone, use a coffee color."

"A coffee color?"

"Yeah. A skin color described by a small black coffee and the amount of cream you put in it." Wallace pointed to a gentleman dressed in a suit standing at the corner waiting for the light to change. "That guy, for example. He's a black coffee with two creams."

"I'll have to get up to speed on my coffee colors."

"All I'm saying is that you can say 'black' as often as you like."

"I don't have any problem using the word black, when it's called for. But we were talking about your age just a minute ago. You look good, but you have plenty of wrinkles and a bit of a double chin. You don't qualify for the 'black don't crack' reference."

Wallace stewed for a moment and then caught his new partner smiling as she turned away and looked out the passenger window.

"Are we going to have a problem, Detective Fields?" Wallace asked.

"Only if you create one," she replied.

Detective Wallace let silence rule the car for a full minute and then asked, "How old are you, Fields?"

"Thirty-one. And you can call me Emily."

"You can call me Wallace."

"Not Earl?"

"Only if you want me looking around for my wife every time you say it."

"She's the only one who calls you Earl?"

"The only one."

"Wallace it is."

"Where are you from?"

"Fairfax."

"Born and raised in the burbs?"

"Fairfax County has over a million people in it, which makes it twice the size of DC. Area-wise, it's four times as large as the District. It has everything. Little Vietnam near Seven Corners, the madness of the Middle East in Bailey's Crossroads, Koreans in Annandale, the best hospital in the region, good schools, and Tyson's Corner, which is basically a city now. You can't pigeonhole it."

"Where in Fairfax did you grow up?"

"Between the beltway and GMU. The white suburbia part of the county, before you ask."

"Why did you become a detective?"

"I lost my father when I was twelve. He was a chemical engineer. Worked at a big company everyone has heard of. Did business all over the world. Was robbed at gunpoint in Sao Paulo, Brazil. He was in a taxi cab, stuck in traffic. Two guys on a motorcycle robbed my father and two of his colleagues. Took everything they had. Money. Passports. Jewelry. And then they fired five shots into the car as they drove off. The guys were never found. My father's company put pressure on the State Department to put pressure on the Brazilian authorities, but nothing ever came of it. A little bad press and then the storm blew over. Brazil moved forward. My father's company hired a replacement, and life continued."

"But not for a twelve-year-old girl."

"No. For my brother, my mother, and me, things would never be the same."

"Sorry for your loss."

Emily nodded. "Doesn't take Freud to figure out it was my father's unsolved death that drove me to this profession."

"As long as you're aware that solving a hundred other murders won't bring your father back. Probably won't even help the pain much."

"Maybe not. But I will be making a difference."

"One death at a time. One life at a time."

"I like that. You should put it on a bumper sticker on the back of the car. Maybe add a little skull and crossbones. Copyright it."

"The DC Metro Police is not big on personalizing public property. I think a bumper sticker would be frowned upon."

"Just a thought. Where are we headed?"

"To the medical examiner's office."

"What's the case?"

"Lawyer shot through the chest on the doorstep of her home."

"The one up in Spring Valley?"

"You pay attention."

"It was on the news."

"The news can be your friend or your enemy."

"Which is it in this case?"

"Don't know yet."

CHAPTER 4

D R. LEWIS WAS celebrating three decades of death. As a veteran
medical examiner for Washington DC, he had survived the crack
epidemic and the narcotics turf wars that tore the city apart for
twenty years. Then re-gentrification came knocking, led by yuppies with
pit bulls who wanted a shorter commute and a house they could afford,
regardless of what the property may have been in a previous life.

Dr. Lewis watched the city's demographics change before his eyes, one
visitor at a time to his stainless steel table and refrigerated drawers. With the
changes in the city and the decimation and incarceration of ten thousand
crack war soldiers, the number of murders per year plummeted. The last
twelve months had produced the fewest murders since the last US president
to be assassinated was reportedly sleeping with a leggy Hollywood blond.

As was customary, Wallace announced his arrival as he pushed his way
through the swinging double doors. Emily followed, taking note of Wallace's comfort level.

"Doc, I have a new partner for you to meet," Wallace said.

Dr. Lewis closed a manila folder he was reading and placed it on the
counter. "A new partner? That's progress."

"It wasn't voluntary," Wallace added.

Emily extended her hand. "Nice to meet you. Emily Fields. I'm the
unwelcome new detective. I think it has a nice ring to it. I might put it in
quotes on my business card."

"She's into personalization," Wallace added. "Wants to put bumper stickers on the squad car."

Dr. Lewis felt the female detective's grip and glanced down at her hands. "Strong hands. Welcome. My door is always open. If you need access, it can be arranged, twenty-four hours a day, seven days a week."

"A fellow all-nighter," Wallace chimed in.

"I was actually thinking about removing the door. Be like one of those establishments in the French Quarter that's been open for forty years straight," the ME said.

"The good doc here went to his first Mardi Gras last year. It obviously left an impression," Wallace added.

"I really went for a Medical Examiners' conference. I just stayed an extra week to see what the hubbub is all about."

"How was the hubbub?" Emily asked.

"After my wife saw the pictures on my cell phone, she made it clear there would be no encore."

Emily smiled and Wallace pressed the conversation forward. "What do you have for us, Doc?"

"Maybe nothing, but that's for you to decide." The ME walked to the table on the far side of the room and turned on the overhead lights. The body on the table had undergone a full autopsy and was dulled by the pallor of death—all life and blood vacated.

"This is the victim who was shot on her front doorstep the day before yesterday in Spring Valley. An otherwise healthy twenty-eight-year-old female. Not much of a mystery on this one. Shot through the chest, with a rifle in all likelihood. Partial reconstruction shows the bullet was consistent with a .223 round. The bullet was designed to fragment upon striking the target and the projectile performed as intended. She was dead before she hit the ground. Probably didn't even have time to reach for her chest."

"Anything else in her system?"

"Toxicology isn't complete yet, but her BAC was 0.0."

"An easy day at the morgue for you. No mystery as to the cause of death."

"It was an open-and-shut case, from a purely medical perspective.

I can't speak to suspects, motives, or all the other possibilities the body cannot tell me."

"So what's keeping you up?"

"Well, this open-and-shut case reopened itself when I got to the woman on the next table."

Wallace and Emily turned around and Dr. Lewis took the long way to stand across the table from them. The woman's figure was gaunt, bones pushing against greyish skin as if trying to escape.

"This body was pulled out of the canal the same morning the young woman shot through the chest was murdered. Her name is Beth Fluto and she was the driver of a Town and Country minivan. By eyewitness accounts, she drove off the road, over the curb, and then over the short stone wall that runs along the C&O Canal."

"Heart attack?" Emily asked.

"Very good, Detective. That was my initial thought. Or at least at the top of my consideration list. In the good old days, a single car accident was likely the result of a few things. Excessive speed. A sleep-deprived driver. Intoxication. A heart attack."

"And then came the proliferation of cell phones," Emily surmised.

The ME flashed an impressed look in Detective Wallace's direction. "Ladies and gentleman, we have a ringer in the room. The new, unwelcome detective is exactly right. Since the proliferation of cell phones, we have seen a massive spike in single car accidents. Texting is climbing the ranks as a major cause of death. People driving with both eyes and thumbs on their phone."

"Doesn't leave much to drive with," Emily said.

"No, it does not. Simply using the phone is dangerous enough. People pay more attention to the conversation they're having than they do to the road. Jabbering their way through the curve, the stoplight, and into the big oak tree on the corner."

"What is the case with this young lady?" Wallace asked.

"None of the above. She drowned."

"That would be expected if she were found in the canal."

"True, but Beth here is unique. While Beth may have drowned the other morning, she was already dead. Cancer everywhere. Cancer metastasized to her ovaries, liver, lungs, kidneys, stomach. I can't say for sure, but she likely had months or weeks to live. I imagine she was in pain. Very likely on pain medication. Those could have been contributing factors to her death. They could have very easily impaired her driving skills."

Wallace looked at Emily, who seemed to be hoping there was a moral to the story.

"And… ?" she prodded.

The ME moved to the foot of the bed and the evidence in the small basin. A pile of dirty clothes, cut from Beth's body, formed a mound of stench-laden fabric. Dr. Lewis slipped his hand into the corner of the evidence basin and pulled out a single bullet casing.

"You have my attention," Wallace responded as the ME held the brass casing in the air.

"This was found in a pocket of her pants. All of her clothes had been cut off in an attempt to resuscitate. The clothes arrived with the body in an evidence bag."

"What is the caliber?"

".223."

"Are you saying you think this woman killed the woman on the next table?" Wallace asked.

"No, Detective, I'm not. And it would be impossible to match this casing with the bullet used in the attorney's murder. We need the weapon to make a match. That said, the wound on the deceased on the next table is *consistent* with a wound from a .223. Given the fragmented condition of the projectile, however, it would be impossible to say for certain. But what I can say is this: I don't often have middle-aged white females with brass casings in their belongings, much less one that potentially matches the caliber for a murder victim who arrived the same day from the same zip code, and happens to be lying on the next table."

Wallace stared at the body on the table and then looked over at the corpse of the lawyer.

"What was the time of death on the woman pulled from the canal?"

"Seven-fifteen in the morning."

"That's pretty exact."

"The minivan went into the C&O during rush-hour. There were

hundreds of witnesses according to the police report. Over a dozen calls came into 911 immediately after the vehicle entered the water. Her body was found inside the submerged minivan. I assume she didn't come up for air. There wasn't much guesswork involved in the timeline."

"What part of Canal Road did she go in?"

"Not too far outside Georgetown."

"That part of Canal Road is one-way during the morning rush hour."

"One-way coming into the city in the morning. One-way leaving the city in the evening. Why does that matter?"

"Just thinking out loud," Wallace said. "Anything in the police report on a weapon in the minivan? If we assume our girl here shot the lawyer on the next table, then she probably didn't do it with a slingshot."

"There was nothing in the report I received, but it may be worth double checking."

"What about a cell phone?"

"Nothing mentioned in the paperwork."

Emily moved closer to the table and looked down at the woman pulled from the minivan. "You sure about the cancer?"

"Yes, Detective. Her prognosis couldn't have been good."

Wallace alternated glances between both female corpses. "It doesn't look like it was good for either of them."

*

Wallace spent ten minutes on the phone while pacing the lobby of the first floor of the hospital. When finished, he hung up the phone, nodded his head in the direction of the exit, and Emily followed him out the automatic doors.

"What did you learn?" Emily asked.

"There was no weapon found in the vehicle. And no phone," Wallace said. "Between you and me, without a weapon, I'm going to have a hard time believing a woman with cancer in a minivan shot a tree-hugging lawyer on her doorstep. I've seen a lot of things in my time on the force, but that would be a first."

"I would think so."

"And on top of having no weapon, we have a small gap in our timeline for the suspect."

"How's that?"

"The dead lawyer was shot on her doorstep around six a.m. According to the ME and the accident report, the minivan went in the water around seven fifteen. That is a gap of an hour and fifteen minutes."

"Maybe she was driving around."

"The woman with cancer wasn't even from DC. She was from Virginia. I just don't see her coming to DC to shoot a woman on her doorstep and then driving around the neighborhood for an hour. Most people who shoot someone don't stick around."

"So what do we do with the shell casing that the ME found? Ignore it?"

"This is DC. There are a lot of military families in this area. Within a couple of hours of here we have what, a dozen military bases? The Army has Fort Meade, Belvoir, Detrick. The Air Force has Andrews. The Marines have Quantico down Route 95 and the Marine Barracks on the other side of town. The US Naval Academy is thirty minutes away in Annapolis. And of course the Pentagon is the mother of all military installations. Hundreds of thousands of military personnel. Millions of rounds of ammo."

"Meaning?"

"The .223 is a common ammo type for the military. That casing found on the woman could be anything. It could be souvenir, a good luck charm. Something to remember a boyfriend, a husband. And that assumes it was a .223 that killed the lawyer. The ME just said it was consistent with a .223. Tough to prove without a weapon."

Wallace paused and looked out the window before continuing. "But for the sake of being thorough, let's poke around on our dead girl with the bullet in her pocket—see if there's any connection between her and the dead lawyer. Let's also see if we can figure out where she was going when she crashed, and get a look at the minivan for ourselves."

Emily jotted notes in her notebook. "Where do we start?"

"We start with the Duke of Junk."

CHAPTER 5

WALLACE PARKED THE unmarked cruiser next to the trailer at the entrance to Buzzard Point Salvage Yard. Emily joined him in front of the vehicle, looking out over the rows of cars in various states of ill repair. The right hand side of the lot displayed the skeletal remains of automobiles that had been picked through, the organs of the cars ripped out piece by piece and used as transplants for healthier vehicles. The back of the salvage yard sported columns of semi-crushed cars, four vehicles high. Barbed wire ran around the fence, enclosing the three-acre establishment.

"It's like a thrift store for wounded vehicles," Emily observed.

"A combination of store, pawn shop, and auction," Wallace retorted.

A sign on the front of the trailer explained the rules of the salvage yard. It cost twenty dollars to look around. If a customer found something they wanted to purchase, the twenty bucks would be applied to the negotiated purchase price of the item, if a price could be agreed upon.

Emily read the sign and then saw the face of a man peering out between the venetian blinds in the window of the trailer. "You know this guy?" Emily asked.

"Yeah. He handles a lot of the cars for the city of DC. A lot of the police impound vehicles end up here as their final clearing stage."

"If you see something you need to buy, let me negotiate," Emily said. "I have an uncle who has been running flea markets in Winchester since I was a little girl."

The Duke opened the door of the trailer and his eyes immediately danced towards the female detective. The Duke quickly ran his fingers through his graying brown hair and brushed powder sugar off the front of his denim work shirt.

Wallace stepped between the gawking junkyard owner and his new partner. "Good morning, Duke."

"Good morning, Detective. And good morning to your pretty acquaintance."

Emily flashed her newly minted DC detective badge and squelched the Duke's enthusiasm. "You can also refer to me as 'Detective.'"

The Duke acknowledged the badge with a nod. "Come on in," he said, holding open the front door to the trailer. Emily followed Wallace into the small office and the Duke's eyes fell to the back of Emily's slacks as she walked past. The Duke of Junk pulled the door shut and stepped to the desk at the far end of the office trailer.

Wallace and Emily looked around the dimly lit office. An exceptionally large jar of change—mostly quarters, dimes, and nickels—sat in the corner. Filing cabinets ran along two walls. A window air-conditioning unit protruded from a self-made hole in the wall of the trailer. The venetian blinds the Duke had been peeking through moments before, hung unevenly.

"How's business, Duke?" Wallace asked.

"Real good. Counting the days to retirement. I guess you heard the city is buying this place. Yes sir, the development money finally made it to Buzzard Point. They're going to build a soccer stadium here."

"The first thing they need to do is change the name. Buzzard Point just doesn't have a commercial ring to it."

"They can call it anything they want as long as the check clears the bank. You know, I don't understand people who say they'll never sell out to development. I say, when the price is right, take the money and run. They're going to develop with or without you."

"Duke, we're looking for a minivan that was brought in the other day. It was pulled out of the canal."

"I know the one. Stinks to high heaven. Stagnant canal water isn't good for a vehicle. From what I understand, the car was pulled out pretty quickly. But the smell, well, that's going to be there forever."

"Has anyone picked through the vehicle?"

"We don't let people pick through flooded cars. We remove the tires. Pluck out the windshield and mirrors. That's about it. The rest is scrap metal. I can't sell anything on the interior. Can't sell the engine. I mean, the car was submerged. It's not like someone left the moonroof open during an afternoon sprinkle. Flooded vehicles are trouble. All kinds of trouble. Tightly regulated. The insurance guy was out here last evening. We processed the paperwork for a totaled vehicle. The VIN was entered into the system. If that vehicle or its engine were ever found on the road, someone would have some explaining to do."

"And you would be the first person to answer questions."

"Which is why I don't play around with flooded vehicles. Who needs the hassle?"

"Can we see the vehicle?"

"Just a second," the Duke replied. He grabbed the walkie-talkie off the corner of his desk and pressed the button to talk. Deafening machinery roared from the walkie-talkie, drowning out a muffled reply from the person on the other end. The Duke clicked the walk-talkie off and stood from his chair. "Let's take a walk. That car is in the crunch line and the machine is running."

Wallace followed one pace behind and listened to Emily and the Duke chew the fat over the rhythmic pounding of heavy machinery. Emily looked over and pointed at the rusted remains of an automobile. "That's an awesome '59 Cadillac. My uncle had one of those. Too bad it's missing the fins on the back."

The Duke responded. "People are taking the back ends off these cars and turning them into sofas. They put a big frame in the middle and use the fins as the arms of the couch. Some guy showed how to do it on TV. One of those picker shows. The next week I had a line of new clientele full of ideas for turning old cars into furniture."

At the end of the row of cars, the pounding sound of machinery became even louder.

"Here we are," the Duke said, standing among crushed cars, cubes no bigger than the size of large washing machines. He looked down the row of square metal blocks and uttered, "Uh-oh." He stepped forward and ran his hand across the third block of metal on the right. "This is it."

"How can you tell?"

"After a few years, you get pretty good at figuring what's what."

"It's already crushed," she stated.

"Yeah, sorry about that. Didn't think it would have been converted quite yet."

"You usually crush cars this quickly?" she asked.

"Once the insurance has been settled, we can crush them. I can put forty cars on a truck 'boxed up,' as we call it. I can fit twelve whole cars. Economics. Cheaper for me to crush them. And we're trying to thin the herd in here. Everything in this yard has to go by summer, before the developers arrive."

"Was there anything in the vehicle?"

The Duke seemed bothered by the question and both detectives picked up on his discomfort.

"A few things. There was as a baby stroller. Ruined. Some children toys and books. A blanket. There was an empty backpack. A damaged bike rack off the rear. A GPS that was disconnected."

"A GPS?"

"Yeah. One of those aftermarket jobs that sticks to the dash or the windshield. Not many people using them these days."

"Do you still have it?"

"Nope. It was ruined. Tried to plug it in and got nothing. Went in the trash."

"Anything else? Anyone see a cell phone?"

"No phone. There were a couple of miscellaneous items like the owner's manual in the glove box. Some loose change in the ashtray."

"Is that it?"

The Duke of Junk could feel the detectives fishing for a particular answer. "What were you looking for?"

"A weapon."

"What kind of weapon?"

Wallace looked at his partner and she nodded in approval.

"A rifle."

"No. No gun. Hell, I return weapons to the police. Check my records. Check my history. I have returned all kinds of unpleasant finds in the past. Even had a live grenade in the back of a crashed limo once."

"What about any of your employees? Any chance they had their hands in the vehicle?"

"Not this vehicle. I was here when it came in. I handled it. I didn't find a weapon."

Wallace glanced over his shoulder as the top of the crusher fell on the roof of a vehicle in the corner of the yard. The sides of the crusher began to move in and the sound of bending metal overtook the conversation.

The trio backtracked along the same path they had come in on and stopped near the steps of the trailer.

"Sorry I couldn't help you out," the Duke said, speaking in the direction of Wallace while stealing glances at Emily.

Wallace reached into his pocket and removed a business card. He handed the card to the Duke and said, "Let me know if you or your employees think of anything we need to know."

"Yes, sir, Detective."

Wallace turned around and walked in the direction of the squad car. He spoke over his shoulder as he opened the driver's side door. "Keep it clean, Duke."

"Do you believe him?" Emily asked, sliding into the passenger seat and pulling the door closed.

"Yes and no. I don't think he found a gun and I do think he would turn over a weapon if he found one. The juice is not worth the squeeze when it comes to weapons. Not in DC. But I also think he keeps other items of value. Jewelry, cash. Did you notice the large jar of coins in the trailer in the corner?"

"I did. Looked like one of those five-gallon water bottles. Big jar. It's probably too heavy to move by himself."

"If I had to guess, I would say most of that jar is loose change from the vehicles he gets. I would also guess he even finds some drugs on occasion. Probably keeps that or sells it. But he's hiding something. Junkyard owners aren't the most ethical guys in the world. It's possible he stripped that minivan down and sold the engine, or maybe even the whole car, regardless of what he says about the trouble he could get in with a flooded vehicle. I mean, what are the chances anything will happen to him if he's retiring next summer? It's not hard to remove the VIN number from some parts and resell the engine for a couple hundred bucks."

"But you don't think he found the rifle that killed the EPA lawyer?"

"I don't."

"Next step?"

"Let's assume our cancer girl shot the lawyer. We're still on square one. We still need a connection. And we still need a weapon."

"You think she dumped it somewhere?"

"If she's the shooter, that's the next logical assumption. First, we need to call in the water search team and see if they can locate the weapon in the canal near the vehicle crash location. The good news is the canal has virtually no current. The weapon, if there is one, should still be in the vicinity of the crash. We also need to search Spring Valley Park again. We need people poking their heads into the sewers around the neighborhood. You and I can start knocking on doors so the neighbors know to keep their eyes peeled for a discarded weapon. If the minivan driver is our shooter, and the weapon isn't in the vehicle, it has to be somewhere close by."

"And if all that doesn't pan out?"

"Do you have anything black to wear?"

CHAPTER 6

IN THE SMALL bathroom just off the main room of his office, Dan Lord strained his neck to get a view of the still-unhealed wound on his shoulder blade in the mirror. He looked at the dried blood that surrounded the homemade patch job, reached over his shoulder with his opposite hand, and ripped the large piece of duct tape and bathroom tissue off his skin.

Dan picked up the bottle of peroxide from the narrow counter, poured some onto a gauze pad, and pressed it into the wound with minimal efficacy. Struggling with the awkward location of the wound, he spent the next several minutes attaching a series of butterfly Band-Aids, most of which missed their mark.

Unhappy with his self-administered attempt at medical care, he returned to the roll of duct tape and wad of toilet paper.

He plucked his shirt from the small towel rack and cursed at the bloodstain. He opened the tiny bathroom closet where he kept extra clothes, and removed the last clean shirt from the shelf.

Dan exited the bathroom, walked across the open expanse of his second-floor office, and turned off the computer on the lone desk in the middle of the room. The barren décor of the office served two purposes. First, it satiated his desire for simplicity. Somewhere in the midst of two formative adolescent years in Bangkok, he had first heard the Buddhist expression "everything you own, owns you." For some reason the mantra had struck a chord with a lapsed Catholic teenager. Decades later, the expression still resonated. Embracing the motto was especially helpful late at night, with a drink or two in the system, when the power of QVC was at its peak.

The second reason for the barren office was security. Minimal furniture meant fewer places for nefarious elements to plant eavesdropping devices. It was a worry few ordinary people could relate to. But most ordinary people hadn't narrowly escaped an exploding bomb in their workplace within the last year. The explosion, which nearly killed both Dan and his tenant in the art gallery below, was a fresh reminder that being careful was a never-ending endeavor.

Dan waited for the computer monitor to turn black and looked around the room at the exposed brick walls. He swiped his keys off the desk, checked the view from the windows on the front of the building, and headed for the exit. At the end of the office, still on the second floor, Dan pulled the steel-framed door closed, slipped a laser-cut key into the pick-resistant lock, and peered through the door's thick ALON window. Satisfied his office was secure, he punched a code into the security console on the wall and waited for the two-tone beep to indicate the system was armed.

With the first security hurdle activated, he turned and looked down the narrow staircase leading to the ground floor. He glanced up at the closed-circuit security cameras in the stairwell, one at the top of the flight of stairs and one at the bottom. The small red lights on both cameras were functioning. At the bottom of the stairs, Dan stepped through another security door capable of withstanding a direct hit from an RPG. He used another laser-cut key to twist the lock and pulled on the handle to confirm the door was in position. Now standing in the small but secure foyer at the foot of the staircase, Dan placed his palm on the biometric console to open the final obstacle between his office and the streets of Old Town Alexandria.

Dan paused at the threshold, stepped onto the sidewalk, and passed in front of the art gallery that ran the length of the block—the entirety of which he owned thanks to a healthy inheritance that had since partially evaporated. The sign on the front door of the gallery indicated the art establishment was closed for the day, but would be open tomorrow for regular business hours.

Dan walked down two-hundred-year-old cobblestone sidewalks, passing bookstores and law offices sandwiched between restaurants and dessert shops. At the end of King Street he headed for the Old Torpedo Factory on the banks of the Potomac, the brown water of the river swirling in the shadow of the Wilson Bridge.

Dan weaved his way through a group of departing sightseers and entered the old munitions plant turned artisans' lair and tourist trap. He nodded to the potters in the corner and the glass blowers down the hall before stepping into the partitioned floor of the main exhibit hall—a cavernous room that was dissected into a field of semi-permanent booths and stalls.

Dan stuck his head into the first booth on the right and disrupted a young man with wild hair wrestling with a large easel.

Three booths away, Lucia, Dan's lone neighbor and only tenant, popped out from her assigned real estate on the perimeter of the main exhibit hall. Dan smiled as Lucia greeted him with a hug and a kiss on the cheek.

"You're late."

"Sorry," Dan replied. "I had to deal with a small urgent matter," he added, his mind turning to the soreness in his shoulder blade.

"I don't want to know."

"What do you need help with?"

"Hanging pictures," Lucia responded. She reached over to the top of a table and swiped a handful of shiny hooks. She pointed to the wall. "There are wires hanging from the wall. The hooks go on the wires. The pictures go on the hooks."

"Any particular order with the pictures?"

"Smaller ones on top. Larger ones at eye level. Black-and-white on the far side. I may move them around later."

Dan picked up the first framed piece of art and commented, "These are a little different from your usual paintings."

"Yeah, I'm expanding my repertoire. Today's exhibit is for portrait art. The guy I'm dating teaches the subject. He got me interested. The subject matter is a little more concrete than some of my other art."

You could say that again, Dan thought. *Most of your drawings are visual gibberish to me.* "How are things going with your boyfriend?"

"Good. But I don't know if I would call him a boyfriend just yet."

"How many times have you slept with him?"

"None of your business."

"Then he's your boyfriend."

"At this point I'm only looking for nice and normal. I'll worry about the title later. Is that too much to ask?"

"Has your father met him?"

"Are you crazy?"

"Did you do a background check on him?"

"No."

"I'll check him out for you, if you want."

"Why do I get the feeling you're going to check him out even if I don't want you to?"

"Because that's what I do. I can't have someone hanging out in my proximity without knowing who they are."

"Are you saying someone would date me just to get to you? I'm not sure I can deal with that. Dating in this town is hard enough."

"I'll just do a cursory background inquiry."

Lucia fell silent before responding, "I don't need to know everything about him. Just let me know if he's a felon."

"I can do that," Dan replied.

Lucia changed the subject. "You know, you should get a portrait done. There are a lot of talented people in the building today."

"I'd let you take a shot at a portrait some other time. It won't be today."

Lucia finished setting up her booth as Dan hung artwork on the hooks as directed. As Dan placed the last piece of art on the highest hook on the wall, he heard Lucia gasp. He immediately turned, hands rising, as an automatic defensive reaction. Lucia motioned towards Dan's shoulder. "You're bleeding."

Dan strained to look over his shoulder. "How bad is it?"

"You're going to need another shirt."

"Damn it. I liked this one. And it was the last one I had at work."

"Stay here. I'll grab something from the souvenir shop."

*

Lucia returned with a black T-shirt and a travel first aid kit. She set the first aid kit and the shirt on the small table and pulled the curtain across the front of her art booth for privacy.

"Let's have a look," Lucia said.

Dan reached under the back of his shirt and removed his Glock pistol from its holster. He placed the weapon on the table next to the first aid kit. Then he pulled his shirt over his head.

Lucia took an audible breath as she stole her first glance of her landlord's unclothed physique.

"Someone has been working out," she said, distracted from the gun and the bloodied shirt by his well-defined shoulders. Dan turned and Lucia's eyes dropped to his abdomen. "A lot," she added.

"It depends on your definition of working out," Dan replied. He cranked his neck in a failed attempt to see over his shoulder.

Lucia moved in for a close-up of the wound and Dan turned to provide her with a clear view.

"You mind telling me what happened?"

"You wouldn't believe me if I told you."

"Try me."

"I was invited to a party the other night for the Deputy Chief of Mission for the Indian Embassy."

"Easy for you to say. Who is the Indian deputy whatever… ?"

"The Deputy Chief of Mission is the number two guy at an Indian embassy. He lives in Northwest DC. I was investigating a report of illegal workers at his residence."

"There are a million illegal workers in this town. Who cares?"

"This is different. These are citizens of India who are reportedly working under house arrest and without pay."

"How would you know this?"

Dan twisted to look Lucia in the eyes. "Because I do."

"And what happened?

"My exit plan didn't go as smoothly as I had hoped."

Lucia looked closer at the wound. "It's deep. What did you cut it on?"

"Glass from a small window I crawled through."

"Ouch. When did you do this? It looks like it's getting infected."

"Over the weekend, but I reopened it at the dojo last night. I bled on the mats before I noticed. Sensei wasn't happy."

"You will never make it to fifty."

"I just turned forty. Fifty is a long way off."

"And you'll never make it at the rate you're going."

"It could have been worse."

"Did you get what you were looking for at the Indian residence?"

Dan smiled and winked. "It was in the news the other morning, but you had to look quick to catch it. The story was pulled within a couple of hours."

"Does that mean you injured yourself for nothing?"

"Not exactly. The women who were enslaved in the house were on a plane back to India that morning. That is all they wanted."

"Well, good for you."

"Good for them."

"Do you mind me asking who the client was? I'm just curious."

"Enslavement at the Deputy Chief of Mission for India was a pro bono case."

"Of course it was."

"I can afford some pro bono work, as long as I slip a few paying customers in the mix. And as long as my tenants pay their rent on time."

Lucia pulled some gauze from the first aid kit and applied pressure to the open wounds. "You might want to see a doctor."

"I thought I had it under control."

"With duct tape, toilet paper, and butterfly Band-Aids that look like Ray Charles put them on?"

"I'll go to a doctor later."

Lucia applied a thick layer of Neosporin and covered the wound with a series of Band-Aids. "This may not hold very long. But the black T-shirt I picked up should cover the blood until you get home."

"Black shirt? Good idea."

"Family secret," Lucia said straight-faced, making Dan laugh. Her family's ties to organized crime were a running private joke.

A male voice called out for Lucia and the curtain on front of the booth slid open. A man in jeans and a button up cotton shirt paused at the scene in front of him. His eyes fell to the weapon on the table and the bloodstained shirt.

Lucia performed introductions. "Dan, this is my boyfriend, Buddy. Buddy, this is my neighbor and landlord, Dan."

The two men shook hands.

"We're also friends," Dan added.

"I hope so," Buddy said, looking at Dan's exposed upper body.

"Lucia was just helping me with a small medical issue," Dan said.

"I hope it wasn't caused by another bomb," Buddy said.

"You heard about that?"

"I think everyone who watches the news knows about the bomb in Alexandria last year. I wouldn't have made the connection to you, of course, unless I knew Lucia."

"See what I mean?" Dan said, looking at Lucia. "He's working you to get to me."

Buddy responded. "I'm not sure what you're referring to."

"Ignore him. Dan is just being difficult," Lucia said.

An odd silence fell over the trio and Dan reset the conversation.

"It wasn't a bomb this time. Just a flesh wound received in the line of duty," he said.

"Is that from your job as an attorney or a detective?"

"Sometimes it's hard to distinguish between the two," Dan admitted.

Lucia turned Dan around again to look at the wound. Blood had already begun to soak through the patchwork of bandages.

"I'm no doctor, but you may want to find one," Buddy said.

"We'll see," Dan replied, pulling the black T-shirt over his head and sliding it slowly over the dressing. "Lucia tells me you're a teacher."

"Indeed. Art professor at the University of Maryland. Spent the first fifteen years of my adult life as a starving artist before deciding that teaching might pay the bills a little more consistently."

"Lucia says you do portraits."

"Portraits and still life. But I've done a bit of everything at one time or another. Portraits for politicians and athletes. Some murals. Some courtroom sketching. Spent a year doing caricatures at various county fairs and shopping malls."

"Well, there sure are a lot of artists here in the building today."

"I know most of them. Most of the locals anyway. We're a pretty close-knit group."

Lucia interrupted. "I was telling Dan he should sit for a portrait. Maybe even a caricature."

Buddy nodded. "You should. You can give it as a gift to someone."

"I don't know if there's anyone left alive who would want it," Dan replied, bringing the conversation to a screeching halt. He picked his pistol off the table and holstered it.

Buddy changed topics. "Maybe we can all go out for a few drinks some-time. I get the feeling that someone who dodges bombs for a living must have some good stories to tell."

"I would love to," Dan replied turning towards Lucia. "See if you can't get something on my schedule."

"What am I? Your nurse and your secretary? Because if that's what you think, I'm going to need a break in the cost of rent."

"You already get a break on rent."

"Not much of one."

Dan's phone mercifully started to ring and he excused himself from the booth to take the call. A moment later he returned and grabbed his bloodied shirt off the small table. "Lucia, if you no longer need my help, I have someone to see about a job." Dan leaned in and gave Lucia an air kiss on the left side. He turned and shook hands with Lucia's boyfriend. "It was nice to meet you."

"You know it wouldn't hurt to have real stitches put in," Lucia said.

"Actually, it might."

"Funny."

"I'll think about it," Dan replied.

"No, you won't," Lucia said as Dan disappeared into the crowd form-ing outside the booth.

CHAPTER 7

MARCUS LOSH PULLED out the Metro section of *The Washington Post* and opened the last few pages. He twisted the top off the Stoli, the bottle still sweating condensation as it adjusted from the freezer to room temperature. Marcus poured the vodka into a large tumbler, added tomato juice, and stirred it with a celery stalk. He sucked on the end of the celery and when he was done mixing his breakfast, took a crisp bite off the end of the only healthy food he had consumed in the last two days. Unless you counted the tomato juice. Or the barley and hops in the nine beers he drank yesterday during daylight hours. Or the rice in the sake he sipped as a bedtime snack.

*

Most people didn't know the true meaning of the word bender. Marcus flirted with a constant one. His first real bender had been a celebration of his new crutches. The fancy type with the wraparound wrist attachments so he wouldn't drop them when the gyroscope in his head malfunctioned and threw him from the gravitational pull of the planet located between his ears. The crutches were a step up from the walker, and evidence he was on the mend. Eighteen months on the mend. The embarrassment of the walker had kept him close to home, snuggled safely in the all-brick one-bedroom apartment in South Arlington. The new crutches gave him hope. Confidence. The ability to slip onto a bar stool and stash the crutches out of sight. There was no hiding a walker.

His introductory bender had started on a Friday. He had walked out the door of his apartment with his new crutches, a thousand dollars cash, and two credit cards. A couple of beers at the local hole-in-the-wall with old-timers and aging cougars had helped him to regain dormant social skills and given him back some swagger. With false courage in his blood, he called for a taxi and headed into the Ballston-Clarendon corridor—one of the most bar-rich stretches of real estate on the East Coast. A Friday night pub crawl.

He woke up on Monday morning in a hotel room with cocaine on the dresser and a hooker in the bed next to him. Sixty hours had disappeared. A faint memory of the Washington Monument outside a car window fluttered through his mind. Then darkness.

He checked to see if the woman in the bed with him was breathing and then looked around the room for his belongings. He wiped the coke off the dresser with a wet towel, placed a trio of hundred dollar bills on the small desk, and slinked out the door and down the hall to the elevator.

The morning sun greeted Marcus through the revolving doors of the small hotel lobby and he didn't blink. There was no hangover. He was still drunk. High. God knows what else. Probably had a new venereal disease to go with the new vomit stains on the cuff of his pants.

The cab at the front of the taxi stand pulled forward as Marcus exited the lobby of the hotel. He pulled the door open and flopped in the back seat with a cloud of stench the cabbie knew all too well.

"Where to?" the driver asked.

"Columbia Pike, near Four Mile Run," Marcus answered.

"Never heard of it," the driver responded, now turning at the waist to look straight at his fare in the back seat.

"It's in South Arlington. A couple miles from the Pentagon."

"Virginia?"

"Yeah."

"Going to need to see the cash first," the cabbie replied. "That'll run a couple hundred dollars."

"A couple hundred dollars?"

The cabbie realized the problem before Marcus did. "Do you know where you are?" he asked, trying to focus in on his passenger's bloodshot eyes.

"DC."

"No. Philadelphia."

The first bender was the hardest. Then they all blurred together.

*

Marcus's eyes tried to focus on the newspaper, continuing a long-standing family tradition of reading what his mother referred to as the "Irish funnies." He never considered it odd to read the obituaries and death notices. They were in virtually every paper across the country, after all. And what was the point of the newspaper if not to read it? It wasn't until his first assignment in the military, when a commanding officer informed him—through an expletive laden rant—that young men don't read the obits. Especially young men who signed up to serve as soldiers.

Marcus kept reading. He didn't care if the obits were the primary means for the elderly to keep track of who was winning the "I'm still alive award" everyone secretly coveted.

Marcus saw it differently. The faces on the black-and-white pages of the paper were life, death, and the celebrated highlights of everything in between. The best of a person captured in words and presented to the world in one final effort to prove they had mattered. Someone's son. Someone's brother. A husband. A wife. A paragraph to say one final time—for those in the cheap seats—that they had been here. That they were loved. That they were more than the suits that dragged themselves through rush-hour traffic five thousand times over the last twenty-five years to little fanfare. The only sad obituaries were the short ones. A life so mundane, or cared for so little, that embellishment was evasive even in death, the only time and place when no one would call bullshit on statements of grandeur. Only a real dick would spit on the grave of the dead.

As he did every day, Marcus read the paper from beginning to end. He had the time. It was usually a two-drink affair. On Sundays, when the ads where thick and the opinions were plentiful, he would stretch it to three. The obituaries and death notices were always the icing on the cake.

And what had started as a family tradition had gradually turned into an obsession. It had been over three years since he had seen the first face. He remembered it vividly, a moment of clarity in a sea of gray. The photo in the obituary had stared up at him as if daring him to remember. Daring him to recall something he had long ago tried to forget.

Several months later there had been another familiar face. Another face he had tried to wipe from his memory. When the third face surfaced, smiling up from the paper, he got a second revolver to go with the one he already kept stored in the glove box of his ten-year-old Toyota 4 Runner.

Marcus looked at the photograph of the dead EPA lawyer and squinted at the face. He read through the write-up, the usual list of compliments for a wonderful friend, colleague, and daughter. A young environmental lawyer who was on the cusp of greatness. A sharp legal mind who had already plied her skills to the tune of three billion dollars in fines levied against corporations who had done the environment wrong. *Fuck*, Marcus whispered. *Another one.* He tipped the glass up and the remains of the bloody mary disappeared. Then he stared for a moment at the bottle of oxycodone sitting on the small kitchen table, wedged between the salt and pepper shakers, and used more often than either.

The day he saw the first face, he had tried to reach out to her. Unsuccessfully. He called, left messages, and waited. When he called again, the number had been disconnected. When the second face had appeared, he had gone to the house where she had rented a room only to find a young couple living there, the husband pushing a lawnmower across the small front yard while a young boy splashed in an ankle-high plastic pool in the driveway.

He then hired a lawyer to locate the mother of his son under the auspice of discussing visitation rights. The attorney took one look at the strung out, inebriated man in front of him and advised him to get clean before he engaged the legal process again. He was told his current condition was not conducive to a favorable ruling by any sitting judge. Marcus agreed, promised the attorney and himself he would clean up, and then fell on his face in a month of back-to-back benders that stretched from South Carolina to New Orleans. The story never changed. His son was only sobriety away… and it could have been measured in light-years.

Then luck had reared its magnificent head and he rediscovered her in a photo in the newspaper, her stunning black gown in the arms of an up-and-coming congressman from New Mexico. Fortunately for Marcus, while the mother of his child had perfected her ability to melt into the background, to disappear into the social scenery, her new husband couldn't share in her enthusiasm for anonymity. Unknown politicians didn't win elections.

Marcus shut the newspaper and looked up at the clock on the wall. He stood, grabbed his crutches, and ambled towards the door.

CHAPTER 8

ON A ROUGH cobblestone sidewalk outside a townhouse in Georgetown, Marcus appeared from the alley, his crutches clacking as they sought level ground. Stumbling, he nearly crashed into the mother of his child as she briskly hustled down the street.

"We need to talk," Marcus said, trying to keep up.

"How did you find me?"

"Your husband is in the papers. He's a public figure. It wasn't hard."

"You're not allowed to be near me. I have a restraining order."

"I know. It's important."

Sherry Wellington stopped moving, turned and leaned towards Marcus, peering into his soul. She inhaled his presence and easily ascertained his current physical state. "You're on something."

"Only booze."

"It's 9:30 in the morning."

"It's legal."

"I assume you drove here. Drinking and driving is not legal."

"I didn't have a choice."

"All you have are choices. You only need to make a few good ones."

"Not all of us can marry success."

"I wasn't looking for success. I was looking for someone who could be there and be sober. Success wasn't part of the equation. Until you're sober and have completed some form of approved rehabilitation monitored by the courts, you will not see your son. I'm sorry, Marcus."

"I'm sure you are."

"I'm making decisions for my son that real adults need to make. It's easy, Marcus. Do the rehab, see your son."

"I'm not here about my son."

"That's the only thing you and I have to discuss."

"No, it's not," Marcus said.

"What else is there?"

"Something important. Life or death."

"Everything is life or death with you."

"It's serious. Just give me ten minutes."

Sherry looked up and down the street. "Not here."

"Pick a location."

"Starbucks. Wisconsin and S Street."

"I'll be in a back corner with a view of the room. Come find me."

"Give me an hour."

*

Sherry strolled past the half-dozen patrons standing in line and found Marcus sitting at the back table as prescribed. She sat down without looking around, hoping no one would notice her.

"You look great," Marcus said.

"I'm doing great. I opened a little boutique on the other side of Wisconsin last year. I sell high-end, previously owned furniture and clothes."

"Experienced digs and dressers."

"That would be a good name. I went with *Born Again*."

"How is my son?"

"Our son."

"Our son."

"He's good. He's in the first grade. Doing real well. Reads. Can do math."

"I wouldn't expect anything less. I mean, between the two of us, we have as much intelligence as anyone."

Sherry nodded. "What do you want to tell me, Marcus?"

"Do you read the paper?"

"Most days."

"The obituaries?" Marcus asked, placing a folded newspaper on the table.

"I try not to."

"Well, take a look at page eight. Far right column."

Sherry read the page and then looked at the picture.

"Do you recognize her?" he asked.

"I do. I saw it on the news. Shot in Spring Valley. I didn't pay much attention to it after that."

"Neither did I. I'm much better with faces than names. The name didn't mean anything to me. And the photo they showed on the news was more recent. The obituary used a different photo. A little older. A little bit more like I remember her looking."

"So, she was killed? Hardly unusual for this town."

Marcus pulled out a printed page from the Internet. "This is from *The Post* last spring. Recognize the guy at the bottom?"

Sherry nodded as she read. "Says it was an accident. Hit and run. Early morning. Out for a jog."

"But two pieces of each death are the same. No witnesses. No suspects."

"Two random deaths does not—"

Marcus pulled out another obituary from *The Baltimore Sun*. "I got bored. Recognize the woman on the left?"

Sherry's defense of the natural laws of coincidence was eroding.

"Shot in the back. Early morning. No witness. No robbery. Nothing stolen. Not even the Lexus sports car that was on the street with the door open and the keys in the ignition."

"That is three. How many more do you have?"

"Two more."

"Jesus." Sherry wiped a sudden tear from the corner of her eye. "How? Why?"

"I don't know. But I think it's time to be careful."

"Simple advice."

"Or go to the authorities."

"That's not an option. My husband is running for the Senate. I won't jeopardize that." Sherry fell silent and stared out the small window onto S street. "I can take care of myself," Sherry added. "And we have good security."

Marcus nodded. "You'd better. My son only has one parent worth a damn."

"I have to go," Sherry said, standing. "I appreciate you coming. Thank you."

Marcus stood and struggled to remove his crutches from beneath the table. As he grappled with his walking aids in the great production of standing, Sherry reached into her purse, opened her pocket book, and pulled out a photograph. She wrote her cell phone number on the back of the picture and handed it to Marcus.

"That's his school picture from the beginning of the year. My cell phone is on the back. Only call if there is an emergency. If you call and there is no emergency, I will get another number. Nothing has changed. Get sober, Marcus. See your son. Live with the rest of us."

Marcus looked at the picture of his son, staring at the miracle of creation who looked back at him smiling. The water that blurred his vision came in heavy drops. When they stopped, Sherry was gone.

*

Marcus was mesmerized by the picture of his son on the kitchen table. He smiled. He could feel the unused muscles in his face as they produced and held another grin. It was the tenth smile in as many minutes; the first repeated, non-drug-induced enjoyment since he started his fall from grace, a multi-year slip and slide down a rocky cliff named addiction. He had finally hit the bottom, having taken abuse from every protruding stone on his way down. Enough was enough.

Armed with a wallet-sized photo of his son, Marcus felt a hint of strength. He had made two stops on his way home from meeting Sherry in Georgetown, the picture of his son on the dash of his car. The first stop had been a CVS in Alexandria. He had still been buzzing from breakfast. His second stop, with a hangover breaking through, had been at Home Depot an hour later. For the rest of the afternoon—for four hours and seventeen consecutive minutes—Marcus drank water and stared at the picture on the table. No booze. No drugs. *Get clean and get a life. See your son.*

The oxycodone bottle was empty. He looked at his watch and knew his weekly delivery would arrive at 3:00. Twenty pills a week. Brought to his doorstep, procured from sources he didn't want to know about. When his own doctor had refused to prescribe more of the powerful pain reliever, he had turned to the pharmaceutical underworld. It took a week to meet his new "doctor," a white guy in his fifties who drove a Honda and who Marcus never saw again after the initial meeting. Future contact would be at a minimum. A time would be arranged for delivery of the product and the time would not change without paying a fee. It was a precise operation. And an expensive one. The lone interview between the patient and his new doctor of procurement had taken less time than it took to fill out the dozen pages of insurance forms required by his real physician. The whole shebang had been executed in the parking lot of Dick's Sporting Goods in Bailey's Crossroads, just down the street from Marcus's apartment. *The war on drugs was a myth*, Marcus had concluded an hour after the meeting, an unmarked bottle of narcotics in one hand and single pill under his tongue for good measure.

But today was the day he would start over. The dark door of hopelessness had been left open and the light of possibility had slipped in through the crack. He looked at the photograph of his son and swelled with confidence that today would be Day One.

He had a pretty good idea how the story would end. Either a neighbor would call the police, or a distant friend or long-lost relative would take an untimely interest in his well-being. Or the mailman would become suspicious at the growing pile of envelopes in his box. Eventually someone would notice.

But he didn't care. He was looking forward to the pain. *Nothing worth doing is easy.*

But yes, today was the day. His first hurdle would be to turn away the oxycodone man. Pay him for his trouble, send him on his way, and tell him to cancel his standing order.

The moment of truth arrived fifteen minutes early and Marcus walked to the door, his crutches leading the way as if racing to get the rehabilitation started.

"Who's there?" Marcus asked, unlocking the dead bolt on the door.

The deliveryman in the hallway shook the bottle with Marcus's weekly doses and held the bottle up to the security eyehole in the door. Marcus looked through the eyehole and involuntarily licked his lips at the light brown prescription bottle rattling on the other side of the threshold. *Just say no*, he reminded himself. He turned the doorknob and three holes suddenly appeared in his door at chest level. He looked down at his door and frowned at the splintered wood. A small cloud of dust wafted around his waist.

Then the pain hit. He tried to grasp his chest, his crutches still attached to his wrists. His walking aids flailed with his arms, banging into the wall and the bookcase on their respective sides of the doorframe. Moments later, Marcus took his last breath. He'd finally gotten it right. He spent his last five hours sober. Smiling. Only a well-written obituary could improve on his death. It was as good as it was going to get.

CHAPTER 9

"Do YOU ATTEND a lot of funerals?" Emily asked.

"For work, no."

"For pleasure?"

"I try not to," Wallace answered. "But as you get older, you start getting more invites for funerals and fewer for weddings. Haven't enjoyed a funeral yet. They aren't my thing. Probably scarred early. My great aunt died when I was a kid. I was six or so, and I remember my mother dragging me across town so I could get a good look at a dead body. She wanted to show me what happens to us all. Ashes to ashes, dust to dust, and all that. She quoted scripture the entire bus ride. She thought it would be a good experience for me."

"Was it?"

"Hell no. Kids don't need to go to funerals."

"The first funeral I attended was my dad's."

"Shit. Sorry."

"It's okay. I'm glad I went." There was a long uncomfortable pause and Wallace fished through his mind for an appropriate comment.

Emily broke the awkward silence. "But I've never been to a funeral for someone I didn't know."

"You're young."

"And I certainly haven't crashed a funeral as a detective."

"Keep your badge in your pocket. We are just observing. If you need to show your credentials, do it discreetly."

Wallace pulled in behind the main building of the Demaine Funeral Parlor in Springfield, just off Backlick Road. He straightened his tie as he shut the door. Emily shook her skirt and plucked a piece of lint off her black sweater.

"Here's the routine," Wallace said. "In and out in fifteen minutes. Check out the crowd. See if we notice anything or anyone unusual."

"You mean besides us? The unknown white chick with the big black partner?"

"I guess you're getting comfortable with our racial differential."

Wallace held the door open and Emily nodded and smiled as she entered the foyer of the funeral home. A large chandelier hung from the ceiling. The first floor housed four viewing parlors, one on each corner of the large brick establishment. A staircase wound upward from the front of the foyer, leading to four additional viewing rooms on the floor above. Total vacancy for eight quiet customers at a time.

At the far end of the lobby, a table stood near the entrance to a set of double doors. A guest book was splayed open, a gold pen resting in the crevice between the pages. A framed placard with the name Beth Fluto rested next to the guest book. A large monitor flashed photos on rotation, each passing glimpse of Beth straining to capture a life through snapshots.

As Wallace handed the gold pen to Emily, a photo of Beth with her son in her arms flashed across the screen and Wallace felt a twinge of guilt. A life lost. A crime committed. He hoped he was wrong. He hoped there was no connection at all.

Wallace entered the room and nodded at the group in the corner nearest the door. A white woman in her early thirties stepped forward and extended her hand. "My name is Liz. Beth's sister. I don't think we've met before. Did you work with her at the store?"

"Yes. Previously. We both did," Wallace offered, presenting Emily with his palm up. Emily shook hands with the sister of the deceased and felt her grief. The tear on her own cheek caught her off guard and she quickly wiped it away.

"We had a few others from the store stop by at the earlier viewing. Philip was here, of course. You couldn't ask for a more understanding boss."

"Philip was always good to me," Wallace said.

Emily nodded in agreement.

"Thank you for coming," Beth's sister said, looking past the detectives at an elderly couple coming in the door.

"Our condolences for your loss," Emily added.

Liz nodded and then moved in the direction of the elderly couple, leaving the detectives alone.

"I hate this," Emily whispered.

Wallace pointed slightly at the dozen or so bouquets of flowers on the opposite wall, arranged in rows. Nametags and brief messages hung in front of each bouquet, pinched between decorative clips disguised as tree leaves.

Emily stepped past Wallace and approached Beth in the coffin. Her body had been dressed, an expensive wig fitted neatly on her head to conceal the persistent bald spots, which had refused to embrace the end of chemotherapy. Her makeup was artfully applied. Compared to the ashen frame the detectives had seen in the morgue, the Beth in front of them had seemingly moved closer back to life.

Emily wiped away a tear and Earl Wallace closed his eyes and dipped his head. When he opened his eyes again, his partner had moved towards the door and was plucking a handful of tissues from a box.

Wallace walked over, grabbed a tissue, and then whispered. "Get a picture of the visitor's registration on your way out. I'm going to work the room a little."

Emily nodded. She stood in the foyer and waited for two visitors to complete signing in. When they left, she took out her cell phone and snapped a picture of the visitor registration page. She set her phone on the table and flipped to the previous page. Again she raised her phone to take another picture when a young man with blonde hair approached and cleared his throat for affect. Emily looked over and her eyes fell to the pendant on the man's lapel, indicating that he was an employee of the funeral home.

"Can I help you, ma'am?" the young man asked quietly from the confines of a perfectly tailored black suit.

Emily raised the edge of her sweater just enough for the young man to see the bottom half of her gold detective's badge.

"Carry on," the young man replied, heading for the staircase.

*

Emily waited for Wallace in the car.

When he sat down, she punched him in the arm. "Never again."

"Part of the job. Did you get photos of the registration book?"

"Yes. Three pages. Maybe twenty names on each page. Sixty people or so in total."

"Let's run through some of the names."

"Who are you looking for?"

"Someone named Philip."

Emily fiddled with her phone, enlarging the photo she had just taken. "I got it. Fourth line on page two. Philip Rafter."

"I say we go pay Philip a visit at Trader Joe's."

"How do you know he works at Trader Joe's?"

"Because one of the flower bouquets had a sign on it that read, *From her family at Trader Joe's*. And according to Beth's sister, Philip works at the store in the greatest-boss-ever capacity. I think we should pay him a visit."

"Can we change our clothes first?"

"Why?"

"We look like we're coming from a funeral."

"We are."

"It might not be the best choice of clothes for asking questions. I mean, all black, asking questions about a woman that Phillip knows just passed away. Makes us seem like ambulance chasers."

"Hearse chasers."

"You know what I mean."

Wallace looked down at himself and agreed. "Do we look good enough for visiting the EPA and a couple of coffee shops?"

CHAPTER 10

A GUY IN a Hawaiian shirt corralled loose grocery carts from the first lane of parked cars and pushed them to the sidewalk. Another man in an equally offensive color scheme exited the automatic doors with grocery bags in both hands. A pregnant woman walked next to him, directing the employee to her parked vehicle.

The automatic double doors slid open as Wallace and Emily approached. "I think you should take the lead on this," Wallace said.

"Why, because it's a white suburban grocery store?" Emily asked.

"You said it," Wallace responded.

Emily marched across the front of the store, dodging exiting customers with carts full of food. Wood paneling covered the walls. Enough Hawaiian-print shirts for a luau buzzed about, stocking shelves, handing out food samples. Emily rang a bell near the door to an elevated manager's booth in the front corner of the store. A woman's face with dark-framed glasses appeared over the wall above and Emily flashed her badge.

"We're looking for Philip," she said.

"He is in the back," the woman replied.

Minutes later the detectives sat down at a small round table in the break room at the rear of the store.

Philip, the best-dressed employee in the store, sported a goatee and a red paisley shirt with matching red canvas shoes.

"How can I help you, detectives?"

"We wanted to ask a couple of questions about Beth Fluto."

"She was a great lady. And a great mother."

"You knew her son?"

"Everyone at the store got to know him."

"Anything of note in her life that seemed out of the ordinary?"

"Not really. I mean, she was ill. She was out of work frequently. Undergoing therapy. Trader Joe's is pretty flexible. Most of our employees are part-time. A fair number of students. A fair number of married part-timers looking for some extra cash."

"And Beth?"

"She was a full-time worker. A full-time worker who was very ill."

"And you offer decent health insurance? I mean, cancer treatment costs a fortune."

"She started working here before she found out she was ill. So that's not the reason she joined the store. I would like to think it's because it's a good place to work. But a single mother in a yearlong bout with terminal cancer... I think flexibility and insurance would be at the top of your priorities when time is potentially short."

"A single mother with terminal cancer is one tough nut," Wallace said.

"One tough nut, indeed," Philip agreed.

"Was she into anything illegal that you know of? Drugs? Gambling? Prostitution?"

"Detective, I think you just crossed the line."

Emily smiled and tried to lessen the abrasion. "I think what my partner is getting at is whether or not Beth had been acting strange recently. Anything out of the ordinary?"

Philip's goatee did little to hide the sneer he flashed at Wallace. "I think acting strange is relative with someone in her condition. I mean, she worked hard, but she missed a fair amount of time with chemo and radiation. Though, neither seemed to help with the cancer too much. And with chemo and radiation, there are all kinds of side effects that could be construed as strange behavior. I mean, at what point do frequent bathroom breaks constitute strange behavior?"

Emily and Wallace nodded and shrugged, respectively.

"What about her child's father, was he in the picture?"

"I never heard her mention him. I know they were married for a very brief period of time. We aren't legally permitted to ask questions about kids, or marital status, or any of that jazz, as you know. But you learn personal things over time, unless you're oblivious or choose to be oblivious."

"Things like what?"

"Well, for example, I know that Beth and her son were both covered under the company's insurance policy. So that's some indication that the father of her son wasn't around."

"What about a boyfriend?"

"Not that I know of, but…"

Philip faded out and Emily tried to reel him back into the conversation. "But what?"

"Am I violating any confidentiality agreement by divulging what I think?"

"No, for a couple of reasons. The most obvious is that Beth is dead. And if you are only telling us what you think, then it's purely an opinion. Your opinion."

"I wondered once if Beth was being roughed up. I thought maybe it was the father of the boy. I mean, that seemed like the obvious culprit."

"Roughed up how?" Wallace asked as a serious expression washed over his face.

"Well, we have this guy Tom who works stocking the shelves and handling inventory. He does most of the heavy lifting in the back. Here at Trader Joe's, everyone does everything, but if there's something you like to do, as a manager, I'll let you have it as often as I can. Anyhow, Tom, the guy in the back, views moving heavy boxes as a workout. A free workout. A paid workout. He's into martial arts, yoga, reflexology. All that. Good worker too. But one day I come back to the break room, right here at this table, and Tom is strapping Asian medicated hot pads to Beth's arm. He turns to me and says, 'Check these out.' I look over and Beth's upper bicep and shoulder are covered in bruises."

"I asked her if she was all right and she said she was fine, but I could tell she was uncomfortable with the questions. She said she was moving stuff out of the bin in the storage room of her apartment building and a large box fell on her arm. Something like that."

"And you didn't believe her?"

"Let's just say it seemed a little rehearsed. She didn't want to talk about it so I let it go."

"Which arm was it?"

"Right. It looked like maybe someone had reached out and grabbed her. Latched onto her arm and maybe shook her a little."

"It's possible."

"It was a good size bruise. And in a strange location. At first I was a little concerned it had happened here at the store. Workman's comp is a big expenditure for all companies. We are no different."

Detective Wallace scribbled in his notepad for the first time and then returned the pad to his front pocket. Emily quickly opened her notepad and jotted a few sentences. Detective Wallace slipped his card across the table.

"Thank you for your time. It's been helpful."

Philip cocked his head to the side, not sure which part of the conversation the detective was referring to.

Emily also slid her business card across the table. "If you think of anything else, give us a call."

All three stood and exchanged handshakes.

"We have a sale on red wine and a tasting that starts in twenty minutes."

"It's only noon," Wallace retorted.

"We call it early happy hour for stay-at-home moms. It'll be packed."

"We'll pass," Emily said smiling. "Maybe on the weekend."

*

Outside in the parking lot, Emily turned towards her partner and asked, "What do you think? Did you hear anything interesting in there?"

"The story about the bruise on Beth's arm piqued my curiosity. Though a bruise could be from a lot of things."

"It could be. Beth could have been roughed up," Emily responded. She paused before continuing. "Then again, maybe not. You know I had to re-qualify on weapons at the Academy when I transferred from Fairfax to DC. But prior to practicing for re-qualification, it had been a while since I had done repetitive, extended shots with a rifle and a shotgun. I think the bruise the store manager described on Beth could potentially be a bruise from target practice."

Wallace nodded. "Let's see if we can't get an answer to that question."

CHAPTER 11

EMILY WENT OVER Beth's case as they sat in the car on the Belt-way, chugging along at twenty miles an hour in the fast lane.

Detective Wallace took the Annandale exit off the Capital Beltway and merged onto traffic on Braddock Road. Minutes later the car entered the Tall Tree apartment complex, a sprawling development built in the 1960s, comprised of forty three-story buildings with twelve units in each. The grayish brick exterior of the buildings blended with the overcast sky.

Wallace pulled the unmarked detective's car into a space and shifted the vehicle into park. Through the windshield, he could see a woman in a long beige coat playing peekaboo with a young boy. The woman and the toddler took turns hiding their faces behind the trunk of an old tree on the communal ground that ran between the apartments.

Wallace flicked his chin in the direction of the woman and Emily followed his partner's eyes. "That's Beth's sister. You want to take the lead again? This is still your neighborhood," Wallace said.

"Annandale is not my neighborhood. I mean, in high school I think we played Annandale in football a couple times, but that's about it. These days, Annandale is little Korea, all dressed up in suburban clothes."

"Like I said, your neck of the woods."

Emily scowled.

Wallace continued. "And not everyone in Annandale is Korean. Beth wasn't." Wallace pointed at the woman and child outside the car. "And neither is her sister or her son."

"Maybe not, but they are a dwindling minority. Annandale has the largest Korean population outside of Korea. Just drive down the main drag and look at the signs. Don't bother trying to read most of them."

Wallace relented. "Okay. We tag team this. Good cop, good cop."

Emily stepped from the car and the woman in the beige coat scooped up the young boy with strawberry blonde hair. The female half of the detective duo extended her hand as she closed the distance with the woman. Wallace pulled himself from the car and joined them on the sidewalk.

"Thank you for meeting us."

"You're the same couple from the funeral."

"We are," Wallace nodded. "We apologize for the ruse."

"You mean the lie?" Beth's sister raised her hand and waved her finger. "Let me see your credentials."

Both detectives extended their badges and Beth's sister leaned forward to examine them.

"One more lie and you can speak to my attorney, or get a warrant, or whatever it is you have to do."

Emily tried to cushion the second meeting as the two-year-old boy wriggled in the arm of Beth's sister. "My name is Emily Fields and I'm a detective with the DC Police. This is my partner, Detective Wallace."

"I'm still Liz. I'm still Beth's sister. I find it easier to keep track of the truth."

"And we are truly sorry for your loss," Emily added. "And, again, for lying."

"Thank you. You know, nothing prepares you, even when you're prepared." Liz nodded at the boy in her strong embrace. "This is Quinn. My nephew. He's two."

"He's adorable."

"He's a handful. And I don't have my parental stamina yet so he's wearing me out."

There was an awkward pause and Detective Wallace rubbed his hands together.

"We wanted to ask a couple of questions."

"Go ahead. I'll answer what I can. I'm not sure exactly what your interest is in my sister."

"We aren't exactly sure either," Emily replied. "But I thought maybe we would start with a couple of basics. Do you know where she was the morning she was killed?"

"In the canal, *if* you believe the police," Liz said.

Emily felt the sting of the insult.

Wallace ignored it.

The sister continued. "She had a doctor's appointment. She's been seeing a group of doctors at GW Medical Center since her original diagnosis."

"Do you know what time the appointment was?"

"Eight or eight thirty, I think. They open pretty early."

"Did she usually drive herself to her doctor's appointments?" Emily asked.

"If it was just an appointment and it wasn't a treatment day, yes."

"What time did she leave the house the morning of her accident?"

"I don't know. I had Quinn with me at my apartment in Chantilly. The day before was a treatment day and Beth was feeling a bit rough. I was watching Quinn at my place so Beth could rest. Get a good night sleep. She was supposed to pick Quinn up after her appointment."

Emily scribbled in her notebook, and Wallace noted the missing alibi for the precise time of the sniper shooting.

"You wouldn't happen to know the location of your sister's cell phone, would you?"

"I found it in her apartment. Still plugged into the charger on the wall. Looks like she forgot to take it the morning of the accident."

"Is there any chance we can take a look at Beth's apartment?" Emily asked.

"Sure," Liz replied. "Follow me. It's the last building on the left, at the end of the sidewalk."

*

At the apartment door, Liz fumbled with the keys. "You're going to have to excuse the mess," she offered.

The detectives stepped into the apartment and Liz put Quinn on the ground. His small sneakers touched the floor and the boy quickly disappeared into the obstacle course of an apartment in the middle of a move. Toys littered the living room. Half-packed boxes were stacked four feet tall along the wall.

"The week has been crazy. Trying to figure out what to keep. What to sell. Quinn is moving into my place with me. Well, he's already moved in, but we have stuff here, stuff there, stuff in the car."

Liz's eyes bounced around the room and she suddenly seemed overwhelmed.

"I can only imagine," Emily offered.

"You know, the funny thing is I always wanted to be a mom. And I would do it all by myself if I had to... but this isn't exactly what I had in mind. And with my sister's cancer, well, I'd been preparing myself for the eventuality of it, but reality accelerated my timeline."

"So it was decided before your sister passed away that you would be the guardian of her son?" Emily asked.

"That's correct. Beth had a will created after the first round of chemo failed. She was considered terminal, but initially there was hope. As time passed and treatment failed, she became more pragmatic."

"I'm not sure how to broach this subject, so I'm just going to come out and ask. Was her son provided for, financially?" Emily probed.

"Beth had a thirty thousand dollar group life insurance policy through the grocery store. Not much. Enough to cover some expenses. I'm not sure what medical bills she may have had, but you can't collect from the dead. For the last couple of months she seemed less concerned about bills and didn't talk about them. But she was always concerned about Quinn."

"You sure she didn't have money or property stashed away?" Wallace asked.

"I haven't gone through everything yet, but no. As of now, the only thing she had stashed away was a tablecloth collection. Found it in storage in the basement of the building. It's up on eBay right now."

"Was your sister into anything else? Drugs? Bad men?"

"She hadn't dated in a while. Balding and bone thin isn't a popular look with the guys, as it turns out."

"Did you sister own a gun?" Emily asked.

"No. Not that I know of."

"Did she ever go shooting?" Wallace added.

"If she did, she didn't tell me. We were sisters, we talked about everything... but I honestly don't think guns was ever a topic of conversation."

"What about her ex-husband? Was he a gun owner?"

"I can't say. They weren't married long."

"Can we speak with him?"

"He isn't in the picture. At all. I only met him a few times before he skedaddled. Wouldn't recognize him if he walked into the room. Beth had his legal rights removed and he signed the papers. The guy didn't blink. He never paid child support. Nothing. Rumor has it he passed away down south somewhere. Now if he is alive and he shows up looking to be a father, well, that's something the courts will have to decide on."

"What about an old boyfriend? Someone from her past. Did she have someone who may have been interested in guns? Maybe taught her to shoot?"

"Am I missing something? I don't understand the connection between my sister and the questions about money and guns?"

"We're looking into all angles of a murder in the District. The morning your sister died, there was a shooting in Northwest DC. Someone was killed. The medical examiner's office found a .223 bullet casing in your sister's pocket. It is possible the casing found on your sister was the same type of casing for the bullet used in the killing."

"You think my sister murdered someone?"

"We are looking at all possibilities."

"That is insane."

"We can understand why you would think the line of questioning is unusual."

Liz paused. "You found a bullet shell in her pocket?"

"Yes, any idea where it might have come from?"

"I never saw her with a bullet. Or with a gun. And she was definitely not the murdering type. Besides, between cancer therapy, working, and raising a son, she didn't have time."

"Anyone else we should talk to?" Emily asked.

"Talk to the people at her work. Other than that, the only people she spent time with were doctors, nurses, and people in the medical field."

Wallace and Emily both extended their business cards and Beth's sister took them. "If you think of anything that may help, please let us know."

"I'm not sure I understand. You mean if I think of anything that may indicate my sister killed someone?"

Emily felt her face go flush. "If you think of anything that may help us determine her state of mind, anything, really."

Liz shrugged her shoulders. "I can do that."

"Before we leave, can we look in her storage in the basement?"

Liz tilted her head to the side. "Sure. It's downstairs. Across from the laundry room. The second cubicle on the right, on the bottom level. You can help yourself. There's a small lock on the door, the combination is 4-5-6. I assume you can be trusted with that information."

"Thanks," Emily said, turning towards the door and pushing gently on Wallace's shoulder.

*

On the way down the stairs into the basement, Emily chastised her partner. "See what happens when you lie to people? It comes back to bite you in the ass."

"Lying is part of the job," Wallace said, his large frame casting a shadow over his partner as they headed down the stairs.

"That is an awful thing to say," Emily retorted.

"You'll come around to the reality of it."

Emily pushed the door to the storage room open and looked at the small storage cubicles built from plywood. Each cubicle was split horizontally into two. Wallace pointed at the cubicle on the lower level, the second one on the right, as directed by the sister.

Emily entered the combination and pulled the door open. Both detectives bent at the waist and peered in.

"It's empty."

"That wasn't very nice of the sister. Leading us down here to an empty storage bin."

"That's karma," Emily conceded. "You can't really blame her."

Wallace stood. "You can shut it."

"You want to go talk to the sister again?"

"About what? An empty storage bin?"

Emily didn't respond.

Wallace looked around at the two-tiered storage room. "I do think we learned something here."

"What's that?"

"The manager at Trader Joe's mentioned Beth had bruises from boxes falling out of storage, right?"

"Yeah."

"Well, how could that happen with a storage bin located on the floor?"

"It couldn't. Either the manager misunderstood or Beth lied," Emily said.

"And if she lied about that, she probably lied about other things."

"Now you're questioning the integrity of a liar? An interesting turn of events, don't you think, Detective Wallace."

Wallace grunted and scowled. "I'm done talking to you," he muttered, exiting the room.

CHAPTER 12

DAN LORD WALKED down the street, around the block, and then up the alley behind a short row of old townhouses. He completed his lap of the location before finally ducking into Born Again, a used clothing and furniture shop just off Wisconsin Avenue in Georgetown.

Dan noted the security cameras protruding from the ceiling of the store and the sticker in the front window that indicated, in plain print, the presence of an alarm system. Dan stepped forward and ran his fingers along the rack of clothes near the front window as he assessed the business prospects of the store. He checked the handwritten price tag on an Asian step chest in the corner and swallowed. Twelve grand seemed pricey, unless the chest was sporting the first few steps of the stairway to heaven. The candle display in the corner, and the stack of rugs near the rear of the store completed Dan's preliminary assessment.

Sherry, blonde hair cut at shoulder length, was in the back of the store, sitting at a large wooden table with ornate legs that served as the establishment's desk and checkout counter.

Dan could feel the intensity of Sherry's stare as he parted the sea of goods and approached the large wood table. He smiled to disarm and charm, and quickly assessed that Sherry, his potential client, was nervous. She had one hand in plain view on the desk. Her other hand, her right, was hidden under the desktop. Unless the woman was left-handed, Dan assumed his family jewels were in the line of fire. The dominant hand usually fires the gun. And in normal circumstances, the dominant hand would likely be the one on the table.

Dan announced himself as he approached the desk. "Dan Lord. I'm here to meet Sherry Wellington. She called me. I have an appointment."

Sherry sighed slightly, removed her hand from beneath the desk, and stood to introduce herself. She extended her right hand.

Definitely a weapon there somewhere, Dan confirmed to himself.

"Please have a seat. Can I get you a coffee?"

"That would be great. Black," Dan answered, sitting in a chair on the side of the large table so he had a view of the store and the front door.

Sherry Wellington picked up the phone on the table and made a ten-second call, ordering two coffees. She placed the phone back on the table and threw her head in the direction of the wall to her left. "Coffee shop next door. Free delivery. They let me run a tab."

"Nice perk."

"They offered, I accepted."

Dan looked at Sherry's hands and noted their rough texture. Dan moved his eyes from her hands, and then ran his glance up her arm to her face. Her attire was eclectic, a mix of wealth and hippie, a style very much in vogue throughout Northwest DC for women who wanted to be cool without being snobby. But Sherry Wellington's face was the cherry on the sundae. Dan had no doubt that one look at her blue eyes, high cheek bones, pouty lips, and perfect teeth, framed by natural blond locks, made most men weak in the knees. One glance and he understood why John Wellington, congressman from New Mexico, had chosen her. There were trophy wives and then there were just plain trophies.

"How can I help you, Mrs. Wellington?"

"Please, call me Sherry."

"Okay. And you can call me Dan."

"You are a hard man to reach, Dan."

"I'm particular about my clients. Finding me is the first hurdle."

"What are the others?"

"That's what we're here to discuss."

"Good. A mutual interview. I have a few questions to ask you."

"I'm sure you do. You mentioned that the former wife of a certain judge referred you. How is she?"

"Great. She's moved on. Found a good man. Living in the suburbs and loving it. Strip malls on every corner."

"The real American dream."

"For some."

"And for you?"

"I guess I found my own version on the American dream. From waitress to congressman's wife."

"How did that happen?"

"I was working in a restaurant on M Street, known as The Friendliest Saloon in Town. I met my husband when I was doing some catering for the restaurant."

"Some would call marrying a congressman a fairytale. A step up from the American dream."

"I love him. He loves me, too."

"Then very well done."

"Then thank you. I'm glad you approve."

Dan nodded.

Sherry forced a smile. "Excuse my forwardness, but do you know how to keep a secret, Dan?"

"Of course. What's the secret?"

Sherry paused and wringed her hands. "I want you to find out who killed the father of my son."

"I assume we are not talking about the congressman."

"No. John is alive and well. Busy. Running for the Senate next year, but still alive."

"Who is your son's father?"

"Marcus Losh."

"I don't recognize the name."

"There's no reason you would. He was murdered in his apartment earlier this week. The police don't have a suspect yet."

"Why do you think he was murdered?"

Sherry pulled out the Metro section of *The Post* and pushed the folded page in Dan's direction. Dan read the article and handed the page back to Sherry. "I'm very sorry for your loss."

"We were estranged. If you can use that term for people who weren't married."

"You can use the term."

"I have been known to flub the occasional word. Not very good at telling jokes either."

"This is not an English test and I'll handle the jokes."

Sherry smiled, this time it was less forced.

"But I'm afraid I don't understand what the secret is," Dan said.

"I don't want my husband to know I've hired you. I don't want anyone to know I've hired you."

"Then no one will know."

"Good. It's of paramount importance."

Dan nodded, though he was now adding curiosity as a reason to take the job being offered. "Would you mind if I asked you a few questions?"

"Sure. I assume you've already looked into my background."

"I'm a private detective. I did a cursory search. Checked public records. I know you were born in Kalamazoo and moved to DC twelve years ago. It's not important, but I am curious as to why…"

"A chance at a different life. Excitement. Glamour. All the dreams and ideas that bounce around the heads of small town girls."

"So you packed up and moved to DC?"

"I moved in with a great aunt in Takoma Park. I enrolled at the University of Maryland and got a part-time job waiting tables. I had a plan."

"Then what happened?"

"My parents divorced. My father vanished and my mother moved back to Northern Minnesota to live with my grandmother. She died within the year."

"So there was no going home for you."

"Home was erased. At least the home that I knew."

"That can be hard. But it can be motivating."

"I understand the difficult part, but not the motivating part so much."

"Historically speaking, burning bridges as they crossed them was one way for military leaders to motivate their men. Burning ships once they reached new land was another. When faced with no other options, there are no other options."

"Well, my plans for success took another hit when my great aunt also passed away."

"You know, there's also an expression for the plans that people make."

"Oh yeah? What is it?"

"Talk about your plans and the devil laughs."

"I haven't heard that one."

"Just a reminder that life is full of surprises."

"Indeed it is. Anyway, my great aunt had been nursing a reverse mortgage for years. She died broke, as it turns out."

"And there went your second home."

"There went my only home. There went everything. There went school. Suddenly, I needed a place to stay and money to pay the rent. School wasn't in my survival routine. But I always wanted to go back."

"You could now."

"I've considered it."

"What happened next?"

"I waited tables and worked as a bartender. Worked long nights. Barely saw daylight during the winter."

"And then you met your son's father?"

"I did. But my life didn't really change until a bathroom break at the bar where I was working. Nothing is scarier for a single woman than peeing on a little white stick and seeing a pink X in the test result window. I was unmarried and had limited finances. Hell, it took me a half hour to find the strength to pull myself out of the toilet stall. I walked into that bathroom a woman with a few issues and walked out of that bathroom with the weight of the world on my shoulders. Funny how a few minutes can define your life."

"Life can be determined in the blink of an eye," Dan said. "What can you tell me about your son's father, Marcus?"

"He was ex-Army. After he got out of the service, he worked as an electrician. Until he got injured."

"How was he injured?"

"Car accident. Late at night. On one of the exit ramps from 395. It was bad. Broken vertebras. Nerve damage. Bruised kidneys. He never really recovered. Spent the last few years doing odd jobs. Hard to be an electrician when you have to use crutches."

"I imagine."

"How did you two meet?"

"We met online. Match.com. Getting dates wasn't hard, as a waitress. Getting good dates was."

"So you weren't swept off your feet by a man in uniform?"

"More like I was swept off my feet by a man with a keyboard. We fell in love, had a child. One right after the other."

"But never married?"

"No. We talked about it. Until the accident."

"And then?"

"Like I said, he never recovered. Got hooked on painkillers. Oxycodone. Then booze took over to steal the remaining good bits the drugs left behind."

"Oxycodone is some bad stuff. The downside is way, way down."

"It was too far down for him to climb out. I tried. I really did. I wanted it to work. But between the booze and the oxy, well, I just couldn't keep it all together by myself."

Sherry held her stoicism but two streaks of tears betrayed her.

"It's okay."

"Then one night he hit me. We were living off Georgia Avenue, in a small apartment, trying to pull together a couple of lives that were spinning in opposite directions. A neighbor called the police and he was arrested for domestic abuse. I didn't want him to go to jail."

"But the police have no choice on a domestic abuse incident if there is physical evidence."

"Right."

"And then… ?"

"Well, fast-forward half a year and repeat the same scene, the same excuses. Nothing changed for the better. Marcus changed for the worse. I left one day while he was out of the house. Left with a stroller, my baby, and a suitcase. You can imagine where it went from there."

"Tell me anyway."

"Restraining orders. Court appearances. Custody rulings. We were estranged. I had full custody. He maintained no visitation rights. We hadn't spoken in years."

"'Hadn't spoken?' That means you saw him again at some point."

"He ambushed me here in Georgetown last week. The day he was shot, according to the paper. Popped out from an alley and said we needed to talk."

"About what?"

Sherry took a long pause and a knock on the back door shook her from her daze. She looked up at the small security camera screen in the corner and identified her cappuccino specialist from next door. She disengaged the lock on the large metal fire door, pushed it open, and grabbed the two cups of coffee.

Back at the table, Dan prodded her for an answer. "What did Marcus want to talk to you about?"

"He said we may be in danger."

"Why?"

Sherry paused again and Dan knew the big lie was coming. There was always one. Always something hidden in the pile of truths that a person couldn't come to terms with.

"He didn't say exactly. But apparently he was right."

"Drugs? Unpaid debt?"

"Those would have nothing to do with me. Like I said, we hadn't spoken in years."

"Something do to with your husband? Politicians make their fair share of enemies."

"Not that I'm aware of. My husband is a good man. A politician, but a good man."

"I will reserve my judgment on him. I don't want it to interfere with my objectivity."

"He has nothing to do with this."

"I hope you have nothing to do with this either."

"Can you help find out who killed Marcus?"

"I can look into it. The article you just showed me said he was killed in Arlington. I'm sure law enforcement is investigating. They have a competent police force. But I have connections. I'll ask around and see what I can find out."

"How long will it take?"

"For what?"

"To find the killer?"

"You haven't hired me yet, and if I agree to work the case, it's going to take me more than ten seconds to solve."

"If you choose to accept the job, what's your going rate?"

"My going rate for paying customers is four hundred an hour, plus expenses. I only bill for work that I do. I don't typically have more than a couple of clients at a time, so you can estimate twenty hours a week, sometimes more. Figure something in the neighborhood of eight thousand a week. Plus expenses."

Sherry stood from the table and opened the sliding door on the small closet in the back of the store. She removed a large cardboard box concealing a small safe bolted to the floor and entered the combination into the lock. She pulled out several stacks of cash, shut the door to the safe, replaced the cardboard box, and put the money on the table. "That's forty thousand dollars. It should cover the first month."

Dan looked down at the money on the table. "Are you sure you don't want to write a check? You can maintain your anonymity with a cashier's check."

"I don't want to write a check and I don't want a receipt. I don't want any record of us doing business. My husband absolutely cannot find out that I've hired you. When we meet, we meet here, or another location within walking distance of this store."

"Not a problem. You control where we meet, unless I think it's dangerous."

"You ever worked as a bodyguard?"

"No. And I wouldn't be a very good one. I can't do two things at once. It would be hard for me to investigate Marcus's death and protect you at the same time. I can find a bodyguard for you if you like."

"Can they be invisible?"

"Probably not. And the effectiveness of security personnel is limited when they have to be a secret."

Dan smiled at Sherry, who was no calmer now than when he had entered the store. Usually clients showed some sign of relief during the initial meeting. Sharing secrets, asking for help, the first steps in seeking resolution… all of these generally helped relieve some of the anxiety that most clients had bottled up. With Sherry, it did not.

"You any good with that gun under the table?" Dan asked.

Sherry looked down sheepishly. "Never shot it."

"Can I see it?"

Sherry reached under the table and pulled out a .45 caliber Springfield XD semiautomatic pistol. She raised the gun in the direction of Dan, who quickly redirected her hand towards the wall. "The second rule of a firearm is not to point it at anything you don't intend to shoot."

"Sorry," Sherry replied, relinquishing her grasp. "What's the first rule?"

"Always assume the firearm is loaded." Dan took the gun, released the magazine, and then racked the slide. The bullet in the chamber popped up into the air and Dan caught it before it hit the table.

"Quick reflexes."

"I play with guns on occasion."

"That gun is not mine. It's my husband's. I took it from the closet. He doesn't know I have it."

Dan removed the slide, spring, and barrel, and checked to see if the gun had been maintained. He noted a slight sheen to the metal and considered the weapon to be in working order. He slipped the spring and barrel back into place, replaced the slide, and pushed the magazine back into the weapon. He handed the gun back to Sherry without racking the slide. "Take the gun home. Put it back where you got it. You aren't going to hit anyone with that unless you have practiced with it or if they're standing next to you."

Sherry looked at the gun on the table and nodded her head slightly. "You're not what I expected, Mr. Lord," Sherry said.

"What were you expecting?"

"Someone a little more rough around the edges. Less educated sounding. Maybe someone a little scruffier. Meaner."

"It's not the size of the dog in the fight, but the fight in the dog."

"People say that, but it always seems like the big dog wins."

Dan smirked. "Not always."

"I hope you aren't insulted. I wasn't saying you're small or short. I know guys hate that."

"That's true, we do."

"Maybe it was your reputation that threw me off."

"What reputation is that?"

"Someone who doesn't care about the rules."

"I have my own rules."

"And you're an attorney…"

"I have a law license and a private detective license. All of my licenses are a matter of public record. But for work, as I mentioned, I don't advertise and I only work on referrals. Almost all of my clients find me the same way you found me. A friend in trouble asks for help and my name gets mentioned. I don't spy on cheating spouses, find lost dogs, or look for runaways. Unless there are extenuating circumstances that make it worth my while."

"Fame or fortune?"

"Neither. Right or wrong. Black or white. I don't see things in gray scale too well."

"So, do I sign a contract with you?"

"No, we shake hands."

Dan stood and took Sherry's sweating palm into his. The two exchanged cell phone numbers and then Dan took the money from the table. "Do you have a bag?"

Sherry reached behind her and turned back towards Dan with a white paper shopping bag in her hand. "Will this be okay?"

"Fine," Dan replied. "I'll give you a call in a day or two. Let me dig around a little on your baby's father. See what I can find out. Of course you can always call me if you need to."

"What am I supposed to do in the meantime?"

"How about taking some time off?"

"And sit around the house all day with the maids and nanny? No thanks."

"Do you walk to work?"

"I do. It's a straight shot up Thirty-Fourth, right past Volta Park, then up to Q Street. But why do I get the feeling you already knew that?"

"I did a little research. Walking from your residence to this location seemed like the obvious mode of transportation, but you can never tell."

"It would take me longer to find a parking space than it does to walk. Our townhouse is two blocks up, three blocks over. Ten minutes door to door. I'm here in the store from nine to three. I have a couple of part-timers who help out in the evening and on weekends. While I'm here, my son is in school. His school is two blocks up the hill."

"All good information."

"Let me see what I can find out. I'll be in touch. Act normal."

CHAPTER 13

"I'VE HEARD ABOUT this place," Emily said, staring up at the menu board on the wall. The backs of two cooks in white shirts moved up and down the grill, repeating orders over their shoulders without turning around.

"I can't believe you've never been to Ben's Chili Bowl. Any DC detective worth their salt comes here. Hell, they even opened one in Arlington. It's an institution."

"It's also a heart attack waiting to happen."

"You gotta die of something. Besides, today is my day to eat whatever I want. Just the smell of this joint will give me enough willpower to make it through my day of fasting tomorrow."

"I imagine indigestion will see you through tomorrow as well."

"You're not going to order anything?"

"I tell you what. I'll order a chili dog, or whatever it is that you recommend, and you agree to come to one of my yoga classes. It may change your life."

"Deal. Anything a girl can do, I can do."

Emily laughed out loud. "We'll see about that. What do you recommend on the menu for premature death?"

"A chili half smoke."

"What the hell is a half smoke?"

"Really? Every DC native knows what a half smoke is."

"Not the white girl from the suburbs."

"It's like a half hot dog, half sausage. A little bigger. A little spicier. Half beef, half pork. They were initially made just for DC."

"Fine, I'll try one. But hold the onions."

A few minutes later, the detectives sat in the corner, eating chili-slathered half smokes served on orange plastic trays.

"Let's go over what we know about the EPA lawyer."

"Or don't know."

"Or don't know," Wallace agreed.

"You start. Age before beauty," Emily said, squeezing the mustard bottle.

Wallace swallowed a large bite and began. "We have one dead woman and one potential suspect, with no weapon or evidence to support a case against the potential suspect."

"And the suspect is also dead."

"And she's also dead. Personally, I don't think Beth's our shooter. No matter how many ways I spin it, the timeline just doesn't match up," Wallace said.

"Let's walk through it."

"On the morning of her death, the EPA lawyer stepped out of her house at roughly the same time she does every morning."

"Six a.m. More or less. As usual," Emily agreed.

"And from the EPA lawyer's house in Spring Valley to the location of Beth's minivan in the canal, we are looking at three miles. There are only two possible ways to end up on Canal Road heading into DC from Spring Valley. One is through Georgetown and the other is via Arizona Avenue. That's it. In the morning, during rush hour, all lanes of Canal Road are one-way, heading into the city. So that eliminates one of our two possible routes. Unless she had wings, if Beth killed the lawyer, she would have driven down Arizona Avenue. Period."

"Okay, so she drove down Arizona Avenue."

"And we know this assumption alone causes a major timeline problem. On a good day, with traffic, it would only take ten minutes to drive the three miles from the EPA lawyer's house to the spot on Canal Road where the minivan took a swim. On a colossally fucked up traffic day, it would take forty minutes at most."

"Could you define a colossally fucked up traffic day?"

"Godzilla walking down K Street."

"Okay. Good to have that perspective," Emily replied.

"And on the day of the murder and crash, traffic was of the common annoyance variety. Until Beth crashed, which then caused a delay."

"And we have about an hour between the shooting and the diving minivan."

"An hour and fifteen minutes."

"Maybe she was just sitting there."

"With the police, rescue, and the press all converging on the neighborhood? With the sun up? Someone would have noticed. Spring Valley is a nice neighborhood, people would tend to notice a woman sitting in her minivan for an extended period of time. Particularly with sirens going off everywhere."

"Just throwing out the possibility."

"Noted. But assuming she wasn't sitting at the crime scene for an hour, with the murder weapon in her possession, the 7:15 a.m. crash time doesn't make sense. She's too late to be the sniper and too early for her doctor's appointment."

"Unless she stopped for coffee or breakfast before her appointment."

"And we checked both of those options. Starting with coffee, we had three Starbucks, an Au Bon Pain, and two coffee joints on the American University campus. All of these are within a mile or so of the EPA lawyer's house," Wallace said, his eyes drifting towards the door as his mind digested the timeline for the hundredth time.

"And none of them panned out. The staff at Au Bon Pain doesn't remember seeing her on the morning in question, and customer traffic is pretty light that early. Keep in mind that Beth didn't look like the healthiest woman on the block. I'm pretty sure the staff would have remembered her sitting there for an hour in an empty restaurant."

"And the three Starbucks were also dead ends," Emily said.

"That's right. The three Starbucks all had security cameras and video. Beth wasn't on them." Wallace continued thinking out loud. "And her credit card wasn't used for any purchases either."

"And we checked the coffee shops on the AU campus."

"The coffee joints on the American University campus are a lot more difficult to reach. She would have had to park on the street and walk past several security cameras on campus. The campus policy also had nothing on their surveillance systems."

"So we know it's not coffee or breakfast," Emily said, chewing.

"And the only other places open in the neighborhood at that hour are two Exxon gas stations. Neither of which had surveillance of our girl. Not to mention, if you're going to kill someone, you would probably fill up before you did it and not in the middle of your getaway."

"You would think."

"And there are no other establishments between the sniper victim and the location of the minivan accident that are open before seven. Mimi's Convenience Store and Berkshire Food and Drugs both open at nine."

"And we're pretty sure she didn't take a drive too far from the area or she would have appeared on a traffic camera."

"Right. We checked the traffic cameras at the major intersections near the Spring Valley neighborhood. Spring Valley sits in a box between Massachusetts and Nebraska Avenue to the north and east. Nebraska turns into Loughboro Road to the south. Dalecarlia Parkway is on the west. All other roads dump onto MacArthur Boulevard. All of those possibilities have street cameras and we identified every car that passed through those thoroughfares between six and seven that morning. That eliminates virtually all of the 'taking a drive' possibilities. And if we limit the possibilities to roads without traffic cameras, we come back to the original route. And that route doesn't make sense. It doesn't take an hour and fifteen minutes to travel that route."

Wallace bit into a bunch of fries between his fingers. "Long story short, we don't know where Beth was between the time the lawyer was shot and the time she ended up in the canal and neither does anyone else. We have no cell phone records and, more importantly, we never found a weapon."

Emily finished her chili half smoke and wiped her face with a napkin. "And the EPA lawyer's side of the house doesn't get us very far in solving the crime either."

Wallace nodded, shoving another handful of fries into his mouth.

"We know that she worked at EPA Headquarters, right there on Constitution Avenue. We talked to her coworkers and her managers. Everyone seemed genuinely distraught and upset. Everyone was open to answering questions. No one seemed to think she was involved in litigation that anyone would murder for. She was an up-and-coming attorney, but she was still a junior attorney."

"Hmm," Wallace responded, chewing and shaking his head.

"We're pretty sure she isn't dating anyone and her past boyfriends all checked out," Emily said.

"I agree. It doesn't look like it was a boyfriend or ex-boyfriend."

"As far as we know she hadn't received any threats either in her personal life or at work. Neither had anyone she worked with."

Another grunt from Wallace as he picked up his second half smoke.

"But just because she was a junior attorney, I don't think we can dismiss the fact she was involved in legal cases that levied meaningful fines against some well-known corporation. A few million dollars in fines does buy some ill will."

Wallace took a swig from his straw. "I'm not saying it's impossible, but I don't buy the corporate assassin line. Maybe if she were a lead attorney."

"Well, the corporate assassin line may be the only possibility that remains open. And, for the record, you don't see the corporate assassin possibility and I don't see the single mom from Trader Joe's as the killer," Emily stated.

"Well, we know someone killed the lawyer," Wallace said.

"Unfortunately, that is still the only piece of real evidence we have," Emily replied.

"I think it's time we start looking for other suspects."

CHAPTER 14

DAN WALKED THE prescribed route from Born Again to the Wellington home on Thirty-Fourth Street, a block south of Volta Park. He walked the route again from the opposite direction, took a lap around the neighborhood at a two-block perimeter, and returned to a bench in the park. The stench of pooch poop from the dog park on the corner of the block ruined an otherwise perfect location. Dan turned away from the offensive smell and filtered through his list of contacts in his phone.

*

Jim Singleton, Arlington County police detective, answered his phone from his glass-walled cubicle in police headquarters, on the other side of the Potomac.

"Yo, Jim."

"Danno," Jim replied,

"You know I hate that name."

"Someday you're going to warm up to it. What do you want?"

"You make it sound like I always want something."

"Don't you?"

"Are you saying our relationship isn't symbiotic? I seem to recall doing you a couple of surveillance favors; off the clock, off the record, and in conflict with some aspects of the US Constitution."

"We might be running even right about now," Singleton admitted, stroking his beard in the faint reflection of the glass cubicle wall. "But I get the feeling we won't be after this call."

"Probably not. I'm looking for any info you have on Marcus Losh. Killed at his apartment last week."

"The disabled ex-Army vet?"

"Nice recall."

"This is Arlington. We average two murders a year. It's a short list."

"What can you tell me that wasn't covered in the paper?"

"The shooting was pretty straight forward. Tapped three times at point blank range with a .45. Through the door. A partially open door. The chain lock was still engaged when the EMTs arrived. They clipped the chain when they got there. The dead bolt was open. Looked like the victim was opening the door just enough to take a peek."

"Robbery?"

"Doesn't look like it. There was cash on his person. A few hundred dollars. Nothing else in the apartment seemed to be disturbed. The living room was clean, for the most part. There were a dozen or so empty liquor bottles in a recycling box on the floor. A pile of newspapers, about waist high, was neatly stacked in a corner. He may have needed help getting stuff to the dumpster on account of the disability."

"How disabled was he?"

"He had hand controls on his car, but wasn't a paraplegic. He had those big crutches or braces, whatever you call them, with the wraparounds on the wrist."

"I get the picture."

"Anyhow, living room was unremarkable. Just the empty liquor bottles and stack of newspapers.... And then things got a little interesting."

"How's that?"

"There was a roll of duct tape and a pair of police-grade handcuffs on the kitchen table next to a photo of a boy. There was an empty prescription bottle on the kitchen table. Nothing in it. No markings. We ran toxicology on Marcus' body and he had a ton of oxy in his blood."

"Ex-baby momma says he'd been hooked for a few years. She had a restraining order on him. They had custody issues. They hadn't spoken in years, according to my client," Dan said.

"Do you think this ex-girlfriend had anything to do with this? Revenge for past misdeeds?"

"I doubt it. You want to guess who the ex-girlfriend is married to?"

"Already know. Her phone number was found on the back of the boy's photo on the table. And I saw the records for the restraining order in the system. Her husband is John Wellington. Just your average congressman. Someone who can end your career and make life miserable. Don't take this the wrong way, Dan, but you need to get some new clients."

"I'll take it under advisement. And I think the congressman's current title is 'Senator hopeful Wellington.'"

"There you go. Someone who can make life miserable."

"He doesn't know his wife hired me."

"What did she hire you to do?"

"Find who killed Marcus."

"We're working it."

"I know. What else do you have?"

"Well, if the duct tape and handcuffs on the kitchen table didn't throw you for a loop, maybe the bedroom will."

"Kinky sex?"

"More like dirty sex. In the bedroom we found a box of adult diapers in the corner, a rubber sheet on the mattress, and a couple of gallon jugs on the bedroom floor full of water with tubes running out of them. The tubes ran from the bottom of the water-filled milk jugs up to the wrought iron headboard on the bed. The tubes were strapped to the headboard with a thick wad of duct tape."

"Some kind of set up where he could get a drink without having to get out of bed?"

"That was our guess. I mean, he was disabled."

"Right assumption, wrong reasoning. Let me ask a question. Were there any full liquor bottles in the house? You mentioned a bunch of empties. Any full ones?"

"Now that you mention it, no."

"Sounds like he was about to embark on a homemade rehabilitation program."

"What do you mean?"

"I mean, he was getting ready to strap himself to the bed and ride out withdrawals. He would probably start by duct taping his ankles, then lock himself to the headboard somehow with the handcuffs. Adult diapers for obvious reasons. Rubber sheets for overflow and puke."

"Jesus. You heard of anyone doing that before?"

"A couple of times."

"Does it work?"

"Sure. If it doesn't kill you."

"That helps. No offense, Dan, but if the congressman's wife hadn't heard from this guy in years and she had a restraining order on him, why in the hell would she care who killed him?"

"She thinks she's next."

There was a very long pause while Jim considered the additional tidbit of information. "She thinks she's next?"

"She is concerned."

"And she lives in DC, right?" the police officer asked.

"Georgetown."

"Good. Keep her on the other side of the river. DC is not my problem. We like it quiet here in Virginia."

"Very professional. So, who do you like for a suspect?"

"No one yet. We're running the usual possibilities. Drug dealers. Friends. Coworkers. I mean, the lack of a robbery in this case makes it seem a little less random."

"Unless the perp was scared off before he could steal anything."

"Possibly. But between you and me, maybe the congressman's wife is right. Maybe she should be afraid. You know how hard it is to shoot someone in the middle of the afternoon and no one see anything? No one hears anything?"

"Not surprising if the weapon had a suppressor."

"We're assuming it did."

"So where's the surprise? No one heard anything because there was nothing to hear."

"Want to guess the last time a silencer was used in a killing in Northern Virginia?"

"Ten years?"

"Try never."

"So it would be rare."

"Never is very rare."

"The deceased was ex-Army. Could have been an old military acquaintance. It's not that much of a stretch."

"We kicked that idea around the water cooler. We're going through a list of old Army buddies. Most of them are still in the service. So far, all of the men in his unit are either deployed or they have alibis. It was a weekday afternoon, after all."

"Who found the body?"

"The daughter of a woman who lives in the apartment upstairs. Happened to walk by and see part of the body through the cracked open door. Not to mention the bullet holes in the door itself."

"Did you speak with the rest of the neighbors? Maybe they saw something but don't want to talk. Those apartments on the south side of Columbia Pike are full of illegals. They don't like the police."

"We call them undocumented. And they like the police, they're just afraid of us. But, yeah, we sent people in. Every Spanish speaking officer we have. Talked to the whole building and the one next to it. No one saw anything. But, once again, most of the tenants work during the day. Probably fewer people home in the afternoon than any other time."

"It's a curious time for a shooting."

Detective Jim Singleton stood up and looked over the cubicles in the surrounding aisles before sitting down again. "Off the record, here are my top three bets. The most likely scenario is a personal relationship gone bad. Someone pissed enough to just walk up and shoot him through the door without stealing anything. We looked to see if he had called the cops on any of his neighbors. Nothing. We checked to see if he had any recent car accidents. He hadn't. We checked into his coworkers at the last place he had worked. No good suspects there either. Statistically speaking, the most likely scenario is a relationship gone sour. The suppressor, if one was used, throws a wrench into that scenario."

"Unless it's an Army buddy."

"And we are nearing a dead end on those. For the scenario of a relationship gone bad, we first need to find a relationship. And for the last few years, this dead guy has been a bit of a loner. Doesn't get out much. Doesn't have a wide circle of friends. No girlfriends. Not a lot of interaction with the real world. The less time you spend with other people, the harder it is to create ill will. And this guy somehow created enough ill will that someone decided to off him with a silenced weapon…"

"Only takes a second to piss someone off."

"It's possible, and statistically speaking it's the most likely possibility, I just don't think that's the deal with this guy. If it was an acquaintance, something will turn up. But so far we have nothing."

"What's number two on your list of possibilities?"

"The second most likely scenario is a drug deal gone bad. But if you follow the drug deal gone bad scenario, why is the dead guy the one with the money on him? Usually, and I mean virtually always, the killer takes the money in a drug deal gone bad."

"Unless it was vindictive in nature. A revenge killing."

"Revenge for what? For not paying? So then why did they leave the money behind?"

"Just to make a point."

"To who? Who are they making a point to? This guy is a recluse."

"You've got me there. What's option C?"

Officer Singleton sighed. "I think it could be a professional hit."

"Besides the suppressor, why?"

"A couple of things have been bothering me. First off, why shoot the victim through the door? If the guy is opening the door—and he's your friend, acquaintance, whatever—why not wait for him to invite you in? At least invite you through the door where you can get a clear shot. Why through the door, leaving it cracked open?"

"Not sure."

"And if you're not going to wait for him to invite you in, why wait for the door to open a crack? If you're the killer, why give the guy a chance to see your face? Who would risk that?"

"Someone he didn't know. Someone he couldn't identify."

"Right. So now we're talking about someone he didn't know, who wasn't interested in stealing anything, who was using a silencer, shooting through the door, in the middle of the afternoon."

Dan paused. "Someone did their homework on this guy."

"Yes they did."

"But there's also a problem with the professional hit scenario," Dan said.

"What's that?"

"A professional would confirm the target has been eliminated. As a hired assassin, I would take a chest shot or two as soon as the door opened and then follow that up with a couple of shots to the head. But not this killer. This guy does all his homework, all the surveillance, gets a suppressor, allows the door to open a crack and then shoots the disabled vet through the door. But he doesn't check to see if the job has been completed. People get shot and survive all the time."

"True."

"So shooting someone through the door doesn't allow for a clear confirmation of the kill. It smells like a professional hit in many ways, but a messed up one."

"Maybe it will prove to be a random. Once again, statistically speaking, a random murder is what, a thousand times more likely than a professional hit?"

"Something like that."

"So then answer me this. Why did a congressman's wife hire you and give you some story about her baby daddy warning her she was in danger? Add that to the equation and you can throw statistics out the window. The likelihood of this being a random killing *and* a nervous congressman's wife hiring you with a story about her baby daddy being worried is virtually zero."

"Keep me posted," Dan replied after another long pause.

"What's your next move?"

"Going to find a junkie."

"We've put the squeeze on most of the oxy dealers. No one knows anything about this guy."

"I guess you're not talking to the right person."

CHAPTER 15

DAN PARKED ON the street next to a car repair shop and weaved his way across two lanes of traffic without waiting for the light to change. On the opposite side of the road, two guys standing on the sidewalk at the edge of the public housing development perked up. When Dan turned in their direction and showed no sign of changing course, the men huddled together and whispered to one another.

Dan closed the gap with a measured, steady pace. The two men stopped whispering and stared menacingly down the sidewalk as Dan approached. Dan made eye contact and considered the likelihood of a confrontation. The larger man with the blue do-rag on his head stood two inches taller and outweighed Dan by at least fifty pounds. Mostly muscle. A little chub. The skinnier man was about Dan's height and perhaps thirty pounds lighter. *Someone has been stealing his friend's lunch*, Dan thought.

Dan focused his gaze on the larger man in the do-rag and the skinnier counterpart moved from his position, distancing himself from his friend and creating two angles for Dan to defend. *Not today fellas*, Dan thought. *Tactically a correct move, but not today.*

"Good evening. Have either of you gentleman seen Darren C. around?"

"Who the fuck is asking?" the larger man with the blue do-rag asked.

"Dan Lord. Attorney. I represented Darren a while back. I have business with him, but he moved from his old place off Route 1. I heard he was in the neighborhood."

"Dan who?"

"Lord."

"As in Lord have mercy?"

You have no idea. "Fellas, this can go easy, or this can go hard. You won't like the hard route. I guarantee it."

The man with the do-rag looked up at the setting sun in the distance. "You have about an hour before you don't walk out of here without some kind of backup."

Dan didn't blink, staring straight into the man's eyes. Without warning, Dan snapped a fifty between his fingers, the cash appearing as if by magic. "Why don't you keep an eye on my car for me? It's just across the street. I'll give you fifty now, and another fifty when I get back. In the meantime, get Beanpole over there to take me to Darren C. I know Darren is around somewhere because you didn't ask who he was when I mentioned his name."

"Fuck you."

Dan mentally measured the distance between himself and the man before he offered a one-syllable chuckle and slipped the money back into his pocket. "Okay, big boy. You have a decision to make. A quick hundred, or a quick ass-kicking. A hundred won't even cover the cost to remove the teeth I break."

The man in the blue do-rag slowly pulled up is T-shirt and brandished the handle of a black semi-automatic pistol. "First, you'll have to go through my friend, here."

Dan's eyes dropped to the weapon and then back up to the man's face. "And I don't think *my* friend behind you is going to allow you to pull that weapon," Dan said, motioning down the sidewalk, looking beyond the face of the man with the do-rag. Do-rag shifted his gaze for a split second before seeming to realize he had been duped.

It was too late.

Dan closed the gap between himself and the gun in the waistband before the large man flinched. By the time Do-rag reached his gun, the grip on his weapon was occupied by Dan's left hand. With his left hand firmly on the weapon, Dan moved his right hand upward until his pointer finger pressed into the man's the throat, just above the top of the breastplate and below the Adam's apple. Dan now controlled two locations on the body that were hard for most men to ignore.

"Move and I pull the trigger," Dan said.

"You wouldn't."

"You willing to take that chance?"

Do-rag removed his hand from the top of Dan's hand, the gun still aimed at his manhood. Do-rag scowled at Beanpole who, ten feet away, seemed oblivious to the current circumstance. With slow realization, Beanpole started to move to his friend's aid accompanied by a string of vulgarities. Without moving his torso, Dan offered Beanpole a sidekick to the abdomen for his delayed heroism.

As Beanpole hit the ground, Dan pressed his finger deeper into the neck of the big man, hooking the top of the breastplate. "I assume you don't have a conceal and carry permit. And I'm guessing that chain-link fence around the elementary school down the block is less than a couple of hundred yards away. You know what that means?"

Do-rag said nothing.

"It means you're currently guilty of a class six felony. Brandishing a weapon within a thousand feet of a school."

Dan pushed the weapon a little deeper into the man's Fruit of the Looms. "So, why don't you just make a quick hundred bucks by keeping an eye on my car. I'll bring your gun back when I'm done with Darren C."

Do-rag nodded grudgingly. Then he borrowed Dan's new moniker for his loitering accomplice. "Hey, Beanpole. Get up. Take this man to see Darren. Bring him back so I can get the rest of my paycheck and my gun." Dan pulled the weapon from the man's waistband and then removed his finger from the trigger. He took the money from his pocket and extended the bill in his fingers. Do-rag took the cash and cupped it in his hand.

Beanpole stood, brushed himself off, and took several breaths. He looked towards his taller accomplice and Do-rag nodded. "Go on. Take him to see Darren C."

Beanpole rubbed his stomach and then motioned for Dan to follow him with a flick of the head. Dan pushed the gun into his own waistband and then followed Beanpole down the sidewalk into the heart of the housing project. The small brick townhouses and apartments resembled military barracks, not unlike many places Dan remembered as home, growing up in various locations around the globe. The entire stretch of brick low-rises had been recently updated. New roofs. New heating systems. New paint on the miles of iron fencing that cordoned off various blocks, creating natural boundaries for gangs and thugs.

Beanpole led Dan through a backyard, passing under clothes drying on a community laundry line. He entered the back door to an apartment building and the light from outside vanished as the door shut behind them. The tight hall was dark and Dan's eyes took a moment to adjust to the change. Instinctively he raised his hands slightly, palms facing out.

At the end of the hall, light shone through a small window near the front door of the building. Beanpole stopped under the light and turned towards Dan. "Wait here."

Dan listened as Beanpole's feet stomped their way up the stairs with an authority that belied the man's weight. The stomping was followed by a faint knock on a door.

Beanpole returned to the first floor and nodded as he passed Dan. "Sit tight. Darren will be right with you," he said, disappearing down the dark corridor from which they had just come.

Dan did as instructed and a minute later the door at the top of the stairs opened. More light illuminated the stairwell and Darren C. looked down at Dan from the landing above.

"My man, Dan."

"Darren. Got a minute?"

"Come on up."

Dan stepped into the living room and Darren motioned for him to have a seat. The one-bedroom apartment was meticulously maintained. Twenty-year-old furniture casually decorated the living room, magazines on the coffee table. The TV was on in the corner, the news playing quietly. Darren C. disappeared down the hall for a moment, returned, and then sat down on the chair across the coffee table from Dan.

"You look good, Darren. Real good. The apartment is nice."

"Got a nice girl. She has me whipped. Won't put up with the usual nonsense. Likes to keep the place clean. Doesn't want my boys hanging out here. To tell you the truth, I like it too. A little peace and quiet."

"You working?"

"Doing some drywall work. Real job, real pay, all legal."

"Good for you."

"Yeah, it is. Did skinny man give you any trouble?"

"Beanpole? No, he wasn't any trouble. But the big guy with the do-rag and I had to come to an understanding."

"I'm sure he enjoyed that."

"He's watching my car. Earning a hundred to keep it safe. I told him I was an attorney of yours, in case anyone asks."

"Good one." Darren C. pulled a joint from the pocket of his shirt and put it on the table. "Smoke?"

"No, I'll pass. I was wondering if you could get me some information."

"What kind?"

"Anything on oxy dealers."

"Don't tell me you got a problem with the ox?"

"Not me."

"Better not. Hillbilly Heroin. Bad news."

Dan peeled off five one hundred dollar bills and placed them on the table next to the joint.

"I need a question answered. I need to know who was supplying ox to a white guy in Arlington who ended up on the wrong end of a gun ten days ago. Name is Marcus Losh."

"You're asking me about a white-guy problem?"

"He was disabled and ex-military. They shot him through the door of his apartment. No one deserves that. Especially not someone who served this country. Regardless of what happened after he got out of the military."

"What's your connection?"

"An ex of his wants to know what happened to him. I told her I'd look into it."

Darren C. picked up the five hundred dollars and put it in the pocket where the joint had been.

"Give me a couple minutes. I'm going to the bedroom. Make a few calls."

"Take your time."

"There's a lighter and ashtray in the drawer on the side of the coffee table. Hit that jay if you want."

"Thanks."

Dan flipped through a magazine as he waited, Darren's muffled voice wafting down the short hallway. Ten minutes later the front door opened and an attractive thirty-something woman walked in with a bag of groceries in her arm. Dan stood and introduced himself.

"My name is Charlene. I heard we had a visitor."

"News travels fast."

"You staying for dinner?"

"I don't want to impose."

"Not an imposition for me. I'm cooking either way."

"I'm good, but thank you just the same."

Charlene set the grocery bag in the kitchen. "Can I at least get you something to drink? Apparently my boyfriend is out of common courtesy. We have ice tea, lemonade, and water."

"Tea."

"Coming right up." The freezer door opened, ice cubes clanked into a glass, and Charlene delivered the tea to the coffee table. She placed a coaster on the wood top and paused when she saw the joint.

"That yours?"

Dan stammered.

"It better be. Darren is not allowed to smoke weed. Especially not in this house."

Dan plucked the joint from the table and stuck it behind his ear. "Sorry. I didn't know."

"Well now you do."

Charlene slipped down the hall and entered the bedroom. Darren reappeared a few seconds later. He sat back down on the chair in the living room and noticed the joint behind Dan's ear.

"You should know better than to bring weed over here, Dan," Darren said for effect, raising his voice above normal conversation level. He shook his head in silence and motioned for Dan to give him his joint back. Dan tried not to laugh and flipped the object of friction back to its original owner.

Darren C. leaned forward and Dan slipped his butt to the edge of his seat. "Took me a couple of calls. The cops have been all over this case. Here's the deal. The dead guy who was shot through the door was getting his drugs from a dealer in South Arlington named Doc. Clean record. Only deals in prescriptions. Rumor has it, he used to live in California and went by the street name Dopey. Not sure what happened out there, but apparently he moved, went upscale, and changed his name. Doc runs a tight operation, primarily dealing in oxy these days, but will handle anything prescription. Has a couple ways of getting drugs, but gets most of his stuff from real prescriptions for real people who are selling for profit."

"Doc into shooting his customers?"

"No, Doc doesn't do violence. He's a white guy who lives in Arlington and drives a Honda. You do the math."

"But Doc was providing the guy with oxy?"

"That's the word. Doc is paranoid. As paranoid as you are, Dan. He will meet with a customer but he will never deal himself. He has runners who deal with other runners. Constantly changing runners and routes. Anyhow, word is the man who was killed was on the delivery list. The deliveryman was there the day the man was shot. He was at the apartment to make the delivery but your man was already dead. The guy arrived with the drugs, saw a commotion with ambulance and police lights, and boogied."

"How reliable is the source?"

"As reliable as any. Doc doesn't allow his runners to carry weapons. Doesn't want the unneeded risk. Oxy buyers in Arlington are mostly affluent, upper-class lawyers and housewives. No offense."

"None taken. Haven't been a housewife in a while."

"Anyhow, all that being said, it doesn't look like Doc is your man. He has the reputation for running a clean operation. No guns. No loans. No consignment. You don't pay, you don't get your drugs. You don't pay, he cuts you off. That is the best info five hundred dollars can buy."

"Thanks Darren," Dan said standing.

"Pleasure doing business with you. Did it help you out?"

"Sure. It was helpful. The fact that Dr. Oxy didn't do the shooting likely means there is a professional killer out there who doesn't mind shooting a disabled vet through a door."

"Well if you're looking for him, I get the feeling, somehow, he's going get what he deserves."

CHAPTER 16

THE PAIN HAD started in Amy's lower back, just above the waistline. With a lifelong aversion to doctors inherited from her father, she chose self-medication and popped three Advil every four hours for two weeks before switching to once-a-day Aleve. At the end of a month of discomfort, Amy grudgingly admitted she had joined the ten million Americans with back pain, if you can believe late-night pharmaceutical commercials.

Her aversion to doctors and desire for relief led to a bi-monthly chiropractic intervention. Three hundred dollars later, the discomfort in her back gave way to abdominal pain and she was deemed cured by the chiropractor. Amy was simply thankful for an alternate location of her affliction, though her abdomen was now pushing her pain tolerance thresholds.

Her second month of pain came with the welcomed side effect of weight loss, not surprising given her unabated abdominal ache and diminished appetite. Then, as autumn neared, she was afflicted with an insatiable itch on her skin. She readily attributed the dermatitis to her life-long allergy to leaves, triggered by the onset of fall. A single glance at the nascent foliage outside her apartment's kitchen window was the only proof she needed. The pharmacist at Rexall's Drug pointed her in the direction of relief on aisle seven, and Amy emerged from the store with a bag of empty promises.

Then, one bright Monday morning, Amy woke to a yellow tint in her skin and she got scared. Most people with a real fear of doctors can rationalize common medical ailments, connecting the dots between pain and its likely cause. An awkward sleeping position and the crick in the neck. The oversized suitcase yanked out of the trunk and the pulsing pain in the shoulder. Prolonged indigestion and the dirty plates at the local taco joint.

Jaundice was different. It was hard to rationalize a yellow skin tone as anything acceptable. Something was wrong and Amy realized it wasn't going to be repaired by skeletal manipulation or over-the-counter concoctions.

Her primary care physician, a nice woman in her mid-thirties, took one look at Amy, reviewed her recent medical history, and promptly sent her to an internal medicine specialist. Swollen lymph nodes and a possible blocked bile duct was the original diagnosis, partially confirmed by a rush CT scan. Upon receipt of the CT scan, the internal medicine specialist referred Amy to an oncologist who ordered an MRI.

In a twenty-four hour period, Amy had been swept into a tornado of medical attention moving at a speed she didn't know was possible. There were no more queues, no more delays. No one asked her to make an appointment for the following month. Medical assistants were on the phone to her insurance company, handling everything before she arrived at her next destination for her next test.

Amy left the MRI center at eight p.m. and her newly referred oncologist called a half hour later. "Don't eat anything after ten tonight. Tomorrow at seven we're performing an endoscopic ultrasound and a fine needle aspiration biopsy. Then we're going to do a full-body PET scan."

"Sounds like fun."

"GW Hospital. Be there by six. You will need a ride home."

Amy looked over at her daughter, asleep on the sofa in the living room, and wiped away a tear. "Okay," she managed before hanging up the phone.

Less than forty-eight hours later, Amy waited for the results of her tests at a small coffee shop near Uptown Theatre. The call from the doctor arrived at three and the request for an immediate, same-day consultation told Amy everything she needed to know.

She was screwed.

Thirty minutes after receiving the call from the doctor, she signed her name on the piece of paper attached to the clipboard at the patient sign-in window. She looked around the waiting room and watched a young boy playing with the toy box in the corner, his mother asleep in the chair, perched over the boy's position. An elderly couple in the corner whispered to each other with concerned looks on their faces. Amy forced herself to turn away, to divert her mind from her own mortality. The clock on the wall ticked and Amy stared at the second hand, listening to CNN as the newscasters reported the day's death, dismemberment, and accident tallies.

Sitting in the chair, watching time slip by, Amy had her second epiphany. The tornado of rapid medical attention had stopped. She had now spent thirty minutes in the waiting room watching CNN. Yesterday, it would have never happened. Not to the old Amy. The medical autobahn and the ability to race by slow-moving patients was a thing of the past. She was back on the residential streets of medical care, chugging along at twenty-five miles per hour. Amy knew the fast lane of medicine was still out there, still moving at the speed of light for patients with a possibility of being saved. She reluctantly snuggled up to the reality that they didn't waste the speed and efficiency of the medical care autobahn on a patient with no hope for recovery.

The medical assistant called Amy's name and she floated from her chair and followed the middle-aged woman in scrubs through a labyrinth of identical hallways.

Dr. Smithson smiled as the medical assistant opened the door and Amy could feel the forced nature of the greeting. Dr. Smithson stood, extended his hand, and Amy smelled death in the air.

She sat down in the leather chair across the desk from the doctor and her eyes slowly passed over the dizzying array of diplomas on the walls. Dr. Smithson organized folders on his desk, pinpointing his attention on one in particular, placing it face up, open.

"What do you know about the pancreas, Amy?"

"I know you need it."

"Yes, and no. On the simplest level, the pancreas produces hormones and enzymes. These can be substituted with varying degrees of success with natural and synthetic alternatives."

"No offense, but can you just give me the news, doc?"

"You want the good or the bad?"

"You're an oncologist. My guess is your news is usually bad. In fact, I would be willing to bet you give good news over the phone."

"Well, the good news is that we know what has been ailing you. The test results on the biopsy confirmed you have pancreatic cancer. As a result of the cancerous mass, your bile duct was obstructed. That caused jaundice as well as your abdominal discomfort."

Amy stared stoically ahead. "Okay. Let's rip it out."

"I'm sorry?"

"If I don't need the pancreas, cut it out. I won't miss it. Get in there and tear it out."

"It's not that simple. The CT scan and MRI show the location of the cancerous mass is inoperable. It has a very low resectability, as the medical terminology goes."

"Okay, so zap it. Chemo and radiation."

"That is the normal course of treatment."

"Let's start."

Dr. Smithson paused a moment too long and Amy's defensive armor cracked with the first stream of unwanted tears.

"We can start a regiment of chemo and radiation tomorrow. But I need you to understand that any gains we see in that treatment will be temporary. They are not a cure. The cancer has metastasized to your liver, your lungs, your colon. Your cancer is advanced. The two-year survivability rate is near zero. You may have far less time."

"How much time?"

"It's hard to say."

Amy wiped at the moisture on her face. "Dr. Smithson, I have a daughter. I need a number."

"Only God knows for certain."

Months of stress surged to the surface and Amy quickly moved past the first stage of grief, arriving at anger in full storm.

"Answer the goddam question! I want a number. You hang these diplomas all over your wall to show people you're a doctor. Time to buck up. Don't pawn this off on God. I want a fucking number."

"Best guess, two months. Your case is advanced. Very advanced. I am sorry."

Amy looked down and her shoulders started to shake. Her head dipped further and she sobbed.

CHAPTER 17

DAN STARED AT the computer screen in his barren office in Old Town Alexandria. Outside, the streetlights were on, the yellow hue arcing upward, the light illuminating the ceiling of the office. The faint sound of traffic could be heard through the thick security glass.

Behind the computer screen, Dan had already finished his background investigation into Lucia's boyfriend, Buddy. His tenant's man-toy was indeed an artist and, unless Dan had missed something, he was neither a convicted felon nor a threat to anything except the bedsprings on Lucia's mattress.

Satisfied with Buddy's background check, Dan had moved on to information related to his most recent client's case. At present, he was conducting three searches simultaneously, crosschecking information as he went. So far, the trio of Congressman Wellington, Sherry Wellington, and the deceased Marcus Losh, revealed absolutely nothing of note. Certainly nothing to merit shooting a disabled Army vet through a partially open door.

Taken individually, Congressman Wellington was winning the competition of most interesting background; not a surprise given his hundred million dollar net worth and the benefits of the best upbringing money can buy. There wasn't anything on the résumé of a waitress from the Midwest, or in Marcus Losh's Army records, that could eclipse John Wellington's dossier.

The Senate hopeful was born in Santa Fe, New Mexico, to wealthy parents. He had attended private schools, earned good grades, and was a star athlete on the track, football, and baseball teams. After high school, he attended Stanford University and then stayed on for another three years to earn his law degree from Stanford Law. As a young man with a new law degree, he joined a prestigious firm in Redwood City working eighty hours a week serving high tech clients in Silicon Valley. Two years of dissatisfaction later, John Wellington moved to Oakland and started working with the people, first on pro bono cases and then for large non-profits serving the masses on cases of inequality. And that track, as a man who was willing to help the little people, was his first step into politics.

Twelve years later, John Wellington had concluded his first term as a member of the House of Representatives and was on the cusp of running for a Senate seat.

Dan clicked through various newspaper articles on the congressman and followed him through his public life in the District. Another thirty minutes into his search, Dan was staring at a photo of Congressman John Wellington, arm-in-arm with Sherry Wellington, posing in front of a large window with fresh oysters on ice as the backdrop.

He read the caption under the photo, looked up at the name on the restaurant, and then re-read the article in its entirety.

"Now why would you lie about something like that?" Dan said out loud. He leaned back in his chair and ran his hands through his hair. He checked the time on the corner of the computer screen, stood, and headed for the door.

*

J. Paul's had taken up the middle of the block on M street since the early eighties. The number of self-proclaimed dignitaries, politicians, and athletes who had passed through the threshold were only surpassed by the count of scoundrels. The oysters on the half shell on ice, prominently displayed in the front window, beckoned tourists from the sidewalk. The ornate wood bar with the high ceiling and soaring mirrors lured the fashionable drunks. Men and women in their forties and fifties bellied up to the bar in search of the same alcohol the homeless guy in the alley sought, without the brown paper bag.

Dan slipped between a parting foursome and sat on an empty bar seat. The bartender with the bowtie wiped a glass and leaned in for Dan's order. Dan scanned the names on the tap handles on the far side of the bar and made his decision.

"Sam Adams, draft."

The bartender nodded and turned to grab a glass.

Dan glanced up at the muted TV and a bowl of peanuts appeared on the bar. A small square napkin landed squarely in front of him and his beer took up residence on the makeshift coaster.

Dan casually looked around, checking his surroundings. The large mirror behind the shelves of liquor in the bar gave him a large panoramic view of the restaurant without having to overtly turn his head.

"You want to keep the tab open?" the bartender asked on his next pass.

"For a while," Dan replied. He sipped the top of the foam off his beer and assessed the pace of the restaurant and the bar. Every restaurant had its own cadence, dictated by the clientele, the waitstaff, and the kitchen. A symbiotic relationship with different measures of success. J. Paul customers were willing to wait longer for better food and didn't mind paying for it. Ties were optional and those being worn had been loosened. Whereas the students from GW and Georgetown flooded the more raucous establishments along M Street, J. Paul's was the kind of place where the parents of students could seek refuge. A restaurant that aimed for a perfect balance between stuffy and casual. Dan counted the tables, estimated the seating capacity, and then did a quick headcount of the bar. For a weeknight, business seemed good.

The bartender made a tray of cocktails and moved the drinks to the end of the bar for pickup by a waitress. On his way back to the center of the bar, Dan raised his finger.

"Another?" the bartender asked.

"Not yet. I was wondering if you can answer a few questions for me," Dan said, placing a twenty-dollar bill on the bar.

The thirty-something bartender with dirty blonde hair looked down for a moment, then slid the twenty off the bar and into his pocket. Then he nodded.

"How long you been working here?" Dan asked.

"Three and a half years. Off and on. Quit once. Worked down the street at a couple of places. Did the Tombs for a while. Came back here for a better schedule. Closes an hour earlier here. Fewer students. Better pay. Better clientele. Bigger tips. Why you asking?"

Dan placed another twenty on the bar. "Looking for someone who may know something. Looking back at least five years now. Who here has been around the longest?"

"You a cop?"

"Do I look like one?"

"You look like something. Not sure what exactly. Got a vibe about you that's hard to place. If you were a little more uptight, I would say you could be Secret Service. Off duty."

"Interesting guess. I'm not a cop. Or Secret Service." Dan placed his hand on the bar and lifted it again, leaving behind a folded twenty as a handprint. "Who has been here the longest?"

"Carla. The waitress in the section by the windows in front. The good-looking black lady. Hair pulled back in a ponytail. She's been here forever. Or seems like it."

Dan dropped another twenty on the bar.

"After Carla, the only other person who has been around that long is Frank, the manager. He's really been here forever. He'll probably die in the kitchen. Thrives off the madness of crunch time. Dinner rush on Friday and Saturdays are his cocaine."

"Is he around?"

"Not tonight. Usually off on Wednesdays, but he isn't hard to find. He doesn't stray too far for too long. He's even here for some lunches. He's sporting the Kojak look. Not a hair on his head. You can't miss him."

Dan placed another twenty-dollar bill on the bar.

"What about Carla?"

"She works five nights a week. Pretty much a set schedule. Wednesday through Sunday. She takes care of her mother and needs to be home early. Blows out of here by eleven, at the latest."

The bartender leaned close and Dan stretched his neck forward. "She has epilepsy. Can't drive. Has to catch the last bus home."

"How's her memory?"

"Good enough. She's a waitress. It's not like she's working at NASA during the day. If you're looking for a good memory though, Frank the manager is your man. That guy knows the toothpick count at the restaurant on any given day. Memorizes the schedule every week. Knows who is coming, who is going, who is banging who."

Dan nodded. "Who's banging Carla?"

"No one that I know of."

Dan put another twenty on the counter. "Think Carla will answer a couple of questions?"

"You throw twenty dollar bills at her like you are to me, and I imagine she'll tell you what she knows. We're all working here for the money."

"Can you let her know I want to talk to her when she gets off work? Tell her I have a few questions about someone who worked here a while back."

The bartender flipped up the hinged end of the bar and stepped onto the main floor of the restaurant. He returned a minute later.

"She says you can meet her here at ten."

Dan looked at his watch. Four hours. "I'll be back."

*

Carla pulled up a stool at the bar and sat next to Dan.

"Barkeep says you have a couple questions and that you're paying."

"And I'm buying drinks."

"I'll take one. I got about twenty minutes to talk. Then I gotta run. Have to catch the next D6 bus across town."

"Should only take a minute or two." Dan raised his hand and motioned for an order of drinks. Then he reached into his pocket and pulled out a photo of Sherry. He showed her the photo and put a twenty dollar bill on the bar. "You know her?"

Carla took a very brief glance at the photo. "Yeah. I know her. Sherry Wellington. She used to work here. She did well. Married out of this life. Every waitress's dream. Maybe not a dream for the younger ones and some of the students, but for the rest of us, she pulled the fairytale ending."

"That's what I called it. A fairytale ending."

"That's what it is."

"Do you know her well?"

"She worked here. Was a good worker. Showed up on time. Was popular with the men. I mean, she is a looker. She's even more beautiful in person."

"Did you know her outside of work?"

"Not really. I would see her around from time to time, usually here in Georgetown before work, but we weren't friends. Not like we had coffee dates or anything."

"You keep in touch with her?"

"Nope. I've only seen her a couple of times since she moved upscale. Not to say we couldn't be friends, we just aren't."

"Not everyone is a friend. I get it."

"Look. Sherry was a sweetheart. But she is Midwest white and I'm a DC native. Born and raised here. Not a lot of shared interests with a white girl from the Midwest."

"What about any of the other waitresses? Was she friends with any of them?"

"Not that I remember, but she hasn't worked here in what, three or four years? Not many waitresses stick around that long. I think most of the workers around here know about her, but they don't know her. When you go straight from waitress to wife of a congressman, people take notice. Most folks probably know who she is because of who she married."

"What about the father of her baby? You ever meet him?"

"I met him a few times. Back in the day."

"What can you tell me about him?"

"He liked his sauce. Drank like an Irishman at a wedding reception with an open bar."

"Any idea how they met?"

"I don't recall. Might have heard how they met, but I might not have. He did come in once in a while but he didn't really fit in with the clientele here. This bar takes money from all types, but we don't have too many hard-drinking ex-military studs. They usually go somewhere less expensive."

"So she didn't meet him here?"

"Not saying that they didn't meet here, just that I'm not sure."

"And when did she meet Congressman Wellington?"

"Four or five years ago. It was in the papers. Some private party. J. Paul's was hired for the catering. All the waitresses, we all do rotation on private parties. Lucky for Sherry, she got the nod. She must have caught the Congressman's eye. He started coming to the restaurant after that, asking for her by name."

"A congressman slumming it."

"It happens. It did happen. And this place isn't that much of a slum."

Dan placed a fifty on the bar and took a sip of his beer. Carla checked her watch.

"Anything else you want to know? I have to get going."

"Any reason why Sherry wouldn't say she worked here?"

"What do you mean?"

"I mean, she told me she worked at The Friendliest Saloon in Town, but she didn't mention this place."

"She worked there before she worked here."

Dan thought in silence for a moment. Then he put another fifty on the bar. "I might come back, if you're okay with it."

"A hundred dollars for twenty minutes? You can buy my time any day of the week."

CHAPTER 18

D AN RAN CONCENTRIC circles around Georgetown for an hour before he stopped at Volta Park. He performed a round of post-cardio exercises, including a plethora of stretches capped with twenty-five pull-ups on the playground in the corner.

Three blocks away, his client was in her shop, swilling cappuccinos and selling pre-owned goods to wealthy customers. His client's husband was also at work, on the Hill, doing whatever lawmakers do when they are paralyzed by partisan gridlock. Dan dropped from the pull-up bar, laid on his back, and commenced on fifty leg-lifts. By the time Dan's abs starting to burn, he had decided to change tactics on his case. Instincts told him his fastest route to solving the Wellington case was going to be through his client.

For that, he was going to need a new temporary office.

*

Less than an hour later, Dan was looking up a short flight of stairs on the stoop of an old building he had passed three times during his morning run. A *For Rent* sign was attached to the small glass window next to the front door of the building. The small print on the sign indicated the room was on the fourth floor. Dan glanced to the top of the building from the street corner, smiled even more broadly, and opened the front double-doors of the four-story apartment building.

The staircase to the top floor was carpeted in hideous burgundy. The middle of each step was worn pink, the landing of each floor ragged and sagging from decades of tenants. The building was built in the 1800s, two hundred plus years of wear and tear kept at bay with dozens of layers of paint, all visible on the worn handrails of the staircase.

On the top landing, Dan confirmed his destination with another *For Rent* sign attached to the door of Apartment 4B.

He knocked on the six-panel wood door and noticed there was no ventilation in the hall. Summer would be sweltering. Thankfully—catastrophic investigative failure notwithstanding—he was confident he would be done with the Wellington case by the time next year's heat rolled in.

Dan knocked a second time and a tall redheaded young man answered the door in bellbottom PJs and a ratty T-shirt with lettering that was no longer legible.

"Can I help you?" the redhead asked.

"The sign says you have a room to rent."

The Georgetown grad student looked at Dan from shoes to hair. "No thanks, man. We're looking for another student. No parents. We already have those."

Another voice called out from the depths of the apartment. "Who is it?"

A moment later, a second student poked his head into the living room. The curly, dark-haired, good-looking kid tried to get a look at Dan beyond the freckled arm of the redhead who was blocking the front door.

"A potential roommate," the redhead answered.

"Sweet."

"He's old."

"Hey," Dan protested.

Dan reached into his pocket and held up a roll of money. "Paying cash. Paying now. Paying for the rest of the school year."

The door flew open and Dan stepped into paradise.

The stench of paradise threw Dan into a flashback of stale beer and moldy food. An off-putting, yet nostalgic mix of a hundred frat houses.

Dan looked at the pile of shoes in the corner near the door and sniffed. *Corn chips or foot odor?* It was always hard to discern between the two.

The dark-haired, curly top young man stepped forward to introduce himself. "Christian. But my friends call me Croc."

"Why Croc? You from Florida?"

"No. They're my footwear of choice."

"Crocs? Aren't they for old people? And I'm old. I should know."

"Wear them once and you may never take them off."

"Not sure I want to risk it."

Croc motioned towards his roommate. "The tall, warm, welcoming party is named Luke. His friends call him Ginger."

Dan turned and shook hands. "My name is Dan. I'm not a parent, a teacher, or a cop. And I'm not running from the law, before you ask."

"Why are you looking for a room?"

"I need a place to crash here in Georgetown temporarily. How long is your lease?"

"We're locked in until next August. Our other roommate checked out on us last week. Bugged out to live with some girl. Ditched us on the rent."

"What's the monthly damage?"

"Nine hundred," Ginger answered.

"Okay. Here's my offer. I'll pay for the room through the end of the school year, plus utilities. The whole nine yards. I won't need the room that long. You can rent it out again when I'm gone and keep the money. That should give you at a few months of double dipping on the rent for the third room. Not a bad deal. I mean, you're probably screwing me on the nine hundred anyway, right?"

"The last guy paid seven-fifty," Croc admitted.

"Figured. I mean, us old guys, we get a lot of breaks with those AARP discounts and senior citizen deals at Red Lobster. It's only fair we pay a little more for an apartment."

Ginger looked over at Croc and scowled.

"How do we know you aren't some murderer?" Ginger asked.

"You don't. But you can make a copy of my driver's license and vet me any way you want."

The two roommates looked at each other and shrugged their shoulders in agreement.

"Welcome to the hacienda," Croc said. "Your room is on the left, behind the kitchen. My room is in the corner, with the views. The park out one window, a tree lined cobblestone masterpiece on the other side. Ginger has the room on the other side of the apartment, looking east."

Dan walked through the living room and ran his hand along the sagging bookcase on the wall. He slapped the couch cushion and stuffing popped out from the seams. He stuck his head into Croc's room, looked out the huge double windows with the killer views, and made his offer. "An extra five hundred for your room," Dan said.

"No dice," Croc responded.

"An extra five hundred. *Per month*. Paid for the duration. In advance."

"I'll have my stuff out by dinner."

Ginger chimed in. "You sure you don't want to face east? I have the best sunrise."

"You're college students. What do you know about seeing the sunrise?"

"I know it happens every morning and old guys like you are sometimes awake to see it."

"I think I'm calling a moratorium on the 'old man' jokes. Unless either of you want to go a couple of rounds in the gym, winner gets to assign all future nicknames."

Croc shook his head and Ginger raised his hands in defeat.

"Good then. Get a standard sublease form off the Internet. Print it out and I'll sign it."

*

Dan was concluding his interior design efforts on his new room. A double futon was rolled out on the hardwood floor in the dark corner, away from the window. A laptop sat on the floor next to the futon. Two cell phones were plugged into the old outlet on the far wall. There was a short stack of magazines and a book buried on the bottom of the pile. A pull-up bar rested above the door to the room, wood shavings on the floor, remnants from the holes drilled into the doorframe for support.

Dan stood on a stool borrowed from the living room and hung a large basket chair from the massive hook drilled into the ceiling. He spun the chair in place and the rattan basket rotated in tight circles. Dan grabbed the basket chair with both hands and pulled down to confirm it was securely attached. Confident the wood in the ceiling beam would hold an additional hundred and ninety pounds, Dan slipped into the chair. From his perch he could see most of the park in the distance to the right. To his left, he had a decent view of the street leading in the direction of Sherry Wellington's shop. The Wellington residence was just out of view, a hundred yards around the corner from the park.

Croc popped his head into the room. "How do you like it?"

"Love it. Worth every penny."

"Who are you keeping an eye on?" Croc asked.

"What makes you think I'm keeping an eye on anyone?"

"I wasn't, until you hung that big bird cage in front of the window."

"I just like the view."

"We also ran a background check on you," Croc admitted. "You're an attorney."

"I'm also a detective."

"So who are you detecting?"

"Not who, what."

"What are you detecting?"

"I'm detecting too many questions."

"I walked into that one, didn't I?"

"You did. I thought you young guys would be quicker than that."

"Okay, old man. You win that one."

Dan sneered.

Croc smiled. "We're going to grab a beer later, if you want to join us."

"I don't think so."

"Why not?"

"I'm a little old to be drinking with college kids."

"A little what?"

Dan growled. "Old."

"Now the score is tied," Croc said from the doorway. "If you change your mind, we're heading over to McGinney's around nine if you want to join us."

*

Dan sat in the chair, waiting for Sherry Wellington to pass on the street below. *Waiting. The real glamour of detective work*, he reminded himself. Stakeouts were the most boring part of any job. Database digging, interviews, crawling through the underbelly of society when necessary—Dan loved those aspects of the job. The mental stimulation he got sifting through pieces of a puzzle and putting them together to form something meaningful. Stakeouts, on the other hand, always left him feeling as if his IQ had dropped a few points. After the first dozen, he understood why most TV police dramas showed two detectives together on stakeouts. It minimized suicidal tendencies.

But the potential of this stakeout was different. He wasn't going to be spending time hiding behind a dumpster, slipping listening devices into a public toilet, or taking pictures from the top of a building in the middle of the summer with roofing tar bubbling around him. He was in an apartment, in his own room, with a couple of university students who promised to be out most of the day. It was looking like the royal treatment of stakeouts.

Dan swung in the chair and mulled over what he knew about his latest client. The vibration in his pants snapped him back to reality and he pulled his cell phone from his pocket. He recognized the number from Detective Jim Singleton at the Arlington Police Department and pressed the talk icon on his phone.

"Jimbo."

"Danno."

"Took you twenty-four hours to call me back," Dan said. "Not that I'm counting."

"Been busy. A lot of heat over here."

"I'm sure. I have some information that may speed your investigation into Marcus Losh."

"I'll take it."

"Just remember you took it the next time I come asking for something," Dan said.

"What do you have?"

"The guy you are looking for is named Doc."

"The killer?"

"No, the drug dealer. The guy who supplied the oxy to Marcus Losh.

He goes by the name Doc, but he may have a record in California under the alias of Dopey."

"Good name change, but I see a theme."

"Doc is an improvement for sure. Anyhow, word has it that the shooter was not the guy supplying the drugs. Apparently this Doc character keeps his nose clean, uses nonviolent runners, and typically stays white collar."

"Where did you get this info?"

"A source."

"Who?"

"Doesn't matter and I can't tell you. But it's accurate."

"I appreciate the information. I'll throw it into the investigation blender with everything else."

"You find anything on your end?"

"Nothing concrete. Found a couple more Army buddies. A couple of them remember Sherry Wellington. But no good leads there for murder. By all accounts Marcus was a good soldier. It wasn't until the accident that he fell off the deep end."

"That was my read on his military records as well. I got a hold of his DD 214."

"Why am I not surprised you have access to his military records?"

Dan ignored the question. "What's next?"

"I've been assigned to keep digging. Been looking into Marcus Losh's finances to see if there's something about money that may have gotten him killed. Captain also wants to know if I can get an estimate on how big his oxy problem was. Putting together a standard spreadsheet with income and expenditures. See if Marcus was overextended."

"You're barking up the wrong tree."

"And what tree are you barking up, Dan?"

"A rich, beautiful one who has secrets and tells lies."

CHAPTER 19

AMY FELT THE first wave of exhaustion at the elevator. The medical tape on the back of her hand where the needle had delivered the chemo irritated her skin. She looked down at the small purple bruise, and ran the fingers from her other hand over the annoyance. She turned her attention away from her hand and pressed the button for the elevator. Then she waited.

And waited.

For the terminally ill, impatience took on a heightened form of torture. Amy stood there in the hall, staring at the illuminated down button, burning time she didn't have.

When the doors opened, she forced a smile in the direction of the elevator's lone occupant. She entered the elevator and as the doors shut she wondered what ailed the man standing next to her. Colonoscopies were offered on the top floor of the building. Rehabilitation covered the fourth floor. OB-GYNs took up the sunny side of the third, leaving the dark half of the floor to a team of podiatrists treating corns, ingrown nails, and plantar fasciitis. Chemo and radiation, in all their glory and enjoyment, were peddled out of the Oncology office on the second floor.

The elevator moved and Amy registered some nausea. *Please not in here,* she thought. *At least wait until I get to the parking garage.* By the time the elevator reached the first floor of the underground garage, Amy felt better. And tomorrow was a day of rest. A day for new, healthy cells to form. Or so they said. She also knew any new cells would do nothing to save her. The only offer the new cells flaunted was more time with her daughter. Time measured in weeks and days and hours.

Amy felt death closing in. An almost palpable stench of hopelessness permeated the air around her. And she was scared. Frightened of the unknown. But she vowed to show her daughter how to die unafraid. It was something no one even mentioned as a possibility, as a lesson to learn. And for whatever faith shortcomings she had, she rested in the conviction that she had spent the last four years of her life being the best mother she could be. Beyond the tattoos on each limb, dropping out of college, and getting pregnant out of wedlock, she had tried. The father of her daughter had left them both when their daughter was still waking up three times a night to eat and fill diapers. Without warning, he had taken a cue from Amy's mother's parenting handbook and was last seen boarding a Greyhound bus outside of Frederick, Maryland.

After the depression of abandonment dissipated, a small part of Amy was grateful. She had been blessed with a realization: There were shitty fathers and there were shitty mothers. Her baby's father was the former. Her own mother was the latter. And being that both existed, Amy realized she was not doomed to parental failure. She had choices.

And her choices were about to become more difficult.

Amy exited the elevator on the third floor of the basement garage. She slipped behind the wheel of her tired four-door Nissan and felt another wave of nausea. She left the door open for a moment; unsure whether the remnants of the oatmeal she had eaten four hours ago was going to make an encore appearance. Satisfied she wasn't going to be ill, she pulled the door handle. She started the car and tugged on her seatbelt. She checked her mirrors and when the face of a man in the back seat of the vehicle appeared in the rear-view, she screamed.

"Relax, Amy. If I wanted to harm you, you would be harmed already."

"Get the hell out of my car."

Amy heard the racking of a semiautomatic pistol and froze.

"I didn't say I couldn't hurt you. Relax and take a couple deep breaths. Chemo can be draining."

Amy didn't relax but she did breathe. She also moved her left hand slowly in the direction of the door's side compartment while staring at the man in the back seat. A New York Mets hat was pulled down to the man's eyebrows. Large sunglasses filled his face. A beard, either real or fake, covered most of the remaining details of his features.

"I have a proposition for you," the man said.

"What kind of proposition?"

"One that will solve all of your problems."

"All of *my* problems? Do you have a magical cure for cancer? The doctors say I have no chance for survival. I'll need a miracle to see Thanksgiving."

"It's a meaningless holiday."

"Fuck you."

"Okay, Amy. Relax. I have a proposition that will solve all of your problems except for *one*."

Amy squinted slightly, as if trying to see through the man's disguise. "I'm listening."

"Then listen very carefully. We are going to have a short conversation here in this car. If the conversation goes well, you will have a gift in the back seat when I exit the vehicle. A good-faith down payment. Do you understand?"

Amy nodded slowly, never breaking her gaze from the large sunglasses and baseball cap, brim pulled low.

"I know your situation, Amy. I know you're a single mother to a beautiful daughter. I know you have no life insurance. No great amount of money stashed away in a bank account. I also know the little savings you do have are going to be tapped out by the time the end is here. You're probably staying up late at night, wondering what you're going to do with your daughter. Wondering who is going to take care of her. You have limited options."

"Who told you this?"

"I know everything, Amy. Everything. And I can make all of your concerns melt away."

"How?"

"You do me a favor. Do me a favor and I will take care of you and your daughter."

"What's the favor?"

"First we agree to the rules."

"I'm going to need to know the favor."

"In good time, Amy. In good time. Rules first. Rule one: If you mention this meeting, future meetings, or my existence to the authorities, your daughter will not make it to her next birthday. Do you understand the first rule?"

"Yes. Now you can get the hell out of my car."

"Amy, Amy, Amy. We're just talking. Rule one is the hardest one. And the only one that truly matters. The rest of the rules are mere details. Rule two: If you choose to accept the arrangement I propose, there will be no backing out. Once you have agreed, you will follow through. Otherwise, the outcome will be the same as a rule one infraction. Your daughter will not see another birthday."

"You're threatening the only thing that matters to me. It's not a good way to gain trust."

"I'm merely explaining the rules. You follow the rules and no one will touch your child."

"Are you done?"

"Rule three: Once you have agreed to the arrangement, you will receive $100,000 cash. It is yours. Do with it what you want. Well, almost anything you want. Open a safety deposit box at a bank. Stuff it under the mattress. Put it in the refrigerator. Buy what you need. Just don't draw attention to yourself. It is enough money to see you through till the end. You can enjoy your remaining time with your daughter without worrying. For obvious reasons, it would be wise not to do anything extravagant."

Amy nodded again, but her eyes had perked up with the mention of a tangible amount of money. Suddenly, the conversation no longer seemed so ethereal. Cash was on the table.

"Rule number four: Once you have agreed to the arrangement, you will follow directions precisely. Exactly as told. You will not vary from the plan. If you are told to show up at eight o'clock, you will show up at eight o'clock. Consider it the military. The consequences for noncompliance will be grave, as you can now imagine. There will be no whining. No exceptions. Do you understand?"

"Yes."

"Okay. Four rules. One consequence."

"What do I have to do?"

"As I mentioned, our arrangement starts today, here in this car, with a good-faith gift. Just for listening to my sales pitch."

"Like one of those time-share salesmen? You agree to sit for an hour and you win a television. Except you never actually get the television. You only receive an endless amount of bullshit phone calls."

"I'm not selling a time-share, Amy. And I actually pay. So when I leave this car, you will have money. Once you agree to the arrangement, you will receive a larger payment. One hundred thousand dollars. Cash. Play money for the rest of your life."

"And then?"

"And then comes the real money."

Amy embraced the words like a warm blanket.

"Once you complete the task I give you, you will receive one million dollars. Paid into a trust for your daughter. To be used for her education, upbringing. Anything left over from this trust after her education and upbringing will be hers to use, at her discretion, once she is an adult."

"And you pay this money after I'm dead?"

"That's correct. Unfortunately, you will never see this money. For most people, it's not possible to hide a sum of money that large. It has to be passed through legitimate channels, with legitimate lawyers and accountants."

"And what is the favor I have to do for this one million dollars?"

She could already envision how she would spend a portion of the money. Toys. Meals out. A new tricycle. Disneyland.

"You are going to have to kill someone, Amy."

Amy's jubilation ended.

"Who?"

"You will only know after you agree."

"I don't think so. You could tell me I have to shoot someone like the president. I won't risk my child's life for that. Label my child as the daughter of a crazy woman who shot the president. Daughter of a whacko. Forget it."

"I assure you, it will not be anyone famous. No politicians. No actors. No authority figures."

"Then I think we need to include all of those in the rules."

The man laughed and Amy could see his white teeth for the first time.

"Okay, Amy. We can call that rule five. No one famous or well-known."

"Or the authorities. No cops. No FBI agents. None of it."

"Agreed."

There was a long pause. "Then who?" Amy asked.

"Someone bad. Someone who did something bad. That is all you need to know."

"How can I trust you?"

"You can."

"I need proof."

The man smiled. "Check out the story of a woman named Carol T. Sutton. Go somewhere with public Internet access. Google her. See what happened. See how it all worked out for her. See how your story could end. *Choose* how your story is going to end."

"Carol T. Sutton?"

"That's correct. From Maryland. Check last spring."

"So what's next?"

The man in the back seat reached into his pocket with his right hand and removed a business card with a single number on it.

"When you make up your mind, you call this number. Find a pay phone somewhere or buy a prepaid phone with cash and use it once. Don't leave a long message. You will provide me with a yes or no response. This number will only work once. We will take it from there. If your answer is yes, I will find you."

"How long do I have to decide?"

"You have a week to decide."

"And if I say yes, how long do I have for the favor?"

"That, you will have to decide. We will devise a plan that, if followed precisely, should allow you to perform the task you agree to without risk of being caught. But accidents happen. The timing of the task is determined by your health. If you wait too long, you may be too weak to perform the task you have agreed to perform. If you perform the task too early, and you are apprehended by the authorities, you may waste precious remaining time with your child."

"So it's my decision."

"It's your decision. The timing is flexible. There may be some training involved. But the first step is for you to make a decision and call the number on the card. Then destroy the card. Any more questions?"

Amy shook her head.

"The good-faith money is here in the back seat, on the floor on the driver's side. Count to one hundred before you move. Once that is done and I'm gone, it's all yours."

The man got out of the car without warning and vanished into the stairwell near the corner of the parking garage. Amy did as she was told and counted to one hundred. Sweat dripped from her hairline as she tried to focus on the numbers in her head.

At a hundred, Amy got out of the car and looked around the parking garage. She walked to the stairwell door the man had disappeared through and pulled on the knob. The door was locked.

She looked around the garage and then returned to her vehicle. She opened the back door, reached down, and grabbed a brown paper bag. She sat back down in the driver's seat and felt the weight of the bag in her hand. She tore the staple off the top of the bag and peaked inside. She reached in and pulled out a small stack of cash neatly wrapped in rubber bands.

And then she wept, followed by an ear-to-ear grin.

CHAPTER 20

S PYING ON HIS only client wasn't Dan's preferred investigative method. Yet on a beautiful autumn weekday, Dan watched as Sherry left her house and crossed the street in the direction of the park. At a distance of almost a hundred yards, Dan blended into the scenery on a public bench with a cell phone pressed to his ear and a half-folded newspaper secured in his other hand. Dan dipped the edge of the newspaper and watched Sherry as she bisected a portion of the park, crossed the street again, and disappeared around the corner. Dan stood, glanced back in the direction of the Wellington residence, and then turned his attention to the rest of the neighborhood, eyes surveying his surroundings.

For a target, if she was indeed one, Sherry Wellington was easy pickings. She followed virtually the same path to work and home, leaving and returning at roughly the same time. She walked through the corner of a park, and traveled down streets with multi-story townhouses and apartment buildings offering myriad perches and advantageous positions for a possible sniper. Alleyways provided additional pop-out-and-kill alternatives. English basements offered ground level access to the sidewalk. The only thing working in Sherry's favor was the pure wealth of the neighborhood. Even the old apartment Dan was bunking in was next door to a townhouse that had recently sold for two and a half million. And the swanky neighbors who bought it had plenty of company. Security systems were standard on most doors and first floor windows.

Dan followed Sherry at a distance until she reached Born Again. With the shop open for business, Dan stopped and touched his toes. By the time he hit Wisconsin Avenue, he had discarded his newspaper and was finding his stride among the morning foot traffic. He increased his pace as he reached the river and finished his five-mile run thirty-five minutes later with an uphill sprint that terminated near *The Exorcist* stairs in Georgetown.

As the lunch hour began, Dan was sitting at a café on Wisconsin Avenue, a hundred yards away from Born Again. For the last three days, Sherry Wellington had had lunch delivered to her store. Thai, Vietnamese, and Indian. Dan was curious as to the day's lunch selection and considered how easy it would be for someone to eliminate his client while disguised as a delivery person.

As Dan considered the perils of Sherry Wellington's daily routine, his client deviated from her standard operating procedure. At five minutes after noon, Sherry Wellington stepped from the front of Born Again, shut the door behind her, and slipped her key into the lock. Dan placed ten dollars on the table and put the salt shaker on the folded cash so the wind wouldn't take it.

Dan followed Sherry Wellington to the bottom of the hill and watched from a distance as she entered the courtyard of the Georgetown Waterfront. Dan slipped into the ice cream shop with a corner view and observed as Sherry waved to her lunch date. Sitting on a chair under an umbrella, facing the Potomac, Carla the waitress stood and smiled. As Sherry approached, Carla opened her arms and the two women embraced. Dan watched for several minutes as Carla and Sherry laughed, smiled, and ordered lunch.

Don't know each other, my ass, Dan thought.

CHAPTER 21

D AN SAT IN his favorite location in Volta Park and looked down the half block in the direction of the Wellington's residence. At nine thirty p.m., a dark four-door executive sedan pulled to the curb in front of the house. The driver's door opened and a man in a chauffeur's coat stepped from the vehicle. The driver took a cursory glance at his surroundings and opened the rear door. Congressman Wellington exited the car with a slight wobble in his step. He nodded to his driver, entered through the wrought iron fence that surrounded the small front yard, and headed for the front door. Security lights on the outer corners of the townhouse illuminated the front steps. A moment later the congressman vanished into the residence.

At precisely ten o'clock, a light in the room on the upper left corner of the townhouse came on. The white curtains screened two silhouettes in the room, masking bedtime preparations otherwise visible to the world outside. Twenty minutes later the room was cast into darkness. Sitting on the bench just outside the perimeter of the park, Dan checked his watch. He stood, walked slowly up the opposite side of the street, crossed at the corner, and then headed to the far side of the residence.

A congressman and a woman hiding something that could bring him down. A perfect union. He thought.

Dan walked and considered the options regarding the case. At the top of the list of potential solutions was returning to Born Again in the morning and plunking down the unused portion of the cash Sherry had fronted him. Return the money and wash his hands of her. Move on to the next client. Dan had a little black book with hundreds of possibilities. And while most clients sought out his assistance, there were occasions when clients employed his services on a less voluntary basis.

Dan wrestled with his dilemma and forced himself to focus on his own rules. Regardless of whether Sherry Wellington was lying, he was being paid to find who killed Marcus Losh. The fact that the client refused to embrace honesty, or the danger she could be in, was irrelevant to what he'd been hired to do. Dan pushed aside his distaste at seeing Sherry and Carla together. The taste of betrayal watered down by the fact that he had just met them both. Emotionally, he wasn't invested in either of them. Yet. And beyond the betrayal, Dan didn't want to get caught up in the morals of it all. Sherry had a past. There was no question about it. And she wanted to keep that past hidden.

But so did Dan.

For five years of Dan's life, he had disappeared. Completely off the reservation. Unrecorded and unfound. It was something he didn't want anyone poking around in. Everyone has secrets. And everyone has a past. Sherry's past was potentially deadly.

So was Dan's.

The previous year had seen a bomb tear through the building where his office was located. That unpleasantness was followed by the equally enjoyable experience of being drugged, bound, and abducted. His past had teeth, and they kept multiplying. In addition to the joys of being kidnapped and tortured, he had also been arrested and beaten, before being summarily kneed in the balls by a sitting assistant district attorney.

Sherry Wellington had a secret. Dan had a storage facility full. *Do your job. Find who killed Marcus.*

Dan checked his watch and then headed down the hill into Georgetown proper. He was on the clock. And nighttime offered a completely different surveillance environment.

*

Carla threw her white apron in the large canvas basket in the back corner of the kitchen. Moments later she parted the sea between the post-shift cooks sitting on the cinderblock wall behind the restaurant, smoking and chatting.

"Good night, Carla," the head cook said, the end of his cigarette burning orange.

"Good night. See you tomorrow."

*

Dan stood on the opposite side of M Street, the sole of his shoe on the brick wall, his eyes down. He plugged the D6 Metrobus route Carla had mentioned the night before into his smart phone and the blip on the map was followed by a text telling Dan that Carla's bus was ten minutes out. He watched as Carla approached M Street from the rear of the restaurant, appearing from a different location than she had exited the night before.

Curious, Dan thought. *A different door than yesterday*. But with only a single data point, there was no way for him to know if the rear entrance was the door she usually used, or if yesterday's departure through the front door was the norm. Tomorrow would be the tiebreaker.

Carla's bus stop was two blocks up, where the foot traffic was heaviest and the old brick and cobblestone sidewalk narrowed. Dan shadowed Carla from the other side of M street, five lanes of thick traffic between them. On the sidewalk, Dan weaved between students, drunks, think tankers, tourists, and lawyers. Cars, taxis, and buses jockeyed for position on the street, racing twenty yards at a time to fill any opening, honking and gesturing vulgarities as necessary.

Dan grabbed a freebie newspaper of apartment listings from a stack near a storefront, and then found a seat on the wall outside the Old Stone House, a Georgetown landmark.

From his position on the wall, Dan was situated in the middle of the block with a view of the opposite side of the street. With the Old Stone House to his right, he looked straight through the traffic as Carla fell into the queue at the bus stop. Over the next few minutes, a dozen fellow restaurant and shop workers joined her in the lineup near the curb. He watched as Carla put earplugs in her ears, the wire to the source of music disappearing into the front of her jacket. Dan shook his head. *Very mugger friendly,* he thought. It's hard to be aware of your surroundings when you cut off one of your major senses.

Dan's plan was simple. Wait for Carla to get on her bus home and follow her at a safe distance in a cab. Just routine surveillance to see if there was anything suspicious in her life. Something that didn't make sense. Anything that would explain why she met with Sherry Wellington after explicitly stating they weren't friends.

Dan stared at Carla in the bus queue and planned his surveillance route. Once the Metrobus stopped and Carla boarded, he would cross the street and catch a cab on the far side of traffic, heading in the same direction as the bus. There was no hurry. The bus would make a multitude of stops as it dissected the city. The promise of a fat tip would be sufficient for commandeering a cab driver for an hour of investigative services.

Crowded sidewalks and five full lanes of traffic meant the chances were slim that Carla would spot Dan watching her as she stood in line for her bus. Not taking any chances, Dan dipped his head, kept his eyes up, and flipped through the pages of the apartment locator paper he wasn't actually reading.

A moment later he checked his phone, the screen below chin level. He casually looked up and scanned the street and sidewalks. It was an unbreakable habit. Observation at all times.

Dan noted the streetlight nearest the bus stop on the other side of the street was out. He glanced down the road in each direction and confirmed all the other lights were functioning. He filed away the void in illumination and scanned the people in line waiting for the bus, pausing again to marvel at Carla, isolated from the noise of the outside world. He registered nothing but tired, overworked souls looking forward to a ride home and sleep so they could do it again when the sun came up.

Dan's eyes moved from the bus stop queue to the moving masses on the sidewalk. When Dan's eyes returned to the corner near the bus line, his focus was drawn to the illumination of a cell phone screen in the darkened stoop of a closed bookstore. Dan squinted at the figure on the top step of the stoop. He watched as the woman on the stoop alternated glances between the screen on her phone and the direction of Carla in the bus queue, ten feet away.

Dan stood still and watched as the woman in the darkened stoop stepped down two stairs and moved closer to the bus queue. Dan checked his watch and then counted the number of times the girl on the stoop checked her phone and subsequently stared at Carla in line. Twelve times in less than a minute.

Dan's natural paranoia switched on and he consumed the details of the person on the stoop. A young woman in a dark sweatshirt, hoodie bunched around her neck. In lieu of pulling the hoodie over her head, the woman wore a winter ski hat, tugged low, hugging her eyebrows and running horizontally over the top of her ears. Blonde hair rolled from the edge of the hat onto her shoulders, disappearing into the folds of the hood on the sweatshirt. She appeared to have something in her mouth. She was currently standing directly under the out-of-commission streetlight, but had moved three steps down the stoop in steady progression. She was holding her position on the second or third step.

Just a young woman waiting for the bus, trying to stay out of the foot traffic, Dan considered, trying to convince himself his gut was sending a false warning.

As Dan tried to dismiss the young woman in the hoodie, the subject took another slow, measured step down the stoop, like a cat closing in on its prey. On the bottom step of the stoop, she paused and stared directly at Carla.

Carla, earphones still in, turned in the direction of the young woman as if an extra sense told her she was being observed. The young woman in the hoodie looked down and away, stepping backwards up the stoop and melting into the relative darkness from whence she had just emerged.

I think Carla is about to become the victim of a pickpocket, Dan thought.

Dan began processing the threat level of the potential criminal in the infancy of a crime. *Sex*: female—usually not a violent threat. *Stature*: smaller than average. *Attire*: hooded sweatshirt and a winter hat. *Location*: given the broken streetlight above, the location of the bus queue was a concern. *Behavior*: considerably suspicious, which could mean a multitude of things ranging from a physical ailment to drugs or alcohol consumption.

Dan moved from his seated position on the stone wall to a leaning position against a lamppost. He was five feet closer to the street and squinted through the traffic for a more detailed assessment of the situation. Again the girl on the stoop checked her phone and then looked down at Carla. She started her second cat-like descent from the stoop and Dan prepared himself to chase down a pickpocket. He checked his smartphone, and the Metrobus application indicated that Carla's ride home was still three minutes out.

Dan watched as the young woman on the stoop took a final glance of her phone before it disappeared from view. Then she looked up the street in the direction of oncoming traffic and Dan followed the direction of her glance. A red Circulator bus lurched down the street and Dan felt a drop of adrenaline hit his system.

Dan's feet starting moving as the girl in the hoodie descended the last step and disappeared into a large group of tourists mulling over their drinking options on the sidewalk. With the red Circulator bus closing in, the girl in the hoodie reappeared from the group of tourist and stepped in the direction of Carla.

Dan yelled to warn Carla, his voice cutting through the din of traffic noise as he started to run towards the corner. Dan kept his eyes glued to the far side of the street, trying to anticipate which direction the pickpocket would run. Shocked, Dan watched helplessly as Carla's body fell from the curb and was met with a sickening thud. The red Circulator bus had just made an unscheduled stop and Carla's body was now under the vehicle.

Dan winced at the growing cacophony of screams from across the street. Squealing brakes echoed through the chaos. Dan stepped from the curb, the bus blocking his view of the sidewalk as he jumped into traffic. He dodged a still-moving Mini Cooper and slapped the roof of a taxi in the third lane as traffic ground to a standstill. Dan two-stepped it across the double yellow line and then finished his run across the last two lanes of traffic. He hit the sidewalk, pushed through the crowd, peaked under the bus, and pointed to crisis-stricken couple in matching dark wool jackets. "Call 911 guys—911."

Standing up, Dan pushed his way through the crowd and jumped to the top of the step of the nearest doorway. He scanned both directions and then stepped down from his perch and raced to the nearest corner. The side street was silent. He turned around, veered into the first lane of dead-stopped traffic, and sprinted the fifty yards to the end of the next block. As Dan turned the corner, his foot pressed down on the woven winter hat he had just seen on the head of the young woman with the hoodie.

Dan paused, swiped the hat into his hand, and looked down the street in the direction of the Potomac River three blocks away. He scanned the darkness and heard feet pounding the ground straight ahead. Dan returned to a full sprint down the sidewalk. At the next corner, now moving away from M Street and the accident scene, he stopped and picked up a yellow wad of fake hair. *What the hell?*

He turned at the corner of the brick building and was now on the crushed stone alleyway running parallel to M Street, one block to the rear of the accident. *Is she going around the block?* Dan thought as he spotted a discarded hooded sweatshirt. In the distance he heard feet pound up a flight of metal stairs. He grabbed the discarded hoodie and ran in the direction of the sound, arms flapping, a wig and hat in one hand and the black hoodie in the other.

Approaching the next street, Dan glanced up as the shape of a woman zipped across the small bridge that traversed the canal a block off M Street. Dan hit the metal stairs, taking them two at a time. *No chance*, Dan thought. *No way. I did five miles this morning before you were awake.*

But Dan also realized he was going to have to hurry to catch her in the next few blocks. In another quarter-mile the young woman would reach the crowded Waterfront where she could disappear into a ton of evening customers. Buses. Taxis. Hell, she could take a boat to Old Town.

At the top of the metal stairs, with the figure of the woman now heading down the hill in the direction of the river, Dan pushed his legs for the final rundown.

Then all he saw was blackness.

CHAPTER 22

DETECTIVES WALLACE AND Fields handed off the report on the stolen Lexus SUV to police forensics. The car had been dumped hastily two blocks from the National Cathedral and was now being pulled onto a flatbed truck as a result of four flat tires.

Emily shook her head. "I will never understand why someone would steal a car, take it for a joy ride, and then slash the tires."

"There are a lot of things I will never understand," Wallace replied. The radio on his belt chirped, and a string of codes flowed from the wireless device. He listened to the dispatcher and then pulled out his cell phone. He hit a number stored in memory and then turned away from Emily. A minute later he hung up the phone.

"We have to go. Robbery in Georgetown. Someone I know, if dispatch has the story right. Victim claims he was robbed after he witnessed an accident between a woman and a Circulator bus."

"Ouch."

"So far, the woman hit by the bus has survived. We'll have to see if she makes it."

"And you say a guy you know witnessed the crash and was then robbed?"

"That's the story." Wallace lowered himself into the police vehicle while holding onto the edge of the roof with one hand. He started the engine and reached for a fresh piece of Nicorette from the dash.

"You seem agitated," Emily said, eyeing her partner as the car lurched forward.

"Concerned. This guy, if the dispatcher is correct on his identity, is unusual."

"You mean he's crazy."

"Why do you say that?"

"When people say someone is unusual, they usually mean crazy and are just being polite."

"He's not crazy. Well, maybe a little. At any rate, he's a friend. Of sorts. He's unique."

"Well that clears it up. What, are you two secret lovers? I mean it's okay, if that's your thing. Love is love, if you ask me."

"I've been married as long as you have been on this earth. He's not my lover."

"Well, he's *something*. You're chewing your gum like a rabid beaver."

"His name is Dan Lord. He's a lawyer. A private detective. Does legal counseling. Hard to pin down exactly. Works for himself."

"How do you know him?"

"We met in the course of Detective Nguyen's murder investigation."

"Your former partner?"

"Yes."

"I'm not sure I follow."

"He helped with the investigation of Detective Nguyen's death, though it wasn't friendly at times between Dan and the police. Ultimately, Dan deserved a lot of the credit for solving Nguyen's murder."

"And just how does a private eye solve a crime before the police? How does a private detective get the better of a DC detective with a quarter century of experience under his belt?"

Detective Wallace didn't smile and Detective Fields knew she had crossed the line.

"He didn't follow the rules," Wallace finally replied.

Emily looked over, waiting for more information.

"What I'm about to tell you is entirely off the record."

"You mean, 'we are partners and I got your back no matter what'? That type of off the record?"

"Yeah, smart ass."

"Then it's off the record."

"When Detective Nguyen was murdered, a lot of things went ass end up. By the conclusion of Nguyen's murder investigation, there had been collateral damage and the involvement of some other federal agencies."

"Interesting."

"And Dan Lord was in the middle of it. He had lost a nephew and a sister-in-law and he was investigating certain aspects of their deaths. Detective Nguyen was handling their cases from the DC police side. The nephew's death was initially ruled a drug overdose. The sister-in-law's death was ruled a suicide. Both occurred the same night."

"But the private detective didn't believe the deaths were an overdose or a suicide."

"No. And he had met with Nguyen a couple of times before Nguyen died. For a lot of reasons, I suspected Dan had something to do with Nguyen's death. The evidence was there. The motive was not. But he was, without a doubt, a suspect. The only suspect we had," Wallace said, his voice trailing off, as if in remembrance of a regret.

"So, what did you do?"

"Well, I might have thrown him in a cell with a few hardened criminals."

"That wasn't very nice."

"In hindsight, it wasn't very nice to the criminals."

"How many?"

"Seven. There were more men in the cell, but some of them chose not to participate. A good decision as it turns out. Four went to the hospital. Two were there for a while."

"He took out seven men, by himself, unarmed, in a jail cell?"

"In less than twenty seconds. After giving them a verbal warning."

"A man after my own heart. Did he forgive you after that?"

"Eventually."

"That's good, because you're in no shape for an ass-kicking."

"Not from this guy, that's for sure."

*

Detective Wallace weaved through the residential streets and squeezed down an alley to get past the congestion. The nosedive from the sidewalk into the path of the red Circulator bus had paralyzed Georgetown traffic.

The flashing lights from the sea of emergency vehicles illuminated the front of the restaurants and shops on M Street. Rubberneckers and gawkers filled the sidewalk on both sides of the street.

Detective Wallace turned the corner, pulled half the car onto the sidewalk, and threw it into park. Twenty yards down the sidewalk, sitting on a small stone staircase, Dan held a cold-pack to the back of his head. A uniformed officer stood next to him. The madness of the accident was just around the corner, less than fifty yards away.

Wallace and Emily approached the uniformed officer. Wallace recognized him, and flicked his head to the side, motioning for the uniformed officer to step away from Dan.

"Officer Gonzalez."

"Detective Wallace."

Wallace introduced Emily and the two shook hands.

"What do we have?" Wallace asked.

"The witness says he knows you," Gonzalez replied.

"Is he a witness or a victim?"

"According to him, both. But he's a little out of it. Big knot on the back side of his head where it meets the neck. Some blood. He started speaking to me in Spanish after he heard me talk to one of the other witnesses, a dishwasher from a café down the street."

"He speaks a couple of languages," Wallace stated.

"Well, he speaks Spanish better than I do and my mother was from El Salvador. Anyway, he has no ID on him. No wallet. Claims it was stolen. He's refusing medical treatment. Says he will sign a release against medical advice. He called it an AMA, so he obviously knows what he's talking about. Sounds like a lawyer. Doesn't look like one. We have an icepack on him. We were waiting for you. He says he doesn't want to waste time with anyone else."

Emily fought the urge to see how her own Spanish compared. Instead she asked, "Diagnosis?"

"Lucky. Hit with a blunt object." The officer pointed to a place on his own head between the ear and the back of the neck. "A little farther down or back and he could have easily been killed. A whole lot of things can be injured in the neck..."

Wallace nodded. "So we have an accident and a robbery?"

"That's right. The only victims are the woman hit by the bus and your friend here."

"What about witnesses?" Wallace asked.

"We have a bunch of people who saw the woman fall into the path of the bus. People on the sidewalk. People in the bus line. No one saw anything suspicious."

"So we have two victims of two separate crimes, and one of the victims is the only witness?"

"And if that weren't strange enough, your friend here says he witnessed the accident from across the street. Across five lanes of traffic."

"And he just happened to look over and see an accident?"

"So he claims."

"Did you search this block?"

"For what?"

"Other bodies."

"No, sir. Why do you ask?"

"Because the guy sitting over there isn't the type to be robbed quietly. Grab a couple of officers and take a look around the backside of the building again. See if there isn't someone with a broken neck floating in the canal."

Wallace and Emily turned and looked in Dan's direction. His head was still in his hands, cold-pack resting on the back of his head and neck.

"I'll have it checked out," Gonzales said.

Wallace walked over and looked down at Dan. Dan tried to turn his head and winced.

"Dan Lord," Wallace said, bending at the knees and trying to focus on Dan's eyes.

"Detective Wallace. Long time, no see. How's the wife?"

"Still married. How are you doing?"

"Been better."

"How about a ride to the hospital? Get you checked out."

"I'll pass."

"They say you got mugged."

"Something like that."

"Well, seeing that you're refusing medical treatment and you don't have a driver's license, wallet, or money, how about I give you a ride home?"

Dan ignored the question and looked over at Detective Fields' shoes. "New partner?" he asked.

"Yes. This is Emily Fields. She's a new detective with the force."

"I see you followed my lead," Dan said. "You went out and got yourself a young white girl for a partner."

Wallace looked at Emily and shook his head as if begging her to ignore the statement.

"And where is your partner, tonight?" Wallace asked.

"Africa. She's in Tanzania this week."

"Still looking for you know who?"

Dan nodded.

Wallace and Emily each took an arm and readied Dan to get vertical. "Okay. Here we go, Dan. Let's get up."

Twenty unsure steps down the sidewalk and Dan fell into the back seat of the unmarked police car.

"I see you haven't changed the interior of the car since the last time I was back here," Dan said groggily.

Once again Wallace shook his head at Emily, silently pleading with her not to lend any credence to the man in the rear of the car. Wallace started the car and pulled a three-point turn using both sidewalks to complete the maneuver on the narrow street.

"You still at the same place in Alexandria?"

"Nope. I moved. Right up the street in Georgetown."

"You moved to DC?"

"Yep. And I took the bar for the District this year, so I can fully practice law within the city limits."

"I can't say I'm happy to hear that. I thought you had too many enemies here in the city?"

"I do. But I'm only here temporarily. Just working a case."

"Address?"

"Thirty-Third Street. Near Volta Park."

*

Ten minutes later, Wallace and Emily steered Dan Lord up four flights of stairs. Dan fumbled with the key and Detective Wallace pushed the door open.

The two guys on the sofa with their girlfriends passing the bong around looked up when the door opened.

"Detective, these are my two roommates," Dan said. "Ignore the weed."

Wallace and Emily helped Dan down to the futon on the floor of Dan's temporary bedroom and walked back to the living room. The bong and the girlfriends had disappeared.

"Which one of you is the least high?" Wallace asked.

Croc raised his hand.

"Then you're on babysitting duty. You need to wake him up every hour. All night. Set an alarm if you have to. You don't do it and I'm coming back here and busting your ass for possession."

Croc glanced down at the large bag of weed protruding from under the table, looked up, and nodded vigorously.

CHAPTER 23

SHERRY WELLINGTON SLIPPED the key into the lock on the front door of her consignment store and turned it to the right. She stepped through the doorway. Balancing her morning coffee in one hand with the keys, she punched the four-digit security code into the keypad on the wall. The small red light indicating the alarm system was armed and activated faded to black and then began blinking intermittently.

Sherry flicked on the lights near the front window and flipped over the sign on the door, displaying the word OPEN towards the sidewalk and the world outside As she did every morning, she slowly worked her way to the rear of the store, perfecting the displays of wares. She straightened a slightly unbalanced lampshade and paused to refold a pair of matching sarongs left strewn on a side table by a customer from the evening prior.

She reached the back of the store and screamed when she saw Dan sitting at the large wood table. "Jesus. You scared me."

"We need to talk."

"You can't just barge into my place of business."

"I was making a point."

"How did you get in?"

"I picked the lock. Your security code was your son's birthday—month and day. You should try something more random."

"You should try to not break the law and scare the hell out of your clients."

"You mean scare the hell out of clients who lie to me."

"I don't know what you're talking about."

"Sherry. Mrs. Wellington. This is your come-to-Jesus moment. Your life may very well hang in the balance."

"That's why I hired you to find who killed Marcus. Find who killed him and my life won't be in danger."

Dan couldn't get around that line of reasoning and it was pissing him off.

"Carla was seriously injured last night." Dan watched as Sherry Wellington turned ashen. "She had an accident with a Circulator bus. Though I don't think there was anything accidental about it. She's in intensive care with swelling on the brain, among other injuries. They don't know if she's going to make it."

"That's awful."

"It was awful. And I watched the whole accident from across the street."

"You were following her?"

"I was."

"Why?"

"Because you refuse to divulge meaningful information that could help me find Marcus's killer."

"Marcus was murdered in Virginia. Don't you think you should spend your time there? Just find Marcus's killer and resolve this."

"I will. But you could make it a lot easier if you tell me what you're hiding."

"I'm not hiding anything."

"Why weren't you surprised when I said Carla was hit by a bus? Why didn't you ask 'Carla who'?"

Color returned to Sherry Wellington's face in a crimson wave. "I only know one Carla. We worked together at a restaurant in Georgetown."

"When was the last time you saw her?"

"It's been a while,"

Dan checked his watch. "It's been seventeen hours. But I'm curious as to the timing of your lunch meeting. I met Carla the night before last, after work. We talked for a while at the bar. She told me the two of you were not friends. Then, lo and behold, you have lunch together. And later that very same night she's nearly killed."

Sherry Wellington scowled.

"I would like to see your cell phone," Dan said.

"Why?"

"I want to know if you called Carla, or if she called you."

"She called me."

"Phone," Dan replied, extending his hand, palm upwards.

"No."

"Mrs. Wellington, I can have your phone records by the end of the day, but I would rather not have to go that route. It would require calling in a favor and I'd also have to charge you for the additional cost incurred. Not to mention I have a pounding headache thanks to being mugged while chasing down the person who tried to kill Carla. So, please, just let me see your phone. I'm really not in the mood to play games."

"You saw who tried to kill Carla?"

"I did."

"Did you catch him?"

"No. And it wasn't a him. It was a her."

Dan watched as Sherry digested his statement. "Now let me see your damn phone."

"Don't speak to me like that. My husband is a congressman."

"File a complaint with him. But then again, you would have to explain what you're doing with a private investigator. A legal advisor. And you wouldn't want that, now would you? Now for the last time, give me your phone."

Sherry Wellington relented and handed the phone to Dan. He checked the call history and recent calls and confirmed that it was Carla who had called Sherry.

"So tell me, Mrs. Wellington, what about my conversation with Carla was so upsetting that she called you—someone she claimed to have no contact with—for an emergency lunch date?"

"She didn't say."

"And now she may never be able to."

Dan saw Sherry's hand shake slightly.

"Why did you tell me that you met your husband at The Friendliest Saloon in Town?"

"Did I?"

"You did."

"I sometimes misspeak. I told you that."

"You did. As a matter of convenience perhaps. Maybe it was true. But so far, truthfulness has not been one of your strong suits. So I'm going with convenience."

"What does it matter where I met my husband?"

"Exactly."

Sherry looked over at Dan and he registered a sense of anger.

Dan spoke, "You know, I've never dropped a client in the middle of an investigation. Never. But I would be lying if I said the thought hadn't occurred to me this time."

"Dropping me as a client wouldn't look good to other potential customers. Word-of-mouth reputation is a two-way street."

"Indeed. Which is why I've decided to keep you as a client."

"Then it's time you got to work, Mr. Lord."

Dan stood and pushed in his chair. "You know, for the life of me, there is one thing I can't figure out."

"There's more than one, apparently," Sherry retorted.

"I can't figure out why you would rather be dead than have your husband discover whatever secret it is that you're keeping from him."

"There are things worse than death, Mr. Lord."

"Like what?"

"Poverty. At least you can rest in death. Poverty just gnaws at you. All day. All night."

CHAPTER 24

DAN SLAPPED HIS hand against his open mouth and the three painkillers in his palm landed in the back of his throat. He took a swig of water from a plastic bottle and nodded at two uniformed police officers exiting the brick building in front of him. The large sign over the door identified the location as DC Police Headquarters for District Two.

Dan had been in the building once before, on a somber morning when a fallen officer was being mourned by his colleagues. By the time Dan had left the precinct on that gray day, his popularity had waned. Today was his chance to make a second impression. All he had to do was clear the cobwebs in his head and flash a little charm.

He walked across the lobby entrance and introduced himself to the white haired officer standing guard at the check-in booth; a vertical Plexiglas coffin with a bird's eye view of the front door, the waiting area, and the large staircase that led up to the heart of the police station.

"My name is Dan Lord. I'm here to see Detective Earl Wallace."

"Dan Lord?"

"Yes."

The officer behind the glass nodded and Dan noticed a slight change in the man's demeanor. The officer's face softened, and for a split second Dan thought he saw a twitch of the man's lip, a precursor to a smile that didn't follow. "Just a second, Mr. Lord," the officer offered with a subtle undertone of respect.

Moments later, Detective Wallace appeared on the staircase from the floor above. Dan threw his keys, phone, and wallet into a blue plastic basket and passed through the metal detector on the side of the room. He followed Wallace up the stairs and walked along the periphery of the robbery and homicide division in all its outdated glory. Old wooden desks and chairs brandished scratches older than some of the detectives using them.

Near the water cooler, Wallace directed Dan to a short hall on the right. Following directions, he entered the open door at the end of the hall. Inside, Emily was sitting at the middle of a large U-shaped table. A young forensic technician in civilian clothes stood at the front of the room, connecting a laptop to a large screen TV. Dan nodded to the young man and took a seat on the far side of the table, with a view of the door.

Wallace found his seat next to Emily and asked the first question. "How's the head?"

"I'm not sure which is worse, the neck, the head, or the shoulder blade. It's a little hard to distinguish this week's beating from last week's."

"Sounds like you need to learn how to fight better or run faster," Wallace said.

Dan ignored the statement. "Thanks for the ride home."

"You're welcome, but it's the last time I drag you to your bedroom," Wallace responded. "Tucking in big boys is not part of my job description."

"I guess I can find someone else willing to drag me to my bedroom," Dan replied, glancing quickly at Emily who was looking at a folder on the table in front of her.

"And for the record, the two of you scared the shit out of my roommates."

"Tell them to keep their weed in smaller bags. We aren't busting for anything less than an ounce, but that was a pretty large Ziploc I saw."

"I'll pass along the advice on the size of their weed sack."

Emily added her two cents. "I'm not sure which surprised your roommates more—cops busting through the front door or being asked to babysit a forty-year-old roommate."

"For the amount of rent I pay, they can put up with some inconvenience."

The young technician stifled a laugh and Wallace returned the conversation to a more professional tone. "Can we go over what happened last night?"

"As I think I mentioned last night, I was following the lady who was hit by the bus."

"But of course you were," Wallace said. He turned to Emily, who pushed a long strand of hair behind her ear. "When Dan here starts following you, one of two things is going to happen. You are about to be killed, or someone you know is."

"That's not fair," Dan said.

"Tell that to the waitress."

"She's still alive."

"For now. I'm just pointing out the high correlation between you following someone and their impending demise. Based on our history together."

"Why were you following her?" Emily asked.

"It's a long story."

"We'll take the short version," Wallace replied.

"I was hired by the wife of someone prominent to find out who committed a murder in Virginia."

"And this person who hired you lives in DC?"

"Yes."

"But the murder was in Virginia?"

"The murder I was hired to solve, yes."

"Help me fill in the blanks between that statement and what transpired last night with a waitress getting hit by a bus."

"You know how it goes. You pull one small string hanging out of your sweater and the next thing you know, thread is everywhere and you're showing off your belly and distinct lack of a six-pack."

"You could always stop pulling the string," Emily said.

Detective Wallace shook his head. "Not him."

The young police technician paused from his connectivity exercise long enough to take a better look at Dan, the subject of the conversation.

Dan continued. "Anyhow, like I said, my client hired me to solve a murder. I have an acquaintance on the Arlington police force keeping me in the loop with the investigation. In the meantime, I was poking around on a few things my client said that seemed relevant to the investigation. I was kicking around the strong possibility that my client may, in fact, be the key to solving the murder she hired me to investigate." Dan rubbed the back of his head. "In light of last night's unforeseen early conclusion, it seems like I'm on the right path."

"You think your client took a crack at you?" Wallace asked.

"I doubt it. My client is concerned she may be in danger and she doesn't want her husband to know she's hired me."

"Do *you* think your client is in danger?" Emily asked.

"I do. And she paid a lot of money for me to find whoever it is she thinks may be a danger to her."

"You said she's married to someone prominent."

"A congressman."

"That's just wonderful," Detective Wallace replied.

Emily chimed in. "So you have the wife of a congressman who claims she may be in danger, but she also doesn't want anyone to know that she hired you? I imagine that makes hiring a bodyguard difficult."

"Very good, Detective."

"That's quite a dilemma," Wallace added.

"It gets better. Some of the information my client provided was not factual. I can deal with secrecy. That part of the arrangement with the client is fine with me. And to a certain degree, I go into every client meeting knowing I'm only going to hear half-truths. And that's on a good day."

"So this client is living up to your expectations with regard to deception?"

"She surpasses them."

"Apparently lies are a shared occupational hazard for both private detectives and real ones," Wallace said. "What did she lie about?"

"I'm certain she lied about where she met her husband and about knowing the waitress from last night who was hit by the bus. As it turns out, the waitress also had an issue with the truth."

"You met her?"

"Yes. The day before the accident. First my client lied to me, then the waitress. Then the two liars met for lunch. At that point, obviously, I knew there was more to the story than what my client was letting on. I figured I'd take a shot in the dark and put in a couple of evenings following the waitress. Just do a preliminary run up. I was in the process of trailing her after work when the accident occurred."

"And?"

"Like I said last night, I was watching from the other side of the street. Saw the accident happen right in front of me."

"And you saw the person who tried to kill her?"

"I saw someone take off and I followed *her*."

"What did she look like?"

"Hard to tell. She changed her clothes. At the first corner, she ditched the hat she had been wearing. Her hair went flying a few yards after that."

"A wig?"

"That's right. I passed some more clothes in the alley on the backside of the building. By the time I caught a second glimpse of her, she looked different. Mind you, it was dark and she was running away, but she had changed her appearance. On the fly."

"She outran you?"

"She had a head start. I was closing the gap, made it to the top of the stairs near the canal, and that was all she wrote. Lights out." Dan snapped his fingers for affect.

"How did you let that happen?" Detective Wallace asked.

"Keyed up. Didn't expect an accomplice."

"Why an accomplice?" Emily asked.

"Too random to be anything else. I don't like the odds of a near-fatal accident, a clothes-ditching jogger, and a mugging of a third person, yours truly, all on the same city block within a minute of each other. Too many coincidences."

The young technician at the front of the room had stopped working on the connection of the video equipment and waited until there was a pause in the conversation. "Sir, the surveillance videos are ready."

*

The screen on the TV came to life and the picture showed a sidewalk full of people, frozen in time.

The young technician handed the remote control to Wallace who immediately slid the remote control back to the young man. "You drive."

The technician nodded and checked the notes he had scribbled on a yellow legal pad. "We have video from all the surveillance cameras we could obtain. SunTrust Bank across the street from the bus stop. The Junior

League, also across the street. The Barnes and Noble entrance on the same side as the bus stop. Another security feed on each side of the street, farther down the block."

Dan took a minute to digest the picture and then he interrupted. "This is taken from the same side of the street I was on. This is basically what I saw. Can you zoom in?"

"We can, but we lose some definition."

The technician zoomed in. Dan emceed. "Carla, the waitress, is the fourth one in line at the bus stop. You can see she's wearing headphones. The wire runs down the front of her jacket and then disappears into the front seam."

Detective Wallace squinted. "If you say so."

"If you take a look at the stoop and doorway in the background, you can see a young woman hanging out. She's wearing a winter cap and a hoodie. The doorstep is dark because the streetlight is out."

"Intentionally disengaged," Emily confirmed. "It was checked out this morning. There's an access panel on the light pole. It was opened and a wire was cut."

The video progressed and Dan continued to explain what he had seen. "At this point I noticed the girl in the doorway. You can see she's checking the screen on her phone. Then she appears to look over at Carla."

The girl in the video repeated the same action multiple times. Each time she checked her phone, her face was momentarily illuminated by the light of the screen.

"Freeze that picture, right there," Wallace commanded. The technician did as he was told. "It looks like she has something in her mouth."

Dan, Wallace, and Emily leaned towards the screen. "Maybe a straw," Emily stated.

The technician looked hard at the image and spoke involuntarily. "Looks like a lollipop to me."

Dan and the detectives looked at the technician and then back at the screen. Dan tilted his head to the side in consideration. "Maybe."

"I'm going to need a better picture to tell," Wallace said. He squinted, leaned further forward, and shook his head noncommittally. "Continue."

Dan felt a surge of adrenaline as he relived the experience from the night before. "By this point in the video, I was starting to get a bad feeling in my stomach."

"Bad Chinese food bad?"

"Exactly. And you can see in the video, the girl steps down from the doorway and moves in the direction of Carla just as the bus enters the picture."

Wallace grimaced and Emily looked away from the video for a split second. Carla's body absorbed the gruesome impact and the bus came to a screeching halt.

Dan continued to serve as the play-by-play announcer. "Now the bus is blocking the view of the far sidewalk. You should see me enter the scene just about... now."

On cue, Dan ran around the front of the bus, bent over, then disappeared from view. Seconds later Dan reappeared near the corner behind the bus. Moments passed and Dan flashed across the screen, running down the first lane of traffic amidst the chaos.

"So the view from this camera is pretty much the same view you had from your vantage point across the street?" Wallace confirmed.

"Correct. Up until the bus enters the scene, you saw what I saw."

"I saw an accident," Wallace stated clearly.

Dan turned towards Emily. "What did you see?"

"Nothing resembling evidence of anything beyond an accident."

The forensic technician offered a truce. "We have more cameras."

"Let's see them," Wallace said.

The forensic technician explained the additional video feeds. "The second surveillance video is only marginally different from the first in terms of angle and distance. It's from the same side of the street, fifty yards farther up the block.

"The third video is from the same side of the street as the bus queue and the accident. This video was taken from above. From this overhead angle, the top of Carla's head is visible in the bus stop line. The mystery woman in the doorway is even more concealed than she was in the video taken from across the street."

With the video running, all eyes were glued to the screen as the mystery woman stepped down from the doorway and walked past Carla just as the bus entered the scene.

"You can see the woman pass within a foot of Carla," Dan said, staring intently at the screen. "My guess is we have a pusher."

"Her arms are crossed," Emily said. "Our supposed perpetrator has her arms crossed."

"Doesn't mean she didn't push her," Dan countered.

The technician leaned towards the screen along with everyone else in the room. The overhead camera showed the girl from the doorway walk within inches of Carla, arms crossed. For a fraction of second it seemed as if a black object flashed across the screen and then disappeared.

"Did you see that?" Dan asked.

"I saw something," Emily confirmed.

"Replay the last ten seconds," Wallace baritoned. "Slow it down if you can."

They all watched the video three more times, each iteration in slower motion than the last. On the final pass, the technician managed to freeze the frame at the moment the dark object appeared.

Dan stood. "I need a police baton."

Wallace nodded at the forensic tech, who disappeared and returned a minute later with a well-used police baton. Dan arranged for a demonstration and asked Emily to stand in the middle of the U-Shaped tables. Dan assumed the role of the perpetrator and took up his position off to the side.

"I'm the girl in the doorway," Dan said, standing ten feet from Emily. He crossed his arms and buried the baton between his forearms. "I can conceal this baton easily in my crossed arms. You can see my hands without seeing the baton at all. I can walk by Detective Fields here, without touching her, without raising any suspicion."

Dan walked over to Emily and repositioned her with a gentle hand on her hip, turning her slightly so Wallace could have a better view.

"Now imagine that instead of a solid baton, I have a retractable baton. With the press of a button the baton will extend and when I press the button again, it will retract. One click, POW. Another click, gone."

"You're saying the flash of the object is a retractable baton, concealed between the woman's arms?"

"Or maybe up her sleeve. Or maybe in the pocket of her hoodie, which would explain why she was wearing a sweatshirt with a hood *and* a hat, which I thought was odd. At any rate, she doesn't need much room. She only needs to press a button. With a little practice, someone could become quite adept at wielding the retractable baton without anyone seeing. Bam, bam. And she only needs to provide enough force for Carla to fall off the curb."

"We have medical evidence that Carla was epileptic and that may have contributed to her fall."

"I'm not putting my money on it," Dan said, looking at the screen in momentary deep thought. "You have anything looking across the street away from the accident. Anything focused on the location where I was sitting?"

The technician picked up the pile of surveillance discs and flipped through them. "I think we have one here. It's focused across the street. It doesn't show the accident, or the victim, or the possible perpetrator."

"I'm not looking for them."

"Who are you looking for?" Wallace asked. "Or are you feeling the need for additional screen time?"

"You'll see."

The technician found the correct feed and the screen flashed to the video image of the opposite side of the street. The technician fast-forwarded to the appropriate time and Dan entered the picture. The video showed Dan standing for several long minutes, his eyes fixed, as if he was watching something with intense focus.

"There," Dan said. "The guy in the Baltimore Orioles baseball cap with the dark glasses. To my left. Twenty or thirty feet away."

"What about him?" Emily asked.

"He's doing the same thing I am. He's performing surveillance. Look at the movement on the sidewalk there. A steady flow of people in each direction. There are no stores right there, so he is not waiting outside for someone. He's too far away from the bank to be waiting in line for the ATM. And he has a clear view to the accident, or the crime, if you believe I'm not crazy."

Everyone stared at the man in the video.

"There are two suspicious people in that video. Me and the guy with the cap and sunglasses," Dan finished.

Wallace shrugged his large shoulders. "He could be waiting for a bus. There's a bus stop on that same block."

"He could be. But how far away from a bus stop do you stand? My guess is not very far. If you do, the bus might not stop for you. But your point is noted. Now let's play the rest of the tape and see."

They all watched the fourth rendition of the bus accident, this one excluding the incident itself. The video reached the point where Dan stepped forward for a better view across the street and the man with the cap could be seen staring at Dan.

"Uh-oh," Wallace said.

When Dan jumped into the first lane of traffic the man dropped the newspaper he'd been carrying as cover and headed to the corner. A second later he could be seen entering the crosswalk in the direction of the bus stop. The man stopped at the corner, looked down the block, and then disappeared into the darkness of the side street.

"Down that street is where you found me on the curb," Dan said. He looked over at Wallace, whose face grew stern. Emily's mouth opened just a bit.

"Any more doubts?"

"None," the forensic technician offered.

"So this guy disappears around the corner, down the street where we found you, and assaults you as you pursue the perpetrator."

"That's right. What we have is a killer and a spotter. And that combination means they are professionals to some degree."

"Well, if the dead guy in Virginia whose murder you were hired to solve was also whacked by these two, we may be watching the video of serial killers in action."

Dan answered. "Maybe. But serial killers, for all of their fame and glory, are rare."

Emily objected. "You mean, those that are caught are rare. I did a thesis on serial killers. At any time there are estimated to be over two dozen serial killers operating in the US. Unidentified serial killers, lurking out there."

Dan looked over at Wallace. "See if there are any other video feeds with the guy in the cap and sunglasses from any other stores on M Street. Also, see if you can get the tapes for the same time of day on previous days. If I'm right, someone did reconnaissance. They probably watched Carla just as I was starting to do. They didn't plan this in one day. If we can get our hands on the tapes from other days, we might catch them on video."

"I can get to work on that," the forensic technician answered.

"And we need to see if Carla has any injuries consistent with being jabbed by a high-powered auto baton."

"Any other orders I'm supposed to take from you?" Wallace asked.

"Not that I can think of. But while I'm here, can I fill out a crime report for the mugging last night? Just in case my personal effects turn up somewhere."

CHAPTER 25

DAN AND FRANK spoke in the small office of J. Paul's restaurant for five minutes before the manager sprang from his seat to answer a knock at the office door. He whispered to an unseen employee on the other side of the threshold and then cranked his clean-shaven head back towards Dan. "Can you give me a couple minutes? We seem to have a situation."

"Take your time," Dan replied.

"I'll be right back."

*

Dan's eyes danced around the office. From his seat, he perused the schedule on the wall. Then he read the to-do list on the small whiteboard behind the desk. A stack of paperwork leaned precariously on the desk. A change of clothes was balled in the corner on the floor.

Frank returned and shut the office door behind him.

"Sorry about that. Ambushed by a small group of a hundred in two tour buses. But it's early, we can get them fed and out the door in no time. Should make for an impressive evening of sales."

"What's a good number for an evening? Just out of curiosity."

"On a really good night, we can do over forty thousand in revenue. Then you have to pay rent, the staff, overhead. Restaurants don't have huge margins."

"You make most of your money on booze, right?"

"Most of it. Some nights the food does better than break even."

"That's a sign the food is edible."

Frank checked his watch. "Now, where were we?"

"Carla's background," Dan replied.

"Yeah, Carla. She's good. Great. I feel bad. She's sweet. She's also a great worker."

"Is Carla involved in anything illegal? Drugs? Gambling?"

"Not that I'm aware of, but I doubt it. She works hard. She's been here, geez, probably seven or eight years. And I can count on one hand how many times she has missed work. Had the flu once, sent her home after she threw up in the alley out back. Took off for a couple of days when her mother had surgery on her leg."

"The bartender mentioned she takes care of her mom."

"She does. They live together. Has a sister who floats in and out of the house, too. They live in one of those row houses near the old football stadium. Across from Langston Hughes. "

"You have an address for her?"

"I do," Frank answered. He stood, stepped to the desk, and dug through some papers. "220 Twenty-First Street, Northeast. But you can probably find it without an address. The front yard is covered in lawn animals."

"Dogs?"

"No. Fake lawn figures. Those concrete jobbers. Pink flamingos. Shit like that. I dropped her off a couple of times over the years. Carla doesn't drive. Has epilepsy. Anyway, her mother had a bunch of crap out there in the yard. An angel. A skunk. A bear. Some kind of parrot-looking thing. I think there was a fountain in the corner. Those row houses have small yards, too. Makes it all seem a little surreal."

"It sounds easy to find."

"Unless the yard has been cleaned up."

Dan nodded. "I had one final question."

"Sure."

"Do you know Sherry Wellington?"

"I do. Everyone working on M Street knows her. Or knows of her."

"And are Sherry and Carla friends?"

"Of course. Carla got Sherry her job here."

CHAPTER 26

THE ROW HOUSES near the old stadium were once a working man's neighborhood, the housing of choice for neighborhoods in Baltimore, Philly, and northward through Boston. Dan pulled his car to the curb and looked over at the first strip of homes. Ten residences snuggled together before the first access point to the alley broke the monotony and shared roofline. As described, concrete statues littered the yard of the third row house from the corner. The rusted chain-link fence around the tiny front yard had recently been painted silver without any attempt to remove the old rust.

Dan walked down the uneven sidewalk, the concrete slabs cracked from years of exposure and use. He reached the fenced yard and paused to admire the artwork. A fountain was indeed in the near corner. A garden hose feeding the water feature disappeared beneath a bush near the house. Along the fence were a half-dozen Terra Cotta warriors, standing guard over a litter of concrete piglets and a creature that resembled a leprechaun with a cowboy hat.

Holy crap, Dan thought.

He pushed open the gate to the fence and admired the small concrete birdbath on the left. Mildew engulfed the interior of the bowl. He announced himself to no one in particular and set out for the front steps, head scanning left and right. He knocked on the door as he glanced around the porch and back at his car parked on the street.

On the second set of knocks, the front door opened. A young woman in her early twenties stood on the other side of the still-locked security door. She wore jeans and a gray sweater. Her hair was pulled back into a ponytail and Dan noted the resemblance between the woman and Carla the waitress. As Dan performed his quick assessment he could feel the tension in the air.

"Can I help you?" the woman asked without any facial expression.

"My name is Dan Lord. I'm a private detective. I'm investigating Carla's accident."

"The cops were here earlier."

"I'm not a cop. I'm a private detective."

The young lady looked at Dan with suspicion. "Who hired you?"

"A woman who worked at the same restaurant Carla did. I was investigating a related matter and now I'm looking into Carla's accident. I assume I have the right address?"

"You do. I'm Candice. Carla's sister."

"Can I talk to you for a minute?"

Candice considered the question and looked down at her attire before replying. "Just give me a second."

The girl disappeared and returned a moment later with a revolver in her hand, the smooth wood on the gun's grip protruding past her pinkie finger.

Dan's eyes dipped and then slowly rose again to meet Candice's. He hoped his deliberate movement let Candice know he was fully aware of the weapon.

Candice shrugged her shoulders. "You look honest and all, but around here, you can never tell. You still want to talk?"

"I do."

Candice nodded and opened the door. Dan entered the living room. He kept his hands visible and moved slowly.

"You can sit on the sofa."

Dan did as suggested. "I'm sorry about your sister. I met her the other night at the restaurant. She seemed real nice. Real kind."

"My momma is a mess. She's got diabetes and a bad heart. She's over at the hospital now. Been back and forth all morning. I'm going to pick up her up in a little while."

"Are you the designated driver?"

"My momma hasn't driven in so long, I can't remember. Nerve damage in her legs from diabetes. Carla used to drive, then she started having seizures. They let you slide on the first one. But after a couple more seizures, they took her driver's license away. I've been driving Momma to the doctor and the grocery store. Sometimes I drive Carla to work. I'm working nights now, myself, so Carla has been taking the bus back."

"Were you here when the police came?"

"Nope."

"Do you know what they asked?"

"They wanted to know if Carla is having any problems. Asked if either Momma or me had seen anything strange."

"What did your mom say?"

"Probably nothing. Carla works and takes care of Momma. That's all she does."

"Do you live here, too?"

"Now I do. I moved out a couple years ago but I came back in the summer. Just couldn't afford rent on my own. We have three bedrooms. Me, Momma, and Carla. It's all right."

Dan looked across the room at the shelves in the corner. Photographs littered each shelf, picture frames climbing and clawing over one another.

"You mind if I take a look at the photographs?"

"Not if you don't mind me sitting in this chair with this gun in my lap."

"Fine by me."

Dan stood and again moved slowly and deliberately to the shelf in the corner. There was a picture of Carla in her prom dress, a purple gown that touched the floor. A young man in a tuxedo stood next to her with a broad smile.

"Who's the guy in the photo?"

"Jerome Watkins. Everyone called him Jay. Sometime after high school people started calling him Jelly. Then Jelly Donut. After that, JD."

"What do they call him now?"

"Dead."

"I like JD better," Dan replied. "What did he die of?"

Candice shrugged her shoulders. "Died of the same thing every other decent guy dies of around here. Bad friends. Wrong place, wrong time. Bad dope."

Dan eyeballed another shelf of photos as Candice watched him.

"My mom said the cops think it might not be an accident. What happened to Carla. They said at first they thought maybe she had a seizure. Maybe she fell off the sidewalk. But Momma said the white female detective was having different thoughts."

"I don't think it was an accident."

"You going to find who's responsible?"

Dan rubbed the back of his head and the lump that was still pulsating slightly. "I'm going to do my best."

Dan turned around to look at Candice. Tears ran down her cheeks, and her hands caressed the revolver in her lap.

Dan took a box of tissues off the small coffee table and handed it to Candice. He turned slowly back towards the photos before raising his eyes to the rest of the room. He took inventory of the TV, the DVR, and the phone in the corner. He looked over his shoulder and eyed the kitchen and its appliances.

Candice watched as Dan eyeballed the interior of the home. "You see anything you like?"

"Just looking around. Is your sister dating anyone?"

"No."

"What about an old boyfriend? Anyone since Jelly Donut?"

"She had a couple of no-goods here and there. Probably a man or two I didn't know about. I mean, Carla is a woman. She gets the itch every now and then."

"Nothing steady?"

"Nah. Carla and me don't bring boys around the house. Momma is just too hard on dates. You could bring Obama in here and she would tell you he ain't good enough for her girls."

"You ever hang out with any of these no-goods, as you put it?"

"Every once in a while. If they stuck around long enough."

"How many of them stuck around long enough?"

"Not too many. But like I said, she doesn't introduce most of them to me or Momma. A while back I think she was dating a guy named T-Daddy."

"T-Daddy?"

"I never met him. Not sure what his real name is. I heard her talk about him on the phone. Might have been an older guy. Talked about how T-Daddy had given her a few things."

"Anything suspicious in her life you want to tell me that maybe your mother didn't tell the cops?"

"Nope."

Dan reached into his pocket and produced a business card. He handed the card to Candice, who read it and then put it on the table.

"How about giving me a call if you think of anything?"

CHAPTER 27

HIS NAME WAS Angel and he was no good. He had lost all goodness before he realized he had had any. A lifetime ago. An exotic, lucrative, but equally soul-damning lifetime ago. Yet Angel was at peace. For him, there would be no redemption. No rehabilitation. Hell was his final stop. And his certainty in his own damnation made life bearable. He didn't fret over the future. It had been decided. He slept well and looked in the mirror without flinching. There were no visions of spiritual grandeur. All had been vacated.

Angel sat on the sofa in the living room of the simple rambler, a hundred yards from the two-lane county road just outside of Warrenton, Virginia. The long gravel driveway leading to the house was in need of another load of rocks, most of the initial layer consumed by the earth over time. With five acres of undeveloped forest surrounding the house, the location was perfect for the homeowner and his sole roommate: a large Rottweiler named Peso with a physique and growl that scared away most visitors. The few guests that did make it to the door never realized the real danger was not the dog, but its owner.

From his position on the sofa, short stacks of white paper filled the coffee table in front of him. On the corner of the table, a half-empty glass of scotch stood next to a nearly full bottle. A large plastic canister of canine jerky treats rested on the sofa cushion next to him. Angel twisted the top off the jar and tossed a jerky treat into the air. Peso's large mouth slapped together in a mix of powerful muscles and dog slobber.

"Are you ready to get to work?" Angel asked Peso. The ninety-pound canine responded with a single bark as if she understood she was being beckoned.

Angel picked up the top piece of paper from one of the short stacks and started reading out loud. "First up is Katherine Hyde. Age forty-one. Stage four breast cancer. Estimated longevity less than five months. She works in a plumbing supply office. Makes forty grand a year. Has two children. No husband. No ex-husband. Last intel on the father showed him shacked up with a casino card dealer outside of Vegas. No known life insurance policy. No known religious affiliation."

Angel turned towards Peso and tossed the dog another jerky treat. "I see potential. No insurance and no religious affiliation. That's always good. We certainly don't need any churchgoers, now do we, girl?" Angel asked. Peso again responded with a single bark.

"Yes, Peso, she is a strong candidate. Let's call her 'Killer Katherine.' A little more vetting and we may have a winner, here."

Another jerky treat. Another bark. Angel reached for his glass of scotch and took a sip.

"Next up, we have Sarah Turner. We'll call her Sniper Sarah. Another case of stage four breast cancer. Nasty stuff, this breast cancer. Doctors really need to find a cure, don't you think, Peso?"

Another bark of agreement.

"Sniper Sarah is the mother of one. Has a single surviving family member, a brother in Utah who has joined a radical, end-of-the-world religious sect. She is currently working at a day care center in Maryland. No baby daddy mentioned anywhere in her child's birth records. She has competed in several half-marathons, according to her Facebook page. That's good. Physical condition is very important. It leaves open more possibilities for planning and execution…"

An hour later, the stacks of white paper had been whittled down to three finalists. Angel shoved the unchosen dossiers through the paper shredder and then threw handfuls of the paper strips onto the logs in the fireplace. Peso was asleep on the floor next to the sofa, satiated by three-dozen jerky treats and exhausted from voicing her opinion.

*

Angel turned on the TV in the corner of the room and found the DVR menu. He checked to be sure the news had been recorded and clicked on NBC to start his news scan for the evening. He finished his fourth glass of scotch and poured another. He ran through the playback of the news broadcast, switched to FOX, and became excited when he saw the breaking update from News 5 at 5. The image of the red Circulator bus and the caption on the bottom of screen told Angel all he needed to know. By the time the newscaster confirmed the death of a waitress standing in a bus line on her way home, Angel had walked to the desk in the corner of the living room and removed a mobile phone and a plastic bag full of SIM cards. He shoved a new SIM card into the back of the phone, waited for the service to initiate, and then sent a text.

"Payday."

CHAPTER 28

ANGEL STOPPED ON the side of the Blue Ridge Parkway and rested his backpack on the ground. He put the sole of his boot on the silver metal guardrail and retied his Vibram-bottomed, professional-grade footwear. Standing upright, he slipped his arms through the straps of his backpack, wiggled his hips once to settle the bag, and then checked his watch. He gave a final glance to his car parked at the small lot on the other side of the two-lane thoroughfare and then disappeared into the woods.

The hike to the cabin was four miles downhill. It was a distance Angel could cover in a half-hour on the treadmill. But without the luxury of running shoes, level ground, and a TV for distraction, he was planning on two hours down followed by three hours for the uphill return leg.

Dangerous switchbacks zigged and zagged, slithering down the rocky slope for the first mile of the trail. When Angel checked his watch at the forty-minute mark, the first drops of rain were falling through the remaining colored leaves overhead. The rain, the leaves on the ground, and rocks combined for a treacherous second mile. *The descent is always worse,* he reminded himself. The skies above seemed to rumble in response and the rain fell harder, as if Mother Nature was indicating she would have the final word in which leg would be more arduous. Ten minutes later Angel took his first fall, his backpack cushioning the impact. His second fall was soon thereafter and Angel's thoughts turned to the contents of his bag.

The third mile of the trek was only marginally better than the first two, with a small break in the rain that was just long enough to offer hope there would be a more permanent reprieve. The thunder and sheet-like rain that accompanied Angel on the last mile of level ground put to rest all dreams of an afternoon with dry clothes.

Angel arrived at the clearing near Corbin Cabin thirty minutes later than planned. The cabin—a three-room shack without electricity or water—was the lone habitable structure in the Shenandoah National Forest. The splintered and rotting remains of various other buildings dotted the valley floor; time and the elements having taken their toll and rendering them unsafe. The lone survivor of the original settlements, Corbin Cabin was maintained by a nonprofit trail preservation outfit in Vienna, Virginia. The small organization rented the cabin for twenty-five dollars a night, transportation and amenities not included.

Angel climbed the wood steps to the porch of the cabin and slipped the key into the padlock that secured the front door. He pushed his way inside, removed his dripping jacket, and used a stack of wood in the corner and jar of matches on the mantle to start a fire in the stone hearth in the main room. Ten minutes later, with warmth edging out from the fireplace, Angel sat in a chair at the large wooden table in the middle of the room and began removing the contents of his bag, confirming that each item had survived the early November deluge and his challenges to remain upright.

His forty-liter pack was a quarter-full with a day's worth of provisions. Angel removed two ready-to-eat meals and confirmed the packaging was not punctured. He examined a large Ziploc bag of energy bars and checked the seal. Satisfied, he moved to the next bag and confirmed that his flashlight and emergency water filter were unscathed. The few items on the table, combined with the two water bottles on the sides of his pack, accounted for most of the bag's weight. The remaining weight was attributable to the Glock handgun and two fully loaded seventeen-shot magazines.

Angel checked the most important tool of survival without removing it from the bag. He knew well that a man could survive two days without water and two weeks without food. But injury and illness notwithstanding, he knew he could survive most anything else with the company of his favorite sidearm. Real survival could easily be decided by the man with the most bullets. Just ask the Native Americans.

With the cabin prepared for his guest, Angel took a seat on an old chair on the covered front porch. He listened to the stream babble near the edge of the clearing and remembered camping with his older brother as a youngster. Relaxed, his mind trotted through his teens and twenties. When his jog down memory lane reached the thirty-year mark, he turned his attention back to his work, to past dirty deeds... and to dirty deeds that lay ahead.

*

The man Angel had simply nicknamed "Dinero" reached the clearing in the woods near the cabin from the direction of a well-maintained trail. The trail offered a leisurely two-hour stroll from the nearest parking lot, hugging a stream that ducked and dodged in and out of hollers named for settlers who were driven from the land when the government arrived with their plan for a national park.

Angel watched as Dinero arched his back at the edge of the clearing and slipped the backpack off his shoulder. Dinero's short frame tilted to the side as he grabbed the pack with his right hand. Angel continued to monitor the man's approach to the cabin, the backpack tugging at Dinero's right shoulder, almost pulling him down. The strain of the hike with the heavy backpack grew apparent on Dinero's middle-aged face as he neared the cabin. Passing the stone-rimmed fire pit in the clearing around the cabin, the man's slowing gait melted into a shuffle.

Angel waved his hand slightly as Dinero approached. Angel stood from his chair as the man climbed the stairs to the porch.

"I need to warm up," Dinero said, dropping the bag on the wooden porch for Angel to grab.

Angel gently slapped the man on the shoulder as he passed. Dinero responded to the gesture with a spasm of thick coughs. Angel followed him inside and shut the door, placing the bag on the floor near the table. The newly arrived visitor slowly removed his rain-soaked jacket and hung it on a wall hook fashioned from deer antlers.

"I wasn't sure if you got caught in the storm or not," Angel said. "The forecast was for partly cloudy skies."

"You can't believe the weatherman," the man replied, rubbing his hands near the fire like a character in a children's story.

Angel moved to the far side of the table and sat down so that he had a view of the door. Dinero fumbled with the zipper on his middle layer of clothing and coughed again. Angel heard the man curse under his breath and spit in the direction of the fire.

"You okay? Angel asked.

"I will be."

"You don't look well."

"Have you expanded your expertise into medical advice?"

"No. But sometimes I feel like I could."

"Perhaps that's true. Regardless, don't worry about me. I'm fine. Damn cold. The weather doesn't help."

"Did you see anyone on your way in?"

"Passed a couple of kids. Maybe university students. They were on their way out. Probably caught in the rain. There were a few cars in the parking lot south of Sperryville. Nothing out of the ordinary. Most of them probably on their way to hike Old Rag."

Dinero sat down and reached for his pack. He plucked a thick hiker's guide to the Shenandoah from his backpack and placed it on the table. A single white piece of paper was folded in the book.

"A hiking book?"

"Been carrying something related to the park every time we have met here. Sometimes it's a book on trees. Maybe flora. This time it's a hiking book. Makes for a plausible story. I even bookmarked the section that references this cabin. Dog-eared a couple of other locations for authenticity."

Angel reached over and opened his Ziploc bag of energy bars.

"How about you? Did you see anyone on your hike down?" Dinero asked.

"Not a soul. But then again, I have the route no one wants to take."

"When you start bringing the cash, we can switch paths."

"Fair enough."

Dinero pulled a few more items from his bag and placed a bottle of water and a tightly wrapped sandwich on the table. He put a small stack of napkins next to the sandwich and wiped his hands with one. A minute later, half of the sandwich and most of the water had disappeared.

Angel finished his second energy bar and looked down at Dinero's backpack on the floor of the cabin. "We need to discuss some developments."

"What kind of developments?" Dinero asked.

"The last two assignments have had complications."

"I followed both stories in the press. The shooting of the lawyer seems to have gone off without a hitch. The police have no suspects. No leads. Other than the curiosity of a possible urban sniper, there's nothing unusual about the investigation or indication the authorities have figured anything out. And the waitress who was hit by the bus, well, she didn't die immediately, but she did pass. I think it provides a nice twist, actually. Makes her death seem even more accidental."

Dinero paused and Angel nodded slightly.

"So, what are the complications?" Dinero asked.

"As you're probably aware, the shooter for the lawyer had an automobile accident after executing her assignment. She perished. It was in the news, but it was not in the news in connection with the shooting."

"I heard. But I didn't see any connection between the lawyer and the slightly premature demise of our terminally ill sniper-for-hire. Other than both of them dying on the same day."

"The same morning."

"Has someone made a connection?"

"Not yet. It appears that everything has worked out. But the police did investigate. They did ask around. They could work it out. That's our first complication."

"If they had something, we would know."

"Maybe. Maybe not. Our insulation in these occurrences is a two-sided coin. The upside is that we have no previous connection to any of our hired help. No past dealings. No record of electronic interchanges. No history. This is our advantage. Hell, no one in the US has ever even seen you and me together. We are completely insulated even from each other. Isolated. Compartmentalized. But the other side of the coin is that insulation from our hired help prevents us from monitoring potential investigations. We only know what we hear in the media."

That's what you think, Dinero thought. "Following an investigation doesn't concern me. It's wasted energy. What would worrying about that achieve?"

"I would like to know."

"The hired help for the EPA lawyer perished in a car accident, correct?"

"Yes."

"The lawyer is also deceased, correct?"

"Yes."

"Then neither of them will be talking," Dinero said simply, taking another bite of his sandwich. "And we never met anyone else related to either of them."

"True, but…"

"Good. The lawyer's case is closed. What was the complication with the waitress who was hit by the bus?" Dinero asked. He reached for his water bottle and twisted the top with his thumb while coughing into one of his napkins.

"Someone was watching the waitress the night she was killed. Someone saw it happen."

"It was on a busy street. There were many witnesses. All of who saw nothing. As planned."

"Beyond witnesses. Someone intervened. As a result, I had to get involved."

"Explain yourself."

"The plan was executed flawlessly. But there was a man observing our waitress. He saw our hired help. He pursued her around the block as she changed outfits. I went around the other side of the block to observe. I didn't expect to engage the man, but our woman dropped the weapon, which was not part of the plan. I picked it up, and proceeded to eliminate the threat."

"Eliminate?"

"Incapacitate."

"The police?"

"No. A private detective. And an attorney."

"What was a private detective and attorney doing following the waitress?"

"I'm not sure yet. I have his wallet and am starting surveillance. He hasn't been to his office in a couple of days."

"And the waitress?"

"I don't believe she knew she was being followed."

"I told you I didn't like the idea of using a baton. We should have used a gun."

"It's pretty risky to execute a killing with a firearm on a crowded street surrounded by a dozen witnesses."

"You could have killed the waitress closer to her home."

"Not all of our hired help are proficient with firearms. Not all of our hired help can blend in to any neighborhood, any environment."

Dinero took another sip of water. "So you're saying she was a poor shot with a firearm."

"You could put it that way."

"It's disappointing. For years we didn't have a single hiccup. Now we have two complications in a row."

"You pushed up the timeline. I told you that compressing the frequency of our tasks was inherently dangerous. You want to know why the first few people were easy? Because we were patient. Planning takes time. Training the hired help takes time. Particularly if you don't want to be caught, which is why we operate the way we do. For years we had a steady pace. Everything was perfect. Then you changed that dynamic. If you want speed, then efficiency will suffer."

"Time is no longer in abundance."

"Then perfection is something we can no longer expect."

"As I can see by these last two assignments."

"If you think you can find someone to do it better, be my guest."

Dinero looked over at the fire and stood. He walked to the door and confirmed the latch on the inside was in the locked position. He returned to the table, thrust his hand into his bag, and removed five pounds of cash wrapped in cellophane. The cash thudded on the table and Angel reached for his own backpack. Seven additional stacks of currency landed on the top of the table and Angel quickly transferred the money into his large backpack and pulled the drawstring on the top of the bag.

"That's a million for the dead lawyer and a million for the dead waitress."

"I'll count it later."

"If I had been smart, I would've negotiated payment in Euros. They have a five hundred denomination that would have cut the weight considerably."

"And I would lose money on the exchange rate, in addition to the laundering fee I already have to pay."

Dinero stepped glumly to the fire and said, "This is the last time we will use the cabin."

Angel grunted. "That's not a decision to make lightly. This is the perfect location. No one can tie us together here. We have parked our cars in separate locations that are over forty miles apart via any paved road. As the crow flies, our points of origin are only seven miles apart, but by county and state roads, we are well over an hour away from each other. There is no cell phone coverage to track us. We have a nice little cabin in the woods we can use without being traced."

"The cabin has worked well. Though I was never as sold on its perfection as you were."

"Do you think we would have made it this far if I wasn't careful? The nonprofit that maintains this cabin operates out of a one-room office in Northern Virginia. It's managed entirely by volunteers. In order to get the key for the cabin, you simply need to provide a credit card number."

"I assume you didn't use yours."

"Of course not. When I need to use the cabin, I check online for availability. Once my reservation is confirmed, they send an email to a bogus email account I set up. In the email they provide a code to a lockbox. I can pick up the key to the cabin from the lockbox outside the office."

"So you never have to pick up the key in person…"

"You can. You can even have it mailed to your home. But the organization has a lockbox on the outside of the building for after-hour pickups. I get the key from the lockbox. I drop the key off when I am done, also after hours, and I never have to engage anyone. No one has ever seen my face. Using the lockbox is perfect. In fact, I cannot image a better scenario."

"You don't have to be a member of the trail organization to make a reservation?"

"Therein lies the cherry on the sundae. Because this cabin is in a National Forest, by law, membership cannot be required."

"Like I said, nothing is perfect. Dragging forty pounds of cash through the woods, for one," Dinero said. "But regardless, we'll have to change venues. The next meeting will not be here."

"If not here, then where?"

"I'm working out the details. Something less remote, but just as anonymous." Dinero again reached into his backpack and slid another Ziploc bag across the table. "Here are a couple more prepaid phones. That should be enough for the final two on our list."

Angel opened the bag and removed one of the phones, a basic prepaid model without any bells or whistles. As Angel finished examining the phones, Dinero placed a new Virginia driver's license in the middle of the wooden table. Angel put the phones back into the bag and picked up the new ID. He read the details of the new identity and then Angel's gaze slowly returned to Dinero's face.

"How intimately do I need to become with my new identification?"

"Just remember the name, address, and birthday. You'll need it. Don't lose it. I don't want to have to get another one. They are becoming more difficult to acquire."

Angel nodded, his mind returning to bigger concerns. "Let's discuss the final two targets."

"Yes, let's. We have two targets remaining. The final target is yours, as agreed upon originally. You will handle the final target on your own, without any assistance."

"And payment for the final target is in advance. Also as agreed upon."

"I know the arrangement."

"The final target will be problematic and will require an expedient exit. I won't have time to wait around to get paid. There will be additional press coverage and increased interest from law enforcement. A proper exit will be difficult enough without hanging around."

"I know our arrangement," Dinero said again with conviction. "For the last person on the list, you will be paid in advance. I assume you already have a plan for the last one."

"I do," Angel said, nodding.

"So all we need is one more plan."

"That's correct."

"I would like it done as soon as possible," Dinero said.

"How soon?"

"Weeks, at the very latest."

"Not possible."

"You are paid to make it possible," Dinero retorted.

Angel responded. "Need I remind you that in addition to planning and training, there is also the unknown variable of our hired help? Our inventory of available killers is currently at zero. And even if we did have someone, training is a mixed bag. As we have learned, you can't sign someone up for a weekend shooting camp and expect to churn out a military-grade assassin. There is no substitute for ten thousand rounds of ammunition through various weapons in different environments and situations. Not to mention the impact of stress on breathing and focus. It doesn't take much to induce shaky hands."

"Your point is made."

"Good. As of now, we have zero assistants available. Our last two declined our offer. I have identified another three from the latest list who may be contenders. But there's a lot of legwork to be done with those three before any decision can be made. As of today, if we needed to eliminate a target, we have no one who is trained and operational. No one."

"We do have two people who have been trained and proven that they are trustworthy."

"Reuse the help on a second assignment? That raises our risks considerably. One-and-done is the protocol we agreed upon."

"It may be time to deviate from the existing protocol."

"Easy for you to suggest. Unlike you, I spent time with the hired help. They could identify me. I don't want to reengage any of them. It's a risk I would prefer not to take. Retirement is my goal, not prison. I can get to prison on my own."

"If you're sure about not using old help, then I have another suggestion. Let's double the offer to others. See if any of those who previously declined our offer will reconsider for two million dollars."

Angel considered the option. "That's a better plan than reusing the help from a previous assignment. But I'm not sure increasing the payout is going to solve our problems. A week or two is not long enough for effective training."

"Figure out options that don't require training."

"I'll consider the alternatives."

There was a long silence as the rain started to pound the roof of the cabin.

"As I said, I'm not concerned with the details. That's what you were hired for. That is what you are paid for," Dinero said.

Angel nodded. "What about this private detective?" he asked. "He could be an issue."

"Then you will have to deal with him."

"Do as I please?"

"I'm only concerned about the final two people on the list. How you get it done will not keep me up at night."

CHAPTER 29

D AN DROVE THROUGH downtown Middleburg, the heart of horse country, forty miles west of DC. The main drag was littered with art dealers, real estate offices, swanky coffee shops, and classy restaurants, most residing in two-hundred-year-old buildings with all the modern upgrades. Two banks, a gas station, and a church filled the remaining gaps on the two-lane main road. The working class side of Middleburg was one block over, on a parallel street, where the locals could still find the plumber, the electrician, and the Irish pub that had survived since the end of the Civil War.

Three minutes and one stoplight later, Middleburg was in Dan's rearview mirror. His smartphone rested on the passenger seat and directed him to turn at the second street on the left. Ten minutes farther, with rolling hills and dry stack stonewalls on both sides of the road, Dan turned at a driveway sandwiched between an old oak tree and a large red mailbox.

The long gravel driveway kicked up dust as he approached the house in the middle of an open pasture. With the average size of the Middleburg home approaching nearly ten thousand square feet, the modest, all stone, metal roofed, one-story home on the hill was underwhelming.

The large gate near the edge of the circular driveway in front of the house was the second indication the residence was not simply another home among the foxhunting and steeplechasing majority. A large closed-circuit camera loomed over the gate from a brick column. A black metal security fence ran the perimeter of the yard, its substantial size and girth subdued by well-manicured trees and shrubbery. Another set of cameras peered down on the front yard from the corners of the house. Dan looked closer at the yard and noticed ground sensor alarms at regular intervals.

He rolled down the window of his car and pressed the button on the security panel in the brick column next to the front gate.

A female's voice echoed, "Who is it?"

Before Dan could answer, a familiar male voice interjected, "Drive on up, Dan."

*

Dan climbed the three stairs to the front porch of the house, and the door opened. Tobias, clean-shaven, stepped outside to meet Dan with a handshake. Dan's eyes widened slightly at the sight of the well-groomed Tobias wearing pants and a shirt that hadn't been pulled from the laundry pile.

"Look at you. You clean up well."

"Got a girlfriend."

"A girlfriend?"

"That's right."

"Must be serious. You shaved."

Tobias rubbed his chin. "Not that serious. But she doesn't like stubble. Says it rubs a certain area of her anatomy the wrong way. And she says that if I want a certain area of my anatomy rubbed the right way, then I need to shave."

"Blackmailed."

Tobias turned his neck slightly to show Dan he still had long locks of dark hair pulled into a ponytail. "Now, if she asks me to cut my hair, we are done."

"How did you meet her?"

"I moved out here. She owns the place next door. Was married to a real estate developer. Poor guy died in a steeplechase accident."

"Really?"

"Indeed."

"How does that fit into your death count total? Or have you stopped counting the number of people you know who have died?"

Tobias stared into the distance from the front porch, and then answered.

"My employer has me on Clomipramine. They thought it would be better for everyone if I gave it a try."

"So you aren't counting the dead anymore?"

Tobias leaned in towards Dan and whispered, "I'm still counting. I just count to myself."

"How many are we up to?"

"Two hundred twenty-one."

"Does that include the girlfriend's ex-husband?"

"No, he died before I moved to the neighborhood."

Tobias took several deep breathes of the crisp morning air.

"Nice place you have here. Beautiful view. Good location for security. Nice clean sightlines. A gravel driveway that kicks up dust. Ground sensors. Closed-circuit TV."

"My employers like security. I like seclusion. This is the compromise."

"So you ditched retirement in Belize?"

"Not at all. I'm putting the finishing touches on a nice place in the former British Honduras, as we speak. I have a quarter-acre of waterfront land on the sunset side of the Ambergris Caye. I'm going down there next month for a visit. Going to spend the winter down there."

"A snowbird?"

"I like to think I merely broadened my retirement horizon. Funny how things work out. Who knew organized crime would make me legitimate? I figure with the deal I have with the casinos as an ongoing data consultant, I should be able to launder most of my dirty savings over the next five years or so. Little by little, I should be able to clean years of illegally acquired money. By the end of the decade, I should be entirely legit."

"I'm not sure if I like the sound of you being legit."

"Me either."

There was a long pause and then Tobias cut to the chase. "So, you said you need help looking for something?"

"I do."

"You want to come in and see the new setup?"

"Absolutely."

Dan followed Tobias through the living room, past the large stone fireplace and the matching leather sofas. Near the rear of the house, Dan could see the view from the back was no less spectacular than the view he had just enjoyed from the front. Without warning, Tobias turned left and disappeared down a flight of stairs at the edge of the kitchen. As Dan turned to follow his host, he heard dishes gently clinking together and smelled the faint scent of perfume in the air. It took all the restraint he had not to pass the entrance to the basement and wander into the kitchen just to see what kind of woman would put up with Tobias.

Dan came down the stairs and stood in the middle of a large room filled with computers. Monitors, keyboards, servers, and enough wire to restring the Brooklyn Bridge ran from component to component. Expensive hardware to expensive hardware.

"I have about the same bandwidth here that I did at the other place, but the equipment has been updated," Tobias said.

"All paid for by your employer?"

"Considered as my signing bonus. You want a top-quality product, you have to have top-quality equipment."

"Or know how to hijack top-quality equipment."

"That works too. Hopefully, those days are behind me."

Tobias sat down in a well-worn office chair with wheels and pushed himself in front of a monitor and keyboard. "What are we looking for?"

"I need you to find a connection between three people. And before you ask, one of them is a congressman's wife."

"Which one?"

"John Wellington."

"What is his wife's name?"

"Sherry Wellington."

"Who are the others?"

"The father of Sherry Wellington's son, Marcus Losh. Army vet. Disabled and deceased."

"Which one? He can't be both."

"Deceased. Sorry."

"Who's next?"

"Carla Jackson."

"What's her relationship?"

"She worked with Sherry Wellington at a bar in Georgetown called J. Paul's."

"The place with oysters in the window."

"That's the one."

"Snot on a shell."

"I don't think that's the restaurant's official slogan."

"So where do you want me to look?"

"Everywhere. I tried the usual places. I know Carla the waitress and Sherry Wellington worked at the same restaurant. And I know that Marcus Losh and Sherry Wellington had a relationship, lived together, and had a child together. I'm looking for something else."

"And you don't know what it is."

"I don't, but my guess is there's something. The Army vet is dead. The waitress is also dead. Sherry knows both of them. She says she's scared she may be next. She hired me to find her baby daddy's killer."

"But she isn't telling you the truth."

"She has a problem with the honesty."

"Okay. I can bang this thing off most law enforcement and government databases in just a couple of minutes."

Dan watched as Tobias's fingers danced across the keyboard, interrupted by the intermittent reach for the computer mouse to the right. As Tobias worked his magic, Dan noticed the small basket of prescription medicine bottles sitting just under the main computer monitor.

"You working on anything else you can talk about?" Dan asked.

"Almost finished with the code for picking winners for professional baseball games."

"How accurate is it?"

"It's good. But it's been a lot of work. Baseball has more variables and stats than football. It got a little weedy there for a while."

"Weedy?"

Tobias answered without turning around. "You know, lost in the weeds. Data all over the place. You can't think. Paralysis sets in because you have data and ideas growing up your legs like weeds. Mental overload. You start dreaming about data sets, which is an interruption to your waking hours when you're thinking about data sets. You start talking to yourself. And then you start answering yourself. When it gets really bad, you can forget to go to the bathroom. It can get a little messy at times."

He may be on meds but he's still flirting with instability, Dan thought. "Weedy. I'll remember the term."

Fifteen minutes later, Tobias went over the results of the query. "We do have matches for employment for Sherry and Carla at J. Paul's. Carla worked there first. Sherry worked there for a shorter period of time and joined after Carla. There is no cross-match with Marcus Losh and the restaurant, although he did have a few credit card charges for J. Paul's."

"You can legally get credit card information?"

"Not for all companies," Tobias said. "Not yet, anyway," he added, staring at the screen.

"So there's nothing tying Marcus Losh to Carla the waitress?"

"Nothing."

"And Sherry Wellington and Marcus Losh?"

"Obviously, there are quite a few commonalities. They lived together. They are both on their son's birth records. They had a joint bank account for a brief period of time. They had renter insurance policies on their apartment." Tobias paused. "Are you aware that Sherry Wellington had a restraining order and there was a domestic abuse charge filed against Marcus Losh?"

"Yes."

"Good. If you hadn't found that, I'd be concerned you were slipping."

"Thanks for your concern. Any other ideas?"

"I'm not the idea man. I'm the data man. And the data tells me there is no triangular association."

"How confident are you?"

Tobias spun in his chair and faced Dan. "If it's there, I'll find it. Give me another data point to work with and I'll run it again."

"I don't have one."

Tobias nodded. "Give me a call when you do."

CHAPTER 30

DAN WATCHED AS the light in Sherry Wellington's bedroom went dark at ten. As it had been for three consecutive nights, Sherry was heading to bed without her congressman husband. According to the files Dan was keeping in his head, the Senate hopeful usually arrived home between ten and eleven. But he showed signs of being a husband who tried. Two days prior he had returned home early, with flowers in hand. For his reward, the beautiful Sherry Wellington had pulled the bedroom curtains before nine.

Dan checked his watch and remained on the park bench. In the blocks around Volta Park, the flower of life bloomed early and remained open late into the evening. A week into his assignment, Dan's intelligence of the neighborhood rivaled that of the silver fox gossip who lived a block from the park and who spent her days bending the ear of any warm body she could corner on the sidewalk. Dan had learned to cross the street at the first echo of her cane hitting the sidewalk.

But in many ways, Dan was becoming an equally nosey neighborhood fixture. He knew the man in the expensive suit who walked his poodle, replete with a diamond-studded necklace. He had a detailed mental picture of the young couple in expensive matching running shoes and headbands who generated lethargic, fifteen-minute-miles. He knew the schedule of the thirty-year-old woman next door who arrived home in the wee hours via taxi and wearing sweatpants. Dan was certain he'd seen her swinging on a pole at one of the District's gentlemen's clubs.

Georgetown had it all. The eclectic crowd was as varied as the history, bars, and restaurant options. Dan understood why ten-foot-wide town-houses cost a million dollars and why dive apartments in century-old buildings with dripping faucets cost more than a mortgage on the other side of the river. It was all in the neighborhood.

At ten thirty, Dan checked his watch before he began his goodnight patrol of the Wellington's immediate block. In fifteen minutes Emily was scheduled to meet him at his apartment. Just a late evening drink somewhere in Georgetown. A little chitchat about the possibility of a serial killer in town. Dan exited the alley and turned to the right. He had enough time for one final around-the-block surveillance loop.

Fifty yards from the park, Dan passed three students in various athletic gear with Georgetown Bulldog insignias. Given their location and direction, Dan surmised their most likely destination was the Tombs, a Georgetown student mainstay three blocks down but off the beaten track from the watering holes on M Street.

As the three young men passed, Dan noticed a strong scent of patchouli oil wafting over him. Minutes later, heading in the opposite direction, Dan saw the same three men coming down the sidewalk again, this time walking away from the direction of the Tombs. Dan thought he heard Spanish being spoken and then noticed the three men fell silent as they neared.

Dan's radar emitted a weak warning signal.

Dan and the three men approached each other from opposite directions of the cobblestone sidewalk. The tallest of the three men pressed a phone to his ear. Dan could see a collage of tattoos covering the hand and fingers holding the phone. The pace of the group slowed slightly as the distance between the Dan and the trio closed to ten feet. Dan mentally set his reaction for a hair-trigger response.

The taller man with the tattooed hand removed the phone from his ear and slipped it into his pocket. A dangling earring swung from the earlobe of the man nearest Dan. The shortest member of the trio took up the rear of the triangle. Dan tried to make eye contact as they passed, but all three stared stoically straight ahead. Another blast of patchouli oil filled the air. Dan took several steps, waited for a few seconds, and then turned around, holding his position. He watched as the three men disappeared around the corner, walking back in the direction of Georgetown University's main campus.

Dan again checked the time. *Time to head back and have a drink*, he thought.

*

Five minutes later, Dan was on the darkest section of the block with the outline of the front steps to his apartment building in the distance. In the dim light, a nightcap with a good-looking brunette police detective danced through his mind.

Then he smelled patchouli oil.

Dan heard the footsteps behind him a split second before the man with the tattooed hand appeared to his front, stepping up from the entrance to an English basement of an old townhouse.

Where is number three? Dan wondered.

"Are you Dan?" the man with the tattooed hand asked in the darkness.

Judging by his silhouette, Dan assessed the man as tall and thin, his favorite physical attributes for an adversary in a confrontation without weapons.

"Depends on who wants to know," Dan replied.

"We want to know, asshole," the man with the dangling earring replied from Dan's rear. Dan felt a hand shove him in the back and he stumbled forward for show, taking the opportunity to move to the flank. From his new position, with a townhouse somewhere behind him, Dan now had a dim panoramic view of his two new friends.

"Move," the man with the tattoo said, unofficially announcing himself as the leader.

"Where are we going?" Dan asked.

"That way," the man said, pointing in the direction of a dark street corner opposite Dan's apartment building.

Interesting choice, Dan thought.

"I'm not carrying any money, fellas," Dan said, raising his hands slowly. *And if you want the four hundred dollars in my back pocket, you are going to have to take it. And that means putting hands on me. And that means subsequent medical attention. Maybe for all of us, but certainly for both of you...*

"Put your arms down," the man with the earring said sternly. "This isn't a robbery."

Dan did as he was told and peered into the dimly lit air to count the visible hands of his new friends. Concealed hands usually equated to concealed weapons. A cursory glance allowed Dan to register two visible hands, two concealed hands. *Two perps, each with a weapon*, Dan thought. *And one missing perp, though I'm pretty sure he's anything but missing.*

Dan stepped down the sidewalk in the direction indicated by the man with the hand tattoos.

Nearing the dark street corner, with Dan walking in the middle position between the two perpetrators, a woman's voice cut through the air. All heads turned in the direction of the sidewalk behind them.

"Looks like you could use some help," Detective Emily Fields said, slowly coming into view as she reached the helmet party on the sidewalk. Her badge was hooked to her belt and her service pistol was in her grip. The men on either side of Dan exchanged glances and the man with the earring stepped away, opening space on the sidewalk and giving Emily two angles to consider. She responded by raising her Glock to eye level.

The man with tattoos said something in Spanish and the man with the earring started to laugh.

Dan did the honor of translating.

"They don't care if you're a police officer."

"And my gun doesn't care if I read them their rights." Emily retorted in Spanish.

Dan watched the leader with the tattooed hand and waited for him to realize Spanish would not be a refuge for concealing communication.

"Thanks for the help, Officer, but I think I got this," Dan said, winking at Emily in the faint light.

As Emily slowly stepped forward, pistol drawn, the missing third perpetrator appeared from between two parked cars and raised a knife to the side of Emily's neck.

"Drop it," the shorter, stockier man said, flashing a smile as if the group's backup plan had worked flawlessly.

"I thought one of you was missing," Dan said, hoping that Emily would understand there were no other actors scheduled to make an appearance in the play unfolding on the sidewalk.

Dan locked eyes with Emily and dipped his head as an indication for her to disarm. Emily complied and pressed the magazine release on her gun. She ejected the round from the gun's chamber and it bounced into the darkness. A second later, both the magazine and gun clanked on the ground. The perpetrator with the knife on Emily's neck moved to her rear. Then his desire for a weapon upgrade drove the man to a career-ending decision.

Stooping to pick up Emily's discarded weapon and magazine, the man provided the split-second reprieve Emily needed. By the time he attempted to stand with improved weaponry, Emily had completed a stomp to the top of the man's foot, a knee to the groin, and simultaneous carotid crushing blows to each side of the man's neck. Through fleeting consciousness, the perp warily lunged at Emily and fell. The magazine and her service pistol slipped from the man's hand and returned to the brick sidewalk. The entire assault was over in a matter of seconds.

Dan flashed a look of admiration and then his eye caught the movement of another knife, this one from the man with the tattooed hand in front of him. Dan noted the man's grip on the knife and knew the assailant had experience with the weapon. Dan responded by moving into a standard knife defensive pose, his arms covering the center of his body, alternating high and low positions.

The man with the knife feigned a stab and Dan feigned a flanking move. The man's second thrust with the knife was more accurate and Dan drove his forearm downward onto the wrist holding the knife. Despite the bone bruising impact, the man didn't drop the weapon. Dan quickly tightened his grip on the wrist with the knife. The man fought Dan's grasp as Dan cranked the man's arm, spinning him in the direction of the cars parked along the curb.

*

In the seconds since dispatching the first man, Emily had reacquired the magazine for her service weapon and was reaching for the gun. The man with the earring, having seen his friend disabled, reached the unloaded weapon first and kicked the pistol down the sidewalk. The man followed the kick of the weapon with a kick directed at Emily's head. The intended head shot missed as Emily raised her hands in defense. She blocked a third kick with her left forearm. The perpetrator's subsequent punch was telegraphed and slow, and Emily sidestepped the incoming fist and drove her right elbow to the side of the man's temple. Stunned, the man with the earring reached his hand into the pocket of his jacket. Not waiting to see the pocket surprise, Emily drove a kick to the testicles of the man with the earring, producing a grunt that quickly melted into a whimper. She immediately followed the family-jewel greeting with a knee to the face.

*

The leader of the group still held the knife in his hand and Dan still controlled the man's wrist and arm. The sound of Emily jamming the magazine back into her Glock and racking the slide grabbed the attention of the knife-wielding man. The distraction provided by the loading of the gun was all Dan needed. With a sudden change in direction, Dan forced the perpetrators arm against the natural movement of every joint in the man's limb. A crisp snap was followed by a muffled scream. The danger of the knife ended with the perpetrator's torso crashing into a parked vehicle.

Dan turned and watched as Emily stepped into the space on the sidewalk between the two men lying at her feet. She had both hands on her service weapon, eyes focused down the barrel, her targets at pointblank range. The first man, who had received the simultaneous blows to his carotids, was already ambling to stand.

"Time to call it in, Dan. 911. Tell them you have an officer in need of assistance," Emily said. She moved towards the building to gain a clear shot of the three men in varying states of recovery.

Dan glanced over as the man with the freshly broken arm also struggled to get vertical. Dan raised his foot, stepped on the man's ribs, and pushed him back to the ground. Then Dan pulled out his phone to call 911.

The force of the bullet impacting Dan's chest sent him staggering backwards. A second bullet hit the brick on the townhouse inches from Dan's head. Dan slumped to the ground as Emily dove for cover. Crawling across the sidewalk, Emily reached Dan as his eyes closed. She grabbed his still open phone and completed the call to 911. Placing the phone on the ground as she barked out orders for immediate medical assistance and police backup, she began chest compressions interspersed with mouth-to-mouth resuscitation.

CHAPTER 31

WALLACE PARKED HIS squad car on the curb and ran into the emergency room at GW Hospital. Police shield in hand, he bypassed the half-dozen cases standing in line at the registration desk. The security guard on duty stepped forward to intercept Wallace, noticed the badge, and nodded.

"Dan Lord," Wallace said tersely to the woman in purple scrubs behind the registration desk.

"Room six," the woman replied, pointing down the light blue hall to her left. "He's getting ready to be released."

"You sure?"

"Yes, sir."

Covered in perspiration, Wallace arrived at the doorway of the room and spotted Emily's profile at the curtained partition on the right. Steps later, Wallace tugged the curtain to the side and entered. Dan was sitting upright on the adjustable bed, his pants on, a thick roll of ace bandages wrapped around his chest. A nurse stood next to his right arm, checking the printout of the EKG machine.

"Does someone want to explain exactly what the hell is going on?" Wallace said, pulling Emily to the side. "Dispatch reported he was shot and wasn't wearing a vest."

"He was shot. It hit. Center mass."

"What am I missing? Someone's going to have to start explaining."

Emily tried not to smile. "Dan here has taken to wearing bulletproof clothing." Emily nodded in Dan's direction as if to highlight the living and breathing evidence receiving medical treatment.

"No injuries?" Wallace asked.

"Two broken ribs and one fantastic bruise in the making. But otherwise he's fine."

The nurse who had been checking Dan's vitals turned away from her patient, slipped by Wallace and Emily, and exited while whispering something about men and guns.

"The nurse said I'm free to go," Dan said. "And let me say, I had no idea how fast service at an emergency room could be. Turns out, if you come in with a police officer, you get to cut the line."

"Smart ass. Damn near gave me a heart attack," Wallace said.

"Time to get in shape."

"You think this is funny?"

Emily interjected. "No, we don't think it's funny. We're just a little ahead of you on the emotional roller coaster."

"I don't recall a psychology degree on your résumé. You want to give me the rundown of what happened?" Wallace asked.

"It started with a mugging," Dan said.

"Another mugging?"

"An attempted mugging. Three men. Emily here took out two of them. She left me one for exercise."

Wallace raised an eyebrow. "How considerate. Ever seen them before?"

"No. Well, I saw them ten minutes before on another block. They were walking the neighborhood."

"And you let them follow you?"

"I didn't *let* them do anything. The leader of the group addressed me by name before the altercation. It wasn't random. The guys spoke Spanish."

"MS-13?"

"They weren't MS-13," Dan and Emily said almost simultaneously.

"Why's that?" Wallace asked.

Dan answered. "Because they were Mexicans. Different accent all together. MS-13 members are almost exclusively El Salvadorian."

"I'll have to brush up on my Rosetta Stone Spanish," Wallace said. "Any ideas?"

"I have a few. Starting with the obvious. It was professional hit and whoever shot me wasn't interested in your partner," Dan said.

Wallace turned towards Emily. "You okay?"

"Fine."

"Your new partner can certainly handle herself," Dan chimed in.

"I guess the two of you are a match made in heaven."

"I'll take her in my corner any day of the week. She has a nice range of moves. Incapacitation stuff. Some Krav Maga. Some old school jujutsu. You could learn a thing or two."

"We have a date for yoga tomorrow," Wallace said. "Maybe I'll start there."

"Yoga? That's manly."

"It's a start," Wallace said, again turning towards Emily. "Not that it's any of my business, but what you were doing in the neighborhood at that hour?"

"We were meeting to go over some of the details on the pusher case. Grab a beer. I was off duty."

Emily blushed just enough for Wallace to see the possibility of a real date with Dan was on the table. Graciously, he changed the subject.

"No word on the perps yet," Wallace said. "I heard the BOLO on the radio. We have a description of a getaway vehicle. A neighbor reported three men getting into a car around the corner from the crime scene."

Dan responded. "Keep an eye on the hospitals. One has multiple fractures of his right arm. Heavy hand tattoos. If he ever wants to use his arm again, he is going to need to see a doctor. The other two are suffering from what is known in the medical community a serious ass whooping."

"You want to tell me how they got away?"

"I was performing CPR."

"On a person who had the wind knocked out of him and may have been momentarily unconscious," Dan stated plainly.

"The rules of CPR are clear. Do not stop until you are relieved of your duties or are physically unable to continue."

"Or if the patient starts speaking," Dan added.

Emily grabbed Dan's toe at the foot of the bed and twisted it.

"We were pinned down by a sniper who had us in a location of his choosing. Even if I hadn't been incapacitated and Detective Fields wasn't concerned for my well-being, the suspects probably would have slipped away. Taking cover was the first order of business," Dan said. He moved his feet to the side of the bed and let them hang.

"What about this body armor you were wearing?" Wallace asked.

"It's not body armor. I was wearing a shirt from a bulletproof clothing line." Dan rubbed the ace bandage around his torso. "Fortunately for me it worked as advertised. Miguel Caballero earned my respect tonight."

"Who the hell is Miguel Caballero?"

"A designer of high-fashion clothes. All of it bulletproof. He works out of Bogota, Colombia. You can probably guess the history of his company."

Dan slipped his butt off the mattress and reached into the plastic storage bin on the frame under the bed. He grabbed his jacket and held the garment up to the light.

"There's the hole, right there. Center mass," Dan said. "Went right through the jacket and was stopped by the shirt."

"Taking the Boy Scout motto of 'Be Prepared' a little far, don't you think?" Wallace asked.

"You can never be too careful," Dan replied. "I ordered a few items from Miguel after the little bombing incident at my office last year. It seemed prudent. I told you I have a long list of people in DC who don't care for me."

"I'm starting to not care for you."

"What are you complaining about? I was the one who was shot. And that shirt cost a thousand bucks. I got a deal for ordering in bulk."

"Good thing it wasn't a head shot."

"Professionals go for the torso first on a long shot."

"Lucky for you."

"Indeed."

"You want a lift home?"

"I'll pass. I have a few thing to do."

"Revenge?"

"Not tonight. But there is something you can do for me."

"What's that?"

"Can you keep me in the loop on the ballistic results? I would like to know the caliber of the gun that shot me."

"Will do."

"And another thing... it may be a good idea to stop by the Wellington residence and inform the congressman of the specifics of this little incident face-to-face. He doesn't need to know his wife hired a private detective and that the detective was the one who was shot, but I think everyone should cover his or her ass. This might be a prime opportunity to let Congressman Wellington know of a potential danger in the neighborhood. God forbid something does happen. You don't want to be known as the detective who didn't warn the congressman there was a serial killer on the streets."

Wallace nodded. "I'll make a call, but congressmen and senators fall under the security umbrella of the Capitol Police force, not Metropolitan Police. Everyone is a little touchy about their turf."

"Are you saying they won't do it?"

"I'm not saying that. I'm saying they will do it their way." Wallace paused. "Just like someone else I know."

CHAPTER 32

WALLACE WALKED UP behind Emily in the lobby of the City Gymnasium, which was neither a gymnasium nor in the city. The white building at the top of the hill near Seven Corners had spent decades as various department stores, swapping out names and signage with changes in ownership every few years. It wasn't until the large building had been converted into a health club, and a stream of healthy bodies could be seen crossing the parking lot, that people considered the location as a place to stop.

Emily turned from the front desk and smiled at her partner. Then she handed him a key attached to an adjustable wristband.

"I can't believe I let you talk me into this," Wallace said, small gym bag in his massive grip.

"I didn't. You talked yourself into it with that 'anything a girl can do' comment."

"That part is still true."

"I'm glad you feel that way. Our yoga class starts in fifteen minutes. After that, if you still feel like you need a workout, the wristband lets you do whatever you want for the entire day."

Ten minutes later, dressed in workout battle fatigues, Wallace stood outside the door to the yoga room as sweaty bodies filed out. He leaned into Emily. "These guys sure did sweat."

"Don't they look happy?"

"No, they look like they've been swimming in hell."

"Didn't I mention this was a hot yoga class?"

Wallace's jaw dropped a little. "A hot what?"

"A hot yoga class. Yoga in one hundred and four degrees."

"I'm quite sure you didn't mention it."

"You chickening out?"

"No. But you could have told me to wear swim trunks." Wallace nodded in the direction of a man exiting the classroom completely drenched, his clothes stuck to him like Saran wrap on a microwaved hotdog.

"I have twenty bucks that says you won't make it ten minutes," Emily said.

Inside the room, Wallace sneered and lowered himself to the floor.

"Good idea, partner," Emily said. "Stretch it out. Showtime in five."

*

Sweat dripped from Wallace's face by the time the teacher had introduced herself as Patty from somewhere Wallace immediately forgot. At the three-minute mark, in the midst of a downward dog pose, Wallace's shorts were drenched, hugging his thighs and manhood. His eyes burned from the salt in his perspiration.

At eight minutes, his arms shook and his lungs wheezed. Wallace audibly grunted as the instructor mercifully moved the class into a moment of rest in the happy baby pose. Lying on his back, feet in the air, Wallace was thankful for a position that required neither balance nor exertion. Following the teacher's instruction to grab the soles of his feet while remaining on his back, Wallace instantly understood the meaning of the happy baby. For a brief moment, a peaceful feeling washed over Wallace and he saw a glimpse of the potential of yoga. It was at this precise moment of near Nirvana, on his back with a grip on both feet, that a large gas deposit unceremoniously escaped Wallace's large intestine.

By the time Emily stopped laughing, Wallace had left the room.

*

In the comfort of a seventy degree room on the third floor, Wallace struggled with the controls on the exercise bike. There were twelve buttons on the control pad and a computer screen above the handlebars that allowed gym members to select the scenery to accompany their ride. A tour through wine country? A mountain bike jaunt through the Grand Canyon? A leisurely ride along a beachfront boardwalk?

To Wallace's right, through a large window, traffic crawled up Route Seven, inching past the Koons' Ford-Chrysler-Dodge dealership on the other side of the road. Wallace stared at the line of cars perched on the hill and then glanced back at the computer screen. He shrugged his shoulders, selected the bicycle medley, and left his workout to be decided by the computer Gods. The screen on the exercise bike welcomed him and Wallace smiled as he began to pedal, serenely meandering forward in the direction of a green forest on the virtual horizon.

Now this is what I'm talking about, Wallace said to himself. *To hell with hot yoga.* All he had to do was pedal. Halfway through his programmed ride, he exited the woods for an equally tranquil path through a sea of gently swaying wheat fields.

Wallace ignored the computer screen on the bicycle and averted his eyes to the TV hanging from the ceiling in the corner. With the sound on the TV off, he listened to the steady hum of equipment while he read the closed caption text running across the bottom of the screen. The weather was followed by a reporter covering a rash of bicycle thefts in Northwest DC, including several instances where bikes were stolen off the bike racks of parked vehicles. One unlucky cyclist even had their bicycle stolen from the rear of the vehicle, while their car was stuck in traffic. At the conclusion of the bike theft story, a video clip of a peloton of cyclists raced across the TV screen.

Wallace checked his progress on the computer display of the exercise bike and then returned his gaze to the TV. Moments later he was still staring upward, but his brain was elsewhere. The detective was in problem-solving mode, communing with his subconscious mind. His mind floated from the bicycle theft story and his eyes drifted again to the car dealership out the window.

After a period of silent reflection that a Nepalese monk could appreciate, Wallace broke his silence. "Well, I'll be damned," he said loudly, startling the woman on the bicycle next to him who tried, in vain, to steer away from her suddenly vocal neighbor.

Wallace pressed the red button on the control pad and the computer screen on the bike went dark. He dismounted from the sweat-laden seat, losing his balance in the process, and took long strides down the hall that lead to hell yoga 101. The glass wall at the back of the yoga room was now covered in moisture, allowing Wallace to see only the faintest outlines of the practitioners in the room, asses in the air.

Wallace opened the door and a blast of heat slapped his face.

"Emily Fields, it's time for work. Meet you in the lobby in ten minutes," he bellowed into the furnace before turning away.

*

As they exited the front door of the gym, Wallace pointed in the direction of the car dealership across the street. "It's probably faster to walk."

"Are you buying a car?"

"I was thinking about getting a minivan. You can deck it out for me. Fuzzy dice. A bumper sticker. The whole nine yards."

Emily cocked her head to the side and followed as Wallace skipped across four slow-moving lanes of traffic and a narrow grassy median. Fifty yards later, Wallace opened the door to the showroom and Emily stepped in. Her face was still flush, her body not yet cooled from stretching in the tropics.

The young salesman with the seat nearest the door stood from his desk when he saw Emily. Wallace glanced around the car showroom and quickly concluded the vehicles on display outnumbered existing customers eight to nil.

"Can I help you?" the salesman asked, extending his hand, business card pinched between his thumb and pointer finger. Wallace extended his own hand with his badge cupped in his palm. "Not buying. Just looking."

"What can I help you with, Officer?" the salesman asked.

"We're both detectives," Emily informed him.

"Detectives," the salesman confirmed.

"We're looking for a bike rack," Wallace said.

"For what kind of vehicle?"

"A minivan. Specifically, we're looking for one that fits a Chrysler Town and Country."

"Well, you're in luck. The bike racks we sell for minivans will fit most makes and models. Most dealers sell the same equipment. How many bikes do you need it to hold?"

"Let's assume one or two."

"For single bicycles, the Pro Series Eclipse is hands down the most popular for minivans."

"How does it attach to the vehicle? Specifically to the Town and Country?"

"The Pro Series Eclipse attaches to the rear of the vehicle. The rack fits over the rear door and attaches at the bottom and the top. It's pretty secure. It can hold several hundred pounds. It also comes with multiple locking options for security."

"Are there other ways to attach the rack?"

"There are options for attaching bikes to the luggage rack on the top of the vehicle. But when you are talking about a minivan, there are some clearance issues, not to mention just the physical struggle of getting the bike onto the rack. You would need a ladder in most cases. I'm not saying it can't be done, but it isn't easy. On some of the larger bike rack models, where you can carry up to six bikes, we have components you can attach to the trailer hitch."

"What about bike racks that attach to the front of the vehicle?"

"There's also an option for the front of the vehicle, but I've only seen one or two customers choose that configuration since I started working here."

"So a bike rack that attaches to the rear door is the most popular?"

"For a minivan? Without a doubt."

"How long does it take to attach?"

"The rack to the car, or the bike to the rack?"

"The rack to the car."

"A couple of minutes. Faster if you know what you're doing."

"And can the rear door be used with the bike rack on it?"

"No. You would have to remove the rack to use the rear door."

"Thanks," Wallace said, turning towards the door. Emily smiled at the young salesman as she followed Wallace out. "What did we just learn?"

"Walk through this with me. You are a single mother. You own a minivan."

"I could do one or the other, not both."

"Use your imagination. Why do people buy minivans?"

"A lot of room. Sliding doors. Easy to get in and out of."

"Right. Easy egress and ingress is what I was thinking, but everything else you said is equally true. Most minivans typically have two front seats, two back seats and a third row. So the easy entry and exit is primarily for people. I mean, it's easy to slide the door open and get into one of the seats. The side doors are not as convenient for cargo because once you open the doors, the seats are right there. I mean, imagine you're shopping and you have a bunch of shopping bags, you're probably going to use the back door. Particularly if you're like my wife and you buy your toilet paper sixty rolls at a time from Costco."

"So you're saying that most minivan owners use the sliding side doors for people and the back door for groceries."

"That is my assumption."

"We can go sit in a supermarket parking lot for an hour and prove or disprove that theory."

"We may just do that. But let's assume for a second that I'm right. Most people use the back door for stuff. Now, if I have a bike rack on the back of the van, I can't use the back door."

"According to the salesman."

"Right. Once I put the bike rack on, I sacrifice the back door and some major convenience. And it's not just groceries either. Think about all that miscellaneous stuff parents have to carry around. Strollers. Toys. Diaper bags. Umbrellas. The convenience of carrying all of that around is negated some-what by the bike rack on the back door."

"Okay."

"Which means that people probably only put the bike rack on the back of a minivan when they need it."

"Seems logical."

"Right?"

"Sure."

"So why did Beth have a bike rack on the vehicle the morning her mini-van ended up in the canal?"

There was a long pause and then Emily said, "Because she went for a bike ride so she could dump the weapon."

"I think we just learned what the Duke of Junk was lying about."

CHAPTER 33

DETECTIVE WALLACE KNOCKED on the office trailer and the Duke of Junk opened the door, phone pressed to his ear. He waved the detectives inside the trailer and motioned for them to have a seat at the chairs on the visitor's side of his desk. Wallace and Emily sat, each engulfing the details of the room. The practiced art of observation was a skill shared by all good detectives.

The Duke of Junk turned away from his visitors and checked his appearance in the small circular mirror attached to a gray filing cabinet. As he answered questions on the phone regarding parts for a 1999 Toyota Camry, he brushed his eyebrows with his fingers, and checked the space between his teeth for any breakfast remnants.

"Detectives Wallace and Fields," the Duke said, hanging up the phone and spinning in his chair to face his guests. "I didn't expect to see you back so soon. I hope you're not looking for the boxed up minivan. It's outside Pittsburgh by now, one step closer to a two-thousand degree furnace."

"We are, indeed, here about the minivan."

"I'm not sure I'm going to be able to help you."

"And I'm quite sure you will," Wallace retorted.

A small twitch surfaced just above the Duke of Junk's face. "Anything I can do. You know that."

"When we were here last, you mentioned you found a stroller in the minivan."

"We did."

"And a damaged bike rack. It was on the back of the minivan."

"That sounds about right. Some other stuff in the glove box. Owner's manual. Maybe a handful of change and a pair of sunglasses."

"What about the bike?"

"What bike?" the Duke responded, his voice cracking in betrayal.

"Either you're heading back into puberty, or you know exactly what bike I'm referring to."

"Man, there was no bike."

"Are you looking for an obstruction of justice charge? Clamoring for an investigation into the illegal sale of stolen goods? This can be easy, or this can be hard. You've had a good run. You're close to payday. The developers are getting ready to write you a big check. Retirement is right around the corner. Don't be stupid. Don't fuck things up now," Wallace said matter-of-factly.

The Duke of Junk subconsciously looked over at the large jar of change in the corner of the trailer.

"There was a bike on the rear of the minivan when it came in on the wrecker. It had a lock on it. Had to blow torch the lock off. One of those U-locks with the fancy keys. Pretty sturdy. We ruined the bike rack with the blow torch."

"Was the bike damaged?"

"No, it was in pretty good shape. I figure the minivan probably went into the water nose first. With the engine weight in the front of the vehicle and all. Not to mention the pure momentum. The bike probably never hit the bottom of the canal. Of course, the bike was covered in the little treasures you would expect to find in nasty, stagnant, canal water, but it wasn't damaged."

"And what happened to it?"

"I sold it," he said, his voicing trailing off.

"How? Craigslist?"

"No. Nothing like that. It was weird, man. Real weird. That wrecker arrived at the lot, dropped off the car, and a few minutes after the wrecker leaves, this dude shows up and tells me he wants to buy the bike that was just brought in. Said he happened to see the vehicle on the wrecker as it pulled in here. Said he had the same model of bike at home and that he could use the parts."

"And you believed him?"

"Hell no. I mean, this guy was telling me he happened to look over at a minivan, covered in mud, on the back of a wrecker, and not only is he able to ignore the spectacle of the minivan, but he can identify the bike on the back of it? No way. Uh-uh. I know bullshit when I smell it."

"Don't we all," Wallace said with a glare.

"How much did he offer you?" Emily asked.

"A couple hundred dollars. I turned him down at first."

"Then he offered more?"

"Then he doubled his offer and added a hundred. Pulled the cash out before I even answered. He washed the bike off with the hose outside the door and walked right out the front gate."

"What did he look like?"

"A white guy. Tattoos."

"Tall, short, thick, thin?"

"Average height. But it don't matter."

"Why not?"

"Because I followed that guy to the gate and watched him walk down the street. Halfway down the block he threw the bike into the side door of an older Ford van. He slid the door shut, walked to the front of the van, and said something to the driver. Then the driver drove off. The guy who came into the junk yard with the cash just walked off down the street without the bike."

"What model year was the van?"

"Hard to say. Late nineties."

"Color?"

"White. Dirty but white."

"Did you get a license plate?"

"No."

"Why not?"

"Didn't occur to me. Besides, I don't think I could see that far when I had good vision."

"Any cameras down there?"

"On the outside of a wrecking yard? No. No cameras down there. Got a few cameras on the inside of the yard near the back, but they only show the yard and the back fence line. There are probably a security camera or two in the surrounding blocks, but we are at the end of Buzzard Point, not much else down here."

"Anything else you need to tell me about the minivan? Anything at all? I'm giving you a pass on this little indiscretion. I won't be so generous the next time around."

"I told you everything I know."

As Wallace and Emily exited the trailer, Emily turned towards Wallace. "You want me to canvass the area for cameras?"

"You bet. Run the surrounding blocks. See if we have anything on the van or the driver."

*

Back at the precinct, Wallace pulled out a map of Northwest Washington. Emily stood next to him at the table and stared down. Wallace placed a sticky note on the map next to the EPA lawyer's house and then another sticky note at the location where the minivan went into the water.

"Until we hear back on the security cameras near the junk yard and can identify the van with the stolen bicycle in it, I'm going to assume the guy in the old Ford van wasn't just some random individual buying bicycles."

"What are you thinking?"

"A helper. A cleaner."

"Then Beth the grocery store clerk is our sniper."

"I'm saying it's a distinct possibility."

"I can't believe it."

"I'm going to lay out the morning of the murder. You try to talk me out of my line of reasoning, if you can."

"All right."

Wallace pointed to the first sticky note. "If our grocery clerk is our shooter, then she was at the EPA lawyer's house at six a.m., give or take a couple of minutes."

"Assuming the lawyer was leaving at her normal time."

"Correct," Wallace said. He ran his hand from the first sticky to the second sticky on the map. "Beth the shooter traveled something close to this route to reach the point in the canal where her minivan entered the water. We already checked the coffee shops and gas stations in the area and no one remembers seeing her. She also didn't show up on traffic surveillance cameras anywhere. Everything else is closed at that hour of the morning. We are talking a stretch of primarily well-to-do residential neighborhoods. Not impossible to ditch a weapon there, but also likely that someone would have found a misplaced rifle in their yard. We searched and found nothing."

"Right."

"We also know that Canal Road is one-way heading into the city in the morning at all points after Arizona Avenue."

"So Beth had to be on Canal Road by Arizona Avenue. This is the same conclusion we reached before," Emily said.

"Now, forget the car for a moment. Think about the bicycle."

"She parked her car and rode a bicycle?"

"Yes."

"With a bicycle, she could go in any direction. And she might have been caught on a traffic camera and we missed her. We weren't looking for a bicycle."

"True. We assume she was at the EPA lawyer's residence at six and know for a fact that she was in the canal at 7:15. But let's assume she was on her bike in the time between. She still couldn't have gone too far."

Emily looked down at the map and then over at Wallace.

Wallace dropped his thick index finger down on the map. "We have a couple of off-road options but I am thinking the C&O Canal path is a likely bet. The C&O Towpath runs for a couple of hundred miles from George-town to Ohio. It has less commuter bike traffic than some of the other trails and a lot of places to ditch a weapon. The only hiccup is that at six a.m. the parking lot for the C&O path along Canal Road is closed. There are a couple of places along the side of the road near Fletcher's Boat house where people park after hours to go fishing, but a car would likely be towed pretty quickly during the morning rush hour. But it's still a possibility."

"Other options?"

"There's a pedestrian tunnel not too far from the Georgetown University campus that leads to the C&O trail. There is no vehicle access, but if she were on a bicycle she wouldn't even have to stop to cross the street."

"So you think Beth parked her car somewhere far enough away from the shooting so as to not be suspicious, rode her for bike for a while, ditched her weapon, and then rode back to her car. She put her bike back on the minivan, drove off, and then got in an accident and died."

"That's exactly what I'm thinking."

"I don't know."

"If I put myself in her shoes, I'm thinking I want to dump my evidence in the water. We know she was dying of cancer. According to the ME the cancer had spread throughout her body. She probably didn't plan on dying the day she did, but she was still on her way out. The weapon only has to remain undiscovered for a month or two. Three maybe. After that, who cares if it's found?"

"And she discards the weapon and keeps the bullet casing her in pocket? Why would she do that?"

"Mistake. She worked at Trader Joe's. She wasn't a professional. In the hustle to get away from the murder scene, and all the emotions and adrenaline that would come with that, maybe she overlooked the casing. Forgot about it. Dumped the weapon, came back to the vehicle, and saw the casing on the floor. Stuffed it in her pocket and then crashed."

Emily shrugged her shoulders.

"If we believe she dumped the weapon into the canal, that doesn't exactly limit the possibilities. There's a lot of water in that canal between DC and Ohio."

"And if she was on a bicycle, then the weapon we're looking for was probably disassembled before it was discarded. Someone would notice a woman riding a bike through DC with a rifle on her back. The size of the weapon may be something we need to keep in mind when we send the search boat back into the water again."

"The Duke of Junk mentioned there was a backpack found in the minivan. Probably stuffed the weapon into it before she jumped on the bike," Emily said.

Wallace paused for a long moment and then asked, "How far can you ride in a half hour?"

"Five miles on flat terrain, if I hurry. And she could have gone in either direction. She could have headed towards Georgetown and then back to the minivan, or she could have headed towards Maryland and then turned around for the car."

"Well, five miles in either direction will take forever. Let's call out the dogs. If the dogs hit on anything, maybe we can get a handle on which direction she went. It's a lot of terrain to cover. Canal. River. Swampland. It's going to take some time."

"I'll take my bike out there. Pedal it myself. See if there's anything that jumps out at me. A place to ditch something. Whatever. You want to come?"

"I think we're done working out together. No offense."

"None taken. Tomorrow morning I'll pedal down the canal and check it out."

CHAPTER 34

THE BB&T BANK at Thirteenth and F Street buzzed with perpetual motion. Situated on one of the busiest thoroughfares in the city, on the first floor of a ten-story building that housed over forty companies and three thousand employees, the location had been carefully chosen.

The blonde woman in the long black coat with oversized sunglasses entered the bank at precisely 8:35 a.m. A scarf wrapped around her neck, nuzzling up to her lower lip. A yellow leather purse hung from her left shoulder, creating a stark contrast to her black outerwear. She stared stoically forward, neck bent slightly downward, shuffling her feet in the designated area between the burgundy velvet rope dividers. She didn't look up at the security cameras but knew they were recording her every move. Watching. All twelve of them. She had counted them on three previous occasions, when she had also memorized the layout of the floor and considered her exits.

There were two large cameras at the front entrance to the bank—one on either side of the door. The three overhead cameras located in glass bubbles on the ceiling covered the entire lobby. Cameras near the entrance to the main vault provided views beyond the lobby and the bank patrons. Behind each teller window, additional cameras were affixed to the wall, their focus aimed directly at each customer as they stepped forward and stood at their respective teller window. It was out of particular precaution for these cameras that the woman in the long black coat kept her head down, her chin and scarf almost dipping into the top of her coat collar.

She stared at the tile floor and waited for the next available teller, moving her feet as the patrons in front of her edged forward. At the front of the line the woman subtly clutched her abdomen. The large yellow purse inadvertently slipped off her shoulder. Her oversized sunglasses dipped down her nose as she struggled to regain her composure. Breathing steadily, she pushed her glasses back into place and stood straight. The woman felt the faint rumble of the Metro three stories below as she moved to the next available teller.

She approached the window, pushed the printed note across the counter to the teller, and smiled. The teller read the brief note, looked up at the woman in front of her, and read the note again. Then the teller's face turned white and her hands began to shake. The tall woman in the black coat placed her yellow leather purse on the counter, smiled again, and knocked lightly on the counter to indicate that time was not a luxury the teller enjoyed. The teller nodded in compliance and her hands danced across the top of the open cash drawer, careful not to dip below counter level, per the instructions on the note.

The teller quickly placed three stacks of cash on the counter and the tall woman in the black coat caressed each stack, lifting each to assess their heft. She then flipped through each stack of bills as if running through a deck of cards. She watched carefully as the bills flashed before her eyes, the serial number the only difference between each bill in the new stack. Satisfied, she slipped the three stacks into her yellow leather purse.

The woman in the coat flicked her head to the side and the teller moved to the next window and whispered into her coworker's ear. Seconds later she returned to her teller window with another three stacks of hundred dollar bills. Once again, the robber weighed each stack in her hand and flipped through the end of the stacks, eyeballing each bill as it raced by. She left one stack on the counter and placed the two acceptable piles into her purse. The teller looked down, seemingly disappointed one of the stacks was deemed unacceptable. When the teller raised her eyes, the woman in the black coat casually turned away. Conscious of the note and its instructions, the teller watched as the woman walked past a waiting customer who eagerly moved forward into the space vacated at the teller window.

Seconds later, the woman in the black coat exited the bank from the side door and entered directly into the main lobby of the office building. She fought the urge to rush to the street, the outside world a mere ten paces to her right. *Discipline*, she reminded herself. She turned left down the first hall off the main lobby and walked past a set of doors with the name of a law firm spelled out in gold letters.

At the end of the hall she pushed open the large metal fire door and vanished into the stairwell. When she stepped onto the third floor thirty seconds later, she was four inches shorter with dark brown hair. The black coat, along with her shoes, blonde wig, sunglasses and yellow bag had disappeared into the crevice between the railings of the stairs. She had watched as her disguise thudded to the basement floor three stories below. She was now dressed for the office in a dark cardigan sweater and a long navy skirt. Black flats supplanted her heels. Her large sunglasses had been replaced with library reading glasses. The black bag now on her shoulder hung more comfortably than the yellow one it replaced.

On the third floor, with the bank alarm ringing faintly in the distance, the woman was now a legal professional. The five stacks of cash filled the inside of her small black bag. The pain medication she had delayed for the last few hours in the name of mental clarity was now in her mouth, releasing the nerve numbing magic from its solidified form on the end of the stick.

She took deep breaths to help alleviate the pain. Each step was a step closer to relief. Each second with her medication one second further away from the pain. Slowly, euphoria and adrenaline took over the helm of her emotions. Concentrating on her plan, the woman put distance between herself and the stairwell-turned-changing room. Head up, eyes forward, she strolled purposefully down another long hall, past several smaller law offices.

At the end of the corridor, she turned again. She was now on the opposite side of the building, more than a hundred yards from the bank, three stories above the chaos that was beginning to unravel at street level. At the rear of the building, she entered another staircase and walked down three flights of stairs towards an exit leading to the alley on the backside of the building.

*

A young lawyer smoking a cigarette in the alley heard the bank alarm. Unconcerned with a faint ringing he didn't recognize, he took another drag and held it in his lungs. When police sirens joined the cacophony, the lawyer dropped his habit onto the dirty concrete alley. He extinguished the butt with the sole of his Bostonian and stepped up the small metal staircase to pull on the handle to the rear fire door. Five-hundred-dollars an hour was waiting for him in his office above.

The lawyer pulled the fire door open just as the woman pushed outward from the inside of the same door. Momentum did the rest. When the quick-dressing thief felt nothing but air where the door should have been, the full force of her weight crashed down on the nicotine-satiated attorney. The collision of the real attorney on his way in, and the fictitious legal professional on her way out, sent both parties to the ground in a mass of dark-colored Italian wool.

A grunt and a moan followed, intermingled with a mix of muted curses.

The lawyer fought to stand and a cut above his eyebrow began to bleed. By the time he had shaken the initial cobwebs, crimson trickled freely down his cheek.

The woman rolled over, stood, and dosey-doed around the bleeding attorney, scanning the ground as she moved. For a moment that lasted entirely too long, the woman stopped her search, looked up, and locked eyes with the attorney.

"Are you okay?" the lawyer asked, wiping his cheek. He felt the moisture on his fingertips and looked down at his hand. When he raised his glance he saw the backside of the woman disappear into the mass of pedestrians on the sidewalk ten yards away.

*

A half block away, with the bank's main entrance now in the distance to her right, Amy stepped onto the large escalator heading into Metro Center. She waved her pre-bought subway pass over the gate turnstile and walked down two flights of stairs to the lowest platform. She traversed the platform from one end to the other, weaving slowly through the morning rush hour crowd. At the end of the platform she took another staircase up. From there, she followed the platform to the far end and exited through the fare gate on the opposite side of the station. Without taking a train, she was now a half mile from the scene of the holdup, scrubbed and unidentified. When she stepped foot back on the street level she raised her hand and smiled as the taxi pulled over to the side of the curb.

*

The cellphone in her backpack started to ring with increasing volume and Emily stopped her bike and dismounted.

"You out pedaling?"

"I am."

"You find anything?"

"A lot of area to ditch a weapon."

"How much longer are you going to be?"

"What's up?"

"You want to run a bank robbery?"

"You know I do."

"How long to get downtown?"

"I'm almost back at the car."

"Pedal to the metal. I'll meet you there. BB&T. Thirteenth and F Street."

*

Detectives Wallace and Fields stood shoulder-to-shoulder in the security room of the BB&T bank. The bank manager leaned against the far wall, the extra stress of the morning's security failure already taking its toll, the strain evident by the shaking hands and the nervous tick in the corner of his left eye.

The security guard sat at the controls of the desk, the feed from six cameras on display on the wall, each on its own monitor. The light from the six displays gave the small room a bluish hue, as if staring at an aquarium in the dark. The security guard paused the recording at the beginning of the robbery, just as the suspect entered the bank.

"Is everyone ready?" the security guard asked.

"Run it," Detective Wallace replied.

"Absolutely," Emily chimed. "My first bank robbery."

The security guard handled the logistics of juggling the multiple security feeds as Wallace offered his version of the play-by-play.

"Okay. She walks into the bank at 8:35. She appears to be alone."

The bank manager checked his watch. "An hour and five minutes ago."

"The clock is ticking, I understand," Wallace said.

The security guard continued. "She's disguised. Sunglasses. Long coat. Wig. Scarf. Shoes. Yellow purse. A decent disguise that lets her hide her real height and most of her physical features. All we really have is a flash of her hands and her jaw line. We may get prints off the counter if she wasn't wearing cover to prevent them from being transferred."

"Based on the shoes we found in the stairwell, she seems to be average height. Take away the three-inch heels on the shoes she was wearing and she's in the five foot five range. Five six at most."

They watched as the bank robber handed the note to the teller and then sifted through the stacks as they were placed on the counter.

"How much money is in each stack?" Emily asked, turning towards the bank manager standing in the dark corner with a cell phone in each hand.

"Ten thousand is standard for a stack of hundred dollar bills. We lost fifty thousand dollars."

"She left some on the counter," Emily pointed out.

The manager nodded. "Dye packs. With a little experience, you can detect a dye pack quite easily. The older ones felt heavier and had a hard center. They were very easy to detect. The new dye packs consist of a smaller plastic insert. Harder to detect, but still visible. This woman knew what she was doing. She didn't want the cash placed in a bag by the teller. She wanted the cash on the counter. She wanted to see it. She wanted to decide which stacks she was taking with her."

All parties watched as the woman turned away from the teller.

"She goes out a different exit from the one she used to enter the bank,"

Emily said. "You'd think most people would take the quickest way out of the bank. Straight across the lobby onto the sidewalk, and gone."

Wallace offered his insight. "She did her homework. There's an overhead security camera on the corner of the building. An ATM on each side of the front door. She'd be more easily tracked on the sidewalk in front of the bank."

"But she came through the front door on her way in."

"She didn't care what she looked like then. This woman wanted to change her outfit and then get out of the building looking like someone else. Walking into the bank, robbing it, and walking out of the bank wearing the same outfit is not nearly as effective."

"After she walks out the door into the lobby of the office building, what do we have for surveillance?" Emily asked.

The security guard pointed to the next monitor on the wall. "We have her going down the hall on the first floor. We have nothing in the stairwell."

"Why not?"

"I think there were cameras in the stairwell at one point, but now we only have cameras on every floor. I don't think the stairs see much traffic."

"Fair enough."

The security guard pointed back to the monitor. "We can see the profile of the perpetrator on the third floor as she walks past a camera in the hall near the elevator bank. Only a grainy view from maybe twenty feet away."

"Not much to go on there," Wallace said.

"Not much."

"Less than a minute later she enters the stairwell at the rear of the building."

"A minute later you can see the perpetrator exit the building into the alley. This image is from above, on the outside of the building. This is not a bank camera," the security guard added. "Here is where you can see the collision between the bank robber and the lawyer who was having a cigarette."

All eyes were glued to the screen as the collision unfolded.

"Ouch," Emily responded.

Wallace leaned forward. "You don't see that every day."

"They both get up pretty quickly," Emily added. "The lawyer gets up first. Then the suspect gets up and looks around before she runs off."

"What's she looking for?"

"Maybe she dropped the money."

"If she did, she didn't look for it very long."

The tape ended with a view of the empty alley.

"That's it?" Wallace asked.

"That's all we have. The police, which is you guys, are collecting all the feeds from other cameras in surrounding buildings. I imagine you'll have everything you need in a couple of hours."

"What was the total time from entry to exit?"

"The bank perpetrator was in the building for seven minutes. Four of those minutes were standing in line waiting for a teller."

"Fast."

"Anything else?"

"We have the injured lawyer who got a close up of the perp on her way out of the building."

"Let's meet him."

*

The lawyer touched the Band-Aid over his eyebrow. The windowless branch manager's office was a far cry from the wood-paneled meeting rooms five floors above

Detectives Wallace and Fields walked into the manager's office and the attorney with the Band-Aid over his eyebrow stood. Introductions followed and Wallace pulled out his detective's notebook.

"The bank manager and security guard say you saw the suspect."

"Oh yeah, I saw her," the attorney said. He touched his brow again and added, "Felt her too."

"Can you provide a description?"

"Brunette, dark eyes. Thin. Five four or five foot five. Professional attire. Sweater. Skirt. Librarian glasses."

"Did she say anything?"

"I think we both mumbled a curse or two."

"Anything else?"

"I'm not sure, but I think she was sucking on a lollipop."

Wallace stopped writing and his eyes grew wide. He looked at the attorney and then slowly turned his neck towards Emily. "You hear that partner? A lollipop. The second sucker this week."

"I only saw it for a fraction of a second. It could have been a straw. But I got the impression it was a lollipop. They have a big bowl of them on the counter at the bank. I grab one every once in a while."

Wallace turned towards Emily. "Did you see the perp grab a lollipop in the bank video?"

"Not that I recall."

The lawyer repeated his position. "I'm just telling you what I thought it was."

"When did you see it? Before or after the collision?"

"Before. I opened the back door and stepped up just as this lady was coming out. Those fire doors are thick and they don't have windows so you don't know what's on the other side. At any rate, I was going in, she was coming out, and we collided... and I thought I saw a lollipop."

"And then?"

"We untangled ourselves. My eyebrow started dripping blood. The woman stood, looked around, and walked off."

Wallace nodded. "We need to get your contact information. Stay here."

"I have a meeting in ten minutes with an important client."

"Postpone it. I'm sure the world of legalese will survive without you until lunch."

*

An hour and half after the first bank robbery suspect of Detective Emily Fields' career collided with an attorney, the detective found herself running her gloved hand along the metal staircase in the back alley of the building, her fingers pushing through thick street grime. The scent of urine was strong and she tried to hold her breath. On her second swipe under the edge of the metal step, she brushed away a crushed Burger King cup and a paper bag she hoped she wouldn't need to open.

A moment later, still on her knees, her gloved hand struck gold. "I think I have it," she said, pulling the lollipop from a foot-wide crack near the base of the wall and raising it to eye level.

"What the hell kind of lollipop is that?" Wallace asked.

"I don't know. I've never seen one like it before."

Wallace moved close and stood shoulder-to-shoulder with his partner as she twirled the lollipop. At the bottom of the stick, *Narten Pharmaceuticals* was printed in faded blue letters.

"A pharmaceutical company?"

Wallace put on a latex glove and examined it. "Let's have it processed for DNA and then take it to our friendly neighborhood doctor."

CHAPTER 35

D R. LEWIS OPENED the Styrofoam top on his chicken lo mein delivered from a basement Chinese bodega on the backside of the Verizon center. The tray of noodles and vegetables in the dish was similar to the last meal consumed by the deceased man on table number two. The contents of the man's stomach had already been evaluated, registered, and tossed, but the man's spleen was still sitting in a stainless steel bin at the foot of the table.

Detective Wallace knocked on the double swinging doors and pushed them open before the ME could protest. Dr. Lewis wiped his mouth with a napkin and stood from his desk.

"Detective Wallace and the new detective. How are things turning out in your forced marriage?"

"I'm growing on him," Emily stated assuredly. "Whether he realizes it or not."

Detective Wallace shrugged his shoulders and pulled the evidence bag from his jacket pocket. "We have a drug question for you."

Dr. Lewis looked at the bag and then motioned for his guests to sit at the desk. "Let's take a look and see what we have."

Wallace and Emily sat in the wooden chairs on the other side of the desk as Dr. Lewis pushed his remaining lo mein out of the way. He reached into his desk and slipped on a pair of latex gloves. He slowly removed the lollipop from the evidence bag and held it up to the light.

"Interesting."

"How?" Wallace asked.

"Well, I haven't seen one of these in person."

"Probably because you deal with dead patients."

"And yet you came to me with your question, Detective. Should I just assume you couldn't find a medical professional with live patients to interrupt?"

Wallace smiled. "Didn't mean it as an insult, Doc. What can you tell us?"

"It's commonly referred to as a morphine lollipop," Dr. Lewis replied.

The detectives looked at each other.

"But they don't really contain morphine. They used to. Now they use Fentanyl, which is about a hundred times stronger. One of the strongest pain medications on earth. It's usually used by cancer patients. Terminally ill cancer patients with extreme pain issues."

The hair on the back of Wallace's neck stiffened. He again glanced at Emily, eyebrows raised, and she nodded with understanding.

"Terminally ill cancer patients?" Emily asked.

"Usually. If they're being prescribed correctly."

"That's some mean candy."

"You definitely don't want a child to get a hold of it. Where did you find it?"

"We think someone who robbed a bank this morning dropped it on their way out of the building."

"You should be able to process DNA off it."

"Samples are already on the way to the lab for DNA analysis. What else can you tell me about the drug?"

"I think one of the main side effects is rapid tooth decay."

"Just like real lollipops," Emily stated.

"Worse," Dr. Lewis responded. He flipped his glasses to the top of his head and removed a magnifying glass from another desk drawer. He peered intently at the lollipop from end to end and then hummed quietly for a moment. "You know, I'm pretty sure these have serial numbers on them."

"If it has a number, then we can locate the owner. We can solve this case before dinner," Emily said.

"I didn't see any serial number. Just the pharmaceutical company's name," Wallace said.

The doctor started to hum again and continued for a moment with his eyes dancing over the medication. "Detective Wallace, do you remember the old Tootsie Pop commercial?"

"Sure, how many licks does it take to reach the center of a Tootsie Pop lollipop?"

"In this case, it's how many licks does it take to reach the serial number…"

"You're kidding."

"Not at all. I believe the serial number is on the stick, under the medication. If I remember correctly, these things had a bit of a run as a black market, designer drug of the week. The first version of this medication didn't have a number at all. Thieves were stealing and reselling them. It became a bit of a problem, particularly on the West Coast. In response, the DEA required a way to trace the drug so they added a serial number. Of course, the pharmaceutical companies put the serial number on the handle end of the stick and the thieves just cut the number off. So the drug companies changed the location for the number. And for us to take a look at it, we are going to have to crack the remaining portion of the medication and remove it from the stick."

"I'm sure you have a hammer somewhere in this dungeon."

Dr. Lewis, a man with incredibly thick skin, smirked. "I keep the hammer in my toolbox. But I do have other power tools at my disposal." Two minutes later, with the broken portion of the lollipop in an evidence bag, Dr. Lewis read the number off the end of the lollipop stick.

"I assume you can do something with this number?" Wallace asked.

"Give me a minute. With a little luck and help from a friend, I can tell you where this prescription was filled and by whom."

CHAPTER 36

AMY CONBOY WALKED through the old green doors and into the lobby of the eighty-year old apartment she called home. A block off Connecticut Avenue, a quarter mile north of the National Zoo, her subsidized apartment building was being eyed by a half-dozen developers looking to lure more upscale customers. A wrecking ball, followed by a year of construction, and another old brick building would be replaced with glass and steel, for triple the current rent. Quadruple for a top floor unit with a squinter's view of Rock Creek Park.

Amy checked her mailbox and closed the small metal door, a handful of bills the only correspondence. For now, at least, they were bills she could pay. It was amazing the freedom money could buy. Freedom from worry. Freedom from stress.

Amy stepped aside and pressed her back against the wall as a young man from an apartment on the first floor made his way outside with an aging mountain bike frame on his shoulder. Amy glanced at the young man's glutes as he exited and then she headed in the direction of the old elevator. In the small foyer area near the elevator door, she pressed the up button and smiled at the mixed-race couple sitting on the chairs in the corner.

The couple looked at each other, nodded, and stood.

"Amy Conboy?" the black man asked, approaching with a badge held high in his large palm.

Amy looked down sheepishly at the stack of mail in her hands, all with her name and address on them. Denial was futile.

"Yes."

"You're under arrest for bank robbery."

As she was being read her rights, the female officer stepped behind Amy and gently cuffed her wrists.

CHAPTER 37

DETECTIVE WALLACE OPENED the door to the observation side of the interrogation room and Dan Lord entered. A small table ran the length of the room under the large two-way mirror. A small electronic console filled the corner, replete with video and audio recording capabilities. Six chairs were pushed against the back wall.

"Cozy," Dan said.

"Better than the other side of the glass," Wallace responded.

"No doubt about that."

Emily stepped into the room, smiled at Dan, and then pulled Detective Wallace to the corner. She opened a folder she carried in her hands. Detective Wallace peeked into the folder and then whispered into Emily's ear.

"Don't mind me," Dan interrupted.

Wallace scowled and Emily placed the folder on the table next to a group of other folders differentiated only by the scribble on the tabs.

"So, who's behind the glass?" Dan asked.

"Her name is Amy Conboy. A suspect in a bank robbery this morning."

"A bank robber?"

"Yep."

"And what does that have to do with me?"

"Funny you should ask," Wallace said. He grabbed one of the folders off the table, flipped it open, and showed Dan the photos of the morphine lollipop.

"Our bank robber here was seen leaving the premises of the BB&T Bank on Thirteenth and F, with a lollipop between her lips."

"A lollipop?"

"That's right. A morphine lollipop."

"Fentanyl," Emily corrected.

"Are we assuming this is the same flavor lollipop as the woman who pushed Carla the waitress into the path of the Circulator bus?" Dan asked.

"We don't know for sure. Maybe if you trained cardio a little harder you would have been able to run her down and we would have the answer to that question."

"It wasn't the cardio that got me, it was a blunt object. I assume the morphine lollipop isn't for shits and giggles. They probably don't write prescriptions for those very often."

Wallace nodded at the woman seated behind the two-way mirror. "We don't know exactly what medical ailment she has yet, but the logical choice is cancer. We're working to meet with her doctor. But we do know she has a legal prescription for the morphine lollipop and that prescription allowed us to locate her."

"It still doesn't help us prove the woman who pushed Carla had a morphine lollipop. In fact, the chances are probably slim. A bank robber is quite different from a murderer. There's a big jump in malevolence between the two."

"True. The lollipop itself doesn't prove a link between the bank robber here and the woman in Georgetown. But the lollipop is not the only M.O. This woman here, she also shared the chameleon gene with Carla's pusher."

"How's that?" Dan asked.

"The woman on the other side of the glass there, well, she entered the bank as a tall blonde and she left the building as a much shorter brunette. Sound familiar?"

"Indeed. From a blonde to a brunette."

"She made her escape dressed as a legal professional."

Dan looked through the glass at the woman seated at the table.

"And there's something else," Emily stated.

"I can hardly wait," Dan said.

"If we assume both the lollipop girls are felons, and that they both have cancer, we potentially have a third person to add to the list."

"Another lollipop?"

Wallace answered. "Nothing that cut and dry. But last week we pulled the body of a woman and her minivan from the canal, just west of Georgetown."

"I saw it on the news."

"Are you aware it was the same morning as the sniper killing in Spring Valley?"

"I didn't. And I had no reason to make the connection between the two."

"Well, the woman who perished in that one car accident also had cancer. Terminally ill, metastasized cancer."

"You now have my undivided attention."

"And she may have had help, after the fact."

"An accomplice," Emily added.

"A cleaner."

Wallace explained the demise of the minivan and the man in the old Ford van who bought the bicycle from the Duke of Junk.

"Did anyone at the junkyard see this so-called cleaner?"

Wallace nodded at Emily to add the exclamation point on the evidence. She reached for a folder on the table, grabbed a photo from inside, and held it up for Dan. "This is the guy who bought the bicycle from the junkyard. We knocked on every door for three blocks around the junkyard before we got this off a surveillance camera in front of a Navy Annex building. You can't identify the driver but it's pretty evident that the guy is wearing glasses and a baseball cap."

"This time it's the Yankees. This guy has no loyalty at all. Did you get the tags?"

"We did. Dead end. Stolen off a similar van last year."

"So he's a planner. People usually don't steal license plates a year in advance." Dan rubbed his hand across his cheek. "I don't know about the two of you, but I'm excited."

"About what?" Wallace said.

"About working our cases together. We're all looking for the same person."

"That's what worries me," Wallace retorted.

"Why's that?" Emily asked.

"Because Dan doesn't share information very well."

"That's not fair. You only have a sample size of one. You can't blame me for not sharing information in the Nguyen case. I was looking for someone who murdered my relatives and you were trying to put me in jail."

Wallace smirked and the room fell silent. "Here's your chance to make things right. Let's work this case *together*, as you say. I invited you here for this interrogation out of professional courtesy. I didn't have to invite you, so don't go pissing in the pool."

"I'll keep my bladder in check."

Wallace glared at Dan.

"Oh, and I thought you might want to know they found the three Spanish speaking perps from the other night. All dead. All shot sitting in a car off Georgia Avenue. The guy with the tattoos on his hands still had multiple arm fractures in need of medical treatment."

"Not anymore."

Detective Wallace nodded.

"Then I don't have to worry about them coming back around," Dan added. He turned his neck and glanced over at the woman at the table in the interrogation room on the other side of the glass. "Are we going to ask her questions, or just leave her sitting in there?"

"Stay here with Detective Fields. Let's see what she has to say."

"Make sure she knows her rights before you get started," Dan said as Wallace pulled the door open.

"Thanks for the advice, Counselor, but I got this."

CHAPTER 38

DAN NODDED IN the direction of the two-way mirror and watched as Detective Wallace entered the interrogation room and placed the stack of manila folders on the table. The woman in the cold metal chair sat emotionless. Her face was thin. Her brown hair was cut short, revealing a tattoo of a butterfly that poked out from the collar of her shirt, threatening to fly up her neck. She sat straight in the chair, eyes forward, with a level of confidence Dan deemed enviable. Dan smiled slightly as Wallace stalked the table with a couple laps of obligatory drama, eyeing the suspect from all sides as he paced.

Dan looked at Emily. "Fifty bucks says she isn't going to talk."

"What makes you say that?" Emily replied.

"Her demeanor. She isn't scared and I don't think Wallace can scare her."

Dan watched Wallace's lips move without sound and Emily fumbled with volume on the speaker control. A second later, Wallace's voice echoed from the speakers in the corner of the observation room.

*

Wallace rounded the table for a third lap and leaned his butt against the edge of the table. The stack of folders rested on the tabletop between Wallace's position and Amy in her chair. The suspect looked at the folders and then up at the Detective.

Wallace spoke. "Just to confirm. You have been read your rights and you understand those rights as they were read to you at the time of your arrest?"

"Yes."

"And with those rights in mind, are you willing to speak to me freely without an attorney present?"

"You are free to ask me any questions you like. I may or may not answer them."

Wallace turned towards the mirror wall and winked in the direction of Dan behind the glass. "I'm going to cut to the chase. We have video surveillance of you at the bank and we have additional physical evidence that was left on the scene. As you know, DNA is virtually foolproof." Wallace opened the first folder and moved the up-close photograph of the morphine lollipop into the middle of the table.

"Tempting me?" Amy asked.

"That is a Fentanyl lollipop. Prescribed to you. The DEA likes to keep track of these suckers, so to speak. We know it was prescribed to you by Dr. Smithson."

"So you say."

"So the DEA and the pharmacy say."

"I think all of that has to be decided at a trial, by a jury of my peers. I'm pretty sure that's how our justice system works. You present evidence. The jury decides what to believe."

"We also have a witness who can identify you and place you leaving the building where the bank is located moments after the robbery."

"I don't know what you're talking about."

"Amy, do yourself a favor here. Help me out. We have everything we need to put you away for a very long time."

"Not everything," Amy replied smugly. "I'm not doing anything for a *very long time*."

"How about we start with what you did with the money?"

"What money?"

"The fifty thousand dollars you stole from the bank."

"What bank?"

"The one you robbed this morning. BB&T on Thirteenth and F."

"Like I said, I don't know what you're talking about."

"This can go two ways. You can…"

Amy interrupted. "Detective, take a minute and look at me. Take a good look. It should be obvious this is only going one way. If it's all the same with you, we can skip the detective routine."

Wallace let a moment of silence fall over the room before he spoke. "What's your deal? Do you think you're some kind of tough girl?"

"I'm a single mom with terminal cancer, so yes."

"Why would a single mother be involved in the business of robbing banks?"

"I wouldn't know. But if you asked me why any bank robber would rob a bank, I imagine 'for the money' would be a popular answer."

Wallace tried not to smile. "So that's how you want it?"

Amy looked up at Wallace who was still sitting on the edge of the table. "That's how it is."

Wallace opened a second manila folder and slipped several additional photos onto the table. The first photo was a surveillance shot of Amy, in disguise, at the counter in the bank.

"Doesn't really look like me," Amy replied. "And I'm pretty sure most people on a jury would agree."

Wallace flipped to the next photo, a better shot of Amy after she changed her clothes. The photo was captured from a video feed in front of a Panera, after she had exited the alley. "That one looks like you."

Amy shrugged her shoulders.

"And here we have another photo of you entering Metro Center, another as you walked across the platform, and yet another as you exited the far side of the station."

"I enjoy public transportation. I can't afford a car."

"You never even boarded a train. That's not typically how people use public transportation."

"I was staying underground to keep dry. It looked like rain."

Another photo landed on the table. "And finally, we have a picture of you getting in the back of a cab, which you only took a few short blocks."

Amy looked surprised and Wallace picked up on it.

"You didn't know they were taking pictures in the backs of taxi cabs these days, did you?"

"I would need a lawyer to discuss the legality of that, but hey, if the government is listening to every phone conversation and reading every email, why not take pictures too?"

Wallace opened the last folder and flipped over a picture of the suspected pusher from the bus accident. The photo was a grainy close-up of a woman with a lollipop in her mouth, taken in a doorway in Georgetown moments before a waitress face-planted into the first lane of traffic.

"Do you recognize this woman?"

Amy peered at the photo. "I don't."

"Does the lollipop look familiar?"

"Don't they all?"

"I'm curious, what do you think the odds are of two woman in the same section of DC sucking on lollipops while in the commission of a felony?"

"I wouldn't know."

"Well in my quarter-century of law enforcement, I've never had another case involving a lollipop. This week I've had two."

"Diabetes is rampant. You have any cases with cupcakes? Twinkies? Any criminals involved with those?"

Wallace thought he heard faint laughter from the far side of the mirrored wall. Then he moved the photo of the suspected pusher closer to Amy. Next, he pulled out two photos of the man with the cap and sunglasses. The first picture was taken in Georgetown moments before the waitress's demise. The second photo was of the same man, behind the wheel of a van, near the junkyard after the illicit purchase of a bicycle. Wallace placed the photos next to each other and pushed them slowly closer to Amy. Amy's eyes moved from the suspected pusher to the two photos of the man with the cap and glasses. Her eyes widened and for a split second her tough demeanor cracked.

Wallace noted Amy's reaction. He picked up the photo of the man in the cap and glasses and held it up. "You know this guy?"

Amy stared at the photo. An almost imperceptible tremble surfaced in her fingers.

Wallace pressed. "You know, I've been doing this a long time and I'm pretty good at reading people. I believe you when you say you don't know the other girl with the lollipop. But there is no way you don't know this guy. You look like you've seen a ghost." Wallace turned the photo towards himself and stared at the man in the cap and sunglasses. Then he turned the photo back in the direction of Amy.

Amy's eyes locked on Wallace's. "Do you have children, Detective?"

"I do."

Amy exhaled deeply, ran her hands through her short hair, and rubbed her neck. "Okay. You want me to talk, I'll talk. On one condition."

"What's that?"

"I want to see my daughter."

"We can arrange that after you talk."

"No. You can arrange that *now*."

Wallace stared at Amy for a long moment and realized he was not going to win the battle at hand. He focused on the war and asked, "Where is your daughter?"

"After kindergarten my daughter stays with a sitter down the street. Kay Dines. Kay's Day Care. She keeps a half dozen or so kids."

*

"Did you see that?" Wallace asked, back in the observation room.

"We did," Dan replied. "Looks like she knows our man with the cap and sunglasses."

"No doubt about it."

"A silent partner in the bank robbery?" Dan asked.

"Maybe. Maybe she's being blackmailed," Wallace answered.

"Forced to rob a bank?" Emily asked.

Dan nodded. "It wouldn't be the first time. Remember a few years back when some pizza delivery guy robbed a bank with an explosive collar around his neck? The guy was apprehended, or surrounded, and initially the cops thought the whole thing was an act. Authorities were under the belief the man robbed the bank of his own volition and that the whole bomb-in-the-collar was a ruse."

"And then... ?"

"Kaboom. Right on television," Dan finished.

Emily looked through the glass into the interrogation room. "She isn't wearing a collar."

"Oh, yes she is," Wallace replied. "The collar is her daughter."

*

An hour later, Detective Wallace opened the door to the interrogation room and a four-year-old girl in a pink dress walked in, all smiles. Amy opened her arms and the child scurried into her mother's embrace. A tall woman from child protective services followed the child into the room and Wallace shut the door. The woman exchanged pleasantries with Wallace and let the embrace between Amy and her daughter run its course.

"Mommy, I'm hungry," the girl said. "Can I have a snack?"

Amy's eyes welled up and she ran her hand along her daughter's cheek.

The woman from protective services knelt down, eye-to-eye with the child. "If your mommy says it's okay, I think I can find something for you."

Amy smiled and nodded. "Go with the nice woman and I'll see you a little later."

With another long hug between Amy and her daughter, Wallace danced the fine line between being a detective and being a dick. The professional detective won out and Wallace waited until the child left the room.

"Amy, I don't want to seem insensitive, but we had a deal."

Amy wiped at her wet cheeks with the palms of her hands. "What happens to my daughter now?"

"We will need a family member to pick her up. Or a family friend. If not, she'll be remanded into the custody of child protective services."

"For how long?"

"That depends on you."

Amy stared at the folders on the table.

Detective Wallace broke the silence. "You asked to see your daughter and she's here. You said you wanted to talk, let's talk."

"Thank you, Detective. And I thank you for my daughter who is too young to understand what it means."

"I'm just doing my job."

"Your job as a cop or a parent?"

"Both."

"Some things only a parent can understand. Wouldn't you agree? I mean, as a parent, you would do anything for your child, right?"

Wallace thought about the answer. "Almost anything."

"Then you will understand what I'm going to say next…"

Wallace again looked over at the two-way mirror and nodded in anticipation of the flood of forthcoming evidence. All he received was a drip.

"I said I would talk. But I didn't say I would talk to you," Amy said.

"Excuse me?"

"This conversation is over, Detective. I would like a lawyer at this time. And I can't afford one on my own."

*

Dan stifled a laugh as Wallace entered the observation side of the interrogation room. "Looks like I win the bet no one wanted to take."

"Smart ass. There was nothing funny about what just happened."

"You got played, Detective."

"Technically, she didn't lie to you," Emily confirmed.

"She lied through intention."

"Cut her a break. She was only worried about her daughter. She's a single mom arrested for bank robbery."

"No excuse."

"Lies are a part of the job, Wallace," Dan said.

"Now what?" Emily asked, looking through the glass at Amy, who was smiling.

Dan adjusted his collared shirt, centered his leather belt buckle, and checked his fly. "If she wants a lawyer, let's give her a lawyer."

CHAPTER 39

DAN GRINNED AS he entered the room and reached for his wallet. He forced his fingers into the crevice of his new billfold and pried loose a rarely seen business card. He slipped the card onto the table so that Amy could read it without needing to rotate it.

Amy read the card out loud. "Dan Lord, attorney at law…"

"At your service. If you would like to hire me as your attorney, I can start right here, right now. Anything you say, if you choose to say anything at all, will be protected by attorney-client privilege."

"This may sound paranoid, but it seems awfully convenient for an attorney to magically appear out of nowhere in the interrogation room of a police station."

"I didn't magically appear. I was on the other side of the two-way mirror observing the earlier questioning."

"Are you a cop?"

"I am a lawyer."

"You have anything beyond the business card? I could make that card on any computer."

"I also have a bar card, but I'm getting a replacement. I was mugged last week. You want to see the scar?"

"Sure."

Dan leaned over and showed Amy the back of his head. Amy looked closely at the healing wound.

"You could have done that in the bathroom. Slipped and hit your head in the shower."

"But I didn't," Dan said. Then he pulled his phone from his pocket and placed it on the table next to his business card. "There's my phone. Take a minute and search for DC attorneys in a database maintained by the court. Look me up. Confirm that I'm not lying."

Amy's head dropped and she picked up the phone. As she typed, Dan continued the conversation.

"Are you always this suspicious?"

"Only when a lawyer pops out of the closet."

"It wasn't a closet."

"You know what I mean. What were you doing on the other side of the two-way mirror?"

"Working on another case. I can't divulge the details."

"What if I hired you? If I hire you as my attorney, can you tell me what you were doing on the other side of the two-way mirror? Does attorney-client privilege work both ways?"

Clever girl, Dan thought. "It does."

Amy nodded. "I don't have the ability to pay whatever your going rate is."

"For a single mother with terminal cancer, my going rate is gratis. Pro bono."

"That means free, right?"

"Right."

Amy finished her inquiry into Dan's background and slid the phone back across the top of the table. "You check out."

"So what do you say?"

Amy looked around the room. She eyed the camera in the corner of the room and glanced down at the files still on the table. Then she glared at the large mirrored wall.

"Deal. You're hired. I'll talk to you, but not here. I don't trust that no one is listening."

Dan nodded in the direction of the mirrored wall and stood. "Give me a second."

A moment later, Dan pushed the door open on the observation side of the two-way mirror. "Everyone out."

"What do you mean 'out'?" Wallace asked.

"I mean out. O-U-T. My client doesn't trust that people won't be listening and quite frankly, neither do I. Out."

"You're not serious about this client business, are you?"

"If you want to solve two murders, get out."

A moment later Dan shuffled Amy into the observation room. She looked through the glass as Detective Wallace and Detective Fields sat down at the metal table where she had spent the last three hours. The social worker with child services joined them in the room and unpacked a backpack of books and toys.

"I like the view on this side," Amy stated. "But you have to admit it *is* a little like a closet."

"Don't mistake this side of the glass for freedom. You're still in custody. And hiring me as an attorney won't change that today."

"How long until you can get me out?"

"Slow down. We're on A, and you're asking about Z. Before we can move through the alphabet, I'm going to need your help."

"One of those situations where you say I have to help you to help myself... ?"

"Something like that."

Amy motioned towards one of the water bottles on a table in the corner. "Can I have one of those?"

Dan grabbed a bottle, opened it, and handed it to her. As she drank from the bottle, Dan eyed her shoes.

"Mr. Lord, have you ever been to a cancer ward?"

"Yes.

"Father, mother?"

"Uncle."

"Pretty sobering, isn't it?"

"It is."

"Lots of sick people. Halls without hope. People are dying of cancer every day, everywhere. Most of them you don't know about. Most of them you don't want to know about. Cancer is an equal opportunity offender. It doesn't care about skin color or background. And all these people, people like me, we are all on meds. Lots of meds. Meds for pain. Meds for nausea. Meds for constipation. Meds for skin conditions associated with radiation. Pills, liquids, gamma rays, lollipops. All bargaining chips for the chance of another day and to withstand the discomfort."

Dan could see his client wanted to talk. To someone. To anyone. "How bad is it?"

"They don't give Fentanyl to healthy people. It's used in addition to other pain medication, which I'm due for in another hour or so."

"I'll see to it that you receive your medication. The police cannot withhold that from you."

Amy smiled weakly. "Thanks. And you know, from a legal perspective, all of these medications have serious side effects. Mind-altering side effects. Mood-altering side effects."

Dan peered curiously at his new client. "How long are the doctors giving you?"

"Less time than I would like."

"You know, there's always the chance for a miracle."

"No. There's no chance for a miracle. Christmas would be a miracle. And that would be enough." Amy again peered over at the detectives through the glass. "Mr. Lord, have you ever heard that cats know when they're going to die and sometimes they will just disappear. Walk off to die alone."

"I've heard that old wives' tale, but I don't know if it's true. I never had a cat."

"It's not an old wives' tale. And I did have a cat growing up. His name was Nuts. Lived until he was fifteen years old. We grew up together, me and Nuts. He was the closest thing I had to a sibling. Anyhow, one day I noticed Nuts didn't want to eat. Then he started acting lethargic. My parents didn't have the money to take him to a real vet, so we took him to Mrs. Carter on the next street over. Mrs. Carter had a million cats. At least it seemed that way when I was a kid. Anyway, Mrs. Carter took one look at Nuts and told me that he wasn't going to make it to summer. Sure enough, one day in late spring I opened the door when I got home from school and Nuts made a break for it. Never saw him again. He knew it was his time."

"I'm sure that was hard on you."

"It was. But now I completely understand. I'm just like Nuts. He knew his time was short. And I can tell you this, as sure as Nuts was about his predicament when he slipped out the door and boogied across the yard and into my memory, I can tell you that death is on me. I'm not going to escape. There will be no miracle cure. No recovery. All I have is a stopwatch constantly ticking in my head and the love for my daughter."

"Have you made arrangements for your daughter?"

"The best I could."

"If there is anything you need help with, let me know. As a lawyer I can draft documents. Wills. Trusts. Whatever you need. We can go over some options later if you like."

"Okay."

"Good. I'll prepare a checklist for getting your affairs in order. Is there anyone you have in mind to handle your affairs after you..."

"Die. You can say it. At first, it took me a while to spit it out. You have to ease into it. But after you say it a few dozen times, it becomes just another word."

"I won't hesitate next time." Dan paused and then continued. "Now, I would like to ask you a question or two about today. You don't have to answer me. That is your choice. But it would help me to know where I stand. It may help me to get you back on the street. Anything you say, anything at all, can never be divulged to anyone else. Do you understand that?"

"You go ahead and ask. Maybe I'll answer."

"Fair enough. But I hope my Q & A turns out better for me than it did for Detective Wallace."

Amy smiled and Dan could see dimples in her sunken cheeks.

"Did the lollipop the detectives find belong to you?"

Amy nodded but didn't verbalize her answer.

"And this Dr. Smithson that the detective mentioned, did he prescribe the medication to you for terminal cancer?"

Another nod.

"And would it be reasonable to conclude that your DNA may be on the lollipop they found at the scene?"

Amy didn't nod but looked into Dan's eyes with complete surrender.

"Well, that is certainly a strong chain of evidence that wouldn't work in your favor. In the case of a trial, that is. Bank robbery is a crime, you know."

"It may be a crime, but it's not like killing someone."

Dan digested that statement as Amy continued. "I mean, we bailed out the entire banking world a couple of years ago. The automobile industry. Fannie Mae. Wall Street. Whoever whined the loudest. So I figured, to hell with it. Banks are insured. Fifty thousand here. Fifty thousand there. It won't make a bit of difference to anyone in the long term. That's the cost of a work conference in Vegas for a couple of days for these companies. No one is going to blink at a few thousand dollars."

"Except for the police. They don't really care about the relativity of the amount in question."

"And I don't really care about the authorities."

"They care about you."

Amy nodded her head slowly and then hacked once, her hand finding her midsection.

"Do you still have access to the money from the bank?"

"I never admitted to robbing any bank or having money from a bank robbery."

"That's fine. But you should know there's a good chance the police will locate the stolen money if you choose not to return it voluntarily. Don't take this the wrong way, but I think I have a good idea where the money is, and I haven't even looked for it yet."

"You do, do you?"

"Rock Creek Park. You live in Cleveland Park. The bank is near Metro Center. It's the logical choice. And you have dirt on your shoes."

"Did you know that Rock Creek Park is the largest urban park in the country? Did you know that the entire island of Manhattan or the entire downtown of Tokyo would fit inside the park?"

"I don't know the dimensions, but I do know the police can probably narrow down your location based on soil samples. If they're paying attention. From what I understand about your current outfit, you're wearing your third set of clothes for the day. The first outfit was on your way into the bank. Your second outfit on the way out of the bank. And the third outfit is what you're currently wearing. So you dumped the clothes you were wearing when you exited the bank somewhere between the spot where the taxi dropped you off and your apartment."

"You pay attention, Mr. Lord."

"I try. I wish I didn't have to, but honesty just isn't a strong suit in today's society."

"A thief is not necessarily a liar."

"Duly noted," Dan said. "Out of curiosity, do you have any idea what the federal sentencing guideline is for bank robbery?"

"Do you know what the sentence is for stage four pancreatic cancer with a zero survivability rating?"

"I would guess considerably shorter than the sentence for bank robbery."

"Mr. Lord, let me be very clear. There will never be a trial. I will never be found guilty. I will never go to jail."

"You're already in jail."

"It's now your job to get me out. I know you can."

"You just met me. What makes you so confident?"

"You're talking to a woman with terminal cancer, a mother of a young child, someone who poses no flight risk, and someone in need of medical attention. In addition to that, any actions that may have taken place today could have been the result of current medication, which is largely considered to be the most powerful painkiller available. I think this is what my dad referred to as a slow pitch over the middle of the plate. You should be able to knock it out of the park. If you can't, find me another lawyer and take what I told you to the grave."

"Best case scenario, you will be in custody for a few days. The first step will be getting you moved to GW hospital for medical care, mental evaluation, and observation. It's better than jail, though you'll still be under police observation."

"You mean under arrest."

"Yes. I'll pull some strings, call in a favor or two, and you should be in your own hospital room by lunch tomorrow. After that, I'll start looking at legal options and precedence for getting you home. Maybe I can even keep you home. At least until Christmas. I can probably have you back with your daughter, with an electronic monitoring device, in a week at the latest."

"Whatever. If they charge me, they charge me. No jail. No trial. I don't care about anything else."

"I'll do my best. But don't think about changing your mind on the possibility of a miracle recovery. If you do, I may not be able to keep you out of jail forever."

Amy again showed both dimples and a glimpse of teeth. "I'll try to die in a timely fashion."

"There's one other thing. I want to ask you about the photographs Detective Wallace showed you."

"I assume you heard me tell him I didn't know the other girl with the lollipop. I can't be the only person in the city with one."

"I'm not talking about the woman in the photos. I'm talking about your reaction to the man in the cap and sunglasses."

Amy stared at Dan. "I've never seen that person before in my life."

Why is it so hard to find an honest client? Dan thought.

"You know, I've seen him before," Dan said, pulling his shirt up from his waist. The ripe, black and blue, web-shaped bruise across Dan's torso made Dan's newest client wince.

"Ouch."

"I owe him one. Or two."

"Looks like you could use a lollipop."

"I'd rather just know where I can find him."

"I can't help you with that," Amy said before sighing. "But hypothetically speaking, what would you do if you locate him?"

"When I locate him."

"Fine, when you locate him. Hypothetically speaking, I may not be around to testify. Not that I would."

"I didn't say anything about testifying. I'm talking about unofficial retribution," Dan answered, clenching his jaws.

Amy flashed a look of surprise, turned towards the mirrored-wall and peered at the detectives in the interrogation room. She looked back at Dan. "You mean that figuratively, right?"

Dan shrugged his shoulders. "This conversation is protected by attorney-client privilege. Trust is a two-way street."

Amy stared at Dan for a few long seconds. "So what's next?"

"I'll get your meds and start the ball rolling on your relocation. I'll check in with you tomorrow. If you need to reach me, you have my card."

Amy paused as if she had something profound to say.

"Are you going to be all right?" Dan asked.

"Just get me out. Give me time with my daughter."

"I'll do my best."

Amy started to speak again. Her mouth opened and only silence escaped. She took a deep breath and managed to say, "Counselor…"

"Call me Dan."

"If something happens to me or my daughter, please know that I didn't have anything to do with it."

Dan paused. "What are you trying to tell me?"

"Nothing. Forget it."

"You're going to have to help me to help you," Dan said with a wink.

"You know how you just asked me who to contact in case anything happens to me?"

"When you die."

"Yes."

"I remember."

"Well, if something does happens to me, I want you to locate an old friend of mine. Her name is Carol T. Sutton."

"Do you have any contact information for her?"

"You'll have to get that yourself."

*

Dan watched as the handcuffs were tightened on Amy's wrists and Detective Fields led her away down the hall. Wallace waited until Emily turned the corner with the suspect and then he grabbed Dan by the arm and pulled him into the interrogation room.

"You mind telling me what that was all about, Benedict Arnold?"

"Attorney-client privilege. No can do."

"Sometimes you can be a real asshole."

"And you need to learn to trust people."

"I give trust when trust is earned."

"No. You only give trust when trust is earned the way you want it to be earned. Don't confuse the two. Don't forget who nailed Nguyen's murderer. You didn't trust me then and I proved you wrong."

"I'll tell you what. Prove me wrong one more time."

"I will. But I'm going to need your help with a few things."

"Like what?"

"I want my client at home with her daughter."

"In exchange for what?"

"The guy in the cap and sunglasses."

"She's going to give him to us?"

Dan lied, answering, "She is willing to provide additional information after posting bail and she is home."

"I don't think anyone is going to agree to that."

"Yes they will. In the meantime, I want my client moved to GW hospital for care, observation, and a mental evaluation. With visitation rights. I was thinking tomorrow morning would be good for a transfer."

"She's a bank robber who was caught on video and identified by a witness. No one is going to let her go free."

"This woman will never make it to a trial. I'm prepared to file every motion available, and invent a few more. She is under heavy medication, extreme stress, and suffering from terminal cancer. I can have any number of medical doctors attest to her condition. In addition to her medical state and diminished condition, she is a single mother and the sole provider for her child. She is also willing to provide meaningful information that may aid in solving two active murders."

"Christ."

"I don't think my client is religious."

"I still can't let her walk."

"I'm not saying walk. I'm saying walk with a limp. Let's get her home detention. Push for a trial date that is, say, six months from now. Allow her to continue her treatment and milk every day of life she has left with her daughter. We get our information. We solve some murders. We save the taxpayers some money."

"And in return?"

"In return, I'll arrange for the return of the stolen money and maybe even give you some suspects on a couple of cold murder cases."

"Just how are you going to do that?"

"If I'm right, I should be able to tell you something tomorrow. Come by the apartment in the afternoon. Bring your sidekick."

"The one you're sleeping with?"

"I haven't slept with her yet, but as soon as this case is over, anything is possible."

"I'll keep that out of mind."

"So we have a deal, right? Home detention. My client isn't a flight risk. She has a small child, no other family, and she probably doesn't even own a passport. She is very ill. Gravely ill. Getting her home detention should be easy. As my client put it, it should be a slow pitch over the middle of the plate."

"I don't think the captain or the DA are baseball fans."

"And one more thing," Dan said. "Try and keep her name out of the press."

CHAPTER 40

DAN DROPPED TWO folders on the floor of his rented bedroom in Georgetown. Emily sat on the folded futon. Detective Wallace leaned back in the bird cage chair, spinning slightly. Both DC detectives watched intently as Dan removed photos from the top folder and spread them on the floor on the right half of the room.

When he had emptied the top folder, he placed it to the side. He opened the second folder and repeated the process on the left side of the room. When done, two sets of photos divided the old hardwood floor with an open space between them. Dan moved between the photos, adjusted into a cross-legged position, and checked his written notes on a yellow legal pad. Emily moved to the end of the futon closer to the photos. The afternoon sun shone through the window behind her, illuminating her hair.

Dan looked to his audience for approval to begin.

Wallace nodded down from his perch. "Bring it on."

Dan began. "Let's see if you guys can follow my insanity. I spent about eight hours shuffling through obituaries and online death records for the last seven years and hopefully it wasn't a waste of time."

"Obituaries? Those can be a real pick-me-up," Emily chimed in.

"Try reading a couple thousand of them."

"I'll pass."

"At any rate, I was digging for information on one particular list of individuals. People with terminal cancer. Or more specifically, people who died of terminal cancer."

"I think I'm going to need a drink to get through this," Wallace said.

Dan pointed to an opened bottle of black label Jack Daniels sitting on the floor in the corner. "Take a nip if you need one."

"Did you have a head start?"

"It was a full bottle when I started this morning."

Wallace warily leaned out of the bird chair and Emily intercepted him, grabbing the bottle before he could find his balance.

Dan continued. "Based on what we know about Amy the bank robber, Beth the sniper, and Carol T. Sutton, I made a few assumptions to help me get to a manageable number of people with certain characteristics who died of terminal cancer."

"Who is Carol T. Sutton?" Wallace asked.

"She is someone my bank robbery client identified as a friend, but in reality she's another suspect. She is also dead."

"And your client told you this?"

"She told me to contact Carol T. Sutton if anything ever happened to her."

"And of course you checked her out?"

"I did. But the existence of Carol T. Sutton is inadmissible in any legal proceeding. It was offered to me under attorney-client privilege," Dan paused and stared into Wallace's eyes. "And that is what is known as trust and sharing."

Wallace motioned for the bottle of liquor. "Noted. Can I ask why you use the expression, 'terminal cancer'? These people died. Of cancer. So it was terminal by definition."

"I considered that, and if you stick with me, I can explain."

"What assumptions did you use?" Emily asked.

"First off, I limited my search by focusing on deceased individuals with young children. Then I further limited the search criteria to men and women who died younger than fifty years of age. Mathematically, I needed some filters to reach a manageable number and there just aren't that many people over fifty with young children who died of terminal cancer in the given time period. I may have missed some people but, at the end of the day, what I have done should point us to everyone we need to find."

"Seems reasonable. Not foolproof, but reasonable," Emily replied, motioning for the return of the bottle, which she immediately turned bottom up.

"And for the reason Wallace here just mentioned, I also tried to narrow the definition of terminal cancer. I focused my search on obituaries and death records for individuals who were diagnosed with terminal cancer and died within a year. My search wasn't perfect and some of that information I had to piece together, but that is essentially my new definition of terminal cancer for the purpose of this exercise."

"I'll reserve my opinion on your analysis until you're finished," Wallace said.

Dan continued. "Again, I admit it's not a perfect system. One could have terminal cancer for a much longer period of time than a year. But for our purpose, as you will see, a year is sufficient."

Wallace extended his hand in the direction of the bottle and Emily relinquished her temporary ownership, handing it back to her partner.

"And if at any point, either of you has a better idea, let's hear it," Dan said.

Wallace downed his second drink. Emily shook her head.

"Good. Anyone want to take a guess on how many people under fifty, with young children, died of aggressive terminal cancer in the last seven years in the greater DC area?"

Two heads shook.

"Okay. At least the moving of the heads indicates the audience is listening. And the answer is that there were over two hundred and fifty relatively young adults, with young children, who died of terminal cancer in the last seven years in the DC area."

"Is anyone in the DC area having a more depressing conversation than the one we're having right now?" Emily asked.

"Probably not," Wallace answered. "Why seven years?"

"I have my reasons," Dan responded. "But it's pure speculation at this point."

"Can you give us a hint?"

"Because seven years ago Carla the waitress took her mom and sister on a European cruise, followed by a Caribbean vacation, according to the photos in the living room of Carla's house. And judging by the appliances in the house, everything was replaced in that same timeframe. More or less."

"Okay, then," Wallace replied, shrugging his shoulders in defeat.

"How does two hundred and fifty dead cancer victims stack up against the normal terminal cancer population, if there is such a thing?" Emily asked.

"I wondered the same thing, so I contacted an IT friend of mine who, quite by luck, has a death fetish. He did a quick statistical analysis for me and two hundred and fifty fits within a normal standard deviation."

"What does that mean?"

"Given the population and geographical area covered in the greater Washington, DC area, two hundred and fifty is a reasonable number, given my parameters."

"So that's two hundred and fifty in seven years?" Wallace confirmed.

"Well, two hundred and fifty-one, but I'm rounding here. If we do the math, we know that seven years is eighty-four months. Divide two hundred and fifty people by eighty-four months and we are looking at roughly three people per month, give or take. And those are just those people with obituaries and death records. There are countless others I am not aware of, I'm sure."

Wallace stared down as if transfixed.

Dan plowed onward. "Among those identified, the split of the number of men and women who prematurely died of cancer is approximately even. Fifty-fifty."

"Funny how nature takes care of that," Emily said.

"Indeed. Now, if we take Amy the bank robber, Beth the sniper, and Carol T. Sutton—who my client covertly identified—we can whittle that number down further. If we consider marital status as a qualifier and limit the search to people who are single, the number drops to one hundred and forty people who died prematurely of terminal cancer. If we assume the person is not only single, but is also the sole provider of a child, the number drops to forty-five. If we operate on the assumption that finances are the driving force behind the selection of these people, which I will explain momentarily, then we can exclude single parents who make a decent living."

"How much money is enough to make a decent living?" Emily asked.

"There was some subjectivity on that point. I took the average salary of the DC area and focused on the bottom twenty percent. And when you take finances and consider those people in the bottom twenty percent of average salaries, the total number of prematurely deceased cancer victims who meet all the criteria gravitates more towards women. Right or wrong, there are more single mothers than single dads and there are more single mothers barely getting by than there are single dads struggling to make ends meet."

"So what does that give us?" Wallace asked.

"Twenty-three. Twenty-three young, poor, single parents who have passed away from terminal cancer." Dan waved his hand over the list of photos to his right on the floor. "And here is what they look like."

"They look like soccer moms," Emily stated.

Detective Wallace leaned forward and the bird cage chair squeaked in protest. "There are a couple of soccer coaches in there as well," he added.

"Eighteen women and five men," Dan clarified.

"So these are our suspected killers?" Emily said.

"I'm not saying all these people are killers. After all, we know one of these individuals is my client who is merely a suspect in an alleged bank robbery. But I am saying that by using our sample individuals, these photos could include the faces of numerous killers who have yet to be identified."

"No offense, Dan, but there is a lot of speculation baked into that pie you just served," Wallace said.

"What about you?" Dan asked in Emily's direction. "Do you want some of this pie?"

"Wallace has a point. Seven years' worth of terminal patients, under fifty, single, with young children, economically challenged. I mean… it's hardly evidence."

Dan nodded. "Evidence. That always trips me up." He reached in the direction of the whiskey bottle and Emily pushed it towards him. "Well, if you don't like the twenty-three I have here on the floor, maybe you will like the five that I have chosen from those twenty-three."

Dan's hands danced across the pictures of the dead and he removed eighteen photos, tossing them to the side. He arranged the remaining five on the floor. Three women and two men.

"Any reason you chose those five?"

"I threw some bones in the corner, spit rum, and drizzled chicken blood on them. When I was done, that's what the arrangement of the bones told me."

"Good one."

"In order to reach these final five, I used a little thing called evidence." Wallace furrowed his brows.

Dan continued. "Upon their deaths, these five remaining individuals all had trusts established for their children by the same nonprofit organization. They all had accounts opened by the Carry On Foundation—a nonprofit that helps young children of cancer victims."

Wallace stared at the pictures. "Fuck me."

"That's what they call evidence," Dan said.

"You sure about this?" Wallace asked.

"Absolutely. Five people out of two hundred and fifty identified via Dan Lord black magic who matched perfectly to a verifiable financial trail."

"Did you look into the nonprofit?"

"I poked around. It seems legitimate. They've been around for over a decade. They have corporate sponsors. They've given financial assistance to hundreds of individuals. These five are just a small percentage of the total number of people the organization has helped. But there are still a couple of questions that I need answers to. I have an appointment with them tomorrow."

"Unbelievable," Emily said. "What's next? What do we do with a pool of potential killers?"

"I think that's the first part of the mystery. The other question is who are they killing?" Dan said. He waved his hand over the other photos on the other side of the floor. "We have a waitress. We have an EPA lawyer. We have a disabled Army vet. And we have the wife of a congressman who knew at least two of the victims."

"That would make her the prime suspect if not for the fact that we know she isn't the pusher and she was picking her kid up from school when her baby daddy was killed," Wallace responded.

"I'm sure it's disappointing when a prime suspect won't fit the suspect mold you made for them," Dan retorted at Detective Wallace's expense.

"You *were* a good suspect," Wallace said. "Just the wrong one."

Emily interrupted. "Enough. Let's not get sidetracked. I assume you tried to find a connection between the dead?"

"I did. I initially looked into possibilities when I knew there was a connection between Sherry Wellington, her Army-vet baby daddy, and Carla the waitress. I didn't include the EPA lawyer because I didn't know there was a sniper with cancer until you told me. The initial search for a connection landed nothing."

"No connection at all?"

"None. So I called my data guy this morning and he reran the query with the addition of the EPA lawyer."

"Is this data guy the same IT guy you just mention who has a death fetish?"

Dan nodded grudgingly.

"And... ?

"We still have nothing. No connection between any of the parties, outside of Sherry and Carla working together and Sherry and Marcus living together. There are no extraneous connections."

"How good is your IT data death guy?"

"The best of the best. Crazy as hell, but his programming skills are unrivaled."

"I think what he's saying is that his data guy is good," Wallace jibed.

"Which databases did your guy use?" Emily asked.

"The same ones law enforcement uses. A couple of others I'm sure we've never heard of."

"So no connection between the Army vet, the EPA lawyer, the waitress, and the wife of the congressman."

"None of the normal ones."

"What about abnormal ones?" Emily asked. "A gym membership somewhere? A book club? Some kind of class? Maybe a jury?" Emily said.

"I checked out the jury angle and ran their names through the court system with PACER. I found nothing. The rest of those possibilities will require legwork."

"What about something like a swingers' club?" Emily said.

"Wow. Didn't see that coming. Going right for the smut," Dan replied.

"There are swingers all over this city," Wallace said.

"If you don't like the sex angle, how about something like Alcoholics Anonymous?" Emily asked.

"I like the possibility there. We know the Army vet had a drinking problem *and* he was hooked on oxy," Dan said.

"Maybe Sherry Wellington also had a problem. Waitresses and bartenders are known for doing drugs. Something to do with the lifestyle and unusual hours," Wallace said.

"Unfortunately AA and NA don't keep databases. They are anonymous. It's going to be hard to chase down a connection there," Dan replied. "We could go knocking on doors, but it'll take time."

"There could be a drug connection. A shared drug dealer. Maybe Sherry, the EPA lawyer, the waitress, and the Army vet are all in the same drug circle," Wallace said.

"I doubt it," Dan said. "I asked around on the drug front."

All three stared at the photos on the ground.

"They could've also met at a sex addicts' support group," Emily added.

"Easy partner," Wallace replied. "I think we're getting an idea of what kind of girl you become when you drink."

"We have two puzzles to solve. The first puzzle is to find a commonality between the EPA lawyer, the congressman's wife, the disabled vet, and the dead waitress," Dan said.

"And the second puzzle?" Emily asked.

"Find out who is selecting the killers and how. We know the guy in the cap and sunglasses is involved, so the bigger mystery may be the how. Keep in mind I was able to identify and analyze our potential killers because they were dead. I used obituaries, death records, and a couple of other private detective tricks-of-the-trade. But identifying people after they're dead and in the press, and after the information has been posted in public records is easy. But whoever is behind this is compiling a list while these people are still alive, without obituaries and death records. That is something far more difficult to do. The most obvious route to this information is access to the medical records of patients who are still alive. Somehow identifying living cancer patients and then accessing their records."

"We have an appointment with your bank robber's physician tomorrow,"

Wallace said. "We planned on meeting with the doctor to get more information on the medication your client was taking at the time of the bank robbery. We can poke around on how medical records are handled."

"If that doesn't pan out, I can ask a few doctors I know. But tomorrow I have an appointment with the Carry On Foundation tied to our five suspects," Dan said. "Hopefully I can find something else these so-called soccer moms and coaches had in common."

"I know one thing the killers have in common," Wallace said.

"What's that?"

"They're all dead."

"Very helpful." Dan looked down at the photos. The sun was now setting and the room was edging towards darkness. "There is one other possibility to consider with these dead soccer moms and coaches."

"What's that? Wallace asked.

"It may be worthwhile to go through some of the unsolved murder cases in the District. If these three women and two men are indeed killers, then by definition they had to have killed someone. You may be able to check if any of these dead cancer victims were in the neighborhood of any unsolved murders. See if the timeline matches. Maybe you'll find another person who can tie this whole thing together."

"And if we turn up a goose egg, there is still hope," Emily added.

"How's that?" Dan and Wallace responded in near unison.

"All we have to do is keep our eyes on the obituaries. If we're heading in the right direction, our pusher for the waitress and the person who shot Marcus Losh should show up dead in the newspaper in the near future."

"I don't think I want to wait that long," Wallace said.

CHAPTER 41

ETECTIVES WALLACE AND Fields sat in the waiting room next to a large saltwater fish tank with a sunken ship resting on the bottom. A mix of colorful reef dwellers swam around the sunken vessel, dodging in and out like children at recess on an underwater playground.

Detective Wallace looked around the waiting room and felt the palpable air of death. A man with a bad toupee in the corner sat stone faced, his mind seemingly elsewhere. Maybe on his wife, or his children. Or his life. Or the pain.

On the other side of the room, a child rested in her mother's arm. The face of the child was gaunt and pasty.

"Jesus," Wallace whispered, dipping his eyes on the floor. Emily reached over and squeezed his arm gently.

Wallace averted his eyes back to the fish tank, losing himself in nature's rhythm served in a glass square. The sound of water running through the filter nearly put him to sleep before the door at the end of the reception room opened and Wallace and Emily were called back.

Moments later they were in Dr. Smithson's office, offering introductions, flashing credentials, dropping business cards.

"Before we get started, you understand I have patient-doctor privileges. I'm not permitted to divulge information on any of my patients without their consent. We take HIPAA very seriously."

"We totally understand."

"Unless you have a warrant."

"Hopefully we won't need one. As I mentioned on the phone, we apprehended a suspect in a bank robbery in DC the day before yesterday. At the scene of the robbery, we obtained evidence that identifies the alleged suspect as Amy Conboy."

"What was that evidence?"

"A morphine lollipop. As you know, it has a DEA number on it, which pointed us in the direction of the pharmacy that filled the prescription. From there we apprehended the suspect as she returned home."

"I see," Dr. Smithson replied.

"We wanted to ask you a few questions about these lollipops of yours."

"They aren't mine. And they aren't morphine."

"Yeah, we know. They're something called Fentanyl," Wallace said.

"That's correct. Fentanyl is a hundred times more powerful than morphine. Less risk for addiction. Fentanyl is used for breakthrough pain."

"What is breakthrough pain?" Emily asked.

"Pain sensations so strong they power through other pain medication like a hot knife through butter."

"So the worst pain imaginable," Emily stated.

"The worst of the worst," Dr. Smithson confirmed. "Even as a doctor it's hard to understand how much pain someone is in without firsthand experience. Some things have to be felt to comprehend. So, as a physician, when it comes to breakthrough pain, I'm treating something I can't really understand."

"And this patient we apprehended, Amy Conboy, she would have likely been in severe pain."

"Once again, I cannot discuss a particular individual. But, in general, a patient prescribed Fentanyl would suffer bouts of severe pain. Debilitating pain."

"And could the drug cloud their judgment? Impair their ability to act rationally?"

"It's likely. But the effect of medication varies by individual and it can change over time. Everyone is different."

"So it's possible that a bank robbery suspect on these Fentanyl lollipops could have been out of his or her mind on medication?"

"It could cause significant cognitive impairment. But not always." The doctor paused before asking a question. "Have you ever had surgery, Detective Wallace?"

"Sure."

"Before any surgical procedure, the patient has to answer a battery of questions pertaining to past drug usage. Alcohol consumption. Prescription medication. The obvious reason those questions are asked is to ascertain whether there is a likely medicinal or chemical composition conflict with current medication and the anesthesia that is going to be used during the surgical procedure. Allergic reactions are a concern, of course, but not the only one."

"What are the other concerns?"

"Equally important is determining the patient's drug tolerance threshold. You get someone in the operating room who consumes twenty drinks a day, or shoots up regularly, and it can be difficult for anesthesia to work effectively. When I first started out in medicine, as a resident, we had a career alcoholic come in for surgery. It took four times the usual dose of Propofol, administered intravenously, to render him sufficiently unconscious. And even then, when the procedure was over, this particular patient was able to recall certain details that indicated he wasn't as incapacitated as we like when we perform invasive surgical procedures."

"So you're saying that, potentially, a patient could be using the morphine lollipop and be in full control of their faculties."

"Hypothetically, yes. It depends on the individual."

"What are the other side effects of Fentanyl?"

"The lollipop version, as you call it, tends to rot the teeth. Fentanyl, in general, has other side effects. It can cause the shakes. It doesn't react well with some asthma medications."

Wallace scribbled in his detective's notebook. "Changing gears a little, I was wondering if we could ask some questions about the procedures of this office?"

"In the hope of solving a bank robbery where you've already apprehended a suspect?"

"Actually, no. We're looking for information that could aid in several open criminal investigations."

"Sure, though I'm not sure how I can help," Dr. Smithson answered, leaning back in his chair.

"You're an oncologist, correct?" Wallace asked.

"Yes."

"What exactly does that entail?" Emily asked.

"There are several types of oncologists—surgical, medical, and radiologists. Patients often see more than one of us. I am a medical oncologist."

"Do you perform surgeries?" Emily asked.

"I do not perform surgeries. Typically a medical oncologist employs chemotherapy, as well as other medicinal options, to treat cancer. A radiation oncologist, as you can imagine, employs radiation. A surgical oncologist probably needs no further explanation. There are rare instances where doctors have more than one specialty, and there are oncologists who specialize even further within a medical field. For example, gynecological oncologists are pretty prevalent."

"Would you treat someone who has both a brain tumor, and let's say, ovarian cancer?"

"I can treat all cancers, but my specialty is the GI tract, liver, pancreas."

Wallace wasn't sure where to take the conversation next and Emily stepped to the plate for a swing.

"Who in the medical profession would have access to records across different patients with different cancers?"

"Well, electronic medical records were mandated a couple of years ago, so if someone has access to the system they certainly could piece together a patient's history."

"So if I want to know Daisy Duke's medical history I could look her up in the system and see the history of her treatment."

"That is the implied usage, correct."

"And what if I wanted to do that with more than one patient? What if I wanted to know all of the Daisy Dukes out there who have recently been diagnosed with cancer?"

"That is a different question. Medical records don't work that way. Well, not exactly. For example, I can't search for all males with prostate cancer in the United States in the last year. That is not what the medical records are designed to do. There are different hospital systems that share information but there isn't a national medical record system. Not yet anyway. In addition to the cost of such a system, there would be no reason for a medical doctor to access information on that level, outside of research, which a typical doctor with patients wouldn't be involved in."

Wallace looked at the doctor and then over at Emily.

The doctor continued. "This is how medical records work: If the medical records have been entered properly, we can search for patients by name, address, social security number. Most insurance companies have a member ID number as well. But unless I'm missing something, you are asking about a general search for all cancer patients."

"Yes, we are. Specifically, we are wondering if there is a way to obtain a list of all terminally ill cancer patients in a given area."

The doctor scowled as if the sudden gravity of the questions the detectives were asking moved from theoretical to reality. "Why would you be interested in that information? Why would anyone outside of medical research be interested in that information?"

Wallace nodded at Emily. "We have reason to believe that someone is targeting terminal cancer patients for various illegal reasons."

"Identity theft?"

"Sadly, no. We believe someone out there is interested in people with cancer who are still alive. Specifically, we believe someone is hiring terminally ill patients to conduct criminal activity. Perhaps even murder."

"I see," Dr. Smithson said, his face showing disgust at the prospect of the notion shared by the detectives. "Very perverse."

"Can you imagine any way that someone could identify multiple terminally ill people with potentially different types of cancer?"

"Hmm..."

"Put yourself in the mind of a criminal."

Dr. Smithson squinted. "Well, if you wanted to identify potential terminally ill patients, you could always stake out an oncology office. Our waiting room has a large number of such patients. Another alternative would be to find a cancer treatment facility. Identify a radiation or chemical therapy location and try to determine who is ill based on who is receiving regular treatment. It would be traditional detective work, I imagine, but it could certainly be accomplished."

Emily and Wallace both nodded their heads in silence. Wallace jotted notes in his detective notebook.

Emily asked another question. "How many people have access to medical records that would allow them to search by name, social security number, whatever?"

"In the country? A lot. I think the most recent count put the total number of medical doctors in the US in the neighborhood of three hundred thousand. Of course, not all of them would have access to electronic medical records. There are MDs in a lot of different fields that don't deal directly with patients. Education. Research. Conservatively, tens of thousands of people could have access to a single patient's medical records."

Wallace stroked his chin and then backed up to a simpler question. "Doctor, how do *you* know a patient has terminal cancer?"

"We perform tests and do a biopsy."

"You take actual tissue samples and test them, yes?"

"That is correct."

"Do you do that here?"

"Initial diagnosis is done in a lab down the street. If that diagnosis is determined to be positive, or if there are extenuating circumstances, or if the results indicate the possibility of a particularly aggressive form of cancer, then additional tests are ordered."

"What do the additional tests tell you?"

"They confirm the original test results as well as provide insight into the nature of that particular cancer, if available."

"Where is this follow-up testing done?"

"We send most of our follow-up biopsy tissue to Johns Hopkins in Baltimore."

"How many other doctors use this same center?"

"It's one of the major biopsy evaluation locations in the country. Thousands of doctors and hospitals use it."

"So, hypothetically speaking, if I wanted a list of people who were recently diagnosed with terminal cancer, Johns Hopkins would have the list."

"Well, I don't think they keep a master list, per se. But they would have that information."

"For different types of cancer?"

"Yes. Breast. Ovarian. Brain. Prostate. Colon. Pancreas. You name it. But Johns Hopkins is a massive facility, with different departments of specialization. It's not as if there is one person sitting behind a desk who gets a list of all of the tissue results and then stuffs envelopes and licks stamps."

"They don't use snail mail?"

"When you're talking about stage four cancer, time is not a luxury expended on the United States Postal Service."

"So how do you get the information, the actual biopsy results?

"If the news is dire, they will call. Followed by a fax. Updates in the electronic medical system may not show up until a day or two later. Could be a week if there's a backlog."

"Can you give us the address of the lab at Johns Hopkins that provided the results for Amy Conboy?"

"The office staff can provide that information to you."

CHAPTER 42

ACCORDION FOLDER IN hand, Dan strolled through Alexandria, home to more nonprofit organizations than any other jurisdiction in the world. Offices, large and small, littered the old streets where history seeped from the cobblestone and brick sidewalks. In the first half of his walk, Dan passed the headquarters for the Salvation Army and the United Way. On the far side of the block, he passed the main office for the guys who drive the little cars in figure eights at the Memorial Day parade.

Dan checked the address on his phone, looked up at the door without a name, and pushed his way inside. He climbed a narrow staircase and turned the corner into a small waiting room on the second floor. The sign over the paper-filled reception desk read The Carry On Foundation. The sound of the door shutting behind him lured the receptionist from her location in another room.

"May I help you?" the elderly woman asked.

"Yes, my name is Dan Lord. I'm here to see Jeanie Simpson."

"Have a seat, I'll let her know you're here."

Dan sank slowly into the lone chair in the waiting area. The thick burgundy carpet and a large dark bookcase along the wall matched the rest of the room. Dan got the distinct impression the furniture had been abandoned by the previous tenant, which could have easily been a branch of the retirement homeowners association, based on the décor.

Jeanie Simpson appeared at precisely ten and checked her watch as if to prove she was on time. "Good morning, Mr. Lord."

Dan stood.

"You mentioned on the phone that you're a private detective and attorney in need of information?" Jeanie asked with genuine curiosity.

"That is correct."

"Please follow me," she said, starting down the lone hall. She turned left at the second door and Dan followed her into a small office with additional bookcases closing in on three walls. Dan waited for his host to find a seat at the small table, and then sat across from her, placing his accordion folder in front of him.

"I've never met a private detective in real life. But I have watched my fair share of them on television. *Magnum PI* is still a dream. *The Rockford Files. Mike Hammer.* Some of those guys were probably on TV before you were born. I'm also a big fan of the CSI shows, which is a little different, I know. But I loved them all—Miami, New York, Vegas. I was secretly holding out for a DC version. I would even take Baltimore."

"I can't speak to crime scene investigators, but I assure you private detective work is not as glamorous as it seems on television. No Ferrari. No friends with a helicopter."

"I'll take your word for it. Now, how can I help you?"

"I have a couple of routine questions I wanted to ask about your organization."

"Please."

"How many people work at the foundation?"

"The Carry On Foundation has locations across the US. Here in Alexandria, we are the national headquarters for the organization and we handle the Mid-Atlantic from Maryland to North Carolina."

"How many people work at this location?"

"Five. We have a receptionist who answers phone calls and emails. We have a webmaster who handles all of the web activities. Updates to the website. Manages the content. We have a marketing staff of two. They spend time shaking the money branches, if you will. Everyone else works pro bono."

"Who is everyone else?"

"Attorneys and accountants mostly. We have volunteer CPAs and lawyers in almost every state. We are in the business of setting up trusts for the young children of cancer victims. There are a lot of regulations that need to be followed. The regulations can vary by state, so we need regional volunteers, accordingly."

"In total, how many employees do you have, countrywide?"

"On the payroll, we have employees here, in the South, the Northeast, Midwest, and West. Five offices, twenty-two employees. Most are part-time. We have twice as many volunteer CPAs and attorneys."

"How much money does the foundation give away every year?"

Jeanie Simpson paused. "Have you done any research on the Carry On Foundation, Mr. Lord?"

"Just what I read on the website and in the press. But information can get outdated. Things change."

"I see," Jeanie Simpson replied. "Well, the Carry On Foundation doesn't actually give money away. We facilitate the creation of trusts, which are then funded by corporations and individuals. Of course, we do use our PR reach to help influence others to fund these trusts. It is something we do quite well and pride ourselves on."

"Who can say no to the children of cancer victims?"

"You would be surprised. But we do hold a soft spot in the hearts of a lot of people and organizations."

"How many people does the organization help in a year?"

"On a good year, we set up trusts for over a thousand unfortunate souls. The amount of funding each trust receives varies."

"What's the average?"

"I cannot divulge that information. Donations are made from both public and private sources. What I can tell you is that most of the foundation's funding—the money that pays rent and salaries—that comes from corporations and other organizations."

"Can you walk me through the steps for establishing a trust by the Carry On Foundation?"

"Sure. As I mentioned, establishing the trusts is all handled by accountants and lawyers. Every T is crossed. Every I is dotted. We open the trust and provide a webpage where donations can be made to the trust through an independent financial institution. The foundation doesn't handle the money. We merely provide a channel for the money."

"How do you decide who will receive assistance from the foundation in setting up a trust? I mean, there are a lot of people with cancer who have children."

"Most of our trust recipients are identified through nominations."

"Meaning what?"

"Meaning that someone who has passed away, from cancer, is nominated to have the Carry On Foundation open a trust for them. If a proposed recipient fits the bill—and meets the standards of good-standing set by the organization and its bylaws—they will be considered for the establishment of a trust."

"What are the standards of good-standing?"

"A clean police record. No known drug or alcohol issues. Financial need. Once we receive a nominee, our attorneys perform some due diligence and determine their validity."

"So potential trust recipients are received by nominations and they are paid through money from corporations or anonymous donations from individuals."

"Not exactly. The recipients are deceased, so they aren't paid anything. A trust is created for their children, which can be funded."

"Excuse my inaccuracy. Who can nominate an individual?"

"Virtually all of our recipients are identified through existing relationships."

"For example?"

"We have relationships with churches, hospitals, hospices, local companies, other nonprofits, social services. Our corporate sponsors also nominate their own employees from time to time. But there is no favoritism. Everyone is vetted in the same fashion."

"And how do they contact you?"

"Who?"

"The organizations that submit nominations."

"Mostly mail and fax. Some organizations drop off nominee applications in person."

"What about email?"

"Not anymore. For a while we allowed nominations via email. We also allowed the general public to nominate individuals. We tried both of those for a brief period but we were just overwhelmed with submissions. I think the first month after we opened the website to email submissions we had over five thousand nominees."

"That is a big number."

"Yes, and when we allowed nominations from individuals we received an inordinate amount of spam and speculators."

"Speculators?"

"People fishing for money. The number of requests we had to vet to find real candidates was just too much for the staff to handle. Now we have a form online you can print out. The nominee fills out the application and either sends it, faxes it, or drops it off in person. There must be a contact name, a contact number, and a signature on the form. Sometimes organizations go as far as to provide videos of the deceased with their children. We receive photos. Family keepsakes."

"Desperation."

"That's right. That is why the Carry On Foundation exists. To help ease that desperation as best we can."

Dan removed a legal pad from his folder and wrote several sentences before he looked up. "So once you receive this nomination form, you turn it over to your attorneys for the vetting process?"

"That's correct."

"And do you contact the organization who nominated the deceased?"

"We contact whoever is listed as the contact. Sometimes it's the nominating organization, but it can also be the guardian or attorney of the child of the deceased. It could also be another relative. Anyone who can provide the necessary information on the child in order for our attorneys to establish the trust."

"Not necessarily the person who nominated the deceased?"

"Sometimes the nominee does not want to be further involved. Anonymity is the backbone of much nonprofit funding."

I bet it is, Dan thought.

"If I gave you a list of names, would it be possible for you to tell me how they came to your attention?"

"You mean who nominated them?"

"Yes."

Dan reached into the folder and removed a sheet of paper with the names listed. He placed the paper on the table and Jeanie Simpson's eyes dipped downward. Dan watched as she considered the question and squirmed in her chair slightly.

"It's important," Dan said. "A matter of life and death."

Jeanie Simpson gasped quietly. "Life and death?"

"Yes. And as I'm sure you know from all those television shows you watch, the information I'm interested in could probably be subpoenaed, if necessary."

"Are you threatening me, Mr. Lord? I have never been threatened before."

"Not at all. But I'm looking for someone doing some bad things and I'll do whatever it takes to find them."

Jeanie Simpson's fingers shook slightly as she reached for the paper on the table and read the names. "Can you give me a minute and let me make a few phone calls?"

"Take your time," Dan replied.

Jeanie Simpson nodded, stood, and exited the room. Ten minutes later she returned to the office. "I apologize for keeping you waiting. I have spoken to our lead counsel and he is willing to grant your request."

"Thank you," Dan said.

Jeanie Simpson smiled. "Now, let's play detective with those names."

CHAPTER 43

D AN SAT IN his second waiting room of the day, this time at the Capital Community Hospice off Upton Street in the District. He was waiting for Pepper Hines, the director of the facility, who was currently sitting in traffic on the twelve-lane span of the American Legion Bridge. Dan was also waiting for the arrival of Wallace and Fields, who had U-turned on their way to Johns Hopkins in Baltimore.

Between the tardy parties, Dan donated thirty minutes of his life to boredom. The only consolation to losing thirty minutes of one's life in a hospice waiting room was realizing the lost time was far better than being a patient of the facility. Count your blessings where you find them.

During his wait, Dan had learned two things. First, the Capital Community Hospice was eerily quiet. Voices were kept to a whisper. Visitors to the facility moved silently and efficiently to the registration desk before being escorted down the main hall to one of the thirty rooms that stretched to the back of the property.

The second thing Dan learned was that the Capital Community Hospice waiting room was dreadfully bereft of reading material. No *Time* magazine. No *Reader's Digest*. Not a single copy of every waiting room's mainstay—*People*.

Dan sought mental stimulation in a rack of brochures in the corner of the room. Between one titled *Dying with Dignity* another titled *Beating Cancer*, Wallace's voice boomed across the silent room.

"This better be good."

Dan slowly turned. "Shhhhh. They like it quiet in here."

The woman behind the registration desk stood and gave Detective Wallace her best librarian stare down. "Sorry," Wallace mouthed without vocalization.

"Did you learn anything at my client's oncologist?" Dan asked.

"We learned that Dr. Smithson takes his HIPAA seriously and we were educated on how medical records work. We were on our way to Johns Hopkins when you called."

"Then you should be happy I saved you the drive."

"I'll be happy if you tell me what we're doing here."

"This is ground zero. This wonderfully quiet establishment is where our potential killers were identified. All five of the deceased soccer moms and soccer coaches from the pictures."

"All five?"

"All five. They were all patients here at the hospice. Or at least they were nominated through this hospice."

Wallace whistled and the elderly woman at the registration desk gave him another dirty look. "How did you figure that out?"

"The Carry On Foundation. The woman at the nonprofit confirmed the five people I identified in my obituary and death notices analysis had trusts established for them by lawyers and accountants of the foundation. Nothing fishy really. That's what the organization does. They have pro bono lawyers and accountants who set up trusts for the deceased, and those trusts are financed through public or corporate donations. She then explained how their clients are nominated through various channels including church, work, and the medical community. In our case, all of the people we identified were nominated via this hospice."

"This place?" Emily asked. "It looks like a converted elementary school from the outside."

"It was a school. They swapped the name FDR Elementary for Capital Community Hospice. The hospice has thirty rooms on-site, but also provides home hospice care throughout DC, Maryland, and Virginia," Dan added.

"You sound like a tour guide."

"I had some time to read up on the facility while I waited."

"Did you ask Nurse Ratchet at the registration desk to confirm what the woman from the Carry On Foundation said?"

"I did. She told me to wait for the director. And here we are."

"Where is the director now?"

"Stuck in traffic."

"But of course," Wallace said, looking around the room. He nodded in the direction of chairs against the far wall and Dan took a seat next to him. Emily lowered herself into the seat on the other side of Dan.

Wallace spoke again, this time in a whisper. "I assume you heard that your bank robber client is back home."

"I heard. Safe and sound at home with an ankle monitor."

"She got the deal of the century. She gets to spend her remaining time at home with her daughter. Provided she doesn't live too long."

"When you put it like that, it doesn't feel like the deal of the century."

"Better than jail."

"True. For what it is worth, thanks."

"Don't thank me. My captain pushed for it and the DA was sympathetic to a terminally ill single mother. But my captain is expecting this to help solve a couple of murders. Don't make him look stupid."

"That's not my concern," Dan said.

"No, it's not. It's mine. And if this client of yours makes the captain look stupid on this, I'll be the one who has to pay."

"Then let's hope I'm right."

"I hope that hope isn't all we have."

*

Pepper Hines, director of Capital Community Hospice, arrived fifteen minutes later. Introductions ensued and Dan, Wallace, and Emily followed him into a small office with a desk and a circular table.

Pepper Hines spoke as he took off his jacket. His graying hair was slightly combed over. His glasses gave the impression of intelligence. His voice was buttery smooth. Calming. Wallace, Emily, and Dan filled the chairs around the small table.

"What can I help you with?" Pepper asked, finding a seat.

Dan nodded at Detective Wallace. "We're trying to identify someone at this hospice who may have accessed patient medical information without authorization."

"Oh. That doesn't sound good."

"It's not. Have you ever heard of the Carry On Foundation?"

"Yes."

"Have you ever contacted them?"

"Personally, no. But my staff has dealt with them in the past."

Dan removed a nomination form from his folder and showed it to Pepper Hines. "Have you seen one of these before?" Dan asked.

"I have not. What is it?" Pepper asked, his eyes moving left to right as he started reading the document.

"It's a nomination form for the Carry On Foundation. Based on these forms, the Carry On Foundation vets candidates for their nonprofit. If the nominee clears the vetting process, they will set up a trust for the child of the deceased. They will also solicit donations for these trusts."

Pepper Hines' eyes scanned the document. "Like I said, I've never seen this document before."

Dan moved his finger to a line near the bottom of the page. "Is that your signature at the bottom of the printout?" he asked.

Pepper Hines leaned forward and stared at the signature. "It certainly looks like mine."

"But you didn't sign it?"

"No. Not that I recall. What exactly did someone gain by using my signature?" Pepper asked.

Dan stared hard into Pepper's eyes, searching for deceit. Then he answered.

"We don't know. We assume there was some advantage to using the hospice and your name for the nominees' submissions to the Carry On Foundation. And we think the same person who forged your signature also accessed medical records from this location to facilitate criminal activity."

"What kind of criminal activity?"

"The worst type imaginable," Wallace interjected.

Pepper Hines tugged at his tie slightly.

"Who has access to medical records at this location?" Dan asked.

"We have records online and additional records in a filing room down the hall. Only employees can access the online records. We limit that to medical staff, primarily."

"How many employees do you have?"

"We have a full-time office staff of ten, and a full-time medical and nursing staff of thirty. We have an additional staff of twenty that only handles home hospice care."

"And do all of them have computer access?"

"Yes."

"What about the filing room down the hall?" Wallace asked.

Pepper Hines shrugged his shoulders. "It's a filing room. The door has a lock, but anyone with a key can access the room. You can usually locate one of the keys floating around the office."

"Sounds like loose security," Wallace stated.

"Maybe. If what you say is true. But all of the hospice employees have signed nondisclosure agreements. We have never had an issue in the past."

"Not that you knew of," Wallace said. "Do you keep records on all of your full-time employees?"

"We do."

"And that number is currently around sixty people. Ten in the office, thirty on the medical staff here, and another twenty that perform home hospice care," Dan confirmed.

"That's about right. Beyond that, we have hundreds of volunteers."

"Hundreds of volunteers?" Emily asked incredulously.

"I'm not sure of the exact current number on any given day, but we do keep a list. Generally speaking, we have a high turnover rate with our volunteers. A typical volunteer offers their time in response to an ailing loved one who is a patient at the hospice. They come to our facilities, see the dignity we try to provide to those nearing the end, and they feel compelled to volunteer. The length of time they spend here usually coincides with how long they are in mourning. Once volunteers have picked up the pieces of their lives and have sufficiently healed, they gradually reduce their volunteer hours."

"Human nature," Emily said.

"Indeed. And we don't pressure anyone to stay. Of course, we have volunteers who have been here forever as well."

"What do the volunteers do?"

"A variety of tasks. Many help in the office. Some help with assisted care. Some just keep people company. Read books to the dying. Hold their hands. We also have an eleventh hour volunteer program to help those with the final transition. To be a volunteer in that program one must meet training and certification requirements. We also have patient support groups and family support groups. Both are run by licensed medical professionals with the assistance of volunteers."

"Can you walk us through how patients find their way to the hospice?" Wallace asked. Emily nodded her head in seeming agreement to the question.

Pepper Hines answered. "As you would think. A patient typically seeks medical treatment for an ailment, undergoes a series of diagnostic tests, and ultimately is given a rather grim prognosis for recovery."

"A death sentence," Wallace mumbled.

Pepper nodded. "At that point, the doctor would consult with the patient and ask if they would like information on hospice care. If the patient agrees hospice care is an option they would like to discuss, the doctor will send the patient's medical information to us."

"And do you meet with all the patients for whom you receive information?"

"Most, but not all. Hospice care is voluntary. Some patients never follow up with us. Some patients change their minds. Some patients meet us once and decide they're not interested. Other patients can't bring themselves through the door. It is just too real for them."

Dan listened to Pepper answer the question and then opened his folder and started placing photographs on the round table. The top row included Amy, Carla's pusher, and the man in the cap and sunglasses. The second row was the three women and two men identified through the obituary and death records analysis. "Do you recognize any of these people as patients?"

Pepper Hines' head dipped towards the photos as if he were a chicken about to peck at the top of the table.

"Take a good look," Wallace said encouragingly.

After a full minute of concentration, Pepper Hines rearranged the photos on the table. He turned three photos towards the detectives and said, "I recognize these three."

Dan, Wallace, and Emily all looked down at the photos of Beth Fluto, Carol T. Sutton, and Amy the bank robber.

"You've seen these three before?"

"I have," Pepper answered. He picked up the photo of Carol T. Sutton from the group. "This woman was a patient here at this facility last year. Her name was Carol. She was a wonderful woman. Found God near the end of her stay and prayed through her last days on earth."

You bet your ass she did, Dan thought.

Dan looked at Pepper Hines' face and could see tears welling in the man's eyes.

Pepper returned Carol's photo to the table and picked up the photo of Beth. "This is Beth Fluto. She received home hospice care on a part-time basis. She was registered to move to this location when her condition worsened. She perished in an automobile accident."

Voice cracking, Pepper Hines picked up the photograph of Amy the bank robber. "This woman refused hospice care for financial reasons. I met with her and told her there were funds available, if she was willing to fill out the paperwork. She said she would consider it. I never heard from her again. I only remember her because it wasn't very long ago."

Dan, Wallace, and Emily exchanged furtive glances.

Dan waved his hand over all the photos on the table. "Would you mind asking your staff if they recognize any of these other individuals? You can keep these copies of the photos and pass them around to all of the employees and volunteers. See if anyone recognizes them."

"I can do that. Sure. I can do that today."

"That would be helpful," Emily added.

Dan returned to the previous line of questioning. "What kind of information do the doctors send you on terminally ill patients?" Dan asked.

"Basic medical information. Vital statistics. Medical diagnosis and prognosis."

"And how is this information transmitted?"

"Email, usually. Fax is still popular in the terminal diagnosis business. If we get a copy via email or fax, the doctor will follow up with an electronic record or physical copy. We archive the electronic records and keep a physical copy on record for a year after the patient has passed."

"And you keep these records in the filing room?"

"That's correct."

"We are going to need information on all of your full-time employees and the list of volunteers for the past seven years," Wallace said sternly.

"I can have that for you in a few minutes. Let me get my staff working on it," Pepper Hines replied, his voice shaky with emotion.

*

Dan walked with the detectives across the hospice parking lot to the unmarked squad car.

"What do you think?" Wallace asked.

"Just a couple hundred names to go through," Dan replied. "Let's do the research and see if we can find the mystery man in the cap and sunglasses. We probably need to imagine what he would look like without a disguise. We know dressing up is his M.O. We take the list of employees and volunteers, find a photo for each person, and we go face by face."

"You planning on helping with this exercise?" Emily asked.

"Maybe later. Right now, I have a meeting with the police."

"We are the police."

"Someone from the other side of the river."

CHAPTER 44

PHO 75 PAID homage to the Vietnamese staple through simplicity. They served pho and pho, with the main variation determined by meat selection and the size of the bowl. Beverage options were limited to water from a cooler on the counter and Vietnamese coffee, hot or cold. Long tables, pushed together end-to-end, gave the restaurant a cafeteria-like atmosphere. During the lunchtime and evening rush, strangers were forced to break chopsticks with each other, shoulder-to-shoulder, chair-to-chair.

Dan walked through the glass doors at the front of the shop between the lunch and dinner rush. He pointed towards a quiet corner and the lone elderly waiter with a pad of paper and pen in hand, nodded in response to Dan's suggested seating location.

Detective Singleton of the Arlington Police Department arrived five minutes later.

"Danno."

"Slim Jim."

Singleton looked down at his own waistline but didn't respond.

The elderly Asian waiter with the notepad arrived at the table and took their order without a hint of personality before ambling off towards the kitchen.

"What do you have?" Singleton asked Dan.

"The killer of Marcus Losh is a terminally ill cancer patient."

"Just how did you figure that out?"

"A long twisted game of connect the dots starting with Sherry Wellington. The murder of her baby daddy was case number one. Then a former waitress coworker of hers was pushed in front of a Circulator bus and died. We suspect the pusher in that case was also terminally ill."

"You suspect a terminally ill woman? But you don't have confirmation? Is she in custody?"

"No. She got away. But she had help." Dan rubbed the back of his neck. "Someone with a blunt object. I had double vision for two days. I was also shot in the chest, by the way."

"You look good for being shot. Did you lay eyes on the accomplice?"

"On surveillance video. A guy with a baseball cap and sunglasses."

"Any ID?

"Not yet. But I'll find him."

"Do me a favor. Don't find him in Virginia. I don't want to clean up the mess."

"I already had a DC detective ask me not to find him in the city."

"You still have Maryland."

"I'll see what I can do."

"What do you have on the deceased former waitress who was a coworker of Mrs. Wellington?"

"She wasn't just a former coworker. She was a former coworker Mrs. Wellington claimed she had no contact with, but with whom she had lunch on the very day the coworker was killed."

"Now that is curious."

"It gets better. The guy with the baseball cap and sunglasses caught on video when the waitress dove into the path of the bus, well, this guy also showed up to buy a bike from a junkyard in DC."

"A bike from a junkyard?"

"The pedal variety. The bike came off a minivan that went into the canal last week. The driver of the minivan crashed the same morning as the sniper murder in DC. Distance between the killing and the crash is about three miles. And we know from the ME and her doctor that the driver had terminal cancer."

"So you have a guy in a baseball cap and sunglasses who is connected to the suspect in the sniper murder. And you have the same guy in a baseball cap and sunglasses who is connected to the pusher of this waitress. And you think the pusher of the waitress has cancer because… ?"

"She had a lollipop."

"A lollipop?"

"That's right."

"My daughter has a jar of lollipops on top of the fridge at home."

"Not like these. They're morphine lollipops. Except it's not really morphine. It's something called Fentanyl."

"For pain."

"Bingo. Did you see the bank robbery the other day, at the BB&T downtown?"

"Sure."

"Well, as it turns out, the alleged suspect in that case, who now happens to be my client, also had a morphine lollipop in her possession during the alleged bank robbery. When she was shown photographs of the guy in the cap and sunglasses during police interrogation, we hit pay dirt."

"Another person with terminal cancer tied to the man in cap and sunglasses?"

"That's right."

"Did she confess?"

"She didn't divulge anything that is admissible anywhere; thanks to attorney-client privilege."

"Jesus."

"But if I'm right, we have some terminally ill patients responsible for several murders, and maybe a bank robbery, right here in the DC area."

"And you think Marcus Losh was killed by one of these terminally ill patients?"

"It's my best guess. I can't give you a name, but if I'm right, you'll be able to locate Marcus Losh's killer in the newspapers in the next month or two."

"Are they planning to take out an advertisement?"

"No. They'll be in the obituaries."

The pho arrived and the conversation paused. Detective Singleton threw sliced hot peppers into his bowl of noodles. Dan Lord squeezed a large blob of Sriracha across a pile of bean sprouts.

Detective Jim Singleton slurped a mouthful of noodles. "Let's say I believe you're right."

"Do you?"

"Of course not. And if I did, I wouldn't admit it."

"You aren't alone."

"That makes me feel better. Anyhow, let's say I agree with you. Let's say we have terminally ill people with itchy trigger fingers running around the Beltway and that one of them killed Marcus Losh. Why him? What did he do?"

"We believe the killers received financial compensation from a legitimate nonprofit in Alexandria."

"So they kill for money?"

"We think."

"For what reason? What did Marcus Losh do that someone would pay to have him killed?"

"I'm still working on that."

"Well, that is called motive, Danno. It's kind of important."

"Thanks for the reminder. The good news is that we're working on a lot of potential connections. All we have to do is tie Sherry Wellington to the dead EPA lawyer, or the dead EPA lawyer to Marcus Losh. Or the dead EPA lawyer to the dead waitress."

"I get the idea."

"Or any of the above to anyone connected with a potential cold case, which is a list the DC police are working on."

"What have you looked at so far?"

"I have a technical guy who ran all kinds of crosschecks against the EPA lawyer, the congressman's wife, the waitress, and Marcus Losh. Nothing concrete there. The DC detectives and I kicked around some ideas. At first we thought maybe they all met through something like narcotics or Alcoholics Anonymous. Off the record type of connections. I mean, we know that Marcus Losh had both an alcohol and drug problem."

"Big time."

"Our second thought was that they all served on the same jury."

"It seems logical. A jury is something that ties people together from different backgrounds and when the trial is over, the group is disbanded."

"Exactly. Maybe the jury put a bad guy behind bars."

"And now he's out and wants revenge."

"Yep. It's rare, but it happens. I followed up on the idea and I researched the jury information database for Maryland, Virginia, and the federal courts in DC. Ran all the names we had through PACER. I got nothing. Not a single hit on Sherry Wellington, the dead EPA lawyer, the waitress, or Marcus Losh."

"Nothing?"

"Nope."

"That's very curious."

"Why?"

"Because I've been digging through Marcus Losh's financial records. Keep in mind that we only have a couple of murders a year here in Arlington. The heat is on to solve this thing and solve it quickly."

"I can imagine."

"And my captain still thinks there's a possible drug connection with Marcus's death. So, as shit rolls downhill, I was tasked with guessing how much Marcus was spending on drugs versus how much he was bringing in with disability and income. The thought was maybe Marcus was quietly dealing and that's what actually got him killed."

"You mentioned that before. My drug contact says he wasn't dealing."

"That's what you say. But you also just said that Marcus Losh never served on a jury."

"Not in Maryland, Virginia, or in the federal courts, which covers DC. Those three locations are where he lived all of his non-military life."

"Well, I'm pretty sure I have a bank statement that shows he was paid by the federal court for performing jury duty."

"You're kidding me..."

"As I said, I spent a lot of time looking at Marcus Losh's finances. A lot of time with old bank records. Salary paystubs. Disability payments. I'm pretty sure I logged an entry for a payment from the federal court system for jury service. The reason I remember is because the courts are still paying jurors with real checks. Most people don't receive a lot of physical checks these days. Almost everything is electronic. On top of that, deposits are the least common banking transaction. It stuck in my mind."

"When was this check received?"

"Quite a few years back."

"Any chance it was seven years ago?"

"Could have been. If I remember correctly, the check was deposited into an account with Wachovia, before it was bought by Wells Fargo. The account had been closed for a while, but Marcus kept a lot of his bank records in a filing cabinet in the closet. I can double-check when I get back to the station."

"Fuck me," Dan said. He threw twenty bucks on the table and walked towards the door.

"Keep me posted, Danno."

Dan waved his hand above his head as he exited the restaurant.

*

Detective Wallace pulled the phone from his breast pocket on the second vibration.

"Wallace here."

"You sitting down?" Dan asked.

"You planning on giving me a coronary?"

"Maybe. I need a favor."

"You can't have one. You've reached your quota."

"I need you to access the bank statements of the dead EPA lawyer. See if she received payment for serving on a jury sometime over the summer, seven years ago."

"We already checked to see if she served on jury duty."

"I know. I checked. You checked. She didn't. Except that she did."

"How can that be?"

"I think we're going to find she did serve on a jury, but she is not showing up in the PACER database because it was an anonymous jury."

"You have something concrete on this, or should I just close my eyes and jump down the rabbit hole based on a wild hair up your ass?"

"A lead from your colleagues at the Arlington Police Department. They're still working the case of Sherry Wellington's baby daddy. Records show he was paid for serving on jury duty."

"I'll look into it, but don't most lawyers try to keep other lawyers off a jury?"

"They try, but lawyers serve on juries all the time. Besides, seven years ago your dead EPA lawyer was still in college. She wasn't an attorney. She wasn't even in law school yet."

"I'll check it out. Not sure what I'll find. Seven years is a long time ago."

"You may also want to go back and look at the court cases for the summer that same year. See if any heavy-hitters were put away. See if a guilty verdict put someone behind bars who would be a good candidate for revenge killings. We still need motive and we may be able to identify potential cases even if we can't identify the jurors."

"I'm on it. Where are you?"

"I'm going to see a friend at the courts."

CHAPTER 45

DAN STOOD IN line at the counter, overlooking the spread of possible toppings behind the sneeze guard, readying to ambush Jerry who was sitting at a table in the corner of the sandwich shop. A block from the courthouse, the narrow shrine to sandwiches was only open for lunch. Four hours a day, Monday through Friday. The owner, a large man known as Lunch Money to friends and foe alike, was rumored to clear half a million dollars a year. One foot of meat-stuffed bread at a time.

Dan took his sub in a white bag and approached his acquaintance in the corner. Jerry, wavy dark hair flowing to the collar of his dark suit, was flicking his thumb across the screen of his phone while his other hand shoved a tuna sub into his mouth at steady intervals.

Jerry, an employee in the clerk's office for the DC Superior Court, slipped his smart phone into the pocket of his suit jacket and choked down a swallow of Chicken of the Sea.

"Dan. It's been a while. Not ashamed to say it, but a small part of me was hoping I wouldn't see you just yet."

"I'm not sure what *your* complaint is. The last time I saw you, I was handing over three new laptops and enough cash to buy a car."

Jerry looked around and took a sip from the straw in his cup. "What do you need help with today? More importantly, is it going to require staying up for seventy-two hours straight?"

Before Dan could answer, Jerry raised his hand and showed Dan his palm.

"I'm just saying, if it's something that's going to resemble another sleep deprivation study, I'm throwing in the cost of prescription medication."

"I'm looking to find a case for a trial jury that doesn't show up in the official court records."

"You mean you're looking for a case involving an anonymous jury?"

"That's right."

"Do you have a case number?"

"No."

"Perfect. I can't help you."

"Why is that perfect?"

"Because I don't even have to make up some crazy reason for why I can't help you. This time, it's the truth."

Dan cocked his head and raised his eyebrows. "That's it?"

"You don't like the easy answer?"

"I was hoping for a little foreplay."

"Dan, you know I'm willing to push the envelope a little. Get you some information here and there in the name of capitalism, which is, after all, a cornerstone of this great country."

"I'm willing to grease the wheels of capitalism."

Jerry looked away for a second. "I can't help you, but I can tell you that you're not going to get anywhere without a case number. Maybe, just maybe, you could back into the case if you knew who the judge was. But an anonymous jury is anonymous. As you probably found out, the names of those serving on an anonymous jury are not in any database. They are not stored in any computer I'm aware of. The list for an anonymous jury exists in hard copy, *usually* in the locked filing system of the presiding judge for that case. I say 'usually' because there are some cases where even the judge does not know the identity of the jurors."

"I know how it's supposed to work, but how often does the government do anything exactly as it should?"

"In the case of anonymous juries, they come close. And what it means is you can't just go digging around looking for a name until you find it. You need a case number. Then you will need a court order to access the records associated with that case. If you're lucky, there may still be a physical record of the jurors' actual names in the file. Maybe. Maybe not. Sometimes even the original list of jurors is destroyed at the conclusion of the case."

"You're not being very optimistic here, Jerry."

"Optimism has nothing to do with it. And to be clear, even if you had the case number, I couldn't help you. Not without jeopardizing my job and risking criminal prosecution. I couldn't help even if I really, really, really wanted to—which I don't. You can thank the press corps if you don't like it."

"Money?"

"Big cases are big stories and they sell newspapers. Reporters hound the courthouse on big cases and they are willing to pay for information. The courts have reacted, and now information—particularly on anonymous juries—is harder to get than ever before. On top of that, anonymous juries have increased something like eight hundred percent in the last decade. More high-profile cases involving terrorism and homeland security. People on these juries don't want their names attached to these cases. And it isn't just here in DC, it's nationwide."

Dan twisted the top off his water bottle and took a swig. "Can you get me the name of someone who is willing to take a risk and dig around? As I said, I'm paying."

Jerry forced down a bite of sandwich. He took another drag from his straw and cleared his throat. "No, I don't have a name. No, I wouldn't give you one if I did. And, before you ask, no, I'm not going to start asking around."

"I'll make it worth your while as well."

"Are you listening to me? It's a federal crime to reveal an anonymous jury. If you want the information, you need a case number and a court order. Roll the dice there. I mean, there is no reasonable way for me to explain why I'm poking around on a topic I have no business being involved with. In my position, asking about an anonymous jury list would send red rocket flares, not red flags, red rocket flares shooting through the air."

"Red rocket flares?"

"Big ass red flares. Like the Fourth of July."

Dan turned away and glanced at the traffic on the street outside the window. His hand found its way into his sandwich bag and he unwrapped his roast beef sub without looking.

Jerry tried to finish his tuna sandwich in successive quick mouthfuls.

Swallowing the end of his lunch, he spoke again. "Let me ask a question, Dan. How do you know you're even looking for an anonymous jury?"

"Process of elimination."

"What do you mean?"

"I know someone received payment for serving on a jury, but there is no record of that person ever serving on a jury. Process of elimination."

"So you know who this person is?"

"Yes."

"Why don't you just ask him or her what the case was?"

"Because he's dead."

"Why am I not surprised? If they're dead, who's paying you for this?"

"Are you asking who my client is?"

"Well, yeah. You're asking me to break the law."

"A congressman's wife."

Jerry let a nervous laugh escape his lips. "Why don't you ask her?"

"Because she has a problem with telling the truth."

"No offense, Dan, but this is where I get off this bus. This conversation is over and it never happened. Come find me when you have something that's not going to end with me moving to Alaska."

Jerry stood from his seat and stuck out his hand. Dan shook it, still seated.

"Sorry I couldn't help you this time around."

"I'll work it out."

"I have no doubt."

Dan watched as Jerry passed the long line of people standing at the sandwich bar. Three large bailiffs from the court stepped into the sandwich shop in full uniform. Before Jerry reached the door, he paused, looked at the bailiffs, and then turned around and came back to the table where Dan was still sitting. He slipped back into the chair he had just vacated and dropped his voice to a whisper.

"The three guys who just came in gave me an idea."

"The bailiffs?"

"Yep. You have a picture of this dead juror of yours? The one you suspect was on an anonymous jury."

"I can get one."

"Well, it may be a shot in the dark, but if you're talking about an anonymous jury, there is a chance someone may remember the case without remembering the case number. There are a lot of people in the courtroom during a trial. Even during an anonymous jury trial. You have judges, lawyers, bailiffs, court reporters. Hell, there's probably even a janitor or two who may have seen something."

"You have someone specific in mind?"

"No, not really. You're the private detective. You figure it out."

Dan looked over at the bailiffs.

"And that is free of charge. I will roll it into the price of the next job," Jerry said, heading towards the door again.

*

An hour later, Dan stepped up to the front door of the art gallery on the first floor of his two-story brick building in Old Town. The small bell attached to the top of the door jingled as the door swung open, beckoning the resident artist from the rear of the shop. Lucia stepped into the showroom, her smock covered in a plethora of colors.

"Dan, how are you?"

"I'm good. You?"

"Good enough."

"No date tonight?"

"Tomorrow."

"How are things going with the new guy?"

"Fingers crossed, I'm quietly hopeful."

"As am I. He seems like a nice guy. Relatively truthful."

"You didn't…"

"I just poked around a little. You know I can't help myself…"

"I asked you to leave him alone."

"Actually, you asked me to let you know if he was a felon. He wasn't, so I didn't mention it."

Lucia stared at her landlord for a long minute. "You got me there."

"I need a favor. You can say no, but I'm hoping you won't. I wanted to ask your boyfriend if he would take a look at the photos of some people. See if he recognizes anyone in the photos. Maybe have him send the photos around to his friends. People who work the courts."

"Courtroom artists?"

"He said he knows everyone in the art sketch world, let's see who he knows."

"I'll ask, Dan. But I can't guarantee you'll get an answer. And if you don't like the answer, you're going to have to drop it. Go somewhere else. Find another way for whatever it is you're after."

Dan pulled a thumb drive from his pocket. "Your computer or mine?"

"Am I that predictable?"

"Not at all. I'm just that charming."

"No you're not."

Dan jiggled the thumb drive in the air.

Lucia wiped her hands on her apron and motioned for Dan to sit behind the large stone desk. She slid into the leather chair and inserted the thumb drive. Seconds later the screen filled with several photos.

"What are these?"

"Driver's license photos. Photos from a military ID. Stuff from the web. Facebook. Whatever I could get."

"What are they involved in?"

"Dying."

"That's enough information for me." Lucia's eyes danced across the screen again, scrolling from picture to picture.

"You don't recognize any of them?" Dan asked.

Lucia's attention floated from Sherry Wellington, Marcus, the EPA lawyer, and Carla the waitress.

"This woman looks familiar," Lucia said, pointing at a good-looking blond.

"Let's hope your boyfriend or one of his artist colleagues also recognizes her."

Lucia finished looking at the other photos on the screen. "The rest of them I have never seen before."

"That's okay. I only need someone to remember one face."

"Okay. I'll send it."

"And can you call him after you send it and ask him to check his email?"

"You're pushing it."

"I'll owe you one."

"You're damn right you will."

CHAPTER 46

DAN KNOCKED ON the door with a pink stuffed bunny under his arm. He watched as the light through the peephole momentarily vanished and then reappeared. Seconds later the door swung open.

Amy Conboy smiled and Dan noted the weight loss since he had last seen her.

"I brought your daughter a gift," Dan said, extending the pink bunny.

Amy's daughter poked her head over the arm of the sofa and then disappeared back into the cushions.

"Come in," Amy replied. "Can I get you something to drink?"

"Sure. Whatever you have. Coffee, tea, water."

"The coffee was made a couple hours ago, but I can warm it up."

"That works for me. I don't consider coffee old until it has sat in the pot at least two nights."

Dan watched as Amy stepped into the tiny kitchen of the small apartment. She moved slower than he remembered, every step measured, labored. He could see the bones of her arms clearly, her elbows protruding like weapons. His eyes fell to her overly large sweatpants and then dropped further to her ankles.

"How is the home detention monitor?" Dan asked. "You can't see it, for what that's worth."

Amy paused and pulled up the bottom of her pants leg, revealing the black square monitor attached to her left ankle. "It's fine. It's the least of my worries. I'm home with my daughter. That's all that counts."

"I'm glad it worked out."

"It's as good as it gets," Amy said, topping off the coffee mug. She put the mug into the microwave and hit the start button.

"Can I ask a hard question?" Dan asked.

"At this point, no question is that hard."

"Was it worth it?"

"Worth what?"

"The risk."

"It was a calculated risk."

"It could have easily turned out worse than it did."

"Perhaps."

"Anything could have happened. You could have tripped on the way out of the bank. A security guard could have been itching to try out his service weapon."

"You mean I could have been killed?" Amy responded with mock concern, her mouth open.

"Yes," Dan replied, his train of thought coming off the rails with the realization his client had already considered the worst-case scenario.

"I'm already dead, remember? The threat of being killed isn't that daunting."

"No, I guess not," Dan replied. "There is something else I can't figure out."

"What's that?"

"What were you planning to do with the money? You must have had a plan. You must know that when you die, you can't just leave fifty thousand dollars in cash in a suitcase for your daughter. Someone will ask questions. The IRS will want its share."

Amy exhaled with a pronounced wheeze. "I was wondering when you were going to ask that question."

"You were?"

"You wouldn't be much of a lawyer if you didn't. Let me answer your question with another question. What would *you* do with the money? But before you answer, ask yourself that question as if you were a person without means. Without the financial options available to people who do have money. Imagine you don't know anyone who can send the money through a bank in the Caribbean or hide it in a legitimate business venture."

Dan thought about his client's situation for a moment before answering.

"If I had to hide fifty thousand dollars, I would buy a shitload of lottery tickets and hope for the best. If you win, at least you would have an explanation for where the money came from."

"Close," Amy replied, stepping away from the refrigerator to reveal a smattering of artwork, papers, and messages attached to the refrigerator door with dozens of magnets. She waved her hand in front of the room's largest appliance. "Let me know when you figure it out," Amy said, smirking with a painful expression on her face. As Dan's eyes danced around the overloaded door and the myriad objects, Amy removed the coffee mug from the microwave and placed it on the counter.

Dan's eyes stopped moving and came to rest on the promotional poster attached to the middle of the refrigerator door. He leaned over and pulled the poster from the magnetic clip that kept it in place. He held it at chin-level and digested the photograph. The shiny new hotel in the photo was not immediately recognizable, but when Dan's eyes reached the large statue of a face and arm emerging from the sand on the beach in front of the new hotel, he realized what he was holding.

"You work in the Westin at the National Harbor," Dan said, a picture in his mind clearing from the mist.

"That's right. And what's the biggest draw at the harbor?"

Dan's eyebrows rose slightly. "The new casino."

"Very good, Counselor. The casino. I prefer a mix of blackjack and roulette. I did all right for myself."

Dan reached for his coffee as he processed what his client had just told him. With a grip on the handle of the mug, he paused and slowly looked over at Amy. "What do you mean, 'you did all right'? You haven't been out of police custody since the day you robbed the bank. You were arrested, processed, spent one night in jail, and then a couple of days at GW Hospital under police supervision."

Amy shrugged her shoulders and pushed a small jar across the kitchen counter in Dan's direction. "Do you take milk or sugar?"

Dan stared in disbelief at the offer for coffee condiments. "I think we need to talk."

"About what, Counselor? Your job is done."

"I don't think it is."

Amy patted Dan on the shoulder. "It's done. From here on out, no one can help me."

"Don't count on it."

"Not with this."

"Give me a try."

Amy mulled the offer for a long second, her hand tracing one of her daughter's pieces of artwork on the fridge door. She wiped away a tear as it ran down her cheek and then looked over at her daughter on the sofa. "Let me put my daughter to bed. Grab a seat. The TV works but I don't have cable so you'll have to deal with whatever is on."

*

A half-hour later Amy shut the door to the bedroom she shared with her daughter. She turned off the small hallway light, stepped across the living room, and fell onto the sofa before wrapping herself around one of the large cushions. Dan finished his now-cold coffee and placed the mug on the small table in the corner.

"Sorry it took so long. Sometimes getting her to bed can be difficult."

"No problem. It gave me time to think," Dan said.

"What did you think about?"

"I was thinking about how many other banks you've robbed, in addition to the one I know about."

Amy stared stoically at Dan before she looked away, her gaze facing the darkness of the small hallway. "Just one," she said, her voice distant.

"Where?"

Amy answered. "Not far from Manassas, Virginia."

"A different jurisdiction from DC."

"That's right."

"Disguise?"

"The authorities will be looking for a man."

"Smart girl," Dan said. "Crazy, but smart."

"You know most bank robberies are never solved," Amy said.

"And sometimes they are, which is how we met."

"I don't need to be reminded."

Dan sighed and rubbed his hands across the stubble on his jawline. "How much did you get away with?"

"Just over sixty grand. Allegedly," Amy admitted.

"'Allegedly' just disappeared in the rearview mirror."

"Attorney-client privilege. I'm starting to enjoy it."

"And I'm enjoying it less," Dan said, forcing a smile. "So you took the bank in Manassas for sixty thousand. Plus the fifty thousand from the BB&T downtown."

"Yes. A hundred and ten thousand dollars. Two banks. And I was only busted for one of those. A fifty percent success rate."

Dan let the seriousness of the felonious admission sink in for a moment before formulating his next question.

"Was the plan to rob a few banks, play some poker and roulette, and hope you won?"

"All I needed was a little luck. If I won, the casino could cut me a check, the IRS could take their share, and no one would know any better."

"There are a lot of people who think they're going to get lucky at the casino. It's what keeps them in business."

"I was different."

"Why's that?"

"Because lady luck fucking *owed* me."

"Did she?"

"Yes she did."

"Did she pay up?

"I doubled the money from the first bank robbery in a weekend. In my third hour at the roulette wheel I hit on red seven, which pays thirty-six to one. I took that money to the blackjack table."

"And…"

"I doubled it over another six hours."

"You are incredibly lucky."

"Really? I think maybe, just maybe, the universe tried to break even with me."

Dan nodded.

"I could have won a lot more. A lot more. I was trying not to raise suspicion. But if I had started with twenty or thirty thousand dollars the night I won, I could have walked away a millionaire."

"But if you started with twenty thousand dollars, people would have noticed. Hotel maids don't carry around twenty thousand dollars in cash."

"That's right."

"So what did you do with the money?"

Amy didn't respond.

"What did you do with the money? The police searched this place when you were arrested for the BB&T robbery. I didn't hear anything about them finding cash."

"Because it's not in the apartment."

"Where is it?"

"Now is not the time."

"Did you keep the receipt when you cashed in your chips at the casino?"

"I did."

"And it has a date and time stamp on it."

"It does."

"Well, if the police never make a connection to you and the bank robbery in Manassas, your money has been successfully laundered."

"And what happens then? When I die, and you turn into a lawyer again, I don't think the authorities are going to let me keep the money from the casino."

"I wasn't planning on telling them."

"Not while I'm alive."

"By law, I can't tell them. Even after you have passed."

"You are one curious man, Counselor."

"Do you want your daughter to have the money?"

"That was my goal."

"Then you're going to have to tell me where the money is. I'll handle the rest."

"You would do that?"

"With some help," Dan said, plotting his next move. "But the deal is off if they connect you to the other bank robbery."

"They're going to have to hurry."

"You know something I don't?"

"I know what all my doctors know. In all likelihood, in a couple of weeks

I'll be incapacitated. Medicated up to my eyeballs. Unable to recognize my daughter. Bed-ridden in the quiet corner of a hospice somewhere. And that is if I'm lucky."

"More the reason to tell me where the money is. As your attorney, I'll see to it that your daughter receives it."

"I'll think about it. As of now, only two people know the money even exists—you and me."

"You know what they say. 'The only way two people can keep a secret is if one of them is dead.'"

Amy smiled. "Don't rush me."

Dan tried to return the smile and failed. "When did you decide to become a bank robber? It's not the logical criminal choice for someone who works in housekeeping at a hotel."

"Let's just say I was offered a lot of money to do something for someone else. A lot of money to do something illegal."

"And... ?"

"I turned down the job offer. But the idea stuck with me. I couldn't get it out of my head. After a few sleepless nights I figured, what the hell? What's the downside? So I considered my options, did a little research on the computer at the public library, and figured robbing a bank was as good a choice as any. I pulled the trigger a few days later."

"Did this job offer you receive have anything to do with the man in the cap and sunglasses?"

Amy looked Dan squarely in the face. "I never said I knew the man in the cap and sunglasses, and I still don't."

"Okay, Amy. Okay."

"I think it's time you left."

"I had a few more questions."

"Not tonight, Counselor. I've had enough questions for one evening."

"Fair enough. How about I come back tomorrow? Check in on you?"

"Call first."

"I can do that."

"And thanks for the pink bunny."

CHAPTER 47

AMY DRIED HERSELF off in the shower and then wiped the humidity off the bathroom mirror over the small sink. She didn't recognize her own reflection. She ran her hand along her jawline, feeling her cheekbone. Her eyes seemed more sunken, more distant than even the day before. She removed the towel from her body and stared for a moment at her cancer-ravished torso. Her natural curves had been replaced with the muscle tone of a skeleton. She turned slightly in the mirror and peeked down at her bone-thin derriere. For all the times she had wanted to shave a couple of pounds off her butt, her wish was now fulfilled.

Finished with depressing herself for the evening, she slipped on another pair of large sweatpants and an equally oversized sweatshirt. She hung the bath towel on a hook on the back of the door and stepped into the hallway.

With the thought of a glass of wine dancing through her head, Amy stepped into the kitchen and poured herself a glass of water instead. Pancreatic cancer and wine only caused pain. Pain she could avoid. When she turned towards the living room, a muscular hand fell across her mouth. She could feel the strength in the arm, the power almost lifting her off her feet.

"Do you know who this is?" the voice behind the hand asked.

Amy dropped the glass in her hand and it shattered on the floor.

"I asked if you know who this is?" the voice repeated.

Amy nodded her head.

"Good. Then you know you'll have to be quiet when I take my hand off your mouth. Is that understood?"

Amy nodded again.

The man slowly removed his hand from Amy's face. "Be careful," he said. "You aren't wearing any shoes and glass is everywhere."

Amy stared down at her feet and then her eyes rose to meet the man she had seen once, in the back seat of her car. He was now in her home. In her kitchen. The cap and glasses were unchanged and Amy again realized how little effort was necessary to hide one's identity.

"My daughter…" Amy said, her mind in a new panic.

"She is unharmed and asleep."

"I need to see."

"After you," he said. "Watch your feet. Take a big step onto the carpet."

Amy avoided the broken glass and seconds later peaked into the bedroom she shared with her daughter. She could feel the man in cap and glasses behind her. His breath on her neck.

"Now do you see? I am a man of my word," he said. "It is time we talked."

*

Amy was in the same recliner that Dan had been sitting in an hour before. The man was on the edge of the sofa, a pistol in his left hand.

"What do you want?" Amy asked. "I declined your offer. I followed your rules. I never mentioned you to anyone. I never discussed our conversation with anyone."

"I originally came here tonight to discuss business. I came here to make you another offer," he replied. "The amount of money I could have paid you for your help had doubled."

"Has the task changed, or are we still talking about murder?"

"The job has not changed."

"Then I will have to decline your new offer. My decision wasn't based purely on the money."

"I'm glad you feel that way because I'm no longer offering the money."

"Then I guess this conversation is over."

"Not until I get some answers."

Amy's thoughts turned towards her ankle monitor and her pulse increased. "We have nothing further to discuss."

"Oh, but we do. I want to know what business you had with the man who left your apartment earlier."

"Have you been watching me?"

"I wanted to contact you, but I needed to be sure you were alone."

"I'm alone now."

"I know. Tell me about the man who was here. I know he's a lawyer. I know he's a private detective. What I don't know is what he was doing here."

"I hired him to help me prepare my will. To do a trust."

"No offense, Amy, my dear, but what does a woman of your means need with a trust?"

"Everyone can use a will."

"And you said 'trust.'"

"I meant will."

"How did you meet him?" the man asked, peering towards Amy as if the lenses of his sunglasses would spot a lie as it was delivered.

"I found one of his business cards at work. At the hotel. I called it."

The man caressed the gun with his right hand as if it were a pet. "Are you aware that I have met this man before? In fact, I believe he's looking for me."

"Well, if he's looking for you, he obviously doesn't know where to find you. If he did, he would be here with the both of us."

"The *three* of us," he corrected. "We cannot forget your little girl."

Amy swallowed hard.

"It is time for a new set of rules," he said plainly.

"I declined your offer before. I have declined your offer again."

"As I said. It is no longer an offer. It is an order."

"Or what?"

"Or your daughter will be dead before you are."

Amy wiped her suddenly moist cheeks involuntarily. "I don't want to kill anyone."

Angel grunted. "You are in luck."

"I've decided there is no such thing."

"Of course there is. And you are in it, Amy. You're in luck. You won't have to kill anyone. All you have to do is be on time and follow precise instructions."

CHAPTER 48

D AN STEPPED INTO the cozy expanse of Tryst, the multi-faceted coffee shop turned restaurant turned bar in Adams Morgan. He nodded at the young man sitting on a stool near the door then scanned the floor and noted the exits. A sea of sofas and coffee tables filled the establishment. Booze flowed from a counter on the left. Desserts and coffee were doled out from the rear.

Dan moved deeper into the room and saw Lucia waving her hand from the back right corner. Dan returned a quick wave and weaved through the crowd. He arrived at three large sofas nestled around a wooden table and gave Lucia an air kiss in the direction of her cheek. Lucia's artist boyfriend, Buddy, stood and extended his hand.

"How's the shoulder blade injury?"

"Better," Dan replied. "But the gunshot wound to the chest still hurts like hell."

Buddy retracted his hand and cocked his head to the side.

A second man in a *Where's Waldo* sweater stood and shook Dan's hand. "Nice to meet you."

"Thanks for coming."

"You're welcome."

"Interesting place," Dan said.

"You haven't been here before?" Lucia asked.

"Nope. Knew it was here, but have never been in."

"It has a little bit of everything. Coffee, wine, beer, food, dessert. All rolled into one. It's popular with everyone."

"One of those places where you can tie one on in the evening and return the following morning to get you through the hangover with coffee and biscuits," Buddy added.

"Been there," Waldo said, raising his hand.

The waitress arrived and Dan ordered a Smithwick's.

Waldo leaned forward and placed on the table one of the photos that Lucia had sent in an email on Dan's behalf. Staring up from the top photo was the face of Sherry Wellington.

"I recognize your girl," Waldo said.

"You do?" Dan looked around the table. Lucia and her boyfriend nodded and smiled, as if glad to be part of the sleuthing. "Are you sure?"

Waldo looked Dan in the eyes. "Uh, yeah. She's a congressman's wife. She's been in the papers. And she's gorgeous."

Dan could feel his heart rate increase. The adrenaline that arrived with the precipice of finally shedding light on the unknown was the true addiction of his job. "She's unforgettable for a lot of reasons," Dan admitted. "Please tell me you remember the case she served on jury duty for."

"Like it was yesterday. August, seven years ago. Hotter than hell. The weather was hot. The case was hot. The congressman's wife was hot. Though she wasn't married at the time."

"Why was the case hot?"

"A couple of reasons. The defendant was a big-time gangster charged with six murders. The jury was anonymous. To top that off, me and a couple other court artists got hammered by the judge on this case."

"How's that?"

"As you may or may not know, an anonymous jury means cameras are banned. At the time, there was some gray area when it came to courtroom illustrations."

"You weren't allowed to draw?"

"Technically, yes and no. Drawing in the courtroom was banned. *I* wasn't banned. I was able to attend the proceedings."

"I don't follow."

"They told me I couldn't draw *in* the courtroom."

Dan's eyes widened slightly. "Aaah. You sketched outside of the court-room. And that's what got you into trouble with the judge."

"Exactly right."

"How did you do it? Did you draw in the bathroom during breaks?"

"God, no. That's nasty. Those are public city restrooms. I sketched what I saw after I got home."

Dan leaned back into the large sofa and the waitress stooped over his shoulder and delivered his beer. "That is one hell of a memory."

"We can all do it," Waldo said plainly. "Most of us, anyway."

Dan looked over at Lucia' boyfriend, Buddy, who again nodded in agreement. "Some of us are better than others."

"Did you keep any of your drawings from that trial?"

"I did. I kept the originals of everything. Copies of the drawings were actually entered into evidence in a subsequent first amendment infringe-ment suit filed by a bunch of court sketch artists."

"What was the trial, exactly?"

"A drug dealer by the name of Tyrone Biggs. He and his posse were in Club H2O, down on the Waterfront, now called the Wharf. The club isn't there anymore. There was a whole strip of late night joints down there along the marina before the developers came in and built condos. Anyhow, Tyrone Biggs was charged with six murders and a list of ancillary charges that ran a couple of pages. The story, as it goes, is that Tyrone Biggs and his posse had a disagreement with another group of young men at the club. Things escalated and the guns came out. Six people were killed, all of them bystanders. Four of them were rich white kids from the suburbs. Another ten people were shot and survived. Dozens were injured in the ensuing stampede. But in the end, Tyrone Biggs walked. The jury found the attorneys couldn't prove he had fired the shots. Something like seventy shots fired inside the establishment and another handful outside. Some of the shooting was caught on video."

"It sounds vaguely familiar. You say he walked?"

"Biggs walked."

"The jury found him innocent?"

"I think, more accurately, the jury refused to find him guilty. Tyrone Biggs was a scary ass dude. Gave me chills, and I was just watching. He spent most of the trial staring at the jurors. The judge intervened a couple of times to have words with the defendant, telling him to tone down the attitude. But Tyrone's lawyers were quoting legalese about the right to face your accusers. He was looking at the possibility of life in prison after all."

"And you attended the whole trial?"

"All of it."

"Anything else about the case worth mentioning?"

"There were a lot of witnesses. But that's probably par for the course when you're talking about a shooting at a night club. I think everyone was glad when it was over."

"I can't take it anymore!" Lucia suddenly interjected. "Show him the drawings."

Waldo smiled, reached over the arm of the sofa, and pulled out a large cylindrical cardboard box. "You want to take a peek?"

*

The phone on the nightstand vibrated counterclockwise until it came to rest against the fully locked and loaded Glock.

"You up?" Dan asked.

"Nope," Wallace answered.

"I got the case."

Wallace pulled himself upright and looked over at his sleeping wife.

"Sherry Wellington, Marcus Losh, Carla the waitress, and the EPA lawyer all served on the same jury. The trial was for a guy named Tyrone Biggs."

"Tyrone Biggs…" Wallace replied, his groggy voice trailing off. "Well, I'll be damned."

"Be damned all you want, but tell me you know where I can find this guy."

"I know exactly where to find him."

"I'm all ears."

"He's in an urn on his mother's mantle."

"That is not a positive development."

"Depends on who you ask."

"I'm going to need everything you have on the Club H2O trial. All the files. All the court documents that can be pulled. I'll be at the station first thing in the morning."

"I'll make a call and have someone start gathering whatever is there."

CHAPTER 49

D AN CHECKED IN at the District Two Headquarters' entrance and the same officer from his previous visit smiled and pushed the sign-in clipboard under the edge of the bulletproof glass.

"You're here for Wallace, right?"

"Wallace and Fields."

"You dragged them in early. They're expecting you, but judging from what I overheard when they came in, they might not have anything nice to say."

The officer behind the glass motioned for Dan to pass through the metal detector.

Dan gathered his items from the end of the short conveyor belt and disappeared up the stairs with his cylindrical box of drawings. Detective Wallace met Dan at the top of the stairs and motioned towards the far corner of the robbery and homicide division.

The whiteboard in the corner of the floor near Wallace's desk was the nerve center of the sniper, waitress-pusher, bank robber trifecta, as designated by the uneven letters that stretched across the top of the board. Various photos were taped to the whiteboard. Black lines connected some pictures. Green and red encircled others. The haphazard display of evidence offered no clues to anything definite, other than poor penmanship.

The table in front of the whiteboard was stacked with folders. An empty bag of potato chips rested on the corner, threatening to fall onto the floor. Emily arrived at the table a moment later with a cup of coffee in hand.

"Glad we could all be so punctual," she said sarcastically.

"This is going to be good, isn't it, Dan?" Wallace asked, hopefully.

"It is." Dan unfurled the sketches on the table and arranged them in no particular order. "Can I get a drumroll?"

"No," Wallace said as he sat down.

Emily put her coffee on the table and began tapping her fingers. Dan acknowledged the drumroll with a nod of his head. Looking at Emily, he spoke. "You were right about the jury."

"Do I get a prize?"

"Depends on how the rest of the case goes," Dan said, motioning towards the drawings on the crowded table. "Everyone grab a sketch and take a look."

Wallace grabbed the nearest drawing and stared at the faces in the sketch. "Well, I'll be damned. You have drawings of all the jurors from the Tyrone Biggs trial," Wallace said.

"That's right. See anyone you recognize?"

"Carla the waitress is in the front row on the left." Wallace said.

"That's one."

"And Sherry Wellington is behind her," Wallace added.

"Very good, Detective. That's two."

"The EPA lawyer is in the middle. Two down from Sherry," Emily chimed in.

"Winner, winner, chicken dinner for the new detective."

"Who are the rest?" Emily asked.

"The guy at the other end of the front row is a man named Marcus Losh. Also known as Sherry Wellington's baby daddy."

"That's four," Wallace said.

"It looks like the Unabomber is in the back row. Long-haired hippy with a beard," Emily added.

"Not sure how the attorneys let him through," Dan replied.

"So how did we miss the ones we know?" Emily asked. "You and I both searched through the jury database."

"You can search PACER all day and you aren't going to find anything if it's an anonymous jury."

"Do we know who the other eight jurors are?" she asked.

"Not yet. Four is all we know and we only know them because we recognize their faces. We're going to need a court order for the names of the rest."

"Who was Tyrone Biggs and what was the trial?" Emily asked.

Dan motioned for Detective Wallace to provide the necessary background.

"Tyrone Biggs," Wallace replied. "Also known as Biggy Biggs. Sometimes T-Biggs."

"And I'm guessing he's the person Carla's sister referred to as T-Daddy," Dan said.

"Maybe. All these criminals change their names over time. Kill a few people, add an alias. Take over new turf, give yourself a better title."

"What was the case?" Emily repeated.

"A street thug that walked on six murders, though he probably was responsible for ten times that amount in his life. In this particular case, he was on trial for a good old-fashioned shootout at Club H2O. Six bystanders killed. Four of them were rich white kids from Potomac. Shot standing in line for the toilet," Wallace explained.

"Rich white kids slumming it in the clubs along the old Waterfront," Dan added.

"We did it a few times when I was younger," Emily confirmed. "If you want to dance and stay out late, DC is where you come. Bars close earlier in Virginia and Maryland, and they don't have any decent places to dance."

"She's right," Wallace replied. "The good dance clubs now are near Dupont and U Street, but some of them used to be down on the Waterfront."

There was a momentary pause in the conversation before Emily asked the next question. "So we have six bystanders killed. Four of them kids from the suburbs. And the guy walked?"

"Yes. On that one. He ended up in prison a couple years later on a drug charge. Did over a year and was released early for good behavior, of all things. Not too long after he was released, he was shot in front of his mother's house in Anacostia."

Emily looked at Wallace and then turned her eyes towards Dan. "So much for the theory of the angry gang-banger killing jurors because they put him behind bars. This guy was found innocent in the H2O trial. Hard to find motive there."

"That's why I asked for the H2O case files," Dan said.

Wallace pointed to a stack of legal boxes near the far end of the table. "Those boxes over there are everything we have on the H2O trial."

"I guess I have my work for the day." Dan said, approaching the leaning tower of boxes.

"I can help you go through them," Emily offered.

"Why don't you start putting together a list of people interested in the Tyrone Biggs trial who weren't jurors," Wallace suggested.

"As potential suspects?" Emily asked.

Dan nodded. "If Tyrone did kill six people and he was found innocent, that means six people were killed without justice. That may be enough motive for someone to want Tyrone dead. Six people with fathers, mothers, brothers, sisters, husbands, wives, boyfriends, girlfriends, buddies. You name it. Most of the witnesses and the names of the deceased should be included in the transcripts and on the witness lists. Only the juror information is anonymous. Dig around and see what you can find. Who knows, maybe there's a connection to our guy with the cap and sunglasses."

"I'll get started," Emily responded.

"We need names, bios, photos," Wallace added, thinking out loud. "Create a dossier for everyone who was a witness at the trial or is a relative of the deceased. And take a good look at the rich kids. Let's make sure we aren't just assuming they're rich because they're white kids from the suburbs. Let's get a handle on how much money we're talking about."

"We also need to let any surviving jurors know their lives could be in danger. Let the ones who still have their heads know that they may want to keep them down. We need to know who they are and how to reach them, and that's going to require a court order to see the anonymous juror list," Dan said.

"How long will a court order take?" Emily asked.

"It all depends," Dan answered. "Should be less than twenty-four hours. Could be a couple of days. Depends on who is involved. First someone needs to locate the judge. Then we are going to need the judge to approve the order. Then someone is going to need to locate the physical records. A source told me that information on anonymous juries can be hard to come by."

"Let me talk to the Captain and get the ball rolling," Wallace said, looking in Dan's direction. "But just so you know, two court requests in one week with your name attached is pushing my luck."

"While I'm pushing my luck, can I get a copy of the police file on Tyrone's shooting?"

"You want the files for Tyrone's murder?"

"That's right. I want to take a look at it."

"You think the same person who is killing jurors could have killed Tyrone?"

"It seems like a possibility."

"I can get you that file in a few minutes." Detective Wallace stood and then motioned at the stack of boxes. "Start reading."

*

Dan placed the top of the first box on the floor and opened the top folder. He sat down, perused the first page and then began flipping pages at a brisk pace.

An hour later Emily succumbed to curiosity. "Are you reading, or skimming?"

"Reading," Dan answered without looking up.

"You look like you took one of those speed reading courses you see on late night television."

"Just spent a lot of time without good television when I was growing up."

"Where exactly did you grow up?"

"Africa, Southeast Asia, Russia."

"Army brat?"

"Foreign Service."

"It must have been fascinating."

Dan stopped reading and raised his head. "It had its moments. Some of those memories have since been tarnished by reality, but it was a good way to learn about the world."

"So you read a lot?"

"A lot," Dan answered, his eyes dropping back to the folder in front of him.

"Well, I can't read without a break. I'm going to get some more coffee. You want some?"

"No thanks. I'm good."

Emily stood and stepped away from the table. Dan allowed his eyes another momentary break from reading; just long enough to check out Fields' derriere as it moved through the maze of desks. Five minutes later, Emily returned with a file in her hand. "Detective Wallace gave me the police file on Tyrone Biggs's murder. It remains unsolved."

Dan took the folder and read it while standing, flipping pages. Minutes later Dan stopped turning pages in the file. He returned to the previous page, flipped forward again, and then reread the passage that initially gave him pause. He grabbed a yellow legal pad, placed it next to the open folder, and then jotted several notes on the top yellow sheet.

"I'm going to check on something," he said, without breaking pace, heading for the door.

"Want some company?"

"Absolutely not. I'll do better without the police."

"No offense taken, in case you were wondering."

"I wasn't."

"What do you want me to tell Wallace when he gets back?"

"Tell him to hurry up with the court order. We need the jury list."

CHAPTER 50

D AN DROVE HIS four-door sedan down the street with his head on a swivel. He could feel his .45 caliber in the back of his waistband, pressed snugly between the weight of his body and the bucket seat. He also felt the slight gravitational tug of the .38 revolver strapped to his right ankle.

Dan glanced at the address on the Post-It Note stuck to the dash of the car and slowed to read the house number over the door of an old brick building with boarded up windows. The next block sported the skeletal remains of a gas station vaguely recognizable amidst the rust-covered piles of metal and abandoned appliances. Across the street, a high chain-link fence surrounded an empty lot on the corner.

A minute later, Dan pulled to the curb in front of an old wood house. A covered porch stretched the width of the home. Metal bars secured two symmetrical windows. A gate reinforced the front door.

Dan stepped from the car and eyed the small apartment building next door. A dilapidated fire escape dripped down the side of the building, tilting away from the structure as if testing gravity. Freshly laundered clothes, clipped to the fire escape, flapped in a gentle breeze on the upper floors. As Dan's eyes reached the first floor, the face of an old man disappeared behind a set of moving curtains.

Dan returned his eyes to the old house and he approached the porch. At the top of the stairs, Dan could feel the old boards bounce slightly under his weight. The aged wood squeaked and groaned, rusted nails threatening to release their anchors.

Dan knocked on the front door and took another look to his left and right. Movement echoed from the other side of the door. A thud. A flushing toilet. The clanking of glass and metal. Dan knocked again and the light coming through the peephole in the door went dark, indicating someone was peeking out.

"I'm looking for Ernest Biggs," Dan said.

"Who are you?"

"Dan Lord. I'm an attorney."

"We don't need an attorney."

"I wanted to ask you a couple of questions about your brother's death."

A long silence followed, interrupted by the rattling of locks and chains. The internal wood door swung open and a twenty-something young man in a burgundy collared shirt and khaki pants stood on the other side of the heavily barred security door. "Step back. I'll come out and we can talk on the porch. I don't want anyone thinking I'm hiding anything or talking to a cop."

Dan moved over and Ernest Biggs stepped from the house, the front door hinges squeaking in protest. The security door slammed shut with a resounding thud. Dan extended his hand and the young man just stared at the gesture, Dan's hand, frozen in the air, waist high.

"Name is Dan Lord," Dan repeated. "I'm an attorney and a private detective."

"You helping to catch my brother's killer?"

"Maybe."

"You know the cops didn't do shit."

"That's what I want to know. What do you mean? Talk to me."

"I mean when my brother was killed, the cops didn't spend but ten minutes out here investigating. They asked a few questions to some witnesses and they took a couple of pictures, and that was it. The sidewalk was hosed off before my brother's body reached the hospital."

"Sorry for your loss."

"You ever lost a brother?"

"Well, yeah. A few years ago."

Ernest Biggs stared at Dan and slowly nodded his head. "Nice to meet you, Dan. Ernest Biggs."

"Nice to meet you, Ernest. What can you tell me about the night your brother was killed?"

"Are you familiar with the case?"

"I know what's written in the police report. I read it for the first time this morning."

"Then you might know all you're ever going to know. Tyrone is dead. Shot point blank. Right over there." Ernest pointed to a spot in the middle of the sidewalk thirty feet away. "Been dead for two years. Two years last October."

"And they never found the killer," Dan Lord said.

"The cops? Hell no. Nothing unusual around here. We know how it works. Most of the time, no one's even trying to solve a murder in this neighborhood. The cops show up and pose for a little investigating. They bang on a couple doors, take a couple of notes, and then move on to the crimes people care about. Our little corner of paradise known as Anacostia isn't on the police's give-a-shit list."

"You have any idea who killed him? Anything new come to mind in the last couple of years? Anyone bragging about something they might have done?"

"Shit. I don't know nothing for sure. Everybody's got an opinion. Lots of chatter on the street for a while. Tyrone had big business and big business comes with big risks. So if you ask me who killed him, I say business gone bad killed him. Could have been something else too. Jealous friends. Jealous women. The reason don't matter because there isn't always a reason. You can be sitting on your porch and catch one from a car driving down the street. Get a bullet in the back just walking down the sidewalk, minding your own business. The bullets don't care and the people shooting them don't care either."

"How old were you when Tyrone was killed?"

"I was in high school. Senior year. Graduated, too. Didn't get me far, though. I still live here with my momma. Got a government job doing maintenance work at the Department of Education. Work evenings mostly. Trying to stay right-side up. It's hard. In this neighborhood, it's real hard."

"So nothing new from anyone remembering anything?"

"Nothing new. Nothing old. You said you have the police records. Detectives came out and asked around. Everyone saw something. No one saw the same thing. There was a group of boys drinking forties down the block. Shady Tree Eddy was closing up late from fixing a car at the old station three doors down."

"What about the old man next door?" Dan asked, motioning towards the face that was again pressed against the window.

"Old Man Johnson has his nose pressed to the glass all four seasons of the year."

"What did he see?"

"He says he didn't see nothing that day, but he has a theory."

"What's that?"

"He said he thinks a woman did it."

"A woman?"

"A white woman."

Dan looked around. "You sure?"

"That's what he says."

"But he didn't see anything the day of the murder?"

"That's right."

"And, yet, he still thinks a white woman shot your brother?"

"Yep."

"Is he crazy?"

"He doesn't get out much. But I haven't seen him taking a shit in the bushes, which is what the lady around the corner started doing once her dementia got real bad."

"A woman killed Tyrone?"

"Go ask him."

"What did you say his name was?"

"Old Man Johnson."

"What's his first name?"

"Don't know his first name. My momma probably does, but she isn't around. She's out at the beauty salon. Be back later."

"Anything else you can tell me?"

"My brother wasn't no saint. He was a dealer. Rap sheet down to his knees. Made a lot of money, had a lot of friends, had a lot of enemies, and was killed. That is what this neighborhood does. Produces kids with guns and bad friends who learn to rob and sell drugs."

"Did you attend your brother's trial?"

"Which one?"

"Any of them."

"For his murder, there was no trial. No suspects. Nothing. A dead drug dealer, period."

"How about the H2O trial?"

"No. My momma didn't want me to hear all of that. Even though I knew more than she did."

"Did your brother do it?"

"Shoot up the club?"

"Yes. That's my question."

"I wasn't there so I can't say for sure, but when you have something like thirty witnesses, you get the feeling he could have done it."

"And he walked."

"He walked. Yes, he did. But you know what's funny? The system likes rich white people. Doesn't like rich black people as much. Rich white guys with teams of lawyers walk all the time and no one cares. A young black man with money walks and all hell breaks loose."

"I think it has something to do with how the money is gained."

Ernest Biggs looked around. "What options do you see around you? Make money how you can make it."

*

Dan stepped into the small foyer of the apartment building next door. He ran his finger along the nametags on the bank of mailboxes for the building. Apartment A-1 was labeled "Johnson" and Dan stepped to the first door on the left and knocked twice.

"Who is it?" the voice asked through the door, feet shuffling across the floor like slow-moving sandpaper blocks.

"Dan Lord. Attorney and private detective."

"Well, which one's going to be there if I open this door?"

"Whichever one you're more willing to talk to."

Dan listened to unintelligible mumbling through the door as the neighborhood Peeping Tom considered his potential guest. Dan stepped back as the silence was broken by two dead bolts unlocking and a security chain sliding off its rails.

Old Man Johnson offered half a smile of full dentures. His white teeth were multiple shades lighter than the gray hair that covered his head. Thick brown glasses framed a pair of eyes full of suspicion as they groped Dan.

"Attorney and private detective?"

"Yes, sir," Dan answered.

"My name is Claude Johnson. You can call me Johnson. Hell, you can even call me Old Man Johnson, if you want."

"Nice to meet you, Mr. Johnson," Dan replied, pushing his hand out as the elderly man opened the door. Mr. Johnson returned the handshake.

"Well, don't just stand there heating the building, come on in."

"Thank you."

Dan stepped into the perfectly organized bachelor pad. Neat stacks of newspapers rested on the small dining table. An old chair with a knitted blanket rested in the corner, near the front window. The stifling heat forced Dan to unzip his jacket.

"Sit down. I'll make some coffee."

Ice coffee? Dan thought. "Sounds great."

Dan listened as Claude Johnson rattled and putzed around the kitchen.

"So what do you want with an old timer like me?"

"It isn't your age that interests me," Dan said.

"Well, what is it then? I know it isn't my cooking or my youthful appearance."

"You always pay attention to what's going on outside?"

"Sure. Don't you? Shouldn't everyone?"

"Maybe they should, but they don't," Dan said. "If they did, I would be out of a job pretty quickly."

"If people not paying attention covers your rent, then I guess you can't complain too much."

"Guess not. Ernest next door says you pay attention and that you have a theory on who killed Tyrone Biggs."

"I do. I do."

"You want to share?"

"Sure, but let me clear the air about something first. Tyrone got what was coming to him."

"How's that?" Dan asked.

"He was a punk. A know-nothing, do-nothing punk."

"So you didn't have fond feelings for him?"

"I didn't say that."

Dan had an inkling of where this conversation was going and he leaned back in his chair waiting to hear the rest of Old Man Johnson's pontification.

"Tyrone was a punk. And that was on a good day. But he was *our* punk. I mean, he grew up next door. When his career took off, and I use the word "career" with a snicker, he moved out and bought the house two doors down on the other side of the street. His mother didn't want drugs under her roof."

"If I were his mother, I would've asked him to move a little farther away."

"Wouldn't have mattered. Nothing was going to stop him from anything. Tyrone was dealing. Drinking. Did it all right out in the open. Stood on the corner most nights smoking, hanging with his posse. But if anyone tried anything on his turf, he dealt with it. An old man like me can appreciate a little peace."

"Tyrone was a keeper of the peace?"

"In this neighborhood, he was. Took care of business."

Dan nodded.

Johnson continued. "The more peaceful it was, the less reason the police had to come around. And Tyrone didn't need the police to run his business. He needed the *lack* of police."

"I understand where you're coming from."

"That's probably something hard to imagine if you haven't been around it."

Dan stifled the urge to tell him he had seen it before, in a dozen locations around the world.

"So he grew up next door. Did you know him well?" Dan asked.

"Of course I knew the man. I've been here since before he was born. Know his mother real well. Good woman. Real good woman."

"After Tyrone was killed, did the detectives speak with you?"

"You know it."

"Did you tell them about your theory?"

"It ain't no theory. Tyrone was killed by a woman. A white woman."

"A white woman?"

"You heard me right."

Dan took a deep breath. "A working girl?"

"You're kidding, right? A white working girl in this neighborhood?"

"Working girls work all neighborhoods and come in all colors and sizes." Old Man Johnson looked straight at Dan. "She wasn't no working girl."

"A customer?"

"That's what the police detectives thought."

"And you think different?"

"I do. Maybe I didn't see no murder, but the white woman I saw in the neighborhood wasn't buying drugs."

"How do you know?"

"Because she never stopped the car. Saw her on a few occasions driving by. Black car. Nothing unusual about the car."

"Did you see the woman's face?"

"Enough of it to tell you it was a white woman."

Dan looked at Old Man Johnson's thick glasses and surmised that his eyesight and age combined to devalue his police testimony.

"Did you see the white woman the night that Tyrone was killed?"

"No, but I saw the same car I had seen before. A black sedan."

"Did you get the tag number?"

"Nope."

"Did anyone else see the car?"

"I heard some people mention it."

"And all of this was told to the police?"

"Damn right. I told them exactly what I just told you. I saw a white woman in the neighborhood. Saw the car. Saw the same car the night Tyrone got shot."

CHAPTER 51

D AN FOLLOWED A uniformed officer back to the table near the whiteboard in the corner of the robbery and homicide division. Detective Wallace was standing at the front of the makeshift classroom, magic marker in hand. The chicken scratch from the morning had been replaced with a diagram that appeared more coherent. Previously-terminally-ill-and-now-deceased assassins on the left. Known dead jurors—the EPA lawyer, Marcus Losh, and Carla the waitress—on the right.

The table in the corner work area had also been cleared of the morning's display of documents. Stacks of papers and photos now surrounded the perimeter of the work area. A laptop sat open on an empty chair next to the printer.

"Where did *you* go?" Wallace asked.

"I went to check on a few things with the Tyrone Biggs shooting."

"You went to Anacostia?"

"Yep."

"Smart move going during the day. Generally speaking, I wouldn't go there without a partner," Wallace replied. "Back in the early nineties, standard police operations required two marked units after dark."

"Sounds great. Sorry I missed it," Emily said. "What did you learn?"

Dan rubbed his hands together and spoke. "Did you know a witness reported seeing a white woman in the area in the weeks leading up to Tyrone Biggs's murder?"

"I didn't," Wallace admitted. "But like I said, I wasn't working the case.

By the time Tyrone Biggs was killed, I had transferred to the swanky side of town. Any description from this witness beyond 'white woman'?"

"Not really."

"Well, 'white woman' isn't much to go on."

"Uh-oh, here we go again," Emily interjected. She turned towards Dan. "You are about to learn how to appropriately describe a suspect by the color of coffee."

"White is white," Dan said. "And in Anacostia, apparently, I'm not the only one who thinks so."

"Who was the witness?"

"An elderly gentleman who lives on the same block."

"How old?"

"Old enough that he probably wouldn't be a good witness, but young enough that I think he can tell the difference between a white woman and everyone else in the neighborhood."

"Noted," Wallace said.

"What did you two find out while I was gone?" Dan asked.

Emily answered. "There were over fifty witnesses at the Tyrone Biggs H2O trial. Witnesses testified for all six victims as to the impact the murders had on their friends and families. Victim impact statements. Multiple witnesses also testified to the character of the deceased."

"Did you compile a list?"

Emily motioned towards the top of the large table. "We have a list. Another long list. All the mothers, fathers, brothers, sisters, boyfriends, and girlfriends of those killed at Club H2O. We started to compile photos and dossiers for most of the witnesses and family members."

"Have we run across a photo of anyone who could be our man in the baseball cap and glasses?"

"Not yet. But there are a lot of faces to locate and go through. If we include more distant relatives of the deceased such as uncles and cousins, we are in the neighborhood of ninety names. That's on top of the list of potential suspects we got from the hospice, which is another hundred. Add all that together and we are going to need more manpower."

Dan nodded. "Let's see if we can narrow it down. What about the money angle? Which of these young victims from the H2O shooting came from the wealthiest family?"

Wallace answered. "Looks like we're splitting hairs on that front. How rich is rich? We have four wealthy families, all of them very successful. The four wealthy victims all went to high school together at the Bullis School. Very elite. Very expensive."

"How did the families make their money?"

Wallace lifted a piece of paper off the table and held it at reading distance. "We have Michael Downs, the father of Annie Downs, one of the girls killed at Club H2O. Michael Downs worked for twenty years at a defense contractor that specializes in satellite imagery. He currently serves on the board of directors for that same company and lives in Potomac. Three years ago he purchased the house where he and his wife now live for $6.5 million. Apparently it was a cash transaction."

"That would qualify as 'not poor.'"

"He owns a helicopter and has climbed three of the highest peaks in the world for sport."

"Definitely not poor."

"Number two on the list is Richard Porter. Daughter was named Natalie. Mr. Porter doesn't seem to be employed at the moment because he doesn't need to be. According to some old press releases, Mr. Porter started a couple of IT companies, which he later sold to some larger, well-known corporations. His last company specialized in facial recognition software and was sold to IBM for $90 million."

"Okay. Rich Dad number two. Next."

"The third shooting victim was named Camille Okafore. The Okafores made their money in mining. Precious metal mining in particular. They are fourth-generation miners, originally from South Africa. The amount of their wealth can only be estimated as 'a lot.' The Okafore family owns thirty thousand acres of land in Montana and another twenty thousand in Idaho."

Dan whistled.

"The last on the list is George Westing. Mr. Westing lost his daughter, Laura. Mr. Westing runs his own hedge fund. Westing Financial. You may have seen the commercials."

"I've been looking for some place to put my money."

"I'm sure I don't make enough to qualify as a client," Wallace replied. "I'm not sure the DC Police Department in its entirety makes enough to qualify."

"Does anyone from these wealthy families have a criminal background? Anyone who, on the surface, seems as if they could be involved in multiple assassinations?" Dan asked.

"Not yet," Emily answered. "But we've only been banging away at this list for a few hours. And short of someone with a military or criminal background, I'm not sure what someone who employs cancer victims as killers looks like on paper."

Dan paced around the table looking at the stack of faces and dossiers. "Did we bounce the list of family members and friends from the H2O trial and against the list of employees and volunteers from the Capital Community Hospice?"

"Of course."

"So no match?"

"Nothing. We wouldn't be here talking if there was one."

"Did you double check?"

"I double checked by hand and then I put all the names into a spreadsheet and ran a column match search. There were no names that appeared on both the list of friends and relatives of the deceased from the H2O shooting—those people with motive to kill the jurors—and the list of Capital Community Hospice employees and volunteers."

"Curious," Dan said. "Any idea where we are with the court order for the list of jurors?"

Wallace answered. "It's at the courthouse as we speak. We should have something later today. Tomorrow at the latest."

CHAPTER 52

THE CELL PHONE next to the futon on the floor vibrated against the century-old wood. Dan turned away from his laptop computer and reached for the phone, his hand brushing over his loaded handgun, twelve in the magazine, one in the chamber.

"Did I catch you napping?" Wallace asked without introducing himself.

"No. I was going through the backgrounds of the witnesses and family members from the H2O trial."

"Anything interesting?"

"Interesting, yes. Concrete, no."

"You online now?"

"I am."

"Check your inbox. I just sent you the full list of jurors."

"Same-day turnaround on the court order? That's fast."

"Someone may have mentioned the possibility that a congressman's wife was in danger."

"That would get things moving."

"Do you have the document yet?" Wallace asked.

Dan clicked his mouse. "I just opened it. Twelve names. Have you done anything with them?"

"Just got them. Your girl Sherry Wellington is on the list, under her maiden name. The waitress is there. Marcus Losh is also on the list. Ditto for the EPA lawyer."

Dan started scanning the lists, reading each name carefully.

Detective Wallace continued to talk. "First thing we're going to do is run the list through the District's Department of Motor Vehicles, get some addresses, and start making phone calls."

"What if they're dead?"

"They won't answer their phone."

Dan looked away from the list for a moment. "Does the DC DMV flag an individual when they're deceased?"

"Sometimes. Sometimes it doesn't happen for a long list of possible reasons."

"And if they aren't residents of DC? Some of them could've moved out of the city since the trial."

"We'll have to contact other jurisdictions or get some unofficial federal assistance."

Dan returned his attention to the list of juror names and his eyes froze on the last name listed. "I gotta run," Dan said. "Keep me posted."

"Will do."

*

Dan slipped by two groups standing near the glass front doors and passed the hostess stand without breaking pace. He weaved his way through the mostly standing crowd near the bar and edged his way to the end of the large slab of polished wood. The bartender he had met on his previous trip placed a cocktail in front of a woman three seats down and then made eye contact with Dan. The bartender approached, smiling, anticipating the possibility of another hefty tip for a few quick questions.

"Welcome back."

"Thanks."

"What can I get you?"

"Frank."

"If that's a drink name, you're going to have to tell me what's in it."

"It's not. Is he around tonight?"

The bartender stared at Dan and his face seemed to recognize the former dollar-doling patron was on a decidedly different mission. "Give me a minute."

*

Frank stepped onto the floor in his white kitchen apron with his name embroidered in blue thread on the front pocket. Dan stood from his bar stool.

"Dan. I didn't expect to see you again."

"I'm sure you didn't."

"What can I help you with? We're in the middle of the dinner rush."

"It's important," Dan said. "And it should only take a couple minutes."

Frank, a sheen of sweat glistening on his bald head, motioned in the direction of a recently vacated two-seat table in the back corner of the restaurant. Dan sat and pushed the dirty dessert plates from the table's previous occupants to the side. Frank took his seat across from Dan and stole a quick glance around the buzzing restaurant. Dan stared at Frank's profile and facial features, trying to imagine the man with a different appearance.

When Frank turned his attention back towards Dan, Dan said, "I have a few questions for you about Tyrone Biggs and the trial."

Frank's overheated face notched a loss of color.

"I assume the police called you today to check on your well-being. If they haven't, I would expect a call soon," Dan added.

"You probably wouldn't believe me if I asked 'Tyrone who'?"

"No, I wouldn't. That train has left the station. I received the jury list and your name was on it."

"I knew there was no such thing as an anonymous jury. A bunch of bullshit from a bunch of judges and lawyers."

"It was anonymous until a few hours ago."

"And here you are."

"I found you because your life may be in danger. But I think you already know this."

Frank's head dipped slightly in a subconscious gesture of defeat. "Sherry told me what Marcus had discovered in the obituaries. She warned me. The same day she warned Carla."

"Are you worried?"

"There were twelve people on that jury and from what I have heard, a lot of them are dead. So yeah, it concerns me. No one ever mentioned that jury duty can ruin your life."

Dan felt his phone vibrate in his pocket and ignored it. "Tell me about the jury and the trial."

Frank squinted. "What do you want to know?"

"How did a jury with video evidence of a murder find the perpetrator innocent?"

"Do you know who Tyrone Biggs was?"

"I do."

"Then what do you think happened?"

"I think you were paid off."

Frank nodded. "Out of curiosity, are you going to be asking any questions you don't know the answer to?"

"That's a habit I blame on the attorney in me."

"Well, if you know all the answers you can have this conversation without me."

Dan stared at Frank without blinking. "I don't have all the answers and this conversation is over when I say it is. We can have a decent, polite discussion, or I can make a call to the FBI and IRS and see if they need a new case to work. Just so you know, the police are only interested in your well-being. As of now, I'm the only person with any inclination as to what may have occurred seven years ago."

"I can tell you everything I know and you may still go to the Feds."

"I could, but I'm just not that interested in you. I'm interested in finding the person responsible for killing the jury of your peers."

Frank leaned back in his chair slightly.

Dan continued. "Tell me about the payoff. How much did Tyrone Biggs offer you?"

Frank swallowed and began wringing his wrists in tight, short twists.

"I'm going to say it one more time so we are clear. I'm not interested in you, Frank. I don't give a shit one way or the other. But the guy I'm looking for *is* interested in you. So if you want to increase your chances of receiving social security one day, your best option is sitting right in front of you."

Frank puckered his lips and inhaled deeply through his nose. "He paid us a hundred grand each."

"How many of you?"

"Some of us. Most of us. I don't know exactly how many. It's not like we counted a show of hands."

"But you know that Tyrone paid off Sherry, Marcus, and Carla."

"Yes. He paid them off."

"How in the hell did he reach the jurors? You were sequestered, correct?"

"I will ask you the same question I just asked a minute ago. Do you know who Tyrone Biggs was?"

"Yes. He was a gangbanger and drug dealer."

"In his little corner of the world, Tyrone was more of a drug lord than a drug dealer."

"Which is probably another good reason not to let him walk free."

"There wasn't much choice."

"You always have a choice."

"Really? You really think that? Let me ask you this: If someone gave you the option of living or dying, which would you take?"

"Living," Dan replied.

"Easy choice. No strings attached. Now let's change it up a little. If someone gave you the choice of getting paid and living, or dying, which would you choose?"

Dan didn't respond.

"Not much of a choice is it? The money isn't the important part of the equation. Live and get paid, or be killed," Frank said. "Really, Tyrone Biggs didn't have to offer us the money. He could have just given us the option of living or dying."

"I can see your point. The money becomes inconsequential."

"The money was a side decision. At least it was for me," Frank said. "I was offered money to let a drug dealer and murderer go free. That is true. But I was also offered my life in return for letting a drug dealer and murderer go free. And in the end, it wasn't much of a decision. The money was a bonus."

"You could have informed the judge that the jury had been tainted."

"I could have, but Tyrone knew all of our names. He knew where we lived. He knew our family and friends. We were told he would know if we went to the judge. I wasn't willing to take that risk."

"So he had someone in the courts on his payroll."

"I don't know how he got his information, but he knew everything he needed to know about me."

"Now it's my turn to go back to the previous question. How did he reach you? The jury was sequestered."

"We were. We were put up in the Americana Hotel on Sixteenth Street. It's no longer there. A law firm bought it and converted the whole thing."

"I know the place."

"Well, we were sequestered in the hotel. We had uniformed court officers in the lobby and on the second floor monitoring the hall and the stairs. I was on the third floor."

"And were Sherry, Marcus, and Carla on the same floor?"

"They were. There were four jurors on the second floor, four on the third floor and four more on the fourth floor."

"Go on."

"Pretty early in the case, I woke up with a man standing over my bed. He had a gun and an offer I couldn't refuse."

"Did you get a good look at him?"

"A good look? Nope. It was dark and I didn't turn on the light. He told me enough things about myself to let me know he was legitimate. A legitimate threat. I was forced to make a decision right then and there."

"And how did you receive the money?"

"It was in a nice leather bag. The man standing over my bed showed me a picture of it on his phone. The bag was in my bedroom closet, in my apartment. The bag was still there, as promised, at the end of the trial."

"And then?"

"What do you mean?"

"When did you know you weren't the only one who had been paid off?"

"During the trial. After the man visited my hotel room, I got a strange vibe among some of the other jurors. I mean, when you're sequestered, life is pretty boring. You're not supposed to discuss the case. Television is limited. Most of the shows you can watch, you watch as a group. No news is allowed. No Internet. Boring as hell. A couple of the jurors with family were allowed the occasional visit, but for the most part we spent a lot of time watching court-approved movies and engaging in small talk. Spend enough time with anyone and you start to get a feel for them. In the days after the man with the gun paid me a visit, I noticed some of the other jurors were acting differently."

"How?"

"People were less nervous. I noticed that some of the jurors were more relaxed. I noticed it in myself too."

"You weren't more nervous someone was going to find out?"

"If they were going to find out, it wasn't going to be from me, and that was all I cared about. There's a lot of pressure at a murder trial for a drug lord. I was given an out. I knew what my vote was going to be. After I made the deal, the rest of the trial was surreal. It was like I was watching a television drama from the front row."

"You let a guilty man walk free and in the process you became a criminal yourself."

"It turned out just fine."

"How's that?"

"Tyrone Biggs walked free but eventually he was shot and killed. If we had found him guilty in the H2O trial, me and a few other jurors would probably be dead and Tyrone would be in prison for life at the taxpayers' expense."

"Did you know that after the H2O trial, Tyrone did go to prison. After you let him walk, some jury found the balls to do the right thing."

"Or maybe the courts figured out how to properly protect a sequestered jury. Not let gunmen into the hotel rooms."

"I'm not going to say I agree with you, but you do have a valid argument," Dan conceded.

"Look, I spent a few months wrestling with what I did. Then I got over it. I sleep well at night."

"There was no justice for the families of the victims."

"Tyrone is dead. He received street justice. DC doesn't have a death penalty. Our decision to let him walk probably expedited his departure from this planet."

"Judging by the body count of the other jurors, someone doesn't feel the same way you do."

"Apparently."

A waiter slowly approached the table and made eye contact with Frank. Frank looked towards Dan for approval and Dan nodded. The waiter stepped in and whispered in Frank's ear. Frank listened and looked across the restaurant. "I'll be there in a moment," Frank replied to the waiter, who spun and returned to the crowded floor.

Dan felt his phone vibrate in his pocket for a second time and again ignored it. "Just a couple more questions," Dan added.

"Go ahead."

"How much of the money were you able to launder through the restaurant?"

Frank froze. "What are you suggesting?"

"You know exactly what I'm suggesting. After the trial, both Sherry and Carla started working here. Add to that Marcus Losh, Sherry's baby daddy, and yourself, and that makes four jurors all connected directly or indirectly, to this restaurant. I don't think it was entirely coincidental."

Frank dropped his voice to a near whisper, the din of the restaurant almost overpowering his words. "During the trial, Sherry and I became friends. We had adjoining rooms in the hotel, with one of those doors in the wall between the rooms. We weren't supposed to open the door, but we did. Like I said, it was boring. Anyhow, we became friends. We talked a bit and discovered we both worked in Georgetown. She worked down the street at The Friendliest Saloon in Town, and I worked here. It was a common connection that let us relate to each other. At the same time, Sherry had become friends with Carla. Somehow those two connected the dots that each of them had been paid at the trial."

"How did that happen?"

"I don't know. You'll have to ask Sherry. At any rate, Sherry and Carla both knew each other had been paid off, and I assume Marcus told Sherry, who probably told Carla."

"And after the trail Carla started working here?"

"Carla lost her job and Sherry mentioned that maybe I could get her a position. For the waitstaff, the money is decent here. On a good night, a waitress can clear a few hundred dollars in tips alone."

"So Carla started working here first?"

"Carla started and then Sherry quit working down the street. She came on board a few months after the end of the trial."

"How about Marcus?"

"He never worked here. He was an electrician. He was also unreliable."

"And how did Carla and Sherry know you had been paid off?"

"I got involved with Carla."

"You and Carla had a thing?"

"For a while. She eventually told me she had been paid and I told her the same."

"Okay. So we have three people, all jurors at the same trial, working at the same restaurant, and a fourth person in the picture with another hundred thousand dollars. Did you know for sure if any of the other jurors had been paid?"

"Like I said, I only suspected it from their behavior during the trial."

"So the four of you decided to use the restaurant to legitimize your money."

"Yeah. We have five thousand dollars in tips moving through here on any given night. It was a slow process, but a few hundred here, a few hundred there. Spread it out over a couple of years and the dirty money is clean."

"How much is left?"

"None. We finished a couple of years ago. It worked out."

"That's one way to look at it."

"Any idea who's killing the jurors?"

"Wish I did."

"What about the families of the kids who died?"

"None of them stood out as killers. Most of them were wealthy, white-collar types. And I felt for them. I truly did."

"But you felt for yourself more."

"That I did."

"I have one more question. You've changed your appearance since the trial. I obtained courtroom drawings from the trial and none of the jurors look like you. I assume you were the guy we referred to as the Unabomber. Longer hair. Long beard. A bit like ZZ Top, if you remember the band."

"You can thank Tyrone Biggs for the change in appearance."

"Why? Did he take you to the barber?"

"No. Not at all. I saw him once at a basketball game when the Lakers were in town. I got good seats from one of the beer reps that services the restaurant. Tyrone Biggs was there with some of his posse. He was sitting a few rows closer to the floor. At some point during the game he looked back and we made eye contact. He smiled, nodded, and gave me a salute."

"What did you do?"

"I nodded back and then left at the end of the quarter. Shaved my head and beard the next morning."

"But he already knew who you were."

"He knew who I was, obviously. But that doesn't mean I needed him recognizing me in public. I mean, what if I was out with my mother, or a new girlfriend? It was something I didn't want to have to explain."

"So you changed your appearance."

"Well, I couldn't delete myself from his memory, so I figure changing my appearance was the next best thing."

The corners of Dan's eyes tightened and Frank pushed his chair back a few inches. A long uncomfortable silence followed and the waiter who had visited the table minutes before approached again, stopping several feet away.

Frank glanced at his employee and asked Dan, "Do you mind if I step away for a moment? I have a customer who is demanding to see the manager."

"Go ahead," Dan replied, shoving his hand into his pants pocket and removing his phone. "I need to make a call."

*

Dan punched in a phone number from his recent call list and listened to two rings before a deep baritone voice bellowed out, "Detective Wallace here."

"Good evening, Detective. Three calls in ten minutes? It must be important."

"Your girl skipped out."

"Which girl?"

"The bank robber. The one with the home detention monitor. She's out on the town. We received an alarm notification from the transmitter at her apartment that she had exceeded the range for the home detention device. A police unit arrived on the scene about an hour ago and confirmed she is no longer at her apartment."

"What about her daughter?"

"The daughter is home. Apparently your client hired a babysitter before she left."

"Are you tracking her?"

"As we speak."

"Where is she?"

"In Georgetown. Her location is static. Either she ditched the ankle monitor or she's not moving. We are arriving on the scene of the last signal transmission now…"

*

Dan saw the police lights flicker faintly through the front of the restaurant and the hair on his arms rose to attention. Instinctively, he dropped his phone, stood, and pulled his Glock from the holster in the back of his waistband. He scanned the restaurant for Frank, his head moving right and left. Dan's hearing faded as his tunnel vision focused on the kitchen manager on the far side of the floor. Dan's heart rate spiked as he watched Frank approach a small table near the front window of the restaurant, next to the oyster on the half-shell display.

Dan's eyes dipped to the woman seated at the small window-side table and his legs began rushing through the bar. "Down," Dan yelled in a primal command that silenced the massive room, freezing most patrons. "Down," Dan repeated, raising his gun and breaking into a sprint.

Dan cut through the panicked crowd, focused on the table at the front of the restaurant. He saw Amy's mouth gape as she recognized Dan charging towards her. She watched in frozen bewilderment as her attorney covered the floor of the restaurant in quick strides. Frank, who had followed Dan's verbal instruction and lowered his head, slowly regained his posture as Dan parted the sea of scrambling restaurant patrons.

Dan reached the table in time to watch helplessly as the front window shattered and Frank's body began to spin. Amy screamed as Frank's torso hit the old wooden floor and crimson spilled over the chest of his kitchen apron.

A second bullet whistled by Dan's ear and Dan moved in the direction of Amy's chair. He reached his client and grabbed her bone-thin arm in a vise-like grip.

A third bullet hit flesh as Dan yanked Amy out of her seat onto the floor. Dan immediately recognized the baritone voice of the struck victim and looked up as Detective Wallace fell through the remaining glass of the front window and came to rest on the ice-filled oyster display.

CHAPTER 53

THE NUMBER OF emergency vehicles responding to an officer down in the middle of Georgetown was nothing short of spectacular. Police cars with flashing lights blocked every cross street for a half-mile, from the Key Bridge to Foggy Bottom. The six ambulances on the scene were four more than the number of injured, not counting the customer suffering a panic attack and the restaurant's designated oyster shucker who was injured by a shard of flying glass.

For his heroics, Wallace was strapped to the gurney with an oxygen mask and an EMT assigned to each limb. The wound through his shoulder produced copious amounts of blood and curses, neither of which would be fatal.

Dan was providing his statement to two uniformed officers when Detective Fields interrupted. "I need him for a minute." The two officers nodded and moved towards the next available witness, plucking one from a huddled group around a large circular dining table.

"Thanks for the rescue," Dan replied. "How's Wallace?"

"He's going to be fine."

"You should go to the hospital with him."

"I don't think he wants me to."

"You should still go."

"I don't think *he* wants to go either."

"I'm sure of that."

"Are you going to be all right?"

"I'm fine," Dan replied. "But my bank robber client just forfeited the right to spend her remaining days with her daughter, which is sad. I don't think any judge is going to overlook her walking away from home detention for a dinner in Georgetown. Much less for serving as a distraction in a professional hit."

"She probably didn't have a choice. If she helps us find the killer, maybe we can find a sympathetic judge."

"That's a long shot. Do you know what she said to me after I pulled her to the floor?"

"No, what?"

"She said she wasn't worried about leaving the house because she knew I would find her. She thought I would track her if she left her apartment and that I would be there to protect her."

"Technically, you did."

"Technically, Wallace did. I was late. Just ask Frank the manager."

"It wasn't your fault."

"I could have done things differently. I could have let you know I was coming here. I could have told Wallace I recognized Frank as one of the jurors on the list he sent me. I could have told Wallace that I knew he was alive."

"Let it go, Dan."

"When it's done, I'll let it go."

"Well, it's almost done. We finished going through the juror list this afternoon. Frank's death leaves only one juror still alive, and you know who that is. Eleven of the jurors from the H2O trial are dead. But not all of them were murdered. Two died of natural causes. One from a heart attack. One drowned near Rehoboth beach. The nine other jurors were either killed, or died under mysterious circumstances."

"I assume we have someone watching the congressman's wife."

"We have a couple of marked and unmarked patrol cars keeping an eye on things at the Wellington residence."

"Good, because I don't have time to protect her."

"What are you going to do?"

"I'm going to need the list of witnesses and family members of the victims from the H2O shooting. I'm going to take that list back to the hospice."

"Why? We already checked the list against the hospice employees and volunteer list."

"Something Frank said before he was shot made me think. Something about why he changed his appearance after the Tyrone Biggs trial. I wanted to check something."

Emily pulled out her phone, accessed her email, and sent the attachment. "The list is in your inbox."

"Thanks. Do you mind running interference for me? I'll make myself available later if anyone on the force needs anything."

"Sure. But why do I get the impression you're about to go off the reservation?"

"Women's intuition."

*

Dan walked into the waiting area of the Capital Community Hospice and the receptionist behind the desk smiled and spoke. "Pepper is expecting you," the woman said, motioning for Dan to proceed to the director's office. Dan did as instructed and knocked on the open door, his knuckle hitting just below the gold sign with *Pepper Hines* engraved in plain text.

"Come in, come in," Pepper Hines said in his buttery-smooth voice.

"I'm sorry to keep you here so late."

"Not a problem. Not a problem at all. I'm happy to help. You said it was urgent."

"It is urgent. As you may have heard, a police officer was shot earlier this evening in Georgetown."

"I just saw it on the news," Pepper replied. "Horrible. Just horrible."

"You're probably unaware the police officer who was shot this evening was the same one who visited you here late last week. His name is Detective Earl Wallace. He is a good man."

"I wasn't aware. I'm terribly sorry."

"The good news is that his wounds are not life-threatening."

"That is good news."

"The bad news is I believe the person who shot Detective Wallace is the same person behind several other killings. The same person we were looking for in our earlier visit to this hospice."

"I provided you with all the information we had. What else do you need? I'm an open book. You can have access to anything you want."

327

"I don't think that will help."

"Then I don't understand."

Dan reached into his pocket and handed Pepper Hines a piece of paper. "This is a list of family members and witnesses from a trial that occurred seven years ago. It was a murder trial resulting from a shootout at a club on the DC Waterfront called H2O."

Pepper Hines glanced at the paper and Dan continued. "There are nearly ninety names on that sheet of paper. We compared the names on that list to the list of hospice employees and volunteers you provided us. We couldn't identify a match."

"You want to go through the names of the Hospice employees and volunteers again? We can do that right now," Pepper offered.

"No, that won't be necessary or beneficial. But I do want *you* to go through the witnesses and family members of the victims of the H2O trial and tell me if *you* recognize any names."

"Once again, I don't think I understand."

"I think a person clever enough to orchestrate multiple murders was clever enough to keep his name off a list that could identify him or her. I think they deleted their name from your employee and volunteer list."

"I see," Pepper Hines replied.

"Take your time. Read the list from the H2O trial. It's in alphabetical order. Let me know if anyone rings a bell."

Dan watched intently as Pepper Hines methodically read the names on the paper. Halfway through the second column of names, Dan could see Pepper's eyes pause.

"Do you see someone you recognize?"

"I do. Richard Porter."

"Is he an employee or a volunteer?"

"He was a volunteer in the past," Pepper said, sighing loudly. "But currently Mr. Richard Porter is a patient."

"A patient?"

"Yes. He's receiving home care. In fact, I believe he's on the schedule for a visit from our staff this evening. It's my understanding his health has deteriorated rapidly."

CHAPTER 54

THE PHONE RANG in Tobias's basement and the mad computer programmer touched the earpiece in his right ear to activate the call.

"Tobias, it's Dan."

"I know. I recognize the number. Back for another query?"

"Same case, different query. I found the connection between the congressman's wife, the waitress, the Army vet and the EPA lawyer. They all served on the same jury."

"An anonymous jury."

"That's right. You came to that conclusion awfully quick."

"It was the only conclusion to reach. I checked everywhere for a connection. It had to be something offline."

"It was. They all served on an anonymous jury that let a killer walk free. The case involved a shootout at Club H2O on the Waterfront. Six people were killed."

"What do you need?"

"A complete profile on an individual. Phone numbers. Emails. Bank records. Anything you can get as soon as you can get it."

"As if I didn't have other things to do?"

"Are you downstairs in your office?"

"I am."

"Is your girlfriend in the house?"

"She's out."

"You probably have a Dr. Pepper somewhere on the desk, and a bottle of twelve-year-old scotch not too far away."

"I might."

"Then you have time. And I'm not looking for a freebie. Charge me your hourly rate. I'll pass it on to my client as an expense."

"Dan, I'm not doing hourly work anymore. I'm a salaried employee for a legitimate firm."

"And who got you the interview for your new gig?"

Tobias ran both hands through his hair. "You got me there, Dan. You got me there. What's the name?"

"Richard Porter."

"What did poor Dick do?"

"Dick is the father of one of the girls killed at Club H2O. I think he paid to have the jurors from the H2O trial murdered."

"Not a very nice man."

"I haven't met him yet, but on paper, killing a dozen people usually doesn't get you on Santa's nice list."

"What do you want on him first? Phone records are easy. Bank records will take time. Credit cards I can get fairly quickly, particularly if they send their monthly bills to an email account."

"Let's start with everything."

"Of course."

"I want to know who he's been talking to. Anyone and everyone. I'm looking for his accomplice."

"And you don't have a name for the accomplice."

"No."

"Okay. Let me see what I can find out. Are you going to be by your phone?"

"I will be."

"Give me a couple of hours."

*

Dan checked the number on the mailbox and turned down the short tree-lined driveway. As the car reached the edge of the front yard, the one-story home popped into view. In a neighborhood with heated pools and guest-houses, the rambler was the least impressive home on the street.

From the small circular driveway, Dan could see lights through the windows across the front of the house. Dan concluded his assessment of the home and his eyes focused on the white van parked in the driveway. Lettering for Capital Community Hospice arched across the side of the vehicle.

"Pepper Hines may be the last honest man in town," Dan whispered to himself.

Dan exited his vehicle and moments later pushed his finger against the doorbell. A short woman with a dark complexion, whom Dan surmised to be in her mid-fifties, answered the door. A dishtowel rested on her left shoulder. An apron was folded in half and tied neatly around her waist.

"Good evening. My name is Dan Lord. I'm here to see Mr. Porter."

"Mr. Porter is not available. The nurses are here. He is receiving medical care."

"It's important."

"He's not well."

"Is he awake?"

"Yes. But he's resting."

"May I speak with the nurses?"

The woman looked pained by the question and her eyebrows furrowed.

"Please," Dan added. *And this is the last time I'm going to ask nicely.*

"Just a moment," the woman replied before she vanished into the home.

Dan listened to a distant, muffled conversation and the woman returned with a large man at her side. Dan noted the man's attire, physique, and serious demeanor. A white coat draped over the man's broad shoulders. Purple scrubs ran from the bottom of the coat to the top of the man's shoes. A nametag identifying the man as *Peyton Felton, Nurse*, was clipped to the lapel of his white coat.

"Good evening. My name is Dan Lord and I'm here to see Richard Porter."

"I received a call from Mr. Hines. I was told you would be visiting."

"Is Mr. Porter incapacitated?"

"No. He's conscious, though he is on pain medication."

"What kind of cancer does he have?"

"I can't divulge that information."

"Does it really matter at this point?" Dan asked.

The nurse looked down at the short housekeeper next to him and she responded to Dan's question.

"Mr. Porter had a brain bleed several days ago. He was doing okay until then."

"So he has brain cancer?"

"No," the housekeeper responded. "He has colon cancer. It has moved to the brain. Now it is bleeding."

Dan glanced at the nurse, looking for confirmation of what he had just heard. Nurse Felton nodded his head slightly as if to indicate the housekeeper's rudimentary explanation was accurate.

"I would like to speak with him," Dan said.

"If you want to speak with Mr. Porter, you should take it up with his lawyer, in the morning. At a more reasonable hour."

Dan smiled. "Oh, I assure you this is a reasonable hour. And believe me when I say I'm the most reasonable person who is going to visit Mr. Porter any time soon. An unreasonable visitor would point out the penalty for aiding and abetting a criminal."

The nurse again looked down at the housekeeper and then back at Dan. "I don't think my presence is needed for this conversation," nurse Peyton replied before disappearing back into the house.

The housekeeper, left alone at the door with Dan, appeared to become visibly nervous. "I'm not aware that Mr. Porter is a criminal."

"He is a suspect in multiple murders, and we believe he was involved in the shooting of a DC police officer earlier this evening."

"Mr. Porter has not left the house in several days," the housekeeper exclaimed. "He hasn't even been out of bed this evening."

"That doesn't mean he isn't involved. And now that you've been informed he is the suspect in multiple felonies, it's time for you to make a decision."

The housekeeper shed a tear in silence.

"You can either let me in, or let the legal chips fall where they may," Dan added.

*

Dan stood to the side as the housekeeper held the front door open. Nurse Peyton and another member of the home care division of the hospice ambled outside.

"We will be back in the morning," nurse Peyton said to the housekeeper before heading in the direction of the van parked near the garage.

The housekeeper nodded. "Mr. Porter is waiting for you," she said to Dan, open door still in her hand. "He is resting comfortably."

Not for long, Dan thought as he followed the housekeeper to the threshold of the living room and turned right. At the end of the hall, the housekeeper stopped at the doorway.

"Please," she said, motioning towards the open door. Dan stepped into the bedroom and the housekeeper disappeared from view.

The size of the hospital bed in the room caught Dan momentarily off guard. Richard Porter was in the middle of the large mattress, the incline at forty-five degrees. A large water bottle with a flexible a straw was resting against the railing of the bed. A remote control poked out from the sheet near the man's left hand. An IV stand was at the side of the bed. A tube from the IV trailed downward, turned at the railing on the bed, and found its way into the veins on the back of the man's hand. A bedside table was pushed into the corner. A cell phone and a smattering of prescription medication filled most of the available tabletop.

Richard Porter looked towards the entranceway as Dan's presence cast a shadow on the wall near the bedroom door.

"Take off your clothes," Richard commanded from his position on the bed. Porter's voice had a slight slur, though Dan had no point of reference to determine whether it was a recent affliction.

"I'm sorry?" Dan asked, his eyebrows rising. In the hall to his left, the housekeeper reappeared as if by magic and produced a woven laundry basket. Her expression never changed.

"I don't think so," Dan responded.

"If you want to talk, you will lose your clothes, your phone, your keys, wallet. Your weapon too, if you're carrying. Everything. Otherwise, you are free to leave," Richard Porter said calmly and deliberately, one hand inching towards the television remote control on the bed.

Dan exchanged glances with the man in the bed and the housekeeper in the hall.

"Fuck it," he said out loud, reaching for the top button on his shirt. A minute later Dan was down to his underwear. The housekeeper folded each piece of clothing and neatly stacked them in the laundry basket.

"Underwear, too," Richard Porter said from the bed and Dan's mind flashed back to the infamous scene in the movie *Deliverance*. The housekeeper handed Dan a pair of sweatpants and Dan turned slightly away to exchange his underwear for the athletic wear. Finished changing, Dan raised his hands and twirled. "Satisfied?" Dan asked.

"It is not about satisfaction," Richard Porter responded. The man on the bed nodded towards the open door and the housekeeper pulled the knob shut.

"I was going to apologize for intruding," Dan said.

"Well, then I'm glad you weren't forced to lie. And if it's all the same to you, we can discard the niceties. In the interest of time, if you will. As you are probably aware, time is something I'm running short of at this juncture..."

"My name is Dan Lord and..."

"You are an attorney. And a private detective. I didn't ask who you were. I want to know why you're here, standing in my bedroom, threatening my housekeeper."

"I think we both know why I'm here."

"Humor me. My memory isn't what it used to be. The cancer has finally reached my brain. It has run the full circuit. From colon to cranium... if you can believe the scans."

"Do you?"

"I didn't always. I do now."

"What's the prognosis?"

Richard Porter smiled. "Not good."

Dan tried to judge the man's face, to assess his emotion. He eyed the IV bag and the drip.

"Pain killer?"

"Morphine. The good stuff. The headaches have become unbearable."

"I was given morphine once. Years ago. It works."

"Indeed it does. Now, to the point. How did you find me?" Richard Porter asked, his voice steady but weak. His slur never wavered.

"It wasn't easy."

"I tried to make it impossible. I obviously didn't try hard enough."

"You didn't really think you could kill a dozen people without someone eventually taking notice."

"I didn't kill anyone."

"No, you didn't. You hired someone."

"What's wrong with hiring competent workers? You don't think Henry Ford built the Model T himself, do you?"

"I'm not here to discuss automotive history."

"What would you like to discuss?"

"I'm looking for answers to a few questions, and then you're going to tell me how I can locate the man in the baseball cap and sunglasses."

"Don't waste your energy. I don't even know his real name."

"You may not know his real name, but I'm quite sure you can reach him."

Richard Porter succumbed to a coughing fit that sent him rolling onto his side. When he rolled back over, Dan was next to the bed. Richard Porter's eyes widened as Dan unclipped the morphine line from the IV bag and moved the stand in the direction of the wall.

"Let's see how a few moments of clarity can help your mental faculties."

"Is it my turn to be threatened?"

"Not at all. If there's one thing I've learned recently, it's that the terminally ill don't play by the same rules as the rest of us. Threats and rewards don't have the same value."

"You have learned the secret of the ill."

"And you should know. In more ways than one, you are sick. Very sick. Healthy people don't murder a dozen innocent people."

"The only innocent people in this world are children. That's it. The rest of us, well, we are all guilty of something."

"Not something worth killing over."

"Do you have any children, Mr. Lord?"

"I do not."

"Then you don't know a thing about what's worth killing over."

Dan's mind turned to the recollection of a New York mobster and a used garrote he no longer owned. "I may not have children, but I know a few things about killing someone who deserves it."

Richard Porter moved his head to the side as if to refocus his vision on Dan. "The only way to understand complete loss is to lose your own flesh and blood. Someone you raised from an infant. A person you took care of and worried about every day they were on this earth. Once you understand the depth of that relationship, then you can understand the anger parents feel when the person responsible for that loss walks away without retribution. And for those who allowed the guilty to walk free to continue on with their lives, enriched. Experience those circumstances and then tell me how you feel."

Dan nodded and reminded himself... *When someone is willing to talk, let them talk...*

"Seven years ago I lost my life. Today, what you see in this bed is just the final inconsequential moments of my lungs taking breath and my heart beating. Life ceased seven years ago in a club on the Waterfront in DC. My daughter went to go dancing with her friends and never came home."

"I'm sorry for your loss."

"The losses were many. First, I lost my daughter. Then I lost a year of my life. The year after her death. Twelve months of nothing more than a grainy black-and-white film of my daughter on a constant loop. The sun rose. The sun set. Neither penetrated the walls of this house. I didn't sleep without medication. When I did sleep with the help of meds, I would dream about my daughter. Her favorite blanket. Her first tennis racket. Her high school prom."

Dan swallowed hard. "It still doesn't make it right to kill the innocent."

"Don't interrupt. I'm not finished. If you want to judge me, you're going to listen."

Dan motioned with his hands as if to encourage Richard Porter to continue. As he gestured, he looked down at his own naked torso and the pair of ill-fitting sweatpants.

"Do you know what percentage of marriages survive the loss of a child?" Richard asked.

"Ten percent," Dan guessed.

"Something in that neighborhood. My wife and I weren't lucky enough to make the ten percent. By the time the trial began, my wife and I were living apart. My wife moved out. I stayed here. For better or for worse. This is the only house my daughter knew. I didn't want to leave. I still don't. But with the death of my daughter, the glue that held us together as a couple was in the ground, riddled with bullet holes. I started drinking. My wife started drinking. The dark year, I call it. And the dark year ended with Tyrone Biggs walking out of the courtroom into the sunshine, free as a bird."

"He got what was coming to him."

"Eventually someone paid him back. But it was too late for my family and me. A couple of nights after the conclusion of the H2O trial, at the bottom of a particularly expensive bottle of wine, my wife stopped by the house. This house. She wanted to visit her daughter's room, which we had left untouched. Hell, a toothpaste tube in my daughter's bedroom was still on the sink. So when my wife wanted in, I let her in. And while I was in the kitchen making more drinks, my wife blew the back of her skull across my daughter's room."

Dan shook his head in silence.

"It was then I decided everyone would pay. They were all guilty. Tyrone may have killed my daughter, but the jury killed my wife."

"So you say."

"So I know."

"What do you think happened with the jury?" Dan asked. "They had convincing testimony and video evidence as to what occurred in Club H2O."

"I know exactly what happened with the jury. They were paid off."

"What would make you say that?" Dan asked.

"Because I paid them off."

CHAPTER 55

DAN COULDN'T CONCEAL the surprise on his face and Richard Porter immediately recognized it.

"That's right," Richard Porter repeated. "You heard me correctly. I bought the jury. The same jury that let Tyrone Biggs walk."

"You bought them?"

"Eight of them. We couldn't reach the jurors on the second floor."

"Because that's where the uniformed court officers were posted."

"Someone did their homework."

"I try."

"Yes, the court officers had a post in the main lobby and on the second floor near the staircase. But the eight jurors on the third and fourth floors were reachable."

"How?"

"The fire escape in the back. The Americana Hotel was an old-school establishment. According to the private detective I hired during the trial, they used to shuttle the occasional call girl up the fire escape. Back when the hotel was in its heyday and visiting politicians needed a place that was a little more under the radar. At the time the jury was sequestered, there was access to the fire escape through a window in a storage room on the third floor."

"And that is how you reached the jurors."

"It was common knowledge that Tyrone Biggs was a bad guy with bad intentions. I hired someone to follow the jurors once they had been sequestered. That individual, someone much like yourself, was able to confirm the sequestration. Surveillance indicated the jurors may have been contacted by someone working on the behalf of Tyrone Biggs.

"And then you offered them money. You offered the jury money to ensure that Tyrone would be found guilty."

"Yes, the jurors were offered money. They were offered money to fulfill their judicial obligation as jurors. Jurors with indisputable evidence that the defendant was guilty."

Dan thought back to Frank's words of wisdom. The additional offer of money becomes inconsequential when faced with the option of life or death. "But you were outbid. Tyrone Biggs offered money *and* he offered the opportunity for each juror to save their own life. To not to be killed. You merely offered money."

"A lack of forethought on my part. I knew jury tampering was a real possibility. A real possibility. Everyone did. But my offer wasn't enriching enough."

"So, you bought eight people on the jury?" Dan confirmed.

"That's correct. And if a criminal case requires a unanimous decision, then all twelve men and women had to vote for a not-guilty verdict. I know that eight of those people received money. Eight of those jurors took *my* money and then voted not guilty. Those eight people were anything but innocent. The other four jurors somehow looked at a video of a nightclub shooting and let the man who pulled the trigger walk free. I figured they were also paid off by Tyrone Biggs."

Dan nodded, "It's possible."

Richard Porter continued. "So I started planning. I mean, killing a single person is easy. But if you're going to kill multiple people, the only way to do it is to have alibis. To make sure there is no connection in the deaths. That, for those who have contemplated it, takes planning. Planning and money."

"And, in your case, a professional who is willing to train people and clean up the mess."

"It helps," Richard Porter said, shrugging his shoulders.

"And in addition to hiring a professional killer, you used a more traditional killer as well… cancer."

"Yes. Cancer opened my eyes to other possibilities."

"When were you diagnosed?"

"Five years ago."

"And it was terminal."

"Yes."

"And you survived…"

"I was a rare case. My cancer went into remission after a terminal diagnosis. They gave me six months. I stopped treatment three months later with the cancer in remission."

"Lucky indeed."

"It doesn't happen often, but it does happen."

"And then you stuck around the hospice as a volunteer."

"Once again, your summations are on point. I offered my time as a volunteer at the hospice."

"And you used your technical background to gain access to their computer systems."

"It's a hospice. The integrity of their computer system was easy to compromise. I was a computer expert. I helped out with various aspects of their computers in the office. Showed some of the employees how to use basic computer applications. In the process, I made sure I had access."

"And what if your access was denied for some reason as time passed?"

"It happened. The solution was easy. I just contacted the hospice and let them know I was available to volunteer again, which I did. Once I sorted the technical hurdles and regained access, I would stop volunteering."

"And no one suspected anything?"

"It's not a bank. The most valuable information that a hospice keeps is medical records of patients with terminal cancer. By definition, the value of the data they store has a limited shelf life."

"And your access to the system also allowed you access to the volunteer list. Which you astutely kept your name off of."

"The volunteer list was stored on the server. It seemed prudent to keep my name off it. It is a rather long list. No one would miss one name. Except for you."

"And with your computer access you were able to monitor the records of incoming patients and cherry pick those who might have been useful to you."

"Correct. I had ongoing access to the electronic records. Or those that were received via paper and then scanned and stored in the computer. Once digitized, I had access."

"What made you think that cancer patients would ever agree to your proposal?"

"My experience at the hospice. When you are terminally ill, counseling is a large part of the end-of-life transition. When I was first diagnosed as stage four, I also participated in counseling. Group counseling. And do you know what I quickly realized was a big concern for a lot of people?"

"Money?"

"Right. Money. Specifically, the financial well-being of those they would be leaving behind. For those on the lower end of the wealth spectrum, the concern was even more poignant. Of course, most of the group spoke about religion and family, but money was also a big worry."

"And you saw an opportunity."

"I think a reasonable person could see an opportunity to alleviate the financial concerns of the terminally ill."

Another bout of coughing brought Richard Porter into a seated position. When the spasm ended, Richard rested back on the mattress.

"Who is the man with the cap and glasses?"

"I don't know his real name."

"How did you meet him?"

"You're going to have to figure that out for yourself."

"How do you contact him?"

"How do you think I contact him, Mr. Lord?"

"You probably use burner cells. Anonymous email accounts. Spoofed IP addresses."

"That wasn't very difficult to figure out, now was it?"

"How do you pay him?"

"What does it matter? It's untraceable. Anything and everything you're going to think of now is something I had years to consider. You're playing catch-up."

"It's not my first time in that position."

"Forget about this man. You'll never find him because I don't know where he is."

"Oh, I'll find him."

"You say that with confidence. How can you be so sure?"

"Because there's one juror who is still alive. And a man like you… a man who is as full of piss and vinegar as yourself… a man who is also on his death bed… a man like that is going to finish what he started."

CHAPTER 56

TOBIAS ANSWERED THE door wearing pajamas. His bare feet protruded from the hem of his pants. Long, knuckled toes wiggled in the mountain air. He motioned for Dan to follow him.

"I have a glass waiting for you," Tobias said over his shoulder.

"I could use something to take the edge off," Dan replied, following his host through the living room to the edge of the kitchen as he had done on his first visit. Moments later the two men were in the basement, with an array of computer equipment as the backdrop.

Tobias found his chair and motioned for Dan to grab a seat. Dan did as directed and pushed a chair from the far wall in the direction of the computers. Shoulder-to-shoulder with Tobias, Dan looked up at the dual screens illuminated over the desk.

Tobias reached for a small glass and motioned towards the bottle of an eighteen-year-old Macallan just out of reach. Dan obliged, filled his glass, and took a sip. "What did you find on Richard Porter?"

"Maybe nothing. Maybe something. In a lot of ways, Old Dick is pretty boring. He started several companies and sold them for quite a bit of money."

"Doesn't sound boring."

"For the last few years he has been living a quiet life."

"That's what ninety million can do for you."

"He's worth more than that, but does it really matter?"

"What else did you find?"

"I started with his email and phone. He has a wireless router in his home that handles all of the traffic from his residence. His IP address was easy to get. The guy doesn't send many emails. He does have instances where his computers go offline for extended periods of time and his IP goes inactive. He may be using some type of IP spoofing setup. I can look more into it, if you need me to."

"Not now. What else do you have?"

"His phone usage falls into a standard pattern. He makes a lot of calls to his attorney and his financial advisor. A group named Westing Financial. He must have a good deal of his money with them."

"Westing Financial is run by the father of another girl killed at Club H2O. A friend of Richard Porter's daughter."

"You know, Dan, it seems that every time you show up, you're talking about someone else who has died. Have you thought about keeping track of your own death count?"

"Not once. Who else is Dick talking to?"

"He calls his attorney, his financial advisor, a group of doctors, the hospice home care division, and a couple of acquaintances."

"Any calls made to anything that looks like a burner cell?"

"Nothing. But if he's spoofing his IP address intermittently, and he's calling a burner cell, my guess is he would probably call a burner with another burner."

"Did he make or receive any calls this evening?"

"What makes you ask that?"

"Because another member of the jury was killed this evening and I'm guessing Richard Porter and the killer somehow contacted each other."

"Richard Porter made exactly one call this evening. He called Potomac Hills Country Club, where he has been a member for several years. This evening, he called the pro shop. He spoke to someone there for a little over three minutes."

"Is that part of his normal routine?"

"It's not. Not really. I ran a query for all the numbers he called in the last three months, which is how I got my list of typical calls. Richard Porter called the Potomac Hills Country Club on exactly two other occasions. He called the restaurant in September. The conversation lasted thirty seconds.

He also called the pro shop a couple of weeks ago. That conversation was much longer. It lasted fifteen minutes."

After a moment of consideration, Dan spoke. "What does a bedridden man want with the pro shop at his country club?"

"If that's your question, then things are about to become even more mysterious. A couple of days after Richard Porter made the fifteen-minute call to the pro shop, he charged twenty-three hundred dollars and change to his credit card for the purchase of a set of clubs and a bag. The data indicates it was an in-store purchase."

"So, I ask again, what does a stage four terminally ill patient with ninety million dollars in the bank want with a new set of golf clubs?"

"A parting gift for someone?"

"Maybe. Is the pro shop still open?" Dan asked.

"It's probably closed. Call it and see for yourself," Tobias said, pointing at the number on the screen.

Dan picked up his cell phone and called the number. The phone rang several times and then went to voicemail. Dan listened to the message and then hung up. He stood from his chair and paced back and forth on the carpet. "What time did he call the country club this evening?"

"Just after six p.m."

"Right after the shooting in Georgetown."

"Within a few minutes."

A sly smirk slowly stretched across Dan's face. "I guess it's time to go see the club about becoming a member."

CHAPTER 57

THE LONG BLACK Mercedes with a six-figure price tag was run-of-the-mill at the entrance to Potomac Hills Country Club. Angel stopped his car at the guard booth, flashed his driver's license, and then rolled slowly in the direction of the massive clubhouse in the distance. To his right, green fairways stretched away from the main drive, disappearing into the rolling hills just west of DC. The Potomac River hid beyond a grove of trees to the left.

Angel considered parking options as he approached the clubhouse. His plan was short and simple. Spend as little time as possible without raising any undue suspicion. The grand entrance to the clubhouse grew before him, front and center, and a small sign indicated that the pro shop and bag drop were to the right. Angel turned at the designated sign and a young man approached the car as it crawled to a stop in the bag drop zone.

"My name is Luis Gomez. I'm here to pick up a set of clubs."

The young man in a red golf shirt and white pants greeted Angel and then spoke into a walkie-talkie he removed from his belt. A second later the walkie-talkie chirped in response.

The young man turned towards the man in the Mercedes. "Mr. Gomez, you will have to sign for the bag in the pro shop. They are expecting you. You can leave your car here, if you want. Just put the hazards on. I'll keep an eye on it."

Angel considered the young man's pimpled face and then lowered his defenses. He parked at the curb, leaving the engine running. He stood from the vehicle, a Titleist cap snug on his head. The lenses on his light-sensitive sunglasses darkened as they were exposed to the sunlight.

*

The assistant golf pro, decked out head-to-toe in Callaway attire, dragged the oversized golf bag from the back room and pulled it around the counter. He pushed the heavy bag into a standing position next to a sweater display, and then patted the top of the set of clubs.

"Mr. Porter picked this set of clubs because a lot of professionals use them on the tour. The latest from Mizuno. Forged blades. Great clubs. Not for beginners, though."

The assistant golf pro watched as Angel fondled the head cover on the driver in the bag and then asked, "What's your handicap?"

"I don't play. My son plays," Angel responded. "The clubs are for him."

"Your son?"

"That's right."

"Well, it's none of my business, but if your son walks when he plays, he may need a smaller bag. That bag right there is one of the largest bags they make. Mr. Porter filled it with everything you will need for a round. He packed the bag himself when the clubs arrived. Spent an hour in the clubhouse with that bag, making sure everything was just right. He bought tees, balls, some rainwear, even a pair of shoes."

"I'm sure it will be fine."

"Don't get me wrong. It's a great bag. Top of the line. Just like the clubs. Great setup. But it's heavy as hell."

"I'll keep that in mind."

"We are at the end of the golf season for the year, everything is on sale. If you're interested in a smaller bag, I can offer an additional twenty-five percent off."

"Next time," Angel said, picking the bag up by the large leather handle.

*

Outside, the young man in the red shirt hustled towards Angel as he exited the pro shop. "Let me get that for you," the young man said, reaching for the bag as part of his duties.

Angel pulled back and swung the bag away from the young man's grasp. *Keep your cool*, Angel reminded himself. *Make yourself unmemorable.*

Angel smiled, released his grip, and watched as the employee hefted the large bag into position on his shoulder. Twenty paces later, the young man struggled to get the bag over the lip of the Mercedes' trunk. With a resounding thud and rattle, the bag and clubs slipped from the young man's grip and crashed onto the trunk floor.

"Sorry," the young man exclaimed.

Angel grunted and reached into his pocket for a tip. He handed the boy a twenty, mumbled something unintelligible, and then reached to shut the lid of the trunk. As Angel turned back towards the driver's door, his eyes met Dan's, and a look of surprise washed over him.

*

Dan didn't give Angel an opportunity to protest, quickly latching on to Angel's throat, jamming his thumb under Angel's jawline. Angel's glasses fell from his face and Dan stared into the man's eyes, finally seeing his facial features without impediment. Angel's black, soulless eyes were dark enough for Dan to see his own reflection.

Angel winced as Dan increased the pressure of his grip and then instinctively pulled his own hands upward in an attempt to loosen Dan's grasp. With blood flow to his brain waning, he pawed at Dan's vise-like compression on his throat. Struggling to breathe, Angel dropped his right hand to his side and slid it into his waistband, reaching for his weapon. Dan responded with a kick to Angel's left leg. As Angel tried to regain his balance, Dan released the man's jaw and spun him into a standard law enforcement control position. Standing to Angel's rear, Dan glimpsed the weapon in the man's waistband holster as Angel regained his strength and balance.

The possibilities of the next few seconds flashed before Dan's eyes. He could feel the strength of the man temporarily in his control and understood his adversary was no stranger to physical confrontations. The pistol protruding from the back of the man's waistband made Dan's decision an easy one.

"Payback time," Dan announced. Powered by adrenaline, Dan quickly released his grip on Angel's arm, grabbed the back of Angel's head, and drove it into the frame of the car. The force of the collision rocked the vehicle and the body of the man slumped to the pavement.

The young country club employee in the red golf shirt gasped. "Is he okay?" he asked.

"For now," Dan replied. "Go inside and call the number I gave you. Tell the woman who answers the phone exactly what I told you to say."

The young man nodded, feet frozen.

Dan dragged Angel's unconscious body to the passenger side of the car and put him in the passenger seat. Shutting the door and walking around the car to the driver's side, Dan looked over at the young man, still unmoving near the bag drop and said, "Make the call. Just like we talked about."

*

Dan parked the Mercedes in the furthest space of a sparsely filled lot, a hundred yards from the clubhouse. His own car was several places away, among a smattering of more expensive automobiles. Through the windshield, he had a clean view of the main entrance to the club, the guard booth sitting at the crest of a small hill.

In the seat next to Dan, after a series of incomprehensible groans, Angel began mumbling. A pair of handcuffs attached Angel's right hand to the door armrest. A golf cap and sunglasses rested on the floor of the passenger's side.

Dan reached over and patted the man on the cheek. "Time to wake up, pudding." Dan flipped through the contents of the man's wallet and eyed the new driver's license issued by the DMV in the name of Luis Gomez.

"Wake up, Luis," Dan teased.

Angel grumbled. "Fuck you."

"Not this time," Dan said. "You had your chance. Twice, if I'm right. Once with the baton in Georgetown. I'm also guessing you were the one who took a shot at me last week on the sidewalk outside my apartment. I was on to you and you were probably trying to eliminate me so you could finish off the jurors. A job you're being paid for."

"You were lucky," Angel said, cobwebs clearing.

"Or you're not very good. You used three guys posing as muggers to set me up for the shot on the sidewalk. You did the same for Frank the kitchen manager. You used Amy to position Frank just how you wanted him. At a table, near the window."

"Rifle shots in urban environments can cause a lot of potential collateral damage."

"Only if you miss."

"Maybe I didn't want anyone innocent to be killed."

"I don't believe that. You kill innocent people for money," Dan said. "Worse. You train innocent people to kill other innocent people."

"Whether they are innocent or not is up for discussion."

Dan considered the statement for a moment and then said, "I still don't understand why you didn't just let the muggers finish me off on the sidewalk. Give them a gun and let them do the work for you."

Angel smiled. "I can't let others have all the fun, all the time. I actually hit you from nearly five hundred yards out."

"Well, you shot a good man last night. A good detective. Fortunately for you, he's going to live. Unfortunately for you, he is a police officer and shooting him alone will likely put you in jail for life. Add another ten murders to that and, well, you will never see the light of day."

"I wasn't shooting at the police last night. I was aiming for Frank. The second shot was for your client. The hotel housekeeper."

"What did she do?"

"She broke one of our rules."

"And that makes her guilty enough to kill?"

"Rules are rules."

"It's a good thing you like rules, because there are a lot of rules where you're going."

"I don't think so. I assure you, I won't spend my life in jail. I won't spend a single night in jail."

"And I assure you that you won't spend your life free." Dan looked down as Angel's left hand slipped between the passenger seat and the center console of the vehicle. "Don't bother. I removed the guns from the vehicle. One in the glove box. One under the driver's seat. One in the crack between the passenger's seat and the console. One in the pocket on the back of the passenger seat."

"Very thorough," Angel replied without emotion.

"As are you," Dan replied. "I also relieved you of the gun on your person. All of the weapons, save one, are in the trunk, unloaded. A little arsenal sitting back there with the golf clubs and the golf bag."

"You can keep the clubs," Angel said. "I hear they are top-of-the-line."

"They may be top-of-the-line, but the bag is where the real money is. I figure there's a couple million in the false bottom of that bag. Not a bad sum at all. But you won't be taking it with you."

"How did you know I would be here?"

"It was hard to imagine why Mr. Porter wanted a set of new clubs with such little time left to live. I mean, he already has a set of clubs. Two sets, in fact. Both of them are stored here at the country club. What would a man on his deathbed need a third set of clubs for?"

"I never liked the idea of coming here."

"You should have stuck with your gut."

"What now? If you wanted to kill me, you could have. And if you wanted to arrest me, the police would be here already. What now?"

"Well, I assume you aren't the talking type, but I thought I'd give you the opportunity just the same. I'm pretty sure your name is not Luis Gomez. That driver's license was issued last month and it's not you in the picture, though there is a resemblance."

"You were right in your assumption. I'm not the talking type."

"This is your last chance to say something that may not be used against you in a court of law. Hell, you could even hire me as an attorney."

"I'll pass."

"Then we have nothing to discuss. The police are on their way. Your fate is sealed."

Dan opened the door to the driver's side and stood next to the vehicle. He reached into his waistband and removed the weapon that Angel had attempted to defend himself with minutes before. Dan ejected the empty magazine and threw it on the driver's seat. Then he checked the chamber of the weapon to ensure it was clear before placing the pistol on the seat next to the empty magazine.

Angel looked at the handcuff on his right hand and then down at the weapon and magazine on the seat next to him. Nodding slowly, he looked up at Dan. "Do you like dogs?" Angel asked.

"I do," Dan said. "I do like dogs."

"I have a sweetheart of a Rottweiler named Peso. A three-year-old with a perfect temperament. See to it that she gets a good home."

"You have an address?"

"591 Quarry Pine Road. Warrenton."

"I'll see to it that she is taken care of."

"Thanks."

Dan pointed in the direction of the police lights coming over the hill near the guard station. Then he reached into his pocket, pulled out a single bullet casing, wiped it on his shirt, and threw it onto the driver's seat.

"I figure you have enough time to load the weapon and get one shot off, if you hurry. Don't waste the shot on me. I'll be out of the line of fire before you can aim.

"See you around," Dan said, shutting the door and jogging for cover.

*

Dan sat in Detective Fields' unmarked police car in the last parking spot of the far lot as the FBI, state, and local police swarmed the scene. He stared through the windshield as Emily worked the officers on the scene, letting them know she was available for briefings on the case. Dan watched as Emily pushed a few strands of hair behind her ear and flashed her dimples to the men in blue who were just as mesmerized by Emily's looks as they were by the crime scene. Moments later, Emily joined Dan in the car.

"What's the word?"

"This is Maryland. I'm a DC detective. I'm in the queue."

"I imagine if you keep flaunting your dimples, they'll bump you up in the line."

"I don't know what you're talking about."

Dan smiled. "Maybe you do, and maybe you don't."

Emily returned the smile, dimples on full display. Then her demeanor turned serious. "What you did was dangerous."

"I don't know what you're talking about."

"This isn't a joke. You gave a professional killer a gun and ammunition while you were standing there."

"He only had time for one shot and he said wasn't going to spend his life in prison. It was an educated guess he would use the bullet on himself."

"Well, he did," Emily replied. "But what you did was still dangerous."

"I won't do it again."

"Good," Emily said. "And there may be some question as to why the man was handcuffed to the door of the vehicle."

"I did what I thought I had to do to ensure the safety of the members of Potomac Hills Country Club. He was secured in his vehicle and we were waiting for the arrival of the authorities. I think I can handle that inquiry."

"You think you have an answer for everything."

"And yet, the law allows me to not answer any question I'm not interested in answering."

"See what I mean about having an answer for everything?"

"I'll work on it."

There was a long pause and then Emily asked, "Now that this case is over, what's next for you?" she asked.

"What makes you think this case is over?" Dan replied, reaching for the door handle on the car. "There's one more murder to solve."

CHAPTER 58

DAN PULLED THE chair out and sat down at the wooden table in the back of Sherry Wellington's shop in Georgetown. An open bottle of wine rested in the middle of the table. Two glasses stood next to the bottle. Sherry Wellington leaned back in her chair and Dan could see her eyes were slightly bloodshot.

"Are we drinking tonight?" Dan asked.

"I didn't have any champagne to celebrate. You want a glass?" Sherry asked.

"Sure."

Sherry poured and Dan swilled the red wine in the glass.

"You said you located the person I hired you to find. The man who killed Marcus?"

"I located the man responsible for the murder."

"Where is he?"

"Dead. He chose to take his own life, as opposed to going to prison."

"Who was he?"

"I don't know his name yet. All indications are that he was hired to kill the jurors from the Tyrone Biggs trial. You are the only one left."

Dan stared at Sherry, waiting to see some kind of reaction.

A moment later Sherry stoically answered, "Should I feel lucky being the last one?"

"I would."

"Are you sure he's dead?"

Dan thought back to the scene in the parking lot of the country club and the unsightly mess in the dark Mercedes. "Pretty sure."

"And you said he was hired. What about the person who hired him? The person responsible?"

"He's still alive. But not for long. He's receiving end-of-life hospice care. He's bedridden. The end is near. He is of no concern to you. He is not a threat."

"Unless he hires someone else."

"Possible, but unlikely. There was a lot of planning involved with what he did."

"Who was he?"

"Someone you might recognize," Dan said, pulling a folded picture from his pocket.

Sherry glanced at the photo and recognition washed over her perfectly symmetrical face. "He's one of the family members of the deceased. The dad of one of the girls killed at H2O."

"That's right."

"You know, I always felt bad for the families."

"Just not bad enough to overcome fear. Fear and a really big bag of cash."

Sherry paused mid-drink. "What do you mean?"

"I mean I know everything, Sherry. I know you were paid off in the Tyrone Biggs trial. That you received payment to let Tyrone Biggs walk."

Sherry stared into a dark corner of her store. "I don't know what you're talking about."

"Sherry, don't."

Sherry gulped the rest of her wine and refilled her glass.

"Are you going to turn me in? Hand me over to the authorities?"

"I had something else in mind. How about you tell me everything and we both walk away."

"Walk away? I don't think you'd allow that to happen."

"I will, on one condition. You tell me everything."

"Everything, what?"

"Everything."

Sherry Wellington didn't speak.

"I'll start," Dan offered. "You should know I stole one of the bullets from your gun. The gun you had under the table, here, the first time I came to see you."

"I noticed one was missing later."

"I'm sure you did. I learned a lot digging through Marcus's background. The Arlington police learned even more. As it turns out, a couple of Marcus's old Army buddies recalled that you were a pretty good shot with a pistol."

"Did they?"

"They did."

"They must have had me confused with someone else."

"Probably not. They were pretty detailed in their description. I never really thought about it before, but one of the downsides to being gorgeous is that people remember you. For better or for worse. Good when you are talking about tips as a waitress. Bad when you want to kill someone without anyone noticing."

Sherry's breathing momentarily stopped. "I didn't kill anyone."

"I think you did. And if you want me to keep your jury bribery incident quiet, we're going to finish this conversation like two adults. Then we are going to part ways and never speak again. Agreed?"

Sherry Wellington's eyes welled up ever so noticeably.

Dan continued. "You stated the gun you had the first day we met was your husband's gun, correct?"

Sherry Wellington nodded.

"Well the bullet in that gun matched the same make and model as the casing used in the Tyrone Biggs shooting. The bullet that killed Tyrone Biggs. The bullet was a Black Saber."

"I wouldn't know anything about that."

"I believe you. On that point at least, I believe you. I don't think you would have known that the ammunition your husband owns is specialty ammunition from a company that is no longer in business. The company was acquired by a larger ammunition company several years ago. It no longer sells a product under its own name. You probably wouldn't have known this."

"I wouldn't have. So what?"

"Indeed, so what. Ammunition does little without the gun that fired it. And the police investigating Tyrone Biggs's murder never had a weapon. Virtually impossible to prove anything beyond a reasonable doubt with only a sample of ammunition."

"So they say on TV."

Dan paused before the next step in proving his theory. "Where were you the night Tyrone Biggs was killed?"

"I was in Pittsburgh."

"You want to think about that?"

"No, I was in Pittsburgh."

"Are you sure?"

"I'm sure."

"Because I'm not sure where I was on Saturday night three weeks ago, much less a couple of years ago. But you had the answer like that," Dan said, snapping his fingers.

"It's something I remember."

"How did you find out about Tyrone Biggs's death?"

"Marcus told me. He loved to read those obituaries."

"Apparently," Dan said. "What did you do in Pittsburgh?"

"I went sightseeing."

"In Pittsburgh?"

"Yes."

"Now, I know you're lying."

"I was in Pittsburgh. I stayed at the Embassy Suites near the river."

"And I'm going to guess you have a receipt from the hotel."

Sherry nodded. "I'm pretty sure I have the receipt."

"Bravo, Mrs. Wellington. Bravo."

"I don't know what you mean, Mr. Lord."

"Pittsburgh. It's perfect. Four hours from DC. Not too far. You could leave your son with the nanny and drive up for a day or two. You could check in to the hotel, one without valet parking, and go to bed at a reasonable hour. Then you could slip out of the hotel. Drive back to DC, pop Tyrone Biggs, and drive back before breakfast. No toll roads between here and Pittsburgh. It would probably require more than one tank of gas to pull it off, but you could work that out. Pay cash at a gas station outside of town. As long as you don't have an accident, or hit a deer, or have a mechanical breakdown, you could make it work. And heck, if you do hit something, you could say you decided to come home early or take a drive."

"That is an interesting theory, Mr. Lord."

"More importantly to you, and our conversation here, is that it's a theory I haven't discussed with anyone else. But I think with enough time and digging, someone could find a hole in your alibi. Nothing is executed perfectly."

"So you say," Sherry responded. "Then again, who knows, maybe my husband did it."

"I thought about that. But I couldn't really see the motive for your husband. In fact, I had a real hard time coming up with a motive for you. So help me out. Let me help you sweep the past into the past. Pull the carpet over the ugliness of years ago."

"How can I trust you?"

"What choice do you have?"

Sherry Wellington gritted her teeth.

"I'll take a guess if you want me to begin," Dan said.

Sherry didn't respond so Dan continued. "Somehow, someone figured out you took money during the Tyrone Biggs trial. And someone threatened to use that past indiscretion against you. A past you were desperately trying to keep hidden from your congressman husband."

"Not exactly," Sherry said, taking another healthy sip from her wine glass. "No one figured out I had a past. Someone figured out I had a future. And that this new future could come with a payout."

"Tyrone Biggs."

Sherry nodded again. "He saw my face next to my husband's in the newspapers. Then he figured he could blackmail me."

"When?"

"A couple of years ago. After he was sent to prison on drug charges. He got out of jail, and shortly thereafter he paid me a visit. I guess he'd lost a lot of his business while he was in prison and he was looking for some quick money."

"And the statute of limitations on federal jury tampering is five years."

"Yes, five years. I researched that myself when he approached me. Five years. Tyrone Biggs couldn't be charged with jury tampering in the H2O trial so he was free to blackmail me."

"The same statute of limitations applied to you. You couldn't be charged with accepting bribes in the H2O trial either. You didn't have to be blackmailed."

"If I lived in any other city in the US and were married to any normal man, that would have been the end of the story. But not in this town."

Dan nodded.

"Tyrone Biggs understood that in this town, politics don't operate on truths or fact. You only need the whisper of an indiscretion to end a political career. Just a whisper of a rumor."

"And Tyrone Biggs was willing to start that rumor."

"Yes. I don't think he was worried about how it would reflect on him. Legally, he was untouchable on the rumor. As you said, the statute of limitations had passed. But that didn't mean the rumor wouldn't kill my husband's political career."

"So Tyrone Biggs blackmailed you. He threatened to end your husband's political career by starting a rumor that a congressman's wife took a bribe while on jury duty for a drug lord. And in order to keep quiet, he wanted money."

"He knew I had money. Or he knew that my husband came from money. A lot of money. That didn't take a genius to figure out."

"Did you pay him?"

"No. I never did. I figured once I paid him, it was never going to end."

"You were right. It wouldn't have ended." Dan sat in silence for a moment as tears ran down Sherry Wellington's face.

"You are a survivor, Sherry. I'll give you that," Dan said.

"What's next for me?"

"I'll tell you what's going to happen. You're going to say goodbye and then I'm going to walk out of here. With one more caveat."

"Another stipulation?"

"There is another."

"What?"

"If by chance you have done something stupid and kept the weapon you used to kill Tyrone Biggs, you need to lose it."

Sherry sat in unmoved silence before speaking. "What would make you say that?"

"You have an alibi for the night Tyrone Biggs was killed. But I'm guessing if I checked into it, your husband wouldn't have an alibi. I can think of a few scenarios where your husband could find himself in hot water if that gun were found in his possession. It's possible you used one of your husband's guns and returned it without his knowledge. As an insurance policy for your own future."

"Enough," Sherry said, tears streaming.

Dan paused for effect. "Do we understand each other?"

"Yes."

"If I ever hear about that gun in the news in connection with Tyrone Biggs, you will hear from me and so will the authorities. Who knows, maybe I already have a picture of you from a surveillance camera the night Tyrone was killed. A photograph that shows you were driving in the direction of Anacostia when you say you were in Pittsburgh."

Sherry wiped at the tears on her face. "I understand. What I don't understand is why you're letting me walk away."

Dan took a sip of his wine. "Because there are no winners in this whole thing. None. And as much distaste as I have for politicians, your husband didn't do anything wrong. He may well be a good man. He married a waitress who had a child and he gave you an opportunity for a life. We are going to leave that where it is."

Sherry stared off in the direction of the front window and nodded.

CHAPTER 59

DAN PLACED THE cafeteria's plastic tray on the white circular table. Detective Wallace started to stand from his chair for a proper handshake and Dan urged the detective to remain seated. "Don't get up."

"How did you find me?"

"The nurse on your floor told me you were down here."

"Police privileges. Don't have to eat in my room. Not that the cafeteria food is anything special."

Dan sat and looked out the window. Traffic from the GWU campus crisscrossed the quad below. An endless stream of bodies entered and exited the Foggy Bottom Metro station. A line of students stood near the curb by a trio of food trucks. A man with a box of magic paraphernalia sat on a park bench, taking a break.

"You say the food's not good, but the entertainment out the window seems decent. No shortage of things going on," Dan said.

"That's why I'm here. There was a guy selling drugs out there earlier."

"Did you call it in?"

"I did, but he vanished into the Metro as soon as he saw a uniform."

"The nurse said you're going home later today."

"Just waiting for my doctor to sign me out. He's been in surgery most of the morning."

"How's the shoulder?"

"It hurts like hell," Wallace replied, glancing down at the sling on his arm.

"And it may hurt like hell for a while."

"Thanks for the optimism."

"The shoulder is a complicated joint. It may never feel the same."

"You bring any good news with you?"

"Lots. For starters, we're done working together."

"I heard about the guy blowing out his brains all over the inside of his car."

"I was there, it wasn't pretty."

"Did you hear they identified him?" Wallace asked.

"I didn't."

"Angel Reyes. An American, born to undocumented Mexican parents."

"And what was his relationship to Richard Porter?" Dan asked.

"Turns out that one of the companies Porter started and ran was a flash drive manufacturer. A few years ago, before he sold it, Porter moved the company south of the border to take advantage of the lower wages. When he sold the company, it was just outside Tijuana. It looks like Angel had connections with some of the security employees at this Mexican factory. And so did Richard Porter, obviously."

"So Angel was American?"

"Born in Texas but ended up working security in Mexico."

"Security in Mexico? That's an oxymoron," Dan said.

"It gets better. As near as we can tell, Angel had a business relationship with a known drug cartel. He was stopped a couple of times in the US, heading south, with weapons in his vehicle. All of the weapons were legally owned. You can imagine the final destination for the weapons was anything but legal."

"And Richard Porter hired him."

"After Richard Porter lost his daughter and his wife, he started making inquiries. Enough money can buy just about anything. Especially south of the border. Richard Porter apparently dangled a large enough carrot to get the attention of Angel Reyes."

"And the rest is history," Dan said.

"Something like that," Detective Wallace said. A long silence fell over the two men.

"We found the rifle from the sniper killing in Spring Valley."

"Where was it?" Dan asked.

"In the canal. Not far from Chain Bridge."

"Was there a match on ballistics?"

"Still waiting for results. But it looks promising."

"That's good detective work, Wallace. I'm not sure many people would have cracked that case."

"Thanks," Wallace replied, staring out the window. "Before you hear it any place else, you should know I'm thinking about retiring."

"Retiring?"

"Yes. It's been a long run. I'm facing a good chunk of rehabilitation with the shoulder. I think it's time."

"Does your wife think it's time?"

"I haven't told her yet."

"You might want to run that by her first. She may not be ready to have you at home every day."

"I'll have to think about that."

Dan considered his next statement for a moment. "You know, from time to time I could probably use help on the private detective front. If you're interested."

"Are you offering me a job, Dan?"

"Part-time employment."

"I'll have to think about that, too."

"See what your wife says and let me know."

"I will," Wallace replied. "Speaking of asking women for their opinion, what's the deal with Detective Fields?" Wallace asked.

"We'll have to see," Dan said.

"I don't know if you're going to do any better than Fields. She's a looker. She's smart. She can kick a little ass. Might be just what you need in your life."

"We'll see," Dan repeated.

Both men stared out the window and then Dan glanced down at his watch. "I need to get going. I have something to do this afternoon."

"Don't let me keep you."

"Think about the job offer," Dan said, standing and shaking Wallace's hand.

CHAPTER 60

D AN GOT OUT of the car and glanced around the green rolling landscape surrounding Tobias's house on the hill. He inhaled the clean Middleburg air and opened the back door of his car, grasping for the end of the dog leash on the back seat. Without prodding, Peso leaped from the vehicle and began sniffing the ground.

Dan tugged once on the leash and led the large Rottweiler around the rear of the vehicle. At the passenger door, Dan gave Peso the command to sit and the dog complied, drool hanging from one side of its mouth. With Peso by his side, Dan reached onto the passenger seat and removed a black duffle bag. A moment later, Dan was heading towards the front porch with one hand firmly on the dog leash, the knuckles of his other hand wrapped tightly on the handle of the bag.

Tobias appeared at the door before Dan reached the steps.

"Is this the dog?" Tobias asked, stepping outside and looking down at Dan.

"This is her," Dan replied. "Meet Peso, a three-year-old, ninety-pound Rottweiler with good manners."

"And she was previously owned by an assassin?" Tobias asked with a hint of incredulity.

"Is that a problem?"

"Not for me."

"Good. Because it would be odd for a hacker with a healthy disregard for the law to discriminate against a perfectly good dog based on its previous owner."

"Is she trained?"

"Not as a security dog. But it seems she'll put her mind to anything for a jerky treat. Training probably won't take much effort."

Tobias seemed to consider Dan's assessment.

"And I'll take her back if it doesn't work out," Dan offered.

Tobias nodded. "Then I'll take her. On a trial basis."

"That works for me," Dan said, as a woman's voice called out to Tobias from inside the house.

"Did you bring the money?" Tobias asked, pulling the door shut behind him.

"I did," Dan replied, lifting the duffle bag.

Tobias took the bag and unzipped the top. "What's this?" he asked, removing a plastic jar in the shape of a barrel.

"Those are jerky treats. I also brought some dog food with me. It's in the trunk."

Tobias reached into the bag a second time and pulled out a stack of money with a rubber band around the middle. "How much in total?"

"A hundred grand and change. Can you handle it?"

"It shouldn't be a problem. But you're going to owe me one."

"Just make it untraceable."

"Then what?"

"Then it gets deposited into a trust fund for a young girl who just lost her mother to cancer. The trust fund has already been established. Everything on that end is legitimate."

"You never mentioned where this money came from."

"If you believe a recently deceased client of mine, most of what you see in the bag was won at the new casino in Maryland."

"That would make it clean already."

"But I can't guarantee it. There's a chance that a serial number on one of those bills could show up as stolen in a bank robbery. All things considered, I would rather avoid that possibility. Which is why I've come to you."

"A young girl who lost her mother?"

"That's right. For a good cause."

"But not without risk."

Dan nodded.

Tobias zipped the bag closed.

"Let me get the dog food out of the trunk," Dan said, handing the leash to Tobias.

A minute later, Dan lugged forty pounds of dog food up to the porch and set it down near the front door. Tobias scratched Peso on the ear and the big dog licked his new owner's hand.

"I have my doubts about her ability as a guard dog," Tobias said, motioning towards the affection the dog was showing his hand.

"Even if her bark is worse than her bite, that may be enough. Appearance alone should scare away most people."

A woman's voice called out for Tobias a second time.

"I'll give you a call when I'm done with the money," Tobias said, looking back over his shoulder.

"I'll be waiting."

"And then we can discuss the favor you owe me."

"You already have something in mind?" Dan asked.

"I do. And you're going to love it."

Proof

Made in the USA
Columbia, SC
29 August 2017